Human

Mark Sekela

Human

ISBN: 978-0-9879059-6-3

Printed in the United States of America

Please visit www.MarkSekela.com for details about the other books in the Convergence Series.

For Marilyn and Mike – I want to be just like you when I grow up.

ACKNOWLEDGMENTS

As was the case for the first two novels in The Convergence Series, the professional editing and formatting of Mark Hooper and the team at Angel Editing has been exceptional. Thank you so much Chris Eckley and Melissa Gledhill who have both provided far more time and energy to improving my writing than I could possibly express in words. I can't thank Becky Greenhow and Linda Spinosa and Aurora Sekela enough for their professional proof reading and insightful feedback. Once again, it was the support and encouragement I received from my two boys, Luca and Matteo that kept me going. You make being a father easy.

Human

By

Mark Sekela

CHAPTER 1

CHANGE

L ooking into his eyes was like gazing into the abyss. Hollow and lifeless, they captured every ray of light that entered them but reflected none. Their blackness was made even darker by silvery-white eyebrows and matching brush-cut. His sixty-nine years were hidden in his youthful face and only evident in the color of his hair.

Tonino Fabro entered the noisy Vatican cafeteria and paused at the head of the long wooden table glowing white with a tablecloth. The clanking sound of coffee cups connecting with their saucers replaced the loud discussions that had filled the room seconds before. Tonino's gaze silenced the small room so only the snare drum tapping of rain on the terra cotta roof could be heard.

"Wonderful, everyone is here. Thank you for coming on such short notice. I trust everyone has removed their VisText and shut off their tablets?" he asked in perfect English except for a noticeable Italian accent. Tonino scanned the room and saw all but the oldest man at the far end of the table had placed a VisText in front of them. Like most people of his generation, the older man refused to use the device at all.

Tonino's request unleashed apprehension from all of the men except one, Father Sean Black. He was a stocky middle-aged Australian whose rapidly thinning blonde hair gave him the appearance of a schoolteacher rather than a priest. He was the only one of the fifteen people sitting at the table who left his VisText on his ear.

"G'day, sir," Father Black replied, not attempting to hide his accent.

Tonino looked down at him, seated at the end of the table closest to him, and forced a smile to his lips, but he didn't answer. Father Black had worked at the Vatican for more than sixteen years, and he reported directly to Tonino, who controlled the Vatican Secret Service.

Tonino's reputation for intimidation was second only to Father Black's reputation for ruthlessness. The clandestine operation of the VSS had survived unchanged from the earliest days of the Church. Motivated by power, its influence remained unbound by borders or politics.

Before Tonino could continue, another voice interrupted the silence.

"Why do you bring us here again?" said an old man's voice, struggling to speak English through an Indian accent.

Tonino's eyes looked down the long table and focused on the elderly man beginning to stand with the aid of a polished walking stick. His frail body, decrepit with age, barely reached the feet of the life-sized Crucifixion hanging from the wall behind him.

"I'm delighted you asked, Mr. Gill," Tonino replied lengthening the fake smile on his face. But unlike the other world religious leaders seated around the table, Mr. Gill was too old to be concerned about the price he would pay for questioning Tonino.

"We've done as you've told us for decades. Now, our people cannot feed themselves, we have nowhere to live; it only gets worse with the endless rain. Yet you demand we continue—why?" Mr. Gill complained.

Before Tonino could answer, a younger Asian man stood up and continued the dissention in a far less confrontational tone.

"The Democratic Republic of China is worse—we can't continue. I feel it is already too late; we have surpassed three billion people this year," the man said before quickly sitting down.

"Do the rest of you agree?" Tonino asked, searching the room with a menacing stare.

The room remained silent for a second, and then a short dark-skinned man stood up next to Mr. Gill. His navy blue business suit was in complete contrast to the bright orange and yellow dhoti the man next to him wore. Speaking English with a slight accent, the man nervously addressed Tonino.

"With all due respect, Mr. Fabro, most of South America has become reliant on the handouts you provide, and I'm afraid Brazil will soon follow."

The remaining religious heads around the table nodded in agreement, and the two men took their seats.

"Don't concern yourselves; our scientists have developed new capacity in Canada, Egypt and Australia. We can now grow enough to feed double the current population."

"Are you mad?" shouted Mr. Gill. "It's not only food, there's no room! Where would thirty billion people live?"

"It's unnatural, and it's not what God intended for the Earth," said the Brazilian man, shaking his head with the others in disbelief.

"I think it unwise to concern yourselves any further with this; I assure you, the Vatican will continue to provide for your people. Just as we continue to look after you," Tonino snapped.

"Like you did for the others?" Mr. Gill replied, raising his voice and not hiding the sarcasm.

"What do you mean?" Tonino asked, casting a meaningful glare to the end of the table.

"My predecessor, those executives in the pharmaceutical companies, and all those workers in the water-bottling plants rotting away in jail—or dead."

"Ah yes, Mrs. Singh. It was unfortunate she did not agree with our ways. It saddened me to remove her from our Holy gathering. As for those others, I don't know what you're referring to. The Vatican had nothing to do with PharmaScam-2020. I can assure you, Mr. Gill, tainting the world's beverage supply with fertility drugs wouldn't be God's work, would it? It's also unnecessary since you've all dedicated your efforts to helping the Vatican complete the will of God."

Mr. Gill didn't waver in his accusations and pulled his glasses off his face, casting an equally meaningful stare back at Tonino.

"You've not answered my question. Why... Why does the Vatican, or as you say 'God,' wish it necessary to form such blight upon the Earth?" Mr. Gill replied.

Tonino turned and faced Father Black, passing him a glance of indignation before addressing the table.

"Our world is on the cusp of an evolution," he said, methodically turning his eyes to meet his onlookers. "But there are those among us who wish to destroy everything. They're malicious beings, preying off the living, using them as hosts to do their bidding," he continued while pausing for the group to show reaction to his declaration.

"You can't see them... or touch them... but make no mistake, they do exist. They'll infect us without notice; taking over our minds. They communicate without speaking and move among us undetected, spreading like a virus. They're not of this Earth. Only the devil could conjure something so insidious."

"This can't be so! Blasphemy!" cried the Brazilian, unable to restrain the power of his Catholic convictions.

The rest of the table erupted in jeers of confusion and disbelief.

Tonino leaned over the edge of the table, placing both hands on its surface. His movement was a signal for the group to silence their outburst so he could continue.

"Listen to me! Mankind is about to change forever, and if we don't stop them, everything will be lost."

"Who do you speak of?" asked Mr. Gill, clearly not

convinced of the satanic doom Tonino implied.

"They call themselves 'Primoris,'" Tonino said, expecting an immediate response from the group.

The religious leaders said nothing, remaining transfixed on Tonino as if hypnotized by his words.

Surprised by their silence and lack of reaction, Tonino continued, "They spread through the universe infecting life like a disease, taking over our minds and leaving us an empty shell of who we were. There is no way of knowing where they are, or who or what they will infect next. It could be a bird outside your window, a dog running in the park or the person sitting next to you," he said, shifting his glare to Mr. Gill.

"This is nonsense..." "You're crazy..." "What are you talking about?" said multiple voices from the group, filling the room with incoherent chatter.

A loud crack startled the room into silence. Mr. Gill slammed his walking stick on the top of the table, knocking the coffee cups off their saucers on both sides of his stick. With the entire group's attention focused on him, he lifted the stick off the table and spoke.

"What do these Primoris want with us?"

"They require humans to make more of their kind."

"If this is true, then how do we stop them?" Mr. Gill demanded.

"Some of you may remember sixteen years ago, Mr. Gill, I'm certain you do," Tonino said, looking deep into Mr. Gill's eyes before continuing.

"The young couple we scoured the Earth to find. They were Vectors created by the Primoris. The Primoris planted a genetic seed inside their DNA. That is how they infect us. If we hadn't found them, they would have spread their infection, causing an unstoppable pandemic."

"But you found these Vectors, so this threat is no more. What's the reason for drastically increasing the Earth's population?" the Brazilian asked.

"I'd expect you to know better than any of the others. It is

God's will: '*Be fruitful and increase in number; fill the Earth and subdue it,*'" Tonino said, quoting the Bible and parting his lips to form a smile.

"No, I don't understand," replied the Brazilian, shaking his head.

"The Primoris will return; it's just a matter of time. Mankind's only chance of surviving the pandemic is by '*increasing our numbers.*' The more humans there are, the greater the likelihood God will give us immunity."

"You mean a mutation," Mr. Gill said.

"This isn't the time to discuss whether it's Creationism or Evolution."

"How do we know who is infected by one of these Primoris?" the Brazilian asked.

"You will see it in their eyes. All those infected by the Primoris will have crystal-blue eyes. And the Vectors will have the mark—the shape of a fish on the back of their neck."

"How will we know when they have returned?" Mr. Gill asked.

"Leave that to me."

This agitated the Mr. Gill. The wrinkles surrounding his eyes disappeared, and his eyes exploded with anger.

"I don't believe any of this nonsense!" he said, slamming his stick on the table again. "It is rubbish! The Vatican wants all of us to believe this so they can continue increasing their numbers and coffers. I think you exploded the population by adding fertility drugs to everyday products. The PharmaScam-2020 investigators were right; the Vatican did marry big business to secure the future of Catholicism. More people means more Catholics, and more mouths to feed, clothes to buy, houses to build and most of all, more profit for business. This explains the insurgence of Catholics over the last decade in India and China. Did you realize it would push our planet into an environmental death spiral? Did you care?"

Tonino fired his glare across the room like a bullet from a rifle.

"I'm disappointed to hear you no longer support our efforts. Does anyone else agree with Mr. Gill?"

Tonino stepped back from the head of the table, looked down at Father Black and curled the right side of his mouth to form half a smirk.

Father Black stood up and reached into the breast pocket of his suit coat, removing a small shiny metallic device from his pocket resembling a child's toy gun. He adjusted the small round dial on the top of the device before pointing it toward the far end of the table.

A crimson red beam of light, the thickness of a pencil, struck Mr. Gill directly between the eyes, splitting his glasses in two before exiting the back of his head. His body folded forward, collapsing face-first onto the bleached white tablecloth. No blood spilled from the holes in his head left by the laser; the intense heat generated by the light disintegrated his skin when it passed through. The air was filled with the putrid smell of burned hair and flesh.

The group sat stupefied by the sudden murder of one of their members.

"Thank you, Father Black," said Tonino while Father Black returned the laser to his pocket and took his seat.

"Is there anyone else who would like to voice their concerns?" Tonino asked while scanning the room with a large smile on his face.

"Excellent, I'm pleased to know the Vatican can still count on your support."

CHAPTER 2

ANDY AND SANDY

Prophetic clouds concealed the Earth under an eternal shroud, obscuring the crystal blue sky behind a translucent barrier. The late June sunlight struggled to break through the fist of darkness gripping the planet. Nourished by a decade of nearly constant rainfall, the massive yew trees flourished and formed a canopy over the serpentine driveway leading to the stone mansion. Nestled in a private Geneva suburb, the Muller estate glowed like an emerald.

Vibrations shook the gilded lion heads hanging from the black iron gates opening before the bronze-skinned teenager. Two quick beeps of the small car's horn bounced off the towering rock walls surrounding the estate. Bradley Kruger's mother waved her hand out the driver's side of the electric car before speeding silently away.

Bradley dropped his skateboard onto the wet pavement and began propelling himself up the steep incline to the Mullers' home. Each push of his right leg lifted the hair hanging below his helmet off his shoulders. He stopped at the front of the mansion, pausing to remove his helmet and flip his board into his hands with his foot before bounding up the granite steps two at a time. Light green moss covered the edges of the dozen stone steps leading to the front door.

He stood under the covered entranceway peering at his reflection in the small glass window set in the door. For an instant, his eyes shifted to the sliver of light reflecting off the small metallic device hanging over his left ear. He reached out for the doorbell. Just before pushing the button, a chorus of barking emanated from the opposite side of the door—its thunder still intimidated Bradley even after three years.

"Andy, Sandy, that's enough," commanded Gabriel Muller as he approached the door.

The two snow-white German shepherds turned in unison and faced Gabriel, their cobalt blue eyes focused intently on their master's. They immediately stopped barking and took a position on either side of Gabriel like a pair of centurions. He reached for the door handle to greet his friend.

"Gabriel, Bradley's at the door," called his grandmother from upstairs. Tanya Muller's English had a New York accent that had softened over her seventy years.

"I've got it!" Gabriel replied.

Gabriel opened the door and looked up into Bradley's dark green eyes, seeing the lingering concern left from the barking dogs. His navy blue raincoat made his curly hair appear more blonde. Gabriel sent the dogs away and smiled at his best friend.

"Hey, come on in."

"I thought we were going skating? It's not raining," Bradley said with a slight German accent. His family still followed the old traditions and spoke German at home even though English dominated the globe.

"In a minute. I just want to see the M3 launch," Gabriel replied, heading down the hall to the media room.

Bradley put his skateboard on the floor next to the one already leaning against the wall and hung his helmet and raincoat with the others on the row of hooks behind the door. He shuffled down the hall, trying to catch up with Gabriel. The two teenagers sat in the large leather sofa watching the three-dimensional video image covering the wall across from them.

"What's so exciting about a manned mission to Mars?" Bradley asked, but they were interrupted before Gabriel could answer by Tanya entering the room.

"Why aren't you boys outside?" she scowled.

"We will, I just want to see this."

"Hello, Bradley," said Tanya, realizing her impoliteness and switching to her normal soft voice. She then turned to face Gabriel again.

"What are you waiting for? Get outside! It's the first time in months without rain, and you're watching the V-screen. V-screen..." Tanya began, but her command to shut the device off was interrupted by Gabriel before she could complete it.

"Wait, Oma, I want to see the launch," he pleaded.

"You're too obsessed with all this space stuff—get outside before the rain starts again."

Bradley held his laughter inside as Tanya reached for the remote on the coffee table in front of the sofa, deciding to use that instead of a voice command. Her hand moved quickly for her age, beating Gabriel's to the remote. Gabriel jumped out of his seat in protest, his six-foot frame dwarfing his grandmother. Their matching blue eyes locked together.

"Please, Oma, just one more minute. They're leaving the Space Station right now," Gabriel begged while gently reaching for the remote she held behind her back.

"Too bad you don't have a VisText; you could watch the launch *and* be outside," said Bradley as a cheek-to-cheek smile spread across his face. His finger touched the small metal device resembling a hearing aid from half a century ago hanging over his ear.

Bradley knew Gabriel desired a VisText, but his grandfather, Derek, refused Gabriel's constant request for one. Gabriel blamed his grandfather's refusal on his age, thinking that at seventy-five, he didn't understand how important it was for a teenager to have one.

His grandfather insisted it was unhealthy for a computer to link to a child's brain. He always remained steadfast and refused to let his grandson get a bio-neural device even though Gabriel was about to turn sixteen.

Gabriel could hear his grandfather's words repeating inside his head, '*Your Visual Cortex is for seeing not computing.*'

This caused Gabriel continual embarrassment, as everyone he knew could search the E-network, send and receive text, voice and video using their VisText. He was the only student at the International School of Geneva, the exclusive private high school he and Bradley attended, who didn't have a one. This left him no choice but to use a tablet, something only young children did.

Gabriel smiled at Bradley in a display of gratitude for his friend's attempt to support his desire and was about to resume the argument for permission when the V-screen distracted him.

"Look, it's launching," Gabriel said as he pointed to the image.

The room fell silent when the wall filled with an image of the *Frontier* spacecraft. It departed the International Space Station with the Earth as its backdrop. The once blue planet brush-stroked with white lay smothered beneath a uniform mass of ash-grey clouds. Gabriel watched in awe, his radiant blue eyes refusing to blink while the ship drifted away from the station. The voice of the video announcer covering the live launch interrupted Gabriel and Tanya's jostling over the remote.

"Volume increase," commanded Gabriel, and the sound of the announcer's voice increased.

"Volume stop," he commanded when the announcer's voice filled the room.

"For those of you just joining us, thank you for linking to the World News e-Networks live coverage of the M3 launch. We're covering this historic event live. Since the first Marsnik 1 attempt by the Soviet Union in 1960, there have been a total of fifty-four unmanned missions to our red neighbor. But today is truly a historic day as the first manned mission to Mars is now officially underway. Their five-year mission will have them arrive in Martian orbit in approximately two years' time, with expected touch down on the Martian surface sometime in late 2029 or early 2030. Keep your V-devices linked to WNN coverage for live uploads on the progress of the *Frontier* and the M3," said the voice from the V-screen.

"V-screen off," commanded Tanya, and the image instantly disappeared from the wall. "Now you boys get outside this instant and take advantage of a rare break in the rain. Who knows the next time we'll get one?"

Gabriel and Bradley left the media room and headed for the door. Bradley took his helmet off the hook and snapped it on as they both grabbed their skateboards and went outside. They leaped down the granite stairs. The humidity made the early summer day feel like a midsummer afternoon.

"Want a race to the gate?"

"You're on!"

They both tossed their skateboards on the pavement and prepared to mount them as Tanya opened the door.

"You know I don't like you leaving without them," called Tanya, and the two dogs bolted from the door toward Gabriel like a pair of white doves released from their cage.

"Yes, Oma," Gabriel replied, the embarrassment unmistakable in his tone.

"And put your helmet on!" she demanded while waving it in the air.

Tanya wasn't surprised that Gabriel ignored her demand; she blamed his insubordinate behavior on the parents he never met. His stubbornness and obsession with science were gifts from his father, murdered before he was born. His exceptional athletic abilities and charismatic good looks came from his mother, who had died in a horrific car crash shortly after his birth.

"Still?" responded Bradley with a small smirk, referring to Tanya's insistence that Gabriel take the dogs with him whenever he left the house.

"Yah, you'd think I was turning six tomorrow," he said

while reaching down to stroke the head of Sandy, the larger of the two dogs positioning its body next to his.

"Any idea what you're getting? Maybe a...?"

"Not a chance. My Opa still won't let me," Gabriel interrupted.

Bradley understood Gabriel's tone and changed the subject to their impending skateboard race.

"To the front gate—first to touch the lion's head wins."

"You're on," Gabriel replied.

The two teenagers lined the noses of their skateboards up on an imaginary starting line in the middle of the driveway, holding them in place with one foot.

"On the count of three... one, two, three," shouted Bradley, and they both pushed off with all their might to begin the race.

They advanced rapidly down the steepest part of the driveway, crisscrossing paths over the smooth surface; the trail left by their skateboards wove a perfect helix on the surface of the damp pavement.

The large metal gates swung open to allow a vehicle to enter the Muller estate, its electric motor whisper-quiet as it accelerated up the winding driveway. The break in the rain inspired Derek, who was rushing to get home after picking up Gabriel's birthday present. The Mullers gave the house staff the weekends off, preferring to do their own driving and chores.

The dogs followed the racers, running along the narrow strip of grass beneath the yew trees; Andy kept pace with Bradley while Sandy flanked Gabriel. The boys focused on their riding, each crouching through the hairpin turns in an effort to gain an advantage over the other.

The luxury sedan filled the narrow driveway, its wheels inching onto the grass through every turn. Concerned the rain would begin again and anxious to enjoy the unexpected break in the weather, Derek negotiated the car through the turns like a teenager, much faster than usual.

"I've got you this time!" Bradley shouted, attempting to

beat Gabriel through the inside of the approaching turn.

"In your dreams!" Gabriel yelled back, and he squatted even lower on his skateboard as he entered the turn. He directed his skateboard to the left edge of the pavement to cut the corner, and the move put his left shoulder inches from Sandy's body. The sound of her panting grew louder in Gabriel's ears.

The lower profile worked, and Gabriel gained an additional two yards on Bradley. Adrenalin filled Gabriel's veins, travelling faster through his body than his skateboard over the pavement. His heart pounded the walls of his chest, knowing this was the last turn before the straightaway.

A gentle breeze rustled the branches of the trees, starting a cascade of leaves and drizzle. Derek accelerated the sedan in the straightaway, activating the windshield wipers to remove the debris falling from the yew trees. He moved the car toward the right side of the lane as he entered the turn.

Gabriel didn't see the small twig fall to the ground a few yards ahead of him, and the front wheels of his skateboard seized when they met the tiny piece of wood. His skateboard ground to a halt. Like a marionette pulled from a stage, Gabriel's momentum propelled his body into the air as the front of Derek's sedan appeared around the bend.

Time vanished. The sensation of floating in space unleashed an army of butterflies in Gabriel's stomach. His freedom from gravity lasted less than a second, but it felt like an hour. The moment of weightlessness spread through Gabriel's body and replaced the adrenalin rush with exhilaration. The horrific clash of breaking glass and thunder of twisting metal shattered his unnatural euphoria. The impact of the vehicle colliding with the tree was the last sound Gabriel heard.

A sharp pain radiated from his forehead, and Gabriel's eyes filled with a sea of white. Suddenly, blackness engulfed the white, collapsing it from all directions, compressing it into a single point of light until it vanished.

CHAPTER 3

CONSCIOUSNESS

Gabriel's body lay motionless on the left side of the driveway, his face buried in Sandy's snow-white chest. The sedan came to rest against the trunk of a yew tree with Derek's head smothered inside an airbag. Bradley lifted his body off of the wet grass where he had landed after leaping from his skateboard. He ran to Gabriel.

"Call an ambulance!" the words rang inside Tanya's mind.

"What's wrong? Where are you?" Her questions shouted inside Derek's mind while she stood frozen with fear in the kitchen.

"It's Gabriel!" he replied, the words even louder inside her mind.

Overwhelmed with shock, Bradley stood looking down at the dog's and Gabriel's motionless bodies on the pavement. Andy leaped in front of Bradley, nearly knocking him over, and dropped his head to Gabriel's chest.

"Gabriel, you all right?" Bradley called, stunned by the scene before him.

The sounds coming from the vehicle wreckage pulled Bradley's attention away from Gabriel. He snapped out of his confusion and ran to the smoking car. The driver's side window was streaked with lines of blood where Derek's left arm was pinned against the window by the airbag.

Bradley tried to initiate a call for an ambulance, but his VisText wasn't connecting. He reached up to his head and felt under the rim of his helmet for the device. It had fallen off when he landed in the grass. Bradley raced across the pavement, found it on the lawn and replaced it behind his ear. He darted back toward the car while calling for help.

"*Herr Muller,* are you okay? I've called for help," Bradley said, panic still flooding his body like an incoming tide.

"How is he?" demanded Tanya, the terror evident in her tone.

"I'm checking his breathing." Andy tilted his head toward Gabriel's chest to hear that the rhythmic sound of Gabriel's breathing was clear.

Sandy's body was motionless and remained silent. The lifeless dog's eyes faded from glacial blue to smoky-grey. A flash of bluish-white light, resembling a puff of smoke, emanated from Sandy's body and disappeared inside the car wreck.

"I'm coming," said Tanya, her words spilling over with anxiety. She raced down the long driveway to the accident scene.

Confused as to what to do, Bradley left the car and returned to Gabriel. He rolled Gabriel onto his back and slid him off the German shepherd's body.

A small trickle of blood snaked down Gabriel's cheek from the crescent-shaped cut where his forehead had collided with Sandy's head. The force of the impact had knocked him unconscious and snapped the dog's neck, killing her instantly.

Andy sat at attention next to Gabriel's body, as if waiting for a ball to be tossed. His eyes locked on Tanya's as she approached.

Tanya's eyes met Andy's. "He's alive," she heard in her head.

"What happened? Was he hit?"

"No, he fell off his board just as the car rounded the turn. We intercepted him, preventing him from hitting the car."

Tanya knelt at the side of Gabriel's unconscious body and began assessing his injuries. She pulled his long blonde hair off his face and saw the blood dripping down his cheek. She wiped it with her hand.

Bradley went back to the wreckage, covering his nose with his hands in an attempt to shield himself from the smell of the smoldering car engine.

The distant wailing of emergency sirens grew louder as they approached. Bradley pulled open the driver's side door and reached under the air bag and around Derek's body to undo his seat belt, helping him out of the car.

"*Herr Muller,* you better sit down until help arrives—you're bleeding quite badly," Bradley said, so nervous that he was unaware he was speaking in German.

Derek's arms were covered in blood, shards of glass from the windshield still sticking out of his flesh. His left arm was noticeably broken from the unnatural angle of his wrist. Blood streamed down his face from the two-inch gash on his forehead, and his normally brilliant blue eyes were hidden beneath the scarlet blood flooding into them, making it impossible for him to see Tanya and Gabriel.

"How is he?" Derek demanded.

"He's still breathing but—" replied Tanya.

She turned her attention from Gabriel and looked at Derek, unable to focus clearly because of the tears rolling from her eyes.

"I don't know. He's got a cut to his forehead, but that's all I can see."

"*Frau Muller*, the ambulance is here," Bradley said.

"Get the gate. The remote is in the car between the sun visors," demanded Tanya. Bradley went back to the car and activated the gate opener.

"Have the ambulance look at him first," Derek replied.

The ambulance stopped behind the car wreck. A male and a female paramedic walked to the back of the ambulance to retrieve their emergency kit while each pulled on gloves.

"Please, over here!" shouted Tanya while waving her hands for them to attend to Gabriel.

They approached the accident scene together then split up. The male paramedic approached Derek, and the female went to Gabriel. Bradley left Derek's side when the paramedic arrived and started walking back to check on his friend.

With her attention switching between Gabriel and the large German shepherd watching her every move, the female paramedic conducted her primary assessment of Gabriel and began asking Tanya questions.

"Do you know him?"

"Yes, he's my grandson."

"What's his name?"

"Gabriel."

"Gabriel, can you hear me?" she asked as she continued to assess his condition.

"Did the car hit him?"

"No," said Tanya.

"What happened then?"

Tanya paused before she answered in order to hear the details of how Gabriel had hit the twig and then crashed into Sandy.

"Ma'am, did you hear me, are you okay?" asked the attendant, confused by the delay in Tanya's response and looking to see if the pause was on account of a VisText. Like her husband, Tanya refused to use one.

"Yes, I'm fine, just concerned for my grandson."

"What happened?" the paramedic repeated, her eyes looking over Tanya toward Bradley as he approached from behind her. Bradley was about to speak when Tanya began explaining what happened.

"He was racing down the driveway on his skateboard with his friend when he hit a piece of wood. His skateboard stopped suddenly, and he went flying into the air just as my husband came around the corner."

Tanya pointed to Sandy and continued, "One of our dogs, Sandy, was in front of him at the time, and he landed directly on top of her. Is he going to be okay?"

"He took a good hit to the head, enough to knock him unconscious, so he'll need to go to the hospital. I can't see anything else, but he'll have to be looked at by a doctor."

A small light on the side of the paramedic's VisText began to flash, indicating she was communicating with someone, and she turned her eyes away from Tanya out of politeness, as was customary when sending a message with a VisText.

"I've called for another ambulance; it's only a couple of minutes away."

A police car drove up and pulled off the driveway between the yew trees. The lone officer ran over to the wreckage where the paramedic was assessing Derek's injuries. The paramedic pointed to Bradley, and the officer began walking over to him. He called Bradley to the side and removed his tablet from his pocket to begin taking notes.

Bradley repeated the version of events exactly how Tanya had described them without including the part about hitting a piece of wood—he hadn't seen it.

After the officer was finished with his questioning, Bradley walked back to Tanya and the paramedic to find that Gabriel was slowly recovering consciousness. Their attention turned to Derek, who was arguing with the male paramedic.

"Take my grandson first, I'll be fine," he demanded while the paramedic escorted him to the back of the ambulance.

"He'll be fine. We need to get you to hospital, please *Herr Muller*, get on the stretcher."

"No, I insist you take him first," Derek demanded as the faint sound of the second ambulance could be heard.

"They're here. He'll be right behind us," the paramedic assured.

When the second ambulance arrived, the two paramedics helped put Derek on a stretcher and in the back of the first ambulance. They wheeled the second stretcher over to Gabriel and lifted him on to it. After strapping his body down, they placed him in the back of the other ambulance, accompanied by Tanya. The sirens faded as they accelerated away from the Muller estate.

"Do you need a lift home?" the police officer asked Bradley as he walked back to his cruiser.

"No, thanks. I've called my mother, and she's on her way," Bradley replied.

"I'll be here until the tow truck arrives if you change your mind..."

"Thanks."

The magnitude of the day's events, combined with concern for his friend, muddled Bradley's thinking. Tanya's words repeated over in his mind: *'He hit a piece of wood.'* But *he didn't,* Bradley thought. *He just fell off.* The thought simmered in his mind at first, clouding his other thoughts while he watched the tow truck driver connect the cables to the back of the car wreck.

Bradley's mother was five minutes away when the thought came to a boil in his mind. He had to know so he searched the area for Gabriel's skateboard.

He located it partially covered in glass and debris from the wreckage at the base of the yew tree where the vehicle was being removed. It was still sitting right side-up. Bradley picked it up and turned it over to look at the front wheels. Just as Tanya said, there was a small piece of wood from a yew branch jammed in the front wheels, locking them in place.

Bradley's face crumpled from the confusion streaming through his thoughts. His heart pounded like he was racing down the driveway again. *How did she know?* he thought, looking around for a surveillance camera or some other way she could have seen Gabriel fall.

Andy gave a friendly bark when Bradley's mother pulled up the driveway, before running back to the mansion.

CHAPTER 4

HAPPY BIRTHDAY

G abriel moved between consciousness and unconsciousness the entire night, never fully gathering his faculties until morning. He awoke on his birthday in the hospital to an unexpected surprise, a throbbing in his head so excruciating it felt like someone was driving a white-hot needle through his skull. The smell of antiseptic burned his nostrils when he inhaled, forcing him to breathe through his mouth. The faint beep of the monitoring equipment stationed next to his bed rang in his ears, causing him to wince with each sound.

"How are you feeling?" Tanya asked, positioning herself on the side of his bed and lifting his right hand in hers.

"What happened?" asked Gabriel, the pain causing him to squint with each word he said.

"You don't remember?" she asked, unable to hold back the concern in her voice.

"I was racing down the drive with Brad when I fell off my board. I think I hit Sandy?" he said with uncertainty.

"Can you remember anything else?"

Gabriel lifted his left hand to his head, hoping to somehow reduce the agony as he strained to recall the last moments prior to his blackout. Tanya turned and faced the door when it opened.

"Good day. I'm Dr. Morrison, how are you feeling, Gabriel?"

Tanya looked at the doctor for reassurance but was unable to conceal the concern in her eyes. He pulled the electronic chart from the holder hanging at the foot of the bed and tapped the screen.

"I understand you took a bit of a fall?"

"Yah," said Gabriel, still rubbing his forehead.

"Is that bothering you?" Dr. Morrison asked, pointing to the bandage.

"My head's killing me."

"Here, I'll give you some painkiller; it'll help."

He pulled a silver pen-like instrument out of his lab coat and pressed it to Gabriel's temple, clicking the end. A small vibration spread across Gabriel's forehead like a weak electric shock, instantly dissolving the throbbing in his head.

"How's that?"

"Wow, thanks, way better."

"What can you tell me about your fall?"

"I was racing my friend down our driveway when my board went flying out from under me. The last thing I saw was Sandy right in front of me—that's it."

"Sandy?" asked Dr. Morrison, turning to face Tanya.

"She was one of our dogs," said Tanya, her voice dropping to a whisper.

"What, Oma? Was? What do you mean *was*?" Gabriel demanded, stunned by the news.

Tanya looked at Dr. Morrison for guidance, concerned that the shock was too much for Gabriel. Dr. Morrison lifted his hand and gestured it back and forth.

Tanya paused and turned to Gabriel, her face confirming Gabriel's concern.

"Do you remember anything else?"

"That's it."

"Can you tell what day it is?" asked the doctor.

"Saturday."

"And what's today's date?"

"June 19th, 2027. Why?" he asked, realizing something

wasn't right by the disturbing look on Tanya's face.

"You took a pretty good blow to the head. Take a look."

Dr. Morrison held the tablet containing Gabriel's medical file in front of him and tapped the screen to produce the three-dimensional image of the inside of his head.

"You've suffered a mild concussion." He dragged his fingers over the image on the tablet, enlarging a bright red area. "Nothing too serious, but I'm going to keep you here for the night just to make sure."

Relief flooded through Tanya's body, lifting her spirits and her smile. The positive diagnosis was welcome after a sleepless night.

"From what I understand, you owe your life to your dog. If your head had hit the pavement with the same force it collided with your dog, you likely would've met the same fate."

Like ripples from a coin tossed into a fountain, sadness swept through Gabriel, reaching every part of his body. The thought of Sandy's death pierced his heart like a dagger; she was the sister he had never had. Andy and Sandy were always there for him, since he was an infant, true siblings to Gabriel. The pain in his chest was a thousand times stronger than the one in his head, and no amount of painkiller could quell it.

"I suggest you consider a helmet in the future; they really do work," Dr. Morrison said with a sarcastic smirk, and he returned the chart to the holder.

Gabriel looked at his grandmother, who was using all her might to hold back her words, knowing it wasn't the best time to discuss his poor judgment. Dr. Morrison reached for the door handle to leave the room, but he turned and faced the bed.

"Try and stay awake for the next few hours if you can. I'll come back and check in on you before I leave."

"Thank you, Dr. Morrison," Tanya said, referring to the helmet suggestion more than the medical advice.

"Oma, is she really gone?" Gabriel asked, forcing the words from his quivering lips.

"I'm so sorry," Tanya replied and put her hand on his leg.

Gabriel turned his head away so she couldn't see the tears pooling in his eyes. Having never known his parents, this was the first time Gabriel had experienced the loss of a loved one and the emotional pain that can only be triggered by death.

An ache emanated from his heart and filled his chest, shortening his breaths with each passing second. Like standing at the entrance of an undiscovered cavern, Gabriel hesitated to explore the emptiness within him. An unfamiliar need for closure grew inside his mind. He struggled to hold his emotions inside and paused for a moment before looking for answers.

"Oma, what do you think happens when you die?"

"That's a difficult question to answer."

"Why? Is it because we don't go to church?"

"Why do you think that?" Tanya asked, taken aback by his question.

"We don't belong to a church, and isn't that where you learn about what happens when you die?"

Tanya took a moment before she answered. For the first time in his life, Gabriel was displaying some of her own traits towards faith and religion. It caught her off guard, and she paused before answering.

"It's not important whether you do or don't go to church. A church is just a building, a place for people who believe the same thing to gather. It's what *you* believe that really matters."

"Like heaven and hell?"

"If that's what you believe," she said and let a faint smile lift her lips.

"What about Sandy?" he asked, hoping to rid himself of some of his guilt.

Tanya didn't answer but grinned and raised her hand to run her fingers through his hair.

Gabriel searched for something to ease the pain, but without religion, he was left with nothing but his grandmother's words to shape his faith. The contemplation of an afterlife released a panic attack triggered by a horrific and dark thought: *Where's Opa?*

"Where's Opa?"

Tanya slid off the edge of the bed and walked over to the window. She stared at the water droplets snaking down the glass, growing larger each time they connected and accelerating to the bottom of the window.

"He's asking about you. Shall I tell him?"

"How's he feeling?" Derek replied.

"A mild concussion, otherwise okay."

"Good. Tell him; we don't have a choice."

"Okay."

Tanya turned and faced Gabriel. He was watching her with growing concern.

"What's wrong? Where's Opa?" repeated Gabriel, the mounting concern evident in his voice.

"Relax, he's doing fine," Tanya said in a tone she hadn't used since Gabriel was a toddler in an effort to reduce his growing anxiety.

"Where's Opa!" he demanded.

"He's been in an accident..." started Tanya when Gabriel interrupted her.

"What? Is he okay?"

"He's doing fine; he's on the second floor just getting out of surgery..."

"Surgery!" interrupted Gabriel.

"He broke his arm."

"I want to see him," Gabriel said, throwing the blanket off his legs while starting to turn his body to get out of bed.

"You'll do no such thing," Tanya commanded, racing to the side of his bed.

"Why? I want to see him," pleaded Gabriel.

"You will. After he recovers, I've arranged for him to be

brought here. You two will share a room tonight."

"When's he coming?"

"Soon."

"What happened?"

"Can you remember anything?" she asked, hoping he was regaining his memory.

"No."

"Well, Opa was coming up the drive when you and Bradley were racing. He came around the big turn, you know the one halfway up, and that's when you arrived. He turned the car at the last second and hit one of the yew trees."

"It's my fault, isn't it? It's all my fault!" Gabriel repeated, turning his face away to hide the tears growing in the corner of his eyes.

"No, it was an accident, that's all, an accident," said Tanya, rubbing his arm.

"I killed Sandy and put Opa in the hospital. I'm sorry, I'm really really sorry."

"It was an accident. Forget about it. Now, I have a surprise—"

Before she could finish, the door opened and an orderly put down the doorstop to keep it open while he wheeled in a gurney carrying Derek.

"Opa!" Gabriel shouted.

Derek, still groggy from the anesthesia, turned his head and produced a smile when the orderly wheeled the bed in front Gabriel's. His right arm, immobilized in a splint, was resting on his chest.

"He's going to want to sleep for the next couple of hours," said the orderly as he released the doorstop and left the room.

Tanya walked over to Derek's bed and gazed into his now crystal blue eyes. She rubbed his left hand and smiled. Derek returned the gesture and then closed his eyes to rest.

A quiet knock came from the door. Tanya walked over and opened it to find Bradley dripping wet and holding a small parcel in his hand.

"Hi, Bradley, how wonderful, you were able to get it. Come in."

"Hello, *Frau Muller*," he replied and handed the package to Tanya. He took his raincoat off and folded it in his arms.

Tanya pulled a chair from the corner of the room, dragged it between the two beds and took a seat.

"Hey, G, how's it going?"

"Okay I guess, could be better."

"Can't believe how far you'd go to keep me from winning a race. You know I had you," Bradley said, releasing a nervous chuckle.

"I'll give you this one," said Gabriel, forcing a laugh.

"How's your Opa?"

"Okay. He's got a broken arm."

"Yah, I know, I saw it. Looked bad."

"He just got out of surgery. You know about Sandy?" Gabriel asked, shifting his eyes away from Bradley's face.

"Yah, I think she may have saved your life."

"That's what the doctor said too."

Tanya could see Gabriel's emotions welling up and decided to intervene, pulling him out of his downward spiral.

"I think we should give it to him now."

"Go ahead," replied Derek, his eyes still tightly closed.

"We've got a surprise for you. I was going to wait for Opa to wake up, but I think he'll understand."

She walked over to the same side of the bed as Bradley and handed Gabriel the small package Bradley had brought.

"Open it!" demanded Bradley; an ear-to-ear grin filled his face and his words spilled over with excitement.

Gabriel pulled the paper off the small package, and his face instantly brightened. The sadness building inside him popped like a balloon releasing jubilance. Gabriel's face turned cranberry red, and his cheeks flooded with the warmth of happiness as the grief of a moment ago evaporated. The writing across the outside of the plastic case read: "VisText."

"What do you think?" asked Bradley.

"Well?" asked Tanya.

"I can't believe it! Thanks so much, Oma!"

"Thank Bradley and his mom. They went and got it for you from Opa's car."

"Thanks so much."

"No problem, I did it for me mostly. I couldn't go another day listening to you go on about not having one."

"Do you have any idea what day it is today?" asked Tanya.

Gabriel looked at Tanya, the smile sliding off his face.

"I told you, Saturday," he said with hesitation and a distorted facial expression.

"It's Sunday the 20th," replied Bradley, stunned by Gabriel's answer.

Bradley and Tanya faced each other for a brief moment before turning to face Gabriel, who was looking completely confused by the large smiles on their faces.

"Happy Birthday!" they shouted in unison.

CHAPTER 5

HAPPY NEW YEAR!

"Look at this graph," said the professor as he pointed to the large screen at the front of the auditorium. The crowded class of undergraduate students followed the laser pointer to the steep rise in the line representing the Earth's temperature.

"You can see that over the past decade, the Earth's average temperature has increased five and a half degrees, and this rise in temperature continues to accelerate upward because of the blanket of clouds thickening over the planet with each passing day."

Gabriel tensed in his seat, expecting the usual greenhouse gas explanation to follow, condemning humanity for the rapidly deteriorating atmospheric conditions and some proclamation like a product advertisement to buy more green products to combat the problem. Instead of his blood rising to a boil, Gabriel found himself overcome with elation when the professor continued.

"The dire prediction made by many in the scientific community hasn't materialized; there's been no flooding from a rise in sea level. On the contrary, oceans have fallen, as the Earth's atmosphere has become a sponge, saturated with water in the dense clouds hovering a few hundred yards off the ground. It's these clouds we must thank for the constant rain they unleash. Yes, we must contend with a fair amount of flooding, rivers overflowing, streams bursting their banks, but the benefit far outweighs these minor inconveniences. If it wasn't for these swollen rivers and the unlimited hydroelectric power they provide, how would we have replaced the planet's depleted fossil fuels? And think about this, more than half of the students at this university commute here daily from another country—many from another continent—in that high-speed magnetic monster we call the Tube. That wouldn't be possible if it wasn't for all that electricity. I'll leave you with that thought and see you again next week. Enjoy your commute."

Gabriel left the lecture and headed to the cafeteria feeling as though he had just won a lottery. He knew he had made the right decision about his graduate studies supervisor. Certain of his own future from the moment he had left high school, Gabriel focused his undergraduate work at Geneva University to prepare himself for graduate school. He filled his course load with sciences, concentrating his studies toward a career in physics. It was his dream to debunk current scientific thinking and prove that the catastrophic changes in the Earth's atmosphere were a natural phenomenon and not a result of human activity. He swung the university cafeteria door open and entered the noise-filled room.

He walked through the crowd of students at the entrance and immediately scanned the tables for his friends. The odor of spent coffee grounds and deep-fryer grease distinctive of a fast food restaurant permeated the air. Forty or more tables were randomly positioned throughout the cafeteria, each occupied by groups of students while many more sat on the floor in circles as if sitting around imaginary campfires. A loud chatter similar to a football stadium packed with fans flooded the large room while the mostly first-year students fired pop quizzes across the tables to each other.

Bradley sat at a small round table with his back pressed against the glass of the cafeteria window. His girlfriend, Judie, sat across from him working on her tablet. Her petite frame appeared even smaller with her deep black hair extending down to the middle of her back. She maintained her deep olive skin color by spending countless hours on a D-bed, and her Middle East heritage had provided her with dark chocolate brown eyes.

Judie was a biology major, and this semester only shared a chemistry class with Gabriel and Bradley. She had started dating Bradley over a year ago after they met in a physics class, and since then he had spent most of his free time studying at her flat. Gabriel never missed an opportunity to tease Bradley about the amount of time he spent studying, yet his marks hadn't changed in the last two semesters.

Water cascaded down the outside of the window, forming hundreds of tiny streams, each racing to the stone ledge finish line positioned just behind Bradley's shoulders. Judie held her tablet in one hand while putting her coffee back on the table. Obviously bored with studying, she lifted her eyes from her tablet every time a student walked past the window. A small black figure moved over Bradley's left shoulder, catching the corner of her eye while she continued to read her chemistry notes. Without lifting her head, she glanced upward and released an ear-piercing scream.

"Ahhh!" screeched past her lips, silencing the cafeteria as she shoved herself away from the table.

Startled by the sudden outburst, Bradley looked up from his studying just in time to grab both coffee cups before they toppled from the wobbling table. Bradley remained frozen, leaning over the table with a cup in each hand and a look of complete bewilderment etched onto his face.

"What the hell, Judie?" he said while placing the cups back on the table.

A rush of embarrassment flooded Judie's face from the feeling of hundreds of eyes staring at her. She held her right hand over her mouth while her left pointed out the window behind Bradley.

Bradley turned to face the window, where a rain-soaked

squirrel sat looking through the glass, its cheeks stuffed with bright yellow cloth.

"It's only a squirrel," Bradley said, starting to laugh.

"You know how much I hate those rats. It popped out of nowhere, and I wasn't expecting to see it," Judie explained.

"It's just a squirrel," he repeated, returning to his seat.

"They're all rats to me," she replied, reaching for the table to pull her chair back in.

"Careful, this table is shaky."

"I saw that. Good grab by the way," she said with a hint of a smile.

Judie's shout provided a beacon for Gabriel, and he headed across the floor to their table. Bradley saw him and stood up, waving to get his attention.

"G, over here!" Bradley shouted over the returning noise of the crowded room.

"What was that?" asked Gabriel, standing next to their table.

Bradley pointed over his shoulder to the squirrel still taking refuge on the ledge.

"Oh," Gabriel said, restraining a laugh but releasing a smile.

"I hate those things," said Judie again.

"They're all over the grounds right now. They were nesting in the library ventilation pipes; nearly shut the whole air-conditioning system down. They sent a notice that they'd be on the roof cleaning them out over the next few days."

"That's why there's so many squirrels running around," Bradley said.

"Yup, they're trying to find new places to nest out of the rain," Gabriel pointed out.

"We saved you a seat," Judie said, trying to change the subject, and she began moving her raincoat and purse off the empty seat next to her, hoping Gabriel would drop the topic of the squirrels.

"Thanks," he said and tossed his leather case containing

his tablet on the table so he could remove his jacket.

"No," shouted Bradley and Judie in unison while simultaneously reaching for their coffee cups on the table.

Their effort was futile, and the force of his tablet hitting the top of the unbalanced table toppled their drinks before they could lift them.

"Shit, I'm sorry, you guys. Did I get you?"

"Nope, just missed," Judie said with a tone of relief.

"Good," Gabriel said, looking at Judie before turning to make his way to the cashier area to get some towels to clean up the mess.

He pushed through the crowd of students waiting in line to purchase their food to make his way to the cashier and the napkin dispenser next to her till. He started pulling as many as he could from the dispenser when the young woman working the cash register noticed his frantic actions.

"Had a spill?" she asked in a calm and unconcerned manner.

"Coffee," he responded.

"Where?"

"Over there," Gabriel replied as he pointed to the table where Bradley and Judie where moving their belongings out of the way of the advancing liquid.

"I'll send someone," the girl said, and the light on her VisText flashed red indicating she was in the process of communicating. The light stopped flashing, so Gabriel knew he could speak.

"Thanks."

"They're on their way," she said with a smile.

Gabriel returned to find Judie and Bradley sitting with their chairs pushed away from the table, holding their tablets and watching the liquid drip onto the floor.

"Nice move," said Bradley, unable to resist rubbing it in.

"Sorry, they're sending someone to clean it up."

Gabriel took his seat next to Judie, and she handed him his tablet. He began to unbuckle the top of the case to remove it when a middle-aged woman carrying a mop and bucket approached their table.

Her slender figure was clearly visible through the powder grey jump suit. The top third of the front zipper, which extended from her collar down to her waist, showed unmistakable signs of strain in the chest area. Gabriel's eyes locked onto the shiny gold chain swinging a tiny crucifix that fell out of her ample cleavage when she bent over to wipe the table.

"Hey," said Judie, and she slapped his shoulder with the back of her hand.

"What?" said Gabriel while Bradley laughed.

"Put your eyes back in their sockets and apologize," whispered Judie under her breath.

The cleaner refused to make eye contact with Judie, but flashed a smile toward Gabriel.

"Okay, okay," said Gabriel, and Bradley's giggles disappeared the moment Judie looked at him.

"Sorry about the mess," Gabriel said, hoping he sounded sincere.

"Don't worry about it, this is nothing. I clean messes like this all over the campus," she said, pausing her mopping to face Gabriel.

Gabriel's eyes darted straight to her chest again, but this time it was to read the bright yellow letters embossed on the front of her uniform.

"Thanks again, Angie," he said.

"You're welcome." She picked up her bucket and swiftly navigated her way back through the students littering the cafeteria floor.

The three of them pulled their chairs back up to the table and began working on their tablets when Bradley noticed Sydney Grant, one of the science technicians working in the physics department, standing in the cafeteria food line. Using his VisText so Judie was unaware of his actions, he quickly sent Gabriel a text message.

'Now that's who you should be eyeing!'

Gabriel looked over to Bradley, who discretely nodded his head for Gabriel to look in the direction of the food line. Gabriel looked across the room and scanned the line for a second before he recognized Sydney. He glanced back at Bradley and began texting a response when Judie's eyes caught the flash of his VisText. She looked into Gabriel's eyes to confirm her suspicion before whipping her head around to Bradley.

"Give me a break; you guys aren't still going on about the maintenance woman—she could be your mother!" she said like a parent scolding her children.

"No," said Gabriel.

"Of course not," Bradley confirmed, and they both struggled not to laugh.

"I'm going to the washroom. You guys better be over it when I get back—we've got studying to do," scowled Judie as she pushed herself back from the table.

"I agree," Gabriel responded, looking at Bradley with a snicker as he began working on his tablet.

Gabriel was reading his chemistry notes and decided to ask Bradley a question, as he was a natural whiz in the subject. When he lifted his eyes toward his friend, he noticed Judie talking to Angie at the entrance to the cafeteria.

"You think she's apologizing for us?" Gabriel asked while he nodded for Bradley to turn his head.

"Looks like it," he said when Angie placed her arm on Judie's shoulder.

Bradley turned his head quickly back to his tablet to continue his studying when Judie parted ways with Angie.

"Quick, she's coming, don't let her see you looking at her or she'll give us both hell for staring again," Bradley said, and he and Gabriel returned their attention to their work.

They finished studying with just enough time for Bradley and Gabriel to make it to their physics lab. They raced across the campus, trying to remain dry by using the cover of the library before their final dash to the science building. Gabriel hated to use the main entrance and avoided it whenever he could, but Bradley headed straight toward the double doors.

A battle raged inside Gabriel when he entered the science building. His undergraduate studies left him no choice but to take the physics lab, but a knot formed in his stomach every time he pushed open the large glass doors to the building. The shiny gold MBG plaque hanging in the middle of each door was a constant reminder of the corporate influence over science. This was made even more difficult for him since it was *his* family who donated the funds to the university.

Rikter Muller had opened the first bank in Geneva over two hundred years ago, and now Derek controlled the Muller Banking Group—MBG—a global corporate empire. Their influence was everywhere, including Geneva University, which had named their astrophysics lab the 'MBG Astrophysics Laboratory' after their largest donator.

Derek and Tanya went to great lengths to shield Gabriel from the notoriety of the Muller name and maintain their privacy. All through his childhood, Gabriel remained unaware of the media attention the only son of one of the wealthiest families in the world garnered. Derek and Tanya hid him from the public and media, knowing his name would cast a shadow over him.

Gabriel loathed the fact that he was part of the corporate infrastructure, and it left him with the constant feeling that he was on stage. He struggled to remain anonymous at university and refused to speak about his family to anyone.

He entered the lab and took his seat at the bench to wait for the instructor to arrive. Gabriel knew firsthand the influence corporate funding had on science—and he despised it.

Attending lectures was painful for Gabriel, an unforgiving mental torture that weakened his patience. Unable to contain himself, he questioned his professors, debating openly with them during lectures. He knew their hands were in corporate pockets and their research wasn't without influence, so he couldn't 'just accept' their word.

Nothing aggravated Gabriel more than how science was used to support corporate greed, especially when it involved the environment. He knew his family fortune was based on funding science, and he vowed never to be a part of it. Gabriel had decided that he would devote his life toward proving that the rapid warming of the Earth's atmosphere was a natural phenomenon without corporate support.

His open criticism had gained him a reputation of being difficult and closed-minded, but the professors tolerated him because of his family's influence, and loathed this. Most professors refused to address his questions, considering them theatrical antics to gain attention. This angered him and fueled his desire to conduct research without corporate funding, especially from his family.

His choice to ask Professor Michael Ferrel to supervise his graduate work seemed to be the perfect fit. Dr. Ferrel considered Gabriel's ideas serious and having merit. Dr. Ferrel was a peculiar individual with a reputation of his own. Like Gabriel, he was considered theatrical by the others in the physics department, but mostly because of his unconventional appearance and not his research.

Dr. Ferrel's perfectly round and completely bald head looked like an oversized light bulb from a distance. It was peppered with age spots, which were visible to most, as he stood only just over five feet tall while wearing his shoes. This alone made his appearance noteworthy, but it was his glasses that caused most people sharing a room with him to take a second glace. Like a volleyball with ears, his head always supported a pair of deep-tinted, wraparound sunglasses, making it impossible to see his eyes. He had been forced to wear them as a result of an accident while conducting an experiment on the effects of solar radiation.

He had offered Gabriel a postgraduate position when he finished his undergraduate studies. Professor Ferrel was an expert in solar radiation; something Gabriel had read about since he was in elementary school. It was well known by the students that Dr. Ferrel was the only scientist at the university that wasn't funded with corporate dollars, so working for him was a dream come true for Gabriel, who couldn't wait to begin his graduate work in the New Year.

***

The roar of the crowd outside the Vatican was subdued by the explosions of light overhead. Pelting rain quickly cleansed the air of the burned smell of gunpowder. Bright flashes of green and red reflected off the dense cloud cover, made visible in the night by the constant stream of fireworks. A sea of onlookers cheered as the intensity of the visual display increased, signaling the finale of the New Year's Eve celebrations. The crowd began to disperse from St. Peter's Square when the final sequence of fireworks filled the sky with 'Happy New Year.'

Tonino stood silently staring out his office window, ignoring the festivities outside. He was using his VisText to monitor the progress of the M3 when he received an incoming message. Recognizing the sender as a member of the VSS working within the US Central Intelligence Agency, he interrupted the M3 broadcast to read the encrypted message.

Tonino's face strained from his attempt to hold back all the emotion as he finished reading the information. He deleted the message. Unconcerned about the holiday or the time of night, he called Gino Capozzi, the head of Vatican Security and IT, and Father Black to his office.

Gino arrived first, entering the darkened office completely disheveled, the middle button of his business suit jacket straining from the girth of his enormous waist. Crystal beads of sweat resembling grains of salt glistened in the faint light atop his balding head, dripping down the sides before disappearing into a crown of graying brown hair. Gino pulled a handkerchief from his shirt pocket and patted his forehead dry with his left hand while adjusting his VisText with his right.

Tonino stood motionless in front of the window, aware of Gino's entrance from the reflection on the glass.

"Have a seat. I'm waiting for Black," Tonino said without turning to face Gino.

"Of course," Gino replied, and he pulled one of the two chairs in front of Tonino's desk toward him to take a seat.

"How's your family?" Tonino asked with indifference.

"Very well, thank you," he responded nervously, for Tonino had never shown any interest in his personal life before.

"You have a child, correct?"

"Yes, a daughter."

"She's married?"

"No, sir, studying in university," Gino replied, his voice beginning to crack.

"Oh, yes," replied Tonino, falsely pretending he had just remembered. "Following her father's footsteps I see."

"Not exactly. She's studying the sciences."

"How wonderful," Tonino said disingenuously, and he resumed watching the M3 broadcast while holding the palms of his hands together, joining his fingertips in sequence then pulling them apart as if playing a keyboard.

Ten minutes of excruciating silence was finally broken by Father Black's arrival. He acknowledged Gino with a nod and took a seat next to him.

"We need to act quickly. The IGB has given us less than twenty-four hours," said Tonino, referring to the International Governing Body, as he pulled his chair from behind his desk.

"Why? What is it?" Father Black replied.

Tonino continued, ignoring the interruption.

"Gather the Vatican Council at once. We need to prepare the pontiff."

***

Gabriel and Bradley were part of a small group of university friends invited to celebrate New Year's Eve at Judie's home. Her apartment was old but spacious with large windows and plenty of furniture for a student's flat. It was close to the university, so she frequently had friends over, especially during exams so they could study together.

The small gathering of Gabriel's university friends were transfixed by the live coverage of the 2030 New Year's celebrations broadcast from Rome. Their voices filled the small room, drowning out the Italian announcer's countdown on the V-screen.

"10... 9... 8..." The room was filled with shouts of young partygoers counting down.

"3... 2... 1..." Their voices grew louder with each number until finally climaxing in, "Happy New Year!"

"Happy New Year," said Bradley, offering his hand to his best friend sitting alone on the couch.

"What?" Gabriel asked, unaware that he had missed the countdown and the beginning of another year.

"What are you viewing?" Bradley asked, referring to Gabriel's obvious preoccupation.

"The M3's on final approach," Gabriel told him, hoping the dimly lit room would hide the embarrassment covering his face.

"You're joking! It's New Year's and Syd's here."

"Who?"

"Real funny. Sydney, the tech, you know, the one you couldn't take your eyes off in the cafeteria."

"I know, I know, but the Frontier entered orbit—this is once in a lifetime."

"So is Syd. She may be your once in a lifetime!"

"What?" asked Gabriel, half-listening to Bradley but more focused on the video playing on his VisText.

"Forget it, I can ask Judie to put the landing on the V-screen in the den?" Bradley offered, the sarcasm oozing from his voice.

"No, that's okay. I'll finish watching it here," Gabriel said, unaware that Bradley had no intention of actually following through with his offer.

Bradley shook his head in amazement then smiled at Gabriel.

"Sometimes I think you're more than obsessed with space; it's like some kind of religion to you. Don't you ever get sick of it? That's all you think about."

"Never, I love it," he said, unable to contain his exuberance.

"No, you worship it," Bradley said, and he walked back to the group, enjoying the celebrations and leaving Gabriel on his own.

Bradley was used to Gabriel's insatiable appetite for anything to do with space and his particular obsession with the M3 mission. Gabriel's brilliance in the sciences came naturally; inherited from his father, who had been a celebrated research scientist, but Gabriel's strong convictions came from his mother, who had been a dedicated Catholic.

Gabriel watched as the Frontier neared the planet, its surface rust red and gleaming under the direct sunlight. The voice of Commander Rice, captain of the Frontier, replaced the WNN announcer's coverage of the spacecraft's final approach into the Martian atmosphere.

"M3 Control—Frontier, we're holding orbit, requesting final approach," said Commander Rice, his face visible but broken by poor reception.

"10-4 Frontier—M3 Control, final approach approved. You are cleared to leave orbit for touchdown at your discretion," replied M3 control in a clear and unbroken response.

"Roger, M3. We'll—" replied Commander Rice, but the transmission ended.

"We've temporarily lost our link with the Frontier and will return to our historic coverage as soon as we can determine the cause of the lost signal," said the WNN announcer.

"No! No! No!" chanted Gabriel in disbelief.

"It appears a large solar flare has temporarily knocked out our communication with the Frontier, we'll rejoin their progress as soon as the flare passes," said the WNN announcer.

"Bullshit!" shouted Gabriel, unable to hold in his distress knowing that it couldn't be a solar flare. *They'd have plenty of warning if there's a solar flare*, he thought.

The group gathered in front of the V-screen turned their heads in unison, startled by the unexpected outburst. Gabriel felt the heat rush to his face as his eyes whipped over the group staring at him. The light from the V-screen was just enough to allow him to see that Sydney's hazel-blue eyes had locked onto his through her glasses. Embarrassment surged like a tide through his entire body, knowing he was the unwilling center of attention.

"Are you okay?" Sydney asked, breaking the uncomfortable tension while walking toward him.

"Yes, I didn't mean to be so loud," replied Gabriel, looking over her head at Bradley giving him a thumbs up from the middle of the group, which was now returning their attention to the V-screen.

"What happened?" she asked, her strong British accent lifting a smile to Gabriel's face.

"Nothing," he replied, too embarrassed to say.

"That was a pretty loud nothing," she said, flipping her long brown hair over her shoulders before taking a seat on the arm of the couch.

Gabriel's embarrassment quickly changed to excitement with each beat of his heart. The pounding inside his chest erased the M3 from his thoughts, leaving his attention fixed on Sydney. Her doll-like face and petite frame made her appear much younger than twenty-five.

"What?"

"Why did you shout?"

"Oh that, I was watching the M3 begin their final approach when WNN lost coverage. I didn't even realize I said it out loud."

"Wow, must be really important."

"Not really, but I've been following their progress for the last few years and..."

"Years... I'd say that's pretty important."

"I find it fascinating, that's all."

"You must, 'cause you totally missed the countdown."

"I know, but this is once in a lifetime, and there'll be plenty of new years. What did I miss?"

"Just this," she said. She leaned down and pressed her lips against his, delivering a forceful kiss before slowly parting the embrace.

"Happy New Year!"

CHAPTER 6

A NEW ERA

Powder grey light filtered through the window, struggling to fill the small den while the rain tapped on the glass, its rhythmic beating the only sound in the room. Gabriel remained asleep on the throw rug, his naked body partially covered by the quilt that once lay on the back of the small loveseat at his feet.

Sydney lay next to him, her body fully covered, gently twirling his long blonde hair at the back of his neck. Using a seat cushion as a pillow, their heads rested just inches apart, giving her a close-up view of his birthmark.

Gabriel raised his eyelids slowly then shut them quickly, preventing the light from doing further damage to his head. A moment passed before he realized the sensation originating from the back of his head wasn't coming from the light. His mind was slow to wake; it fought to remain asleep until exploding into consciousness like a match thrown into gasoline. Scenes from the previous night filled his mind, and the images fueled the growing fire inside him.

Gabriel's heart tore at his chest from the inside, returning to the level of excitement it had experienced of a few hours before. He couldn't hide the smile tugging at his lips and struggled to quell the urge to shout. Gabriel rolled over and faced Sydney, now lying on her side holding her head in the palm of her hand. Her elbow was on the seat cushion, and the smile across her face was twice the size of Gabriel's.

"Happy New Year?" she asked, the coyness unmistakable in her tone.

Gabriel nodded his head, unable to stop smiling while he lifted the hair off of her face, tucking it behind her ear so he could look directly into her eyes.

"Wow! I've never noticed how blue your eyes are; guess I've never seen them without your glasses."

"I suppose."

"I better find my VisText. I need to call home; my Oma and Opa are probably going nuts," Gabriel said, searching the pile of clothes on the hardwood floor next to the throw rug.

"I'm sure they're fine."

"You don't know them; I'm surprised they haven't broken down Judie's door," he said with a nervous laugh and stood up to search for his VisText.

"Yah, I live with my parents too. I'm sure they won't have a Happy New Year until I call."

"I thought your parents lived in London?"

"They do."

"Oh, I didn't know you commute."

"Worst twenty minutes of my day," she said, throwing the quilt off her body and standing up to get dressed.

"Wow!" escaped Gabriel's lips, a reflex reaction to her naked body.

"What?" Sydney blurted, turning around to face Gabriel.

"Oh, no, no, no, that's not what I meant, Syd. You're beautiful," Gabriel said, reading the unmistakable look of self-consciousness rolling over her face.

"Then what?" she said, quickly reaching for her clothes.

"Your skin; I never noticed it last night. It's snow-white, and you don't have a single tan line. I thought everyone owned a D-bed."

"My parents do, but I prefer to get my vitamins the old-fashioned way—by eating them. Besides, I despise getting into those solar-microwave ovens," Sydney said, referring to the artificial sunlight showers found in nearly every home to offset the continual lack of direct sunlight.

Gabriel laughed as he pulled his pants on.

"What's so funny?"

"You're a tech in a physics lab, working around radiation every day and you're worried about D-bed radiation? That's funny."

"Not just D-bed radiation, all radiation. My first job was in a biotech lab in northern Canada; I used to commute from London through the Diomede Island Tunnel. That, in itself, frightened me. People just aren't meant to travel under oceans. Besides, I think we're all exposed to way too much radiation—it'll be the death of us all. That's why I hate commuting. What really sucks is that every time I get off, my hair is standing on end," she said with a smile.

"Then why don't you just move here?"

"Now my commute is half as long."

"The radiation?" he said and lifted his right eyebrow.

"I'm trying to save some money to get my own place, and the ten minutes between here and London isn't that bad compared to what I was doing before."

Sydney finished buttoning her blouse and found her VisText on the hardwood under her pants. She attached the device to the back of her ear and waited for the system to connect to the network.

Sydney paused her dressing and stared blankly into the air as Derek spoke to her.

"When will he be returning? There isn't much time," enquired Derek, his words entering Sydney's mind.

"He'll be leaving soon," she responded.

"Good, he'll be safer here. I don't know what's going to happen."

Sydney turned back to face Gabriel and resumed dressing so as not to draw attention to her brief conversation with Derek.

"Seven missed calls and nine e-messages—all from home. That's not as bad as I thought it would be," Sydney snickered while tightening her belt.

Gabriel finished dressing but didn't find his VisText until he lifted the cushion to replace it on the seat. He placed the VisText behind his ear and initiated it.

"That's strange," he exclaimed.

"What, what's strange?"

"Not a single message—not even from my grandparents?"

"You're lucky. Maybe they've finally set you free, wish mine would."

"Yah maybe," Gabriel replied, his voice containing apprehension from the out-of-character lack of concern from his grandparents.

They straightened their clothes before embracing for a final kiss good-bye. Gabriel opened the den door slowly, taking every effort not to make a sound. He was certain Judie was still asleep since the flat remained silent. He stepped into the room ahead of Sydney

Like biting into a fresh jalapeño pepper, a massive surge of heat flashed through Gabriel's cheeks when he stepped into the living room. Judie and Bradley were sitting on the couch facing the den door, each holding a coffee mug and wearing clown-sized smiles on their faces.

"A good morning?" asked Bradley with no attempt to hide his snickering.

"A Happy New Year?" Judie asked in an equally mischievous way.

Gabriel stopped a few steps into the room and bowed his head in embarrassment, and to hide the enormous smile fixed to his lips. Giddiness rushed through his veins like an injection of adrenalin. He reached back without looking and took Sydney's hand, pulling her forward to spread the embarrassment between them.

"Good morning," Sydney and Gabriel replied in unison.

"Oh, isn't that sweet, they're already twinning, and it's only been a few hours!" Bradley said, unable to hold back his laughter.

"Wow, you're right, Brad; they are twins, look at their eyes. I wish you had eyes that blue," Judie said, shifting her gaze back to Bradley.

Bradley's smile waned slightly from Judie's comment about his eyes, sensitive about his appearance.

"All right, that's enough," said Gabriel in a feeble attempt to show concern.

"You need a lift home, G? I called my mom, and she'll be here in a bit if you want a ride," Bradley offered.

"Sure, that'd be great."

"Thanks, Judie, for everything. I had a great time," Sydney said, pulling on her raincoat and heading for the door.

"You're welcome. See you tomorrow," Judie replied.

"Byyyyye, Sydney, see you tomorrow," Bradley said, and he waved from the couch as Gabriel walked Sydney out the door.

Gabriel took Sydney's hand and led her down the hallway to the entrance of the stairwell, the planks of the old wooden steps creaking with each step they took. Gabriel stopped in front of the large glass doors at the entrance to the small lobby of the apartment building and took Sydney's other hand. He pulled her close and delivered a lengthy good-bye kiss.

"Do you want me to walk you to the Tube?"

"No, you'll miss your ride," she said releasing her right hand from his and pointing to the small car waiting at the curb of the building. Then she kissed him on the cheek and left the building.

Gabriel floated up the stairs, high from the last few hours and having the best night of his life. He entered the hall to find Bradley walking toward him with his raincoat.

"See, I told you... once in a lifetime," Bradley said, throwing Gabriel's raincoat at him as he walked past with a large smirk on his face.

"Crap, I totally forgot!" shouted Gabriel, his smile shattering and his heart pounding as adrenalin surged through his body at the thought that he had missed the M3 touchdown.

"Forgot what?" replied Bradley, thinking Gabriel had left something in the flat.

Gabriel was frozen in place, his eyes fixed on Bradley, but his full attention was on his VisText. He activated it and searched the WNN site for an update on the progress of the M3. Relief stymied his adrenalin rush and returned his heart rate to normal.

"What is it? What'd you forget?"

"Nothing," he said and the smile returned to his face as they made their way down the stairs.

Gabriel left his VisText on WNN the entire ride home, hoping the M3 broadcast would resume. He stared out the window at the old stone buildings lining the narrow cobblestone street. Their Renaissance-like splendor was made more notable by their reflection in the glass of the modern office buildings quickly filling the downtown. The rapid clicking of the car tires over the wet stones was rhythmic and was in perfect timing with the windshield wipers. Gabriel's eyes immediately caught the glimmer of the lion heads as the car slowed.

The same sick feeling returned the moment the steel gates swung open. Bradley's mom drove the car slowly up the winding drive toward the Muller mansion. Gabriel held his breath when they drove past the point where the accident had happened.

Through the rain-covered windows, he could see the mark left on the tree where the collision occurred. A fountain of sadness overflowed from his heart, flooding his emotions with the grief of knowing he had caused Sandy's death. Time still hadn't closed the wound at the loss of his childhood companion.

Surprised to find only Andy greeting him at the door, Gabriel developed urgency in his movements as he entered the house. *They would've called if something was wrong*, he thought. The old dog's body was slow to move down the hall, limping with each step from the fused hip joints. Gabriel rushed to the bottom of the stairs and called for his grandparents.

"Opa? Oma?" he shouted up the staircase.

"In here," Tanya said from the media room.

The sound of her voice released the rush of anxiety from Gabriel as if pulling a drain plug from his chest. The concern swirled away with every step toward the media room.

"What are you viewing?" he said, entering the room with Andy trailing behind.

"I thought you'd be watching," Derek replied, his voice softened with his age.

Gabriel looked at the V-screen and his eyes widened. The broadcast erased all other thoughts from his mind but the impending landing. He walked across the room, ignoring his grandparents, who were seated in separate recliners, to take a seat on the couch, never once removing his eyes from the events unfolding on the V-screen. Andy took a spot on the floor next to Derek. The view of the Martian horizon from the cockpit of the Frontier disappeared into a cloud of orange dust when the spacecraft came to rest on the surface.

"Happy New Year, Gabriel," Tanya said, not trying to hide the annoyance in her tone.

"Oh yah, Happy New Year," Gabriel replied with embarrassment, and he jumped off the couch to give her a kiss before turning to hug Derek, who was now standing in front of his seat.

All three of them turned their attention back to the V-screen.

Commander Rice prepared the Frontier's bay doors to launch the Martian rover and place the first human footprints on Mars.

"How long?" asked Tanya in her head.

"Less than an hour," Derek answered.

"Should we tell him?"

"No."

Gabriel remained glued to the M3 broadcast, unaware of the silent conversation occurring next to him. Tears gathered in the corners of his eyes, the direct result of not blinking while staring at the V-screen.

Across every continent and in every corner of the planet, routine activities ground to a halt. Commander Rice donned his spacesuit, continuing the live broadcast from his helmet camera, enabling the WNN to broadcast his point of view of the first manned exploration of Mars.

He and First Officer Donna Wright opened the hatch of the Frontier and stood at the top of the short ramp leading down to the Martian surface. They walked in unison to the end of the ramp, where Commander Rice stopped. The world held its breath in anticipation, and the planet itself seemed to stop rotating when Commander Rice turned his helmet to direct the camera towards First Officer Wright. He raised his arm, signaling her take the first step off the ramp and onto the rust-colored ground.

She turned toward the camera, her eyes barely visible through the reflective covering of the helmet face shield. She lifted her right foot off the ramp and proclaimed, "It's with great honor I take this first human step on Martian soil and begin a new era in space exploration."

In cities and towns everywhere, the air filled with cheers and shouts of jubilation. Long blasts of car horns echoed through the streets, accompanied by the sounds of people yelling and whistling. The jubilation was akin to a country winning the soccer World Cup, but this victory was mankind's leap from the planet Earth.

Commander Rice joined his first officer on the Martian surface, scanning the horizon with his camera to give the WNN viewers a feel for the foreign landscape.

They removed the Martian rover from the opposite side of the spacecraft, extended the two large solar panels on the back and took their seats in the vehicle. Commander Rice drove the rover directly into the amber sunlight blanketing the planet. The external cameras mounted on the Frontier tracked the rover as the polished metal sides reflected the sunlight, giving it the appearance that it was made of gold.

"Look at that," said Gabriel in a voice resembling a child's pointing to animals in the zoo.

"What?" Derek replied.

"The sunlight, something's not right," he said, looking at the current time on his VisText.

"What do mean?" Derek asked, turning his gaze toward Tanya.

"It's exactly 09:37; where they are, the sun should be much lower in the Martian horizon right now," Gabriel said with certainty.

"Are you sure?" Tanya asked, looking back at Derek rather than Gabriel, knowing Gabriel wouldn't be wrong when it came to matters dealing with the sun and space.

"I'm certain, it's Tuesday—well before noon," he said, scanning the information on his VisText.

"So?" replied Tanya.

"The sun shouldn't be above the Martian horizon for another thirty-three minutes, something's not right here."

"Maybe your calculations are wrong," Derek said, hoping this would quell Gabriel's concern.

"Not a chance they're..." Gabriel replied, but he stopped midsentence when he saw the rover come to a rapid stop, sending rust-colored dust into the air.

Commander Rice and First Officer Wright had both spotted the tiny reflection of light from an object on the surface just ahead of the rover.

"Frontier Base this is the Rover. We've spotted an Object of Interest. We're going to investigate," First Officer Wright said over the radio.

"Can you ID the OI?" replied the duty officer back at the spacecraft.

"OI appears metallic, a possible meteorite," replied

Commander Rice, his voice filled with the confidence of a veteran officer.

"Rover, you're cleared to sample."

Commander Rice and First Officer Wright exited the rover and removed a camera and toolbox from the back. Their movements were rendered slow and methodical by the bulky spacesuits as they walked toward the small glistening object.

"Negative on the meteorite," reported First Officer Wright approaching the OI.

"Can you give a positive ID?" requested Frontier Base.

"Standby."

First Officer Wright knelt next to the OI and opened the toolbox while Commander Rice recorded the area with a camera before they disturbed the site. She removed a small hand spade from the toolbox and drove it into the soil a few inches from the exposed tip of the object. The spade stopped dead two inches below the surface.

"Rover, can you confirm OI? Is it a meteorite?"

"Standby," repeated Commander Rice, his voice noticeably apprehensive and lacking its assertive confidence.

First Officer Wright released the spade and began brushing the soil away with her gloves. Commander Rice dropped to his knees next to her and helped remove the soil. Neither officer uttered a word while their hands frantically swept the Martian soil off the OI. A cloud of terra cotta dust obscured the live broadcast, leaving the rapidly expanding audience back on Earth paralyzed with anticipation.

The dust slowly settled, allowing a few rays of sunlight to illuminate a dark grey luster against a backdrop of terra cotta soil. There sat a partially exposed object; its smooth surface stamped with unidentifiable markings.

"I don't believe it!" Gabriel screamed.

CHAPTER 7

A BELIEF

S ilence enveloped the Earth. The eerie calm, born out of disbelief, lasted only an instant as if the entire population of Earth had inhaled a deep breath at the same time. The second of absolute stillness felt like an hour before it was shattered by the global reaction to the discovery.

The first wave of global reaction to the discovery occurred at that moment. Unable to handle the simultaneous surge of ten billion users, the World Wide Wireless network collapsed for the first time in history. The world plunged into a communication black hole. The words 'Transmission Interrupted' filled the solid blue screen visible on the V-screen.

"What's happening?" exclaimed Gabriel, confused by the failed broadcast, having never seen this before.

Tanya looked at Derek for guidance, and he responded without speaking.

"Let things unfold on their own."

"The network must've crashed," Tanya said, turning to face Gabriel, who was standing in the middle of the room adjusting his VisText.

"Network crashed? What does that mean? Even my VisText isn't working."

Tanya and Derek both laughed in unison, realizing that Gabriel had never experienced a network failure. Before they could explain, Gabriel fired questions at them.

"Did you see it? Could it be real? What do you think it was? How did it...?" asked Gabriel, but his questioning stopped when the V-screen started broadcasting and the voice of the newscaster resumed.

"We apologize for the interruption in service and hope to re-establish our audio link as soon as possible. For those just entering our broadcast, the unimaginable has just occurred. It appears the M3 has uncovered evidence of extraterrestrial life on Mars. Hold on... I've just been informed we've regained our live audio."

"Rover, can you confirm?" repeated Frontier Base.

"Affirmative, the OI is metallic," said Commander Rice.

"Viking 1?" requested Frontier Base.

"Negative. Origin: unknown!" said First Officer Wright, her words barely comprehensible through the sound of her heavy breathing.

"This can't be real, I don't believe it," said Gabriel, looking over to his grandparents, his mouth wide open with shock.

Derek and Tanya sat motionless and quiet as if they were watching a weather forecast instead of the most important discovery of humankind. Their complete absence of emotion startled Gabriel.

"What's wrong with you guys, why aren't you saying anything, don't you know what this means?"

"What's it mean?" asked Tanya.

"Oma, are you joking?" Gabriel pleaded.

"Opa, tell her."

"What?" Derek replied.

"I don't believe you guys. This means we're not alone. This is it, there's finally proof, other civilizations do exist," said Gabriel, unable to restrain the jubilation in his voice.

"Why's that so important?" Tanya asked, maintaining no emotion in her voice.

"Are you kidding? It's something I've always believed but never thought it could be true."

The adrenalin shooting through his veins began to wane from his grandparents' total calmness. Confusion replaced his excitement. *Maybe they're too old to understand?* he thought in an attempt to make sense of their lack of enthusiasm.

"Don't you get it, WE—ARE—NOT—ALONE!" he shouted as if saying the words slowly and loudly might free the excitement within them.

"Yes, this is incredible news," Derek said with a feeble attempt to join in Gabriel's excitement.

"Wow, I don't get you two. This is like, like…" Gabriel searched for the words but stopped when he saw V-screen.

Commander Rice panned his helmet camera to the object now extending over a foot out of the Martian soil but no closer to being removed. The camera zoomed in on the unidentifiable markings, which formed a perfect circle at the top edge of the object. They appeared to glow from the red dirt pressed into their depressions.

"Rover, give us a close-up. We're requesting translation support from the International Space Station. Can the OI be recovered?" asked Frontier Base.

"Negative, it's imbedded," replied First Officer Wright.

"Tag and continue."

"10-4," replied Commander Rice.

They returned to the rover after pounding a steel bar holding a locater beacon into the ground next to the partially exposed piece of metal. Commander Rice drove the vehicle slowly around the massive boulders scattered across the surface like giant red and brown marbles.

Progress was slow over the fine Martian sand. Millennia of windstorms had shaped the surface into perfect sand ridges exactly two yards apart, causing the rover wheels to struggle and the vehicle to lurch like a sailboat rolling over rough seas.

Commander Rice's helmet camera bounced down to the red surface ahead of the rover and up to the deep butterscotch-colored sky. They continued to drive, scanning the area for other signs of life.

"It's incredible... Like proving there really is a God," said Gabriel, speaking more to himself than his grandparents.

"Like what?" asked Derek holding back his surprise.

"Like proving there's a God. You know, people have talked about ETs forever, but no one's produced scientific evidence they exist. Like God, no one's ever proven He exists either, right?" Gabriel replied without removing his eyes from the V-screen.

"Really, that big?" Tanya added, glancing toward Gabriel's statue-like body affixed to the broadcast.

The horizon disappeared from view when the rover entered an area where two small rock bluffs grew out of the ground. The sun, still low in the Martian sky, cast long shadows, making it difficult for Commander Rice to maneuver the rover around the increasing number of obstacles in the narrowing path forward. First Officer Wright and Commander Rice took turns giving commentary of their progress while the rover snaked between stone outcrops and miniature sand dunes.

"If we were on Earth, I'd say we're at the bottom of an ocean or in a dry riverbed somewhere in Arizona," Commander Rice said.

"Except the color of the sand is reddish-orange here," First Officer Wright added.

"Take a core," Frontier Base requested.

"Copy," Commander Rice replied.

Commander Rice stopped the vehicle in the riverbed, and he and Officer Wright unpacked the equipment to collect a core sample of the ancient riverbed. They placed the long steel tube containing the Martian soil in the back of the rover and continued their exploration of the landscape.

They followed the ancient Martian riverbed, meandering through the formations as if they were on a Disneyland ride until they rounded a sharp corner. Sun flooded directly into Commander Rice's face shield, blinding him and the camera lens for an instant. He slammed the vehicle to an abrupt halt when he heard First Officer Wright's voice.

"Oh my God!" she shouted.

***

Light from the V-screen reflected off the smooth wooden surface of the desk in Tonino's small Vatican office. He stood in his usual position in front of the window, staring outside while the raindrops raced down the glass. Uninterested in the progress of the M3, he remained with his hands clasped together behind his back, waiting for Father Black to arrive.

The sound of rapid footsteps on the polished marble floor outside his office signaled Father Black's approach. His reflection in the glass was Tonino's cue to turn and address him.

"It was fortunate for us that the IGB time-delayed the M3 transmission," said Father Black, entering Tonino's office.

"They're concerned about the global reaction," Tonino replied.

"Should they be?"

"Is the pontiff prepared?" asked Tonino, ignoring Father Black's question.

"Yes, the Council was able to convince him to read it," Father Black replied.

"Excellent. I want it live. It's got to be genuine," demanded Tonino.

"He's a mess; we could barely get him to read it," Father Black responded, unaffected by Tonino's command.

"This is critical. We've got to maintain control. They've already started jumping from buildings."

"I understand but he's an old man, and the news of the discovery nearly killed him," Father Black replied.

"I don't care!" shouted Tonino. "In a matter of hours, the square will be filled with people looking for guidance; he's got to deliver our message. I want all of our spiritual leaders to deliver our message—understood?"

"Yes, they will. Gino has contacted them—the Muslims, Jews, Sikhs, and everyone else, all have a copy and will deliver it following the pontiff's address."

"We can see the finish line. I'll not tolerate failure."

"Yes, we did everything we could in the time we had."

"It had better be enough."

*****

The camera re-focused and the scene broadcast back to Earth was unimaginable. Rising from the rock bluffs on both sides of the empty riverbed were the remains of a civilization. As far as the camera could see were decrepit ruins protruding through mounds of red and orange dust. Like the ancient city of Pompeii rising from the ashes of Mount Vesuvius, the remnants of what appeared to be an ancient Martian city formed a mosaic across the landscape.

Like listening to a pair of scuba divers during a deep-sea dive, a full minute passed while only the sound of breathing could be heard.

"Frontier, you getting this?" asked Commander Rice, breaking the silence.

"Copy," replied Frontier Base.

A civilization on Mars generated the second global wave of reaction. The realization that intelligent life had existed elsewhere, and Earth's loss of uniqueness in the minds of many, began to take its toll. Temples, churches, mosques, virtually all places of worship saw large gatherings of people. Faith began to crumble.

The elderly were the first to crack under the weight of humankind's first moment of certainty they weren't alone in existence. Bodies fell from the sky as those unable to accept the news leaped from buildings. Others plunged into the torrents of swollen rivers, while entire families hung themselves.

The WNN interrupted the M3 broadcast to cover the emerging story of the mass suicides. The V-screen showed a crowded road in Rome where people were in hysterics over the bodies lying in the street.

"We now go live to Rome, where confusion and panic have spread like a plague infecting the world's religions," said the WNN broadcaster.

"It's started in London," Sydney suddenly spoke in Derek's head.

"I know. Rome too," Derek replied.

"What do we tell him?" Tanya asked while delivering a concerned stare toward Derek. Before he could respond, Gabriel interrupted.

"Are they nuts? Why are people doing that?" Gabriel asked, looking at Tanya, completely unaware of the discussion already occurring.

Gabriel noticed the distressed look on Tanya's face and turned his attention to Derek.

"What's going on, what's wrong?" he demanded.

"Nothing's wrong..."

"Then why does Oma look like she's about to cry?"

"It's a lot to handle; I think we're both in a bit of shock."

"You're not thinking of doing what those idiots are doing, are you?"

"No!" Tanya snapped.

"Good, I still don't get why they're doing it in the first place."

"For some people, their belief in God is all they live for. Without this belief, they have no reason for living. For some, this discovery has shattered their belief and undermined the reason they exist."

"What do life on Mars and the belief in God have to do with each other?"

Gabriel's lack of exposure to religion was evident in his questioning. He had showed no interest as a child, and Tanya and Derek had gone to great lengths to shield Gabriel from all religions, especially the Catholic Church, knowing the Vacare controlled the Catholic empire.

"Up until this moment, all those who believed the words of the Bible to be literally the words of God had all the proof they required to be certain God exists. If God is all knowing, He can't be wrong, these are the words of the Bible, and up until now, the believers were clear on this—we're alone."

"But we're not alone, the Bible was wrong," Gabriel said, his face littered with confusion.

"Exactly, so if the Bible is wrong, then God was wrong. This is impossible; the fact that God cannot be wrong is fundamental to all religions."

"So people are killing themselves because of a mistake in the Bible?" asked Gabriel in disbelief of his own question.

"No, they're killing themselves on account of what they believe," Tanya interjected.

"Wow," Gabriel replied, turning his attention back to the V-screen.

"I'm afraid it could get much worse," said Derek.

"What's worse than killing yourself?" Gabriel asked, turning his attention back to Derek.

"History has shown nothing is more powerful and more destructive than a belief."

CHAPTER 8

WHAT DO YOU BELIEVE?

A patchwork of umbrellas separated brightly colored raincoats in St. Peter's Square. The congregation continued to grow, spilling out of Vatican City and onto the streets of Rome. High-pitched shrieks of crying emanated from the crowd as the faithful gathered to seek guidance from their spiritual leader.

Tonino stood close to the edge of the small stone balcony hanging from the façade of St. Peter's. The rain splashed off of the marble railing, forming crystal droplets on the top of his leather shoes. His charcoal black eyes absorbed every ray of the pewter daylight filtering through the clouds. A smile lifted the corner of his lips when he gazed to the right at the empty Loggia of the Blessings.

A loud creak shrilled from the rusty hinges of the weathered French doors, announcing Father Black and Gino's arrival. The cool interior air rushed from the building, pushing the drapes out the open door. Gino pulled his tablet from its case and began touching the screen.

"He's ready?" Tonino asked, still facing the massive crowd below.

"The other Council members are with him—he's confused," Father Black replied.

"Are you certain he'll read it?"

"He's confused and exhausted, but yes, he agreed to do it."

"Start."

"Right away," Gino replied, and he began working on his tablet while Father Black used his VisText to contact the Vatican Council to prepare the Pope.

The automated three-story V-screen normally used on Sundays to project mass began its rise high above the Basilica roof. Its appearance was the first signal to the crowd of the impending arrival of the pontiff. When the screen reached full extension, it cast a pale blue glow over the square. The anticipation of Pope John Paul IV's arrival subdued the noise of the crowd to a low din.

Two streaks of light flickered across the massive screen like a flash of lightning before the Pope's face appeared. A deafening roar erupted from the square, signaling their overwhelming need to hear from their leader. The Pope's bust filled the entire projection to the midpoint of his miter, giving the crowd a close-up view of the anguish carved into his face.

Without speaking, he labored to raise his hand above his face. His movements were slow when he made the sign of the cross. Gold framed eyeglasses sat low on the bridge of his nose, magnifying his tired and sunken eyes. His eighty-five years left him struggling to begin the Lord's Prayer, his deep voice cracking with the first words. The crowd followed his lead and repeated the prayer, reciting it in unison, drowning the Pope's words.

When the prayer ended, he completed the sign of the cross before lifting his eyes to the teleprompter positioned to the right of the camera. He strained to read the prepared speech, stumbling over the slow scrolling dialogue he didn't want to say.

"People of the world, the time has arrived to renew your belief. We gather today as one planet among infinite planets, one people among infinite peoples. On this day, we realized we are but one of God's many creations. Do not fear, for today we unite for guidance, understanding and spiritual enlightenment.

"Search no longer, as the direction we seek has always been there for us, we can find all that we need in the Bible. Our Lord's own teachings give us the answers. We just need to turn to the book of Genesis. The words written are certain: *'In the beginning God created the Heavens and earth.'* Not a single Heaven but infinite Heavens.

"Others foretold of this miraculous day. We must listen to their word, for if we look further into the Lord's teachings, we can see it has always been clear. It has been our indulgence in our own greatness that has led us astray. We are not his only flock; *'I have other sheep that are not of this sheep pen. I must bring them also. They too will listen to my voice, and there shall be one flock and one shepherd.'* John (10:16).

"Today begins a new era for the faithful. We have borne witness to the Lord's greatness. It is a testament to His wondrousness that He has given us this gift. Our Lord, all knowing and ever-loving of His people, bestowed his faith in us by giving His people the ability to travel to another of his creations.

"But we have strayed from His teachings, reveled in our own greatness and preoccupied ourselves with our own accomplishments. Condemned are those who put faith in man's creations, many of you worship science and not the Lord our God. Science will not bring you salvation! Those who worship this false idol will perish as sure as those who suffered the apocalypse on Mars.

"Just as He created us, our Lord created this message, one that is clear and unequivocal. Merciful and forgiving, God sent us to Mars to deliver a glimpse of our future and give His final warning: the Rapture is coming.

"The image of a civilization on Mars reduced to dust is our future—just as He foretold. Now more than ever is the time to follow the Word of God. Only His teachings will prepare you for the second coming of Christ our Lord.

"Let us pray for forgiveness and thank the Lord our God

for His gift so that we can follow in His footsteps and one day join Him."

The Pope's eyes shifted away from the teleprompter so they looked directly into the camera. He pushed his glasses to the top of his nose, enlarging his eyes to twice their natural size. Ignoring the prepared speech next to him, he continued addressing the billions of faithful with his own message.

"Rid yourself of the evils of our own making and follow the word of the Gospel. It is time for all of those who believe in the Lord our God to rise up and defend His words and rid mankind of those who tempt us with the evils of our own ingenuity."

"What's he saying?" shouted Tonino. "These aren't my words!"

Father Black shouted into his VisText while Gino scrambled to punch commands into his tablet.

"What's going on?" asked Father Black to the Vatican Council members escorting the Pope.

Tonino's frantic shouting contorted his face with rage as he commanded Gino to end the broadcast.

"Stop him, stop him!" he screamed while positioning his body directly in front of Gino's. He stood so close the intensity of his yelling sprayed spit on the screen of Gino's tablet.

"I'm trying, I'm trying," Gino replied, his fingers flying over the tablet screen in a futile attempt to end the broadcast.

"I implore all spiritual leaders around the world to use whatever means necessary to fight back and extinguish those who look to science as their new religion. Only then can the Holy Spirit enter our bodies and give us the eternal salvation we..."

The V-screen flickered, and the Pope's image vanished into the solid blue background at the same time as his words evaporated from the public address system, leaving the crowd momentarily silent.

It was too late. His request conjured an immediate

response. The faithful in the crowd yanked the VisTexts from behind their ears, throwing them to the ground and destroying them.

Like a coin tossed into a fountain, Pope John Paul IV's message started as a ripple in St. Peter's Square that grew into a wave radiating in every direction. A tidal wave of rebellion encompassed the Earth, washing over the planet and dividing the world in two.

***

Gabriel looked at the V-screen in disbelief. He had heard the Pope's address but didn't understand. Like missing the last piece of a jigsaw puzzle, he could see the events in front of him but couldn't put them together or understand why they were happening.

He searched for answers to the questions racing through his mind, but only got more frustrated and confused with each passing moment. His growing annoyance with himself forced him to look for help.

"What're we going to do?" Tanya asked Derek, unable to withhold her concern.

"He can't be left alone. Matteo, Luca, it's time."

"I'll find the Kruger boy at once," Matteo replied, and the old dog struggled to lift its hindquarters from the floor.

"Luca, I need you at the university," Derek commanded.

"Understood, I'll locate his professor," Luca replied.

Gabriel turned from the V-screen to ask for answers. He was surprised to find that Derek and Tanya weren't watching the broadcast. They remained motionless in their seats like a pair of manikins gazing into space while Andy moved between their chairs heading for the door.

"Are you guys all right?" Gabriel asked, jumping out of his seat in concern.

"Yes, we're fine," replied Tanya.

"You're acting strange. You certain everything's okay?" he

asked while walking over to where they were seated. "You looked like you were having a seizure or something."

"It's all happening at once... a bit of shock," Derek replied, trying to deflect Gabriel's attention away from their odd behavior.

"Andy too?" said Gabriel in a snicker, not convinced of Derek's explanation.

"What?" Derek asked, deliberately avoiding his question.

"Even the dog— it was kinda creepy?"

"What's wrong with Andy?" Tanya asked, looking down at the dog in an attempt to look concerned.

"Never mind," said Gabriel in frustration. "Did you guys even listen to the Pope's address?"

"Yes, it's what I was afraid of," Derek said while shaking his head.

"What?"

"Everything is going to change. We must prepare for the worst."

"What does that mean? You're not making any sense," Gabriel complained, looking for concrete answers to Derek's cryptic responses.

"The discovery has shaken the foundation of Christian belief. Not everyone is prepared or capable of accepting that we're not alone. Fear can invoke the religious to go to extraordinary lengths—look at the suicides, that's just the start."

"But the Pope, he made it sound like it was no surprise. It was all written in the Bible."

"What else could he say? He's facing the collapse of the entire Catholic empire."

"Did you understand what he said?" interjected Tanya.

"Not really."

"The Pope has requested not just Catholics but members of all religions unite to actively reject science. He wants them to rise up and renew their belief in God and return to the Bible for answers."

"So?" Gabriel replied. "This still doesn't make any sense to me."

"He's talking about starting a war," said Derek in an elevated voice.

"War? That's crazy; he didn't say anything about war. Besides, there hasn't been a war since the IGB formed—they won't allow it," Gabriel said.

"Yes, but the IGB can't control belief," Derek pointed out.

"Why would they want to control someone's beliefs? People can believe whatever they want... who cares?"

"I wish that were the case," said Derek, pointing to the image on the V-screen of a crowd of people tearing VisTexts off their ears and throwing them on a growing fire in the middle of a street.

Gabriel shook his head in confusion, still not understanding why anyone would condemn science or jump from a building because life was discovered on another planet. Triggered by the thought of the M3, it was at that moment he felt the urge to call Sydney.

"I'm going to call a friend," Gabriel said, walking to the door to find some privacy.

"Say Happy New Year to Bradley for us," Tanya said.

"What? Oh sure," he replied, caught off guard.

Gabriel shuffled past Andy down the cathedral-like hallway toward the kitchen so he could call Sydney in private. The clicking of the dog's nails on the marble floor behind him resembled the ticking of a clock and triggered a thought.

"Hey Boy, you want to go out?" asked Gabriel, who had stopped his progress and waited to rub Andy's head.

Andy lifted his eyes to Gabriel's when they approached the kitchen door. Drizzle coated the paving stone path winding through the garden to the forest at the back of the estate. Gabriel watched Andy limp the length of the path until the large dog's body disappeared in the thick foliage. Gabriel closed the door.

A tingling sensation rolled around Gabriel's stomach

when he activated his VisText. The excitement of the day temporally erased the memory of his New Year's Eve.

"Hi, how was your commute home?" Gabriel asked, his thoughts clouded with nervousness and feeling stupid for not having a better opening line.

"Oh, you know, not the best twenty minutes I've spent in the last twenty-four hours," Sydney said without hiding the innuendo.

"That's good to hear," replied Gabriel, thankful they weren't using a video link so she couldn't see the embarrassment flooding across his face.

"What do you think about the discovery? Amazing, isn't it?"

"I still can't believe it. I think it's incredible," he said with hesitation.

"But?"

"What do you mean?" said Gabriel, trying to play dumb.

"I could hear the skepticism in your tone."

"Something didn't seem right to me, that's all."

"Like what?" she asked.

"Do you ever work in Dr. Ferrel's lab?"

"Every Tuesday, why?"

"You know he's an expert in solar radiation and specializes in solar eruptions?"

"Of course."

"Well, he's documented the solar cycles of eruptions and created a calendar that not only shows the historical events but predicts events into the future."

"I know, I've seen that giant calendar he's got hanging in the back of his lab. What's your point?"

"If you look at it closely, you'll see the next big eruption isn't till sometime in early 2036."

"So? I don't get it."

"The International Space Station claimed the M3 transmission was interrupted by a solar flare," he said in anticipation of a reaction, but there was only silence so he continued.

"Not only that, the sun was in the wrong place."

"You've lost me for good now."

"The sun was in the wrong part of the Martian horizon for the time of day. It was way too high for nine thirty in the morning."

"Wow, you really do take this space stuff seriously," Sydney replied, hoping to stop his dissection of the M3 broadcast with a comment intended to cause Gabriel to realize his obsession with space.

"Yah, I guess so. Have you ever heard of a *'network crash'* before?" he said in a surprised manner.

"No, what is it?" Sydney asked, happy her plan had worked.

"My grandparents said it used to happen in the old days when computers failed or something like that. That's what they called it when our VisTexts stopped working."

"Oh that, that was scary, wasn't it? It's the first time I've ever seen it happen."

"Me too. You know what's really scary? The Pope's address."

"Why?"

"My grandparents said he's calling for a war."

"War. There hasn't been one in ages."

"I know, but he said to follow the words of the Bible, to rise up, reject science and return to the old ways. The Pope blamed people for worshiping science and said the world's going to end."

"Unbelievable," she said, raising her voice to sound surprised.

"I know, I guess we're all going to hell," Gabriel said with a snort.

"You think?"

"When's the last time you... went to church?" Gabriel asked, the sarcasm unmistakable in his tone.

"Never. You?"

"Me either. Guess we're both damned."

"Why?" asked Sydney, pretending to sound concerned.

"'Cause we're scientists," Gabriel replied.

"Do you think it could really happen?"

"After today, I'd believe anything."

CHAPTER 9

SURGERY

Tonino charged past Gino and Father Black through the balcony doors, his shouts of profanities muffled by the chanting crowd. Gino and Father Black followed him inside. Like a cloud drifting in front of the sun, the large room grew darker as Gino closed the burgundy drapes. Tonino placed his hands on the back of one of the two Victorian chairs positioned in front of the mahogany desk on the opposite side of the room.

Subdued by the granite walls, the roar of the crowd penetrated the inside of the façade of St. Peter's, fueling Tonino's rage to the verge of exploding. He released his grip from the back of the chair before facing Father Black; the dim amber light filtered through the Murano glass figures, masking the fury on his face.

"You told me he'd read it!" said Tonino, the words barely audible through his clenched teeth.

"Sir, I told you he was confused and…"

"Confused? Confused?" repeated Tonino, the anger in his voice foreboding. "He's not confused but delusional. It wasn't God who exploded the Earth's population. Nor was it God who put the food in the mouths of these billions and billions of new faithful. It's not God building the dams, powering the light farms or genetically modifying the crops. I won't allow puerile human beliefs to destroy everything I've worked so long and hard for," scowled Tonino like a mad dog locked in a pen.

"He's old and doesn't understand..." began Father Black but to no avail, and Tonino erupted into a raging tirade.

"You told me he'd read it!" he shouted and kicked the chair across the room. The back of the chair slammed onto the floor, releasing an echo into the room as it skidded into the wall. Tonino stepped to the right.

"Why didn't you stop it?" Tonino screamed at Gino, and he kicked the second chair to the floor.

"I tried, but..."

"Shut up!" barked Tonino, getting hold of his temper. "I won't fail this close. We need to fix this before it's too late."

"Fix what?" asked Father Black sheepishly.

"Don't you understand? He's starting a war; if we don't act fast, millions, hundreds of millions of people are going to die, and that will jeopardize everything."

"What can we do?" asked Gino.

Tonino walked over to the French doors and pulled the velvet drapes open to look at the mass of religious followers still milling in the square.

"Look at them; they're lemmings following their leader off a cliff. He must recant his request and call for peace," Tonino said.

"I'll call the other Council members; I'm certain they're still with him," said Father Black, activating his VisText.

"No, take care of it yourself," interrupted Tonino.

"Of course," Father Black replied. He terminated his call and began walking to the door.

"Once you've explained the matter to our pontiff and convinced him of the importance of correcting his request, contact me at once. I'll send you a prepared address."

"Understood," said Father Black, and he reached for the metal door handle on the solid oak door.

"And, Father Black," Tonino said in an out-of-character cheerful tone, "failure is not an option."

Father Black nodded his head and disappeared behind the door. Gino remained motionless, holding his tablet as Tonino approached him.

"We must hurry before the crowd disperses. Start by sending a message to my international friends. They're to take whatever measures are necessary to control their people and quell any uprisings. Tell them the Pope's broadcast failed on account of a camera malfunction and he'll resume his address shortly."

As instructed, Gino spoke out loud so the voice recognition on his tablet could form the message. He confirmed the text and then sent it to government and religious leaders around the world.

"Message sent, sir," said Gino, awaiting further instruction.

"Have this sent to the teleprompter." Tonino began dictating a new speech, emphasizing peace and tolerance, when Father Black contacted him with his handheld.

"Is he ready? We don't have much time," asked Tonino.

"He refuses to do it," Father Black replied.

"He doesn't have a choice. Make him!" Tonino responded, the anger breaking through in his voice.

"He doesn't care."

"Make him!" shouted Tonino.

"Impossible," Father Black replied and the communication ended.

Tonino threw his handheld across the room, smashing it against the same wall as the chair, shattering the device into countless pieces that danced on the floor like a handful of marbles.

Gino stood like a statue, petrified with fear as Tonino cast his eyes toward him.

"Let Father Black know the Council would be wise to prepare the Sistine Chapel for an election."

***

The next five days passed so slowly they felt more like a

month to Gabriel. As he awoke, he struggled to lift his eyelids to find the time. The nightstand clock he had gotten for his fourteenth birthday resembled a miniature V-screen and projected a three-dimensional image of the solar system with all the planets positioned relative to the sun at that moment in time. A line of text scrolled along the bottom of the image displaying: Year 2030 Sunday January 6 – 09:37.

He rolled onto his back, pulled the blanket off his body and lay in bed staring at the dull glow entering his window. Gabriel despised January; the winter sunlight was futile in its ability to penetrate the cloud. Like living in the arctic, there was no difference between day and night, even the temperature remained constant. It was also the time of year when Geneva received the heaviest rains, making it impossible to do anything outdoors.

This year, Gabriel's loathing for winter was nonexistent. Instead, his mind was filled with elation and excitement for the upcoming year. Like being tickled against his will, Gabriel was pleasantly tortured by his emotions; this rendered him incapable of focusing. His thoughts were trapped in a pendulum, constantly swinging between the incredible M3 discovery and the anticipation one gets at the beginning of a new relationship.

He was undecided on what to do on the last day of winter break from classes. Going back to university was something Gabriel looked forward to, especially this semester for two reasons: this was his last semester as an undergraduate, and Dr. Ferrel had asked him to work part-time in the solar radiation lab to prepare for graduate research. This preoccupation left him oblivious to the rapid changes occurring in the world.

Without leaving the bed, Gabriel took his VisText from the nightstand and placed it over his ear. Feeling thirteen again, he struggled to find a reason to call Sydney without appearing desperate since they had last spoken less than ten hours before. Persuaded by his own uncertainty, he decided to call Bradley instead.

"Hey, Brad, what are you up to?"

"Hanging out at Judie's, you—"

"Is that Gabriel?" shouted Judie's voice in the background. "Does he know?"

"Know what?" asked Gabriel, his curiosity piqued.

"No," Bradley replied to Judie.

Judie activated her VisText and Gabriel accepted her request to enter the conversation so he could communicate with them simultaneously.

"You've got to see this!" Judie said.

"What? Brad, what's going on?" Gabriel asked, getting impatient and wanting to know.

"I'll send you a video of—"Bradley started, but before he could finish, Judie interrupted again.

"No, it's something you've got to see in person," she demanded.

Frustrated with the conversation and intrigued by the mystery, Gabriel's patience dwindled.

"What are you guys going on about? Fine, do you want to come here or should I go to your place?"

"We'll go there," Bradley answered.

"Give me a half-hour; I'm still in bed."

"Oh, is Syd there?" Bradley asked, and the sound of Judie laughing filled Gabriel's head.

"Nooo," replied Gabriel, his impatience instantly replaced by embarrassment. "See you guys in a bit," and Gabriel exited the conversation before they could get another question in.

***

Tanya and Derek sat at the kitchen table eating breakfast and discussing the rapid changes occurring around the globe. Derek knew nothing good would come from the Pope's request that all religions have their followers rid the Earth of those who worshipped science.

"I want him out of that university; it's not safe," Derek said.

"Science is everything to him. It's his religion," Tanya replied.

"She's right," said Sydney. "I see him there, and it's his entire life; he will not give it up."

"Even more reason to remove him."

"What do you have planned?" Tanya asked.

"I'll have him take over the business."

"Never. He's embarrassed to even be associated with the MBG," said Sydney.

"I won't give him a choice—"

"No," snapped Tanya, her face lit up with fear.

"I have no choice."

"He can't lose us too; it'll destroy him," Tanya pleaded, knowing Derek would do whatever was necessary to protect the Terminal Vector.

After taking a shower, Gabriel made his way downstairs to the kitchen to get some breakfast. Derek ended the discussion so he could speak with Gabriel.

"Morning," he said, walking past the kitchen table straight for the kitchen door.

"Good morning, do you have a minute?" Derek asked in a voice he reserved for the most serious of topics.

Recognizing the tone at once, Gabriel stopped his progress to the door and returned to the table, standing next to his grandfather. His emotions swung a full one hundred and eighty degrees from the morning's elation.

"What's wrong?" he asked, directing his questions to Tanya even though Derek was closer.

"Have a seat," Derek said, pulling the chair next to him from under the table.

"What's wrong?" Gabriel repeated as his breathing increased and his cheeks flushed with heat.

"Nothing's wrong. We need to talk, that's all."

"It's Andy, right?"

"No, I want to talk about the future and the business—" started Derek, but Gabriel cut him off.

"We've talked about this before—I am not interested!" snapped Gabriel as the concern ripping through his veins transformed into anger.

"It's time; I want you to take over."

"Oma, tell him, tell him I'm not interested. Tell him I don't want to be a banker." Gabriel pleaded with his eyes as much as his words.

"Please listen to Opa. The world is changing, and it won't be safe to be at the university—especially studying science."

"What are you worried about? The Pope's crazy address; a war or something?"

"Yes," Derek replied.

"Yes... what?" asked Gabriel, taken by surprise by Derek's answer.

"All of them."

"I don't care. I won't do it, I won't have any part of the corporate world. Give it all to charity, I don't want any of it," he said emphatically and pushed himself from the table.

Gabriel walked directly to the kitchen door and opened it. He stared down the path, his eyes straining to see any sign of movement as he waited for the anger boiling inside him to cool. Still looking out the door, he changed the subject.

"Any sign of him?" he asked.

"I'm certain Andy won't be coming back," Tanya answered in a tone all mothers reserve for the most difficult discussions with their children.

"How do you know?" Gabriel asked, clinging to the hope Andy would reappear from the woods where he had watched him disappear.

"Andy was at the end of his life. Animals know when their time has come, and many choose to find their own final resting place," Derek said, using little emotion in his tone.

Gabriel's mood took another turn, and this time it came crashing down. His heart filled with a sorrow so powerful it made him nauseous. Andy and Gabriel had shared a special bond that didn't exist with Sandy. When she died, he felt the loss, but it was nothing compared to the agony rushing through his veins at that moment. Gabriel hadn't felt pain rip through his body like this since Derek and Tanya explained how his mom was killed in a horrific car accident in France.

His appetite vanished, as did all other feelings, and Gabriel was filled with emptiness. Tanya struggled to find a way to ease his pain.

"You'll feel better when your friends get here," said Tanya in an attempt to cheer him up.

Derek looked at Tanya, and before he could point out her error, Gabriel interrupted, "How'd you know they're coming over?" He was unable to hide the surprise in his voice.

"I heard you talking to them when I went upstairs to get dressed," Tanya replied, thinking quickly.

"Oh," Gabriel responded, not entirely convinced but too overcome by the loss of his childhood companion to dwell on it.

"I know, but I hate seeing him like this," responded Tanya to Derek, looking over to Derek's concerned gaze.

"He'll be fine," Derek replied in her head.

A tone resembling a doorbell came from the V-screen and an image of Judie's bright yellow car appeared in front of the iron gates.

"Front gate open," commanded Gabriel, and the sound of the warning buzzer and flash of the red warning light filled the V-screen.

"I'll show them in if you want to get something to eat," said Tanya.

"No, thanks. I'm not really hungry anymore," Gabriel replied as he left the kitchen.

Tanya turned toward Derek, concern covering her face.

"You were right. I'm not certain even the death of his grandparents would be enough to keep him from his devotion to science," Derek said.

"What do we do?" Tanya asked.

"We must protect him every minute of every day."

Judie drove the car under the large covered area of the driveway at the front door, triggering the motion-activated lights. The front entrance to the Muller mansion resembled a hotel more than a home. Large manicured shrubs grew out of ornamental pots stationed on both sides of the front door, and dozens of red and white flowers draped over the edge of the massive hanging baskets positioned every few yards.

Gabriel stood in the open front door waiting to greet his friends. The rain pelted the pavement so hard on both sides of the covered area that it made it difficult to talk, so Gabriel waited for them to enter. Judie got out first and made her way to Gabriel.

"Come in," he said and took her raincoat to hang it up.

"Where's Andy?" Judie asked Bradley while bending down to remove her shoes.

Bradley turned to face his friend; Gabriel's crystal blue eyes were welling with emotion and filling with tears. Gabriel looked up at Bradley to find his eyes hidden behind a pair of tinted glasses.

"He's gone," Gabriel said so quietly that only Bradley heard.

"I'm so sorry, I didn't know," Bradley said, and he put his hand on Gabriel's shoulder.

"It's all right; it's just beginning to sink in," Gabriel replied.

"What's wrong, Brad?" Judie asked, confused by their actions and the conversation.

Bradley looked over at Judie with a look intended to get her to drop the conversation, but it went unnoticed under his glasses.

"What is it?" she asked again.

Gabriel paused before taking a deep breath and then answered, "Andy's gone."

"Oh, I'm so sorry," replied Judie in a somber tone, as she also knew how much Andy meant to Gabriel.

"Forget about it, now, please don't tell me you guys rushed all the way over here to show me his goofy glasses," Gabriel stated, and he reached up to pull them off of Bradley's face.

Bradley felt the yank and quickly shut his eyes so as not to get the end of the frame in his eye. Gabriel held the thick, black frames in his hands before lifting them to his face in a motion to place them on.

When Bradley opened his eyes, Gabriel dropped the glasses. A shockwave pierced his body like an electric shock. Bradley's eyes were no longer the familiar dark green Gabriel had always known; they now radiated a brilliant cobalt blue.

"What the hell have you done?" Gabriel asked, desperately trying to restrain a belly laugh.

"Don't you love them?" said Judie.

"Ugh..." Gabriel replied, unable to form a word or take his eyes off Bradley's.

"He surprised me. Isn't that wonderful? He heard me say how much I loved blue eyes, so he went and got them changed," she said, bubbling over with excitement that her boyfriend would have cosmetic surgery just for her.

"Don't say a thing!" Bradley commanded, expecting to hear Gabriel start the ribbing about his relationship with Judie.

"What can I say?" laughed Gabriel, unable to hold it in.

"You wait, you'll be doing the same for Sydney, but I bet it'll be an enlargement of some kind," Bradley snickered, and he picked up the glasses, putting them back on and pretending to need them to recovery from the surgery.

CHAPTER 10

ROSS RADIATION

A low thumping resonated inside Gabriel's heart, growing stronger like the sound of footsteps rushing down a staircase. The pounding originated in his chest but rapidly raced through every part of his body, the intensity so potent it released a surge of adrenalin he hadn't felt since his teenage years racing a skateboard down the driveway. Gabriel's exhilaration gained momentum with each word he read on the tablet in front of him.

The June humidity was stifling, even with the climate control in his room set to reduce the moisture-laden air. Gabriel found it more comfortable to lie on the floor in his bedroom while reading a scientific paper and listening to music. The journal article written by the world-renowned British physicist Dr. David Ross was wildly controversial, contradicting all current scientific thinking. His research purported that it was changes in the sun's radiation and not human activity causing the rapid heating of the Earth's atmosphere, and this radiation reacted in some way with the Earth's atmosphere.

Dr. Ross's lab at the University of Rome had yet to detect the exact wavelength of radiation or what in the atmosphere it reacted with, but he referred to it as 'Ross' radiation. He went on to suggest the sun had been emitting higher levels of Ross radiation over the past hundred years and this was what was responsible for the catastrophic atmospheric conditions blanketing the planet. The scientific community continued to reject his claims since no one had been able to measure Ross radiation or even prove its existence.

Gabriel knew this was exactly what he was looking for, and he wanted to prove Dr. Ross right. Excited by the prospect, Gabriel sent a copy of the article and a message to Dr. Ferrel, informing him of his plans to focus his graduate research on proving that Dr. Ross's radiation theory was correct.

Gabriel's excitement began to wane from the rumbling in his stomach. The aroma of fresh basil and garlic drifted into his room from the kitchen, causing his stomach to growl. Distracted by his hunger, he struggled to finish reading the paper before dinner.

It was Saturday, and only the second weekend in the past six months that he wasn't spending with Sydney. Her absence contributed to his lack of focus, and he fought the urge to call her, knowing she was in London telling her parents about their plan to get an apartment together.

His stomach clenched again, but it was more than his appetite causing the knot to tighten below his ribs. Gabriel glanced at the solar clock nearly every minute, dreading the moment when Tanya would call him for dinner. He too had to tell his grandparents of his plans to move in with Sydney. The anxiety swirled inside his head, causing him to reread the same line of the paper three times without comprehending a single word.

Frustrated by his lack of progress and fueled by his low blood sugar, Gabriel powered off his tablet and tossed it on his bed while he raised himself from the floor. He crawled over the mattress and sat with his head against the headboard and his legs outstretched.

"V-screen on," he commanded.

The device immediately projected an image of a crowd gathering at what appeared to be a fire at a collapsed building. Gabriel commanded the volume to increase, and he watched the broadcast with intent as the voice of the WNN correspondent reported from the scene.

"It is unclear at this moment how many people were in the research lab when the explosion occurred, but I think it is fair to say many lives have been lost here today. As we reported earlier, this is one of three attacks occurring almost simultaneously at different parts of the globe.

"The first was in Moscow, followed quickly by the second in Osaka, and now this one in London, less than a minute after the others. All three attacks were on research labs and all three were intended to completely destroy them. No one has claimed responsibility for these cowardly acts, but we can be certain they were not random."

Gabriel rolled so quickly toward the nightstand to grab his VisText that he nearly fell off his bed. He tilted his head to the right and pulled his shoulder length hair over the side of his head to expose the small shaved patch of bare skin behind his ear used to seat the VisText. Before he could call Sydney, there was a message from her already waiting for him. Gabriel opened the message and read it, 'Don't worry, I'm fine, I'll call you later.'

He read the time on the message and saw it had been sent less than a minute ago; the relief he felt immediately derailed the train of concern rolling through his mind. The text flamed his urge to call Sydney, flaring it into a burning compulsion. Gabriel's mind continued to battle with his heart over the need to hear Sydney's voice when he heard Tanya's.

"Dinner's ready," her soft voice called up the staircase.

"I'll be right down."

Gabriel removed the VisText from his ear and placed it in his pocket, knowing his grandfather forbid the use of any electronic devices during meals. The aroma of basil and garlic was now pungent, reviving the hunger pangs in Gabriel's stomach.

When Gabriel entered the kitchen, he was surprised to find the V-screen on with the volume turned off, but he quickly realized the recent attacks on the research facilities would take precedent over the normal mealtime rules. The look of concern on Tanya's face negated the need for him to ask what she thought.

The familiar ping when the neck of the wine bottle hit the rim of a crystal goblet indicated Derek was pouring the wine.

"Can I give you a hand with anything?" Gabriel asked Tanya before heading to the table.

"No, thanks. Just sit."

Gabriel took his usual seat to the right of his grandfather and struggled to speak. The news of the attacks combined with his need to inform them he was moving out paralyzed his mind. Fortunately, for him, Derek put an end to the battle raging inside Gabriel's head when he spoke first.

"Did you see this?" Derek asked, pointing to the V-screen.

"Yah, I was watching it."

"Now do you understand why I want you to forget about your research and learn the business?"

Gabriel looked towards Tanya in the hope she would intervene and end the discussion before it started. She remained silent as she placed a bowl of pasta in front of Derek and Gabriel.

A burning sensation shot through Gabriel's face. He threw his fork into his bowl, causing a loud clank and slammed his hands on the table. Derek and Tanya stopped their eating and focused their attention on him.

The month of constant badgering, piled on to the stress of telling his grandparents he was about to move out, triggered a rare outburst from Gabriel.

"What does it matter if I'm there or not? I haven't seen you go to the office in months," Gabriel snapped.

"Exactly, you can conduct your business from here, where it's safe," Derek said, caught off guard by Gabriel's outburst.

"You mean as long as I'm not at the university conducting my research."

"Yes."

"That's not going to happen. My research is my life."

"Fine," barked Derek. He lifted the fork and spoon from the table and began turning the fork in the pasta to form a spiral ball in the spoon.

"Please eat," said Tanya.

Filled with the rage at his grandfather's relentless pursuit, Gabriel didn't hesitate and decided to break the news of his departure out of spite.

"Actually, I do have some news for you both," said Gabriel, forming a closed-lipped smile.

Derek's tired and wrinkled face showed its age. His short, snow-white hair barely covered his scalp, but his eyes were untouched by time and still possessed the fire of a much younger man. He locked them on Gabriel's with an ice-cold glare.

Tanya placed her fork on the table and forced a smile to her lips, knowing what Gabriel was about to say. Her age was well hidden under the impeccable care she put into every detail of her appearance; the wrinkles on her forehead were softened by her glacier blue eyes, and her long brown hair was never out of place.

"Sydney and I are moving in together," Gabriel said, and he held his breath in anticipation of an outburst from his grandfather.

Tanya's eyes turned away from Gabriel and focused on Derek's, her expressionless face looking for guidance.

"Let me talk to him," she said to Derek without speaking.

"Okay," Derek replied.

"Well, this is news," Tanya said, returning her smiling face to Gabriel.

Stunned by the lack of a negative reaction from them, Gabriel shifted his eyes between his two grandparents.

"You two are getting serious then?" Tanya asked with a hint of smile showing on her lips.

"We've been getting along really great and Syd really hates commuting so—"

"Where are you going to live?" Derek asked.

"Syd put in an offer on a small flat not far from the university," Gabriel replied, still confused by the lack of emotion from his grandparents.

"Do you need some help?" asked Derek, now returning his attention to his food.

"Syd has been saving, and I can help with the money I make as a teaching assistant," Gabriel explained with a look of surprise flooding across his face.

Gabriel's pride combined with his determination wouldn't allow corporate funding to taint his university research, even if it was from his own family. Gabriel knew he didn't even have to ask his grandparents and his family's wealth would look after his every need.

"Where's the flat?" asked Tanya.

"Right off of Quai Charles-Page, just a few blocks from the university. From the roof we'll be able to see the Jet d'Eau in summer if they ever turn it on again."

"Not likely. The sediment is destroying the pump," Derek replied.

"I know; the lake's the color of coffee," Gabriel said, hoping the change of subject would stick.

"Are you certain we can't help?" asked Tanya, the unmistakable tone of motherly concern overpowering her voice.

"Thanks, Oma, but we want to do this on our own."

"What does Sydney's family think of this?" Derek asked, his tone still cold and hollow sounding.

"Don't know. She's breaking the news to them now," replied Gabriel, the anger once raging through his body now replaced by confusion.

"When will you be moving out?" asked Tanya, struggling to stop the tears from forming.

"Two months maybe, depends when the deal closes on the apartment. We figure by the middle of August or the start of the semester at the latest."

"That soon?" Tanya exclaimed.

"That's more than a month from now, and it's not like I'm moving to the other side of the planet."

"I know, but we hardly see you now—"

"I promise to come home every weekend to see you guys."

"You mean to get some of this," Derek said, pointing to the bowl of pasta in front of him.

Gabriel smiled at his grandfather, uncertain why breaking the news to them had gone so much smoother than he expected. He turned his attention to the V-screen and the images of bloody bodies being pulled from the rubble.

CHAPTER 11

POPE PIUS XIII

Nightfall surrounded the small Vatican cafeteria, smothering the last faint remnants of daylight illuminating the stained-glass windows. The sweet fragrance of fresh-baked biscotti lingered over the long wooden table where Father Black sat nursing the last drops of his espresso. A sharp shrill emanated from the old rusted steel door hinges when the door opened.

Tonino pushed the door closed behind him and hung his long dark rain cloak on the coat hooks next to the door. The soles of his leather shoes clicked along the marble floor as he walked toward the table. His ebony eyes and stone-like face displayed no emotion when he pulled the chair from the table across from Father Black.

"Good evening, sir," said Father Black, placing the small coffee cup on the saucer in front of him.

"I understand the pontiff refuses to recant," Tonino said with an unnatural calmness in his voice.

"Yes, sir. The council has tried everything."

"Then he must be replaced. The attacks are escalating; soon there'll be nothing anyone can do. I want it stopped before there's a war and we start losing serious numbers. Have I made myself clear?" Tonino said as the calmness faded from his voice.

"Yes, sir. Who should replace him?"

"It doesn't matter; just ensure the next Pope follows my

orders better than this one."

"Of course—"

"If he doesn't, I'll replace the entire Vatican Council."

"Understood," replied Father Black, meeting the hollow gaze of Tonino's empty eyes.

Tonino pushed himself from the table and stood up. He looked down the long table to the life-sized Crucifixion hanging from the old wooden beam and watched the final bit of natural light disappear from the face of the stone carving of Christ.

"Remember, Father Black, make sure it's immaculate."

"As always, sir."

Tonino turned and walked away from the table, donning his cloak before leaving the restaurant. Father Black remained seated at the table, gently running his finger around the rim of the espresso cup while sending a message to the other members of the Vatican Council.

***

The long dark corridor of the Apostolic Palace amplified every footstep placed on its stone floor. Pale yellow light entered the hall from the row of windows facing St. Peter's Square, rendering the tapestries hanging between the windows varying shades of grey.

More light than in the corridor entered Pope John Paul IV's sleeping quarters through the two large windows opposite the door. The simply furnished room had high ceilings and a prie-dieu with an oversized Crucifixion above it. Pope John Paul IV lay sleeping in his bed when Father Black lifted the feather pillow over his head.

Little struggle occurred as the last faint remnants of life left the old frail body. Father Black returned the pillow next to the Pope's head before placing the pontiff's arms next to his sides and pulling the blankets up to his chest.

***

Lightning greeted the morning a few hours later. Two rapid flashes of light reflected off the glass protecting the hand-painted mural of Christ hanging over the Pope's bed. The light was followed by a rolling clap of thunder that swept down the long corridor of the Apostolic Palace.

Called by his personal aide, the pope's Camerlengo raced down the hall to the Pope's sleeping quarters, his footsteps clicking on the hard floor like a snare drum as he approached the bedroom door. After his third attempt at calling the pontiff, the Camerlengo sent a VisText to the entire College of Cardinals, beckoning them to the Vatican.

***

Moments later, the sound of the storm was overpowered by the continuous clanging of steeple bells. The ringing resonated outside the large office where three cardinals waited at a table. Their scarlet vestments cast a red hue over the stark white stone floor.

These cardinals represented three of the four members of the Vatican Council, a clandestine group that controlled the Catholic empire. The Vatican Council had existed for millennia. The four bishops or cardinals were each responsible for a different department in the Church: the Department of Diocese, where the day-to-day Church operations were conducted; Vatican Acquisitions, which searched the globe to secure important artifacts of religious significance; Papal-Intergovernmental Relations; and the most powerful department of all was the Vatican Secret Service, controlled by Father Black.

Cardinal Cabot, the eldest and most senior member of the Council, removed his eyeglasses and placed them on the table. Seventy-three years were etched in his face, making it appear cracked and faded like a medieval painting. As Head of the

Department of Diocese, he knew too well what protocols the Church would soon follow after the death of a Pope.

"Why has he summoned us here?" Cardinal Cabot asked the other two cardinals, his voice soft and scratchy from years of saying Mass.

"He didn't say," answered Cardinal Fraser, unable to restrain the apprehension in his voice.

A line of sweat formed at the edge of his salt and pepper hair in spite of the chill in the room from the air-conditioning. Hidden by the table, Cardinal Fraser sat on his hands to prevent the others from witnessing his uncontrollable nervous twitching. This made his already tall and lanky stature more noticeable.

As the newest member of the clandestine group, he still suffered from anxiety when summoned to a Vatican Council meeting. His position as Head of the Department of Papal-Intergovernmental Relations made him responsible for negotiating with other nations on matters of vital importance to the Vatican. Cardinal Fraser had had little success reducing the number of attacks by the faithful around the globe and feared the meeting was to address his failure.

"Stop your worrying Cardinal Fraser; I'm certain we are meeting to discuss the pontiff's death," said Cardinal Popov, his Russian accent made even more noticeable by his deep voice.

"Easy for you to say, you've nothing to worry about. Acquisitions have been good lately... haven't they?" retorted Cardinal Fraser, who continued to watch the door for the first sign of movement.

The room fell silent when the office door opened. Father Black arrived at the meeting wearing his traditional black robes, held in place by a thick crimson rope tied at the waist.

"Put your VisTexts on the table," commanded Father Black.

He walked past the men and over to the large window behind the table in a manner they had seen a hundred times before. He peered down at the massive crowd gathering in St. Peter's Square. Pop-up tents and temporary shelters covered the area as Catholics assembled for the election of a new supreme leader. Still facing the window, Father Black clasped his hands behind his back and spoke.

"Look at them, they are sheep; all so willing to follow without question. We have fifteen days as the College of Cardinals hastens to Rome and the Conclave begins. I want it certain who will replace our dearly departed pontiff," Father Black commanded.

"That's not possible. Even we can't—" snapped Cardinal Cabot.

"Make it happen!" demanded Father Black, his stance frozen in front of the window.

"How?" replied Cardinal Popov.

"There are three of you, I suggest a compromise."

"That hasn't happened for hundreds of years," replied Cardinal Cabot, referring to the election of the Pope by a group of only three, five or seven cardinals who represented all others.

"Use acclamation if you have to, or whatever means necessary, I'll leave that to you," Father Black snarled, squeezing the grip on his own hands with his lack of patience.

"Who do you suggest replace his Holiness?" asked Cardinal Fraser, feeling slightly better the meeting wasn't a result of his failure.

"One of you."

"What?" shouted all three men in unison.

Father Black turned away from the window and headed for the door. He paused at the table. His eyes displayed no emotion, and his face revealed no hint of his intolerance of having to work with others to accomplish Tonino's request.

"I suggest you get to work, the Novendialis has begun and I expect you will encounter much more difficulty during the conclave."

***

Thronged with the faithful, St. Peter's Square rippled like the surface of a small lake as the dedicated moved about in prayer. Pelting rain subdued the waiting crowd, unaware of the proceedings unfolding inside the Sistine Chapel. Most took cover from the deteriorating weather under large umbrellas and makeshift tarps in anticipation of a lengthy vigil.

Late afternoon sunlight struggled to illuminate the rooftops of the Vatican while reams of black cloth draped the exterior of every building as far as the eye could see. It had been four weeks before Pope John Paul IV had greeted his congregation from the balcony above the square, and the gathering was prepared for a similar wait.

The conclave began its deliberation early that morning, sealing themselves inside the chapel following an extensive scan for electronic devices or any other form of communication with the outside world.

Only the College of Cardinals inside the chapel knew exactly what occurred that afternoon, and each was sworn to an oath of secrecy. It was unprecedented when the white smoke poured over the edges of the small chimney atop the Sistine Chapel, sinking to the roof like water escaping from a newly drilled well. No Pope in recent memory had been elected so quickly.

It first began as a distant hum, low and rhythmic like a ship's engine drawing closer. Seconds later, it started to crescendo into a recognizable melody. The crowd released their joy and filled their voices with a *Te Deum* in anticipation of the announcement.

Tonino and Father Black stood in silence looking over the edge of the balcony at the massive gathering of people below them. They, like all the others, waited in anticipation of the announcement from the senior cardinal deacon. The continuous splashing of rainwater off the roofs of buildings disappeared, leaving nothing but the chorus of the faithful. Tonino and Father Black made no attempt to speak, for the singing made it impossible without shouting, even though they stood a few feet apart.

A sliver of a smile parted Tonino's lips when the balcony doors across the square from them began to open. The violet-clad senior cardinal deacon walked to the stone railing of the balcony and prepared to address the crowd. The giant V-Screen rose above the Basilica and projected his image for the entire gathering and the world to see.

Speaking in Latin, his words were slow and deliberate, echoing over the public address system.

"I announce to you a great joy. We have a Pope. The most eminent and reverend Lord, the Lord Cardinal of the Holy Roman Church who takes to himself the name Pope Pius XIII."

The crowd exploded with excitement, releasing a deafening roar as they cheered the announcement. Father Black scanned the sea of people while Tonino remained unaffected by the outburst below, steadfast with patience as he waited for the arrival of the new pontiff.

The senior cardinal deacon left the balcony and the crowd lowered themselves to their knees. Silence spread through the square like a wave moving across the ocean, once again allowing the sound of the rainwater pouring off the rooftops to be heard.

The white vestments could be seen approaching the railing, and like a giant bird about to take flight, Pope Pius XIII lifted his hands to the sky and began the *Urbi et Orbi*. Father Black and Tonino focused their attention on the enormous figure appearing on the V-Screen and smiled when Cardinal Cabot's face filled the image.

CHAPTER 12

A SAFE CHAMBER

Gabriel lifted his head off the pillow and peered over Sydney's body to see the time. The light coming from the sun of his solar system clock interrupted the otherwise complete darkness of their small bedroom. Gabriel rolled his eyes to the back of his head when he read the text at the bottom of the image: 2031 Monday September 1 – 23:31, and he struggled to get back to sleep. His mind was in overdrive thinking of the start of another new school year. *This is going to be a great year*, he thought.

Butterflies fluttered inside his stomach, and his thoughts raced with the excitement of a five-year-old on Christmas Eve. Tomorrow, the first day of the new semester, meant he could finally start his experiments in Dr. Ferrel's lab.

Awakened by Gabriel's movements, Sydney rolled over and faced him. She reached up and brushed his hair off of his face. Unaware she was awake, Gabriel was surprised by her action. His body flinched and released a small bark-like sound, causing Sydney to withdraw her hand as if she had touched the hot coals of a fire. The combined surprise of their reactions released a simultaneous giggle.

"What's wrong?" Sydney whispered.

"Nothing, I can't stop thinking of my research."

"You've got to get some sleep or you'll be a mess tomorrow."

"I know, but I'm too excited," Gabriel admitted.

"Obsessed is more like it. Go back to sleep," Sydney demanded and she rolled her back over to him and went to sleep.

Gabriel continued to stare into the bedroom twilight until he finally fell back to sleep. This time it took hold, and he didn't wake until Sydney pulled the blankets off him in the morning. This was her last of three attempts to get him out of bed before she would give up and leave on her own.

"I'm going to be late. If you want to go together, you better get a move on," she said before leaving for the kitchen to make their lunches.

"Okay, I'm getting up," he said while turning to see the time.

"I can't be late for work. It's the first day of the semester, and I've got a lot to do," Sydney said from the other room.

"Crap, it's ten after! Why'd you let me sleep in?" Gabriel said in a panic while scrambling to find clean clothes for the day.

Sydney spread some jam across a bagel, placed it on a paper napkin and left it on the kitchen table next to the bagged lunch she had prepared for him.

"I've got to go!" she shouted from the kitchen, and she scrambled around the tiny flat gathering her belongings. She picked up her tablet from the living room table before stuffing her lunch bag into its case. Sydney grabbed the umbrella from the holder next to the door and stood impatiently waiting for Gabriel.

"I'm hurrying!" he shouted from the bathroom.

Gabriel finished the bagel while putting his raincoat on. He raced to the door, pulling the lanyard holding his university security card and identification off the hook by the door.

They darted down the crowded sidewalk, dodging the endless flow of people like pylons in an obstacle course. The morning's light drizzle gathered on Gabriel's face while he ran, forming small water droplets on his eyebrows. He wiped his face with the inside of his raincoat and struggled to stay on the sidewalk as they nearly ran toward the university.

They followed their usual route along the River Arve under the cover of the large trees that lined the riverbank. While waiting for the traffic light to change so they could cross the busy intersection, Gabriel's eye was drawn to the unusually high water flowing under the Pont des Acacias crossing.

If it keeps coming up, they'll need to start raising the banks, he thought as they raced across the street.

"Wow, we... made... good... time..." he forced the words out between deep breaths, having winded himself from their rapid pace.

"I want to be early so I can set up the first years' lab this morning," Sydney said, trying to catch her breath.

"Well, I can't wait to get in the lab."

Gabriel and Sydney hustled across the campus to the science building. In his haste, Gabriel nearly crushed a squirrel as it scampered across the walkway in front of him. His heart skipped a beat when he hopped over the animal, uncertain if the adrenalin coursing through his veins was from the near miss or the excitement at setting up the equipment to conduct his experiments.

Gabriel pulled open the door to the physics building so Sydney could enter first. Elation surged through his body as if he were injected with a drug. He quickly kissed her on the cheek and nearly sprinted toward the lab. Gabriel removed his raincoat as he hustled down the hall.

He entered the lab and tossed his coat over the back of a stool. It had taken the entire summer to acquire the specialized apparatus and build the Separated Atmosphere From Environment (SAFE) chamber to allow him to work on Dr. Ross's theory.

Hearing the door open, Dr. Ferrel left his small office at the far end of the research lab and greeted Gabriel in front of the safety glass separating the SAFE chamber from the rest of the lab.

"Good morning, Gabriel. I see you're raring to start," said Dr. Ferrel, his eyes hidden by his glasses, but his smile obvious by the stretching of his chubby cheeks.

"Yes, but I'd really like to discuss the funding one more time," he replied, embarrassed to bring it up again but unable to help himself.

"Certainly, what's on your mind?"

"You're certain your funding isn't corporate?"

"Yes," he said, and his smile disappeared.

"I don't want to be part of anything like the PharmaScam or the sea level screw-up."

A small smile returned to Dr. Ferrel's face. "Gabriel, I was in Australia, and I know Dr. Forestburg personally. When he announced the Pacific Ocean had decreased more than three inches instead of rising, even he didn't expect the global anger that followed."

"What about the whole fuel hoarding nightmare of 2024? It wasn't any better. When the IGB declared the Earth's fossil fuel reserves exhausted—a decade sooner than the so-called leading researchers predicted—the science wasn't wrong, it was corporate greed that kept the truth from us," said Gabriel, the anger building in his tone. "Now no one knows who to believe; science has lost credibility."

"Science hasn't lost credibility—only certain scientists have. You have nothing to worry about."

"Yah, I bet that's what they said back in '26 when the researchers at the Global Greenhouse Gas Research Center in Iceland demanded we use more 'green products' to reduce the cloud cover choking the planet. A lot of good that did; it wasn't three weeks later the last recorded direct sunlight to reach the Earth's surface was recorded in Patagonia."

"Stop worrying. I told you, all of my funding comes from a donor who wishes not to be identified. They're not a corporation, so please stop concerning yourself with this matter and start thinking about your research," responded Dr. Ferrel in a father-scolding-a-child tone.

"I'm sorry, it's just that..."

"I completely understand. With your notoriety, I'd want reassurance corporate funding wasn't influencing my research too. Now go!"

"Thanks," Gabriel replied, the giddiness bubbling from his voice when he left the office to start unpacking the cartons of apparatus.

"You're not going to wait for Bradley?" Dr. Ferrel shouted through the open office door.

"I thought I'd get the set-up started."

Derek had ordered Bradley to stay as close to Gabriel as possible, so Dr. Ferrel had arranged for Bradley to switch his graduate studies from chemistry, his strongest subject, to physics. He had arranged it so they were conducting similar research, thus setting up the perfect opportunity to keep continuous guard over Gabriel.

"Remember, at no time are you permitted to operate the SAFE chamber alone; I don't want you to ruin my perfect accident-free record."

"Yes, I understand," Gabriel said, never directing his attention away from the equipment he was assembling.

Since Gabriel had left the Muller estate, Dr. Ferrel, Bradley and Sydney had continuously monitored his whereabouts. As instructed by Derek, they maintained constant surveillance and communication with each other to reduce any opportunity for Gabriel to be left alone. Gabriel remained completely unaware of his sentinels.

***

"He's in the lab."

Bradley was still at Judie's apartment eating breakfast with her when Dr. Ferrel informed him of Gabriel's arrival. This wasn't a surprise, even though Gabriel and Bradley had arranged to meet at the lab at nine, it was only eight-thirty.

"I'll leave in a few moments," Bradley replied.

"He's already assembling some of the equipment, and I

reminded him about the use of the SAFE chamber, but I don't trust him," said Dr. Ferrel.

"I agree. Sydney and Bradley, I want you there as soon as possible. Dr. Ferrel must leave the lab to give a lecture," Derek commanded.

"I'll be in the physics building shortly," Sydney replied.

"I'm ten minutes away," Bradley said while getting up from the table.

"What's your hurry? I thought you didn't have to be there till nine?" Judie asked, confused by Bradley's sudden departure from the table and obvious rush to get out the door.

"I forgot to tell you, Gabe called last night and asked if we could start a bit early, and I just remembered it myself."

"That guy needs help. I don't know how Sydney does it, his whole life is science," Judie replied, unable to hold back her opinion.

"I know, but I promised him, and this is the first day we can use the SAFE chamber. Gabe's beside himself with excitement," Bradley replied, and he pulled his lanyard over his head before bending down to kiss Judie good-bye.

"I bet he is," she replied in a soft but sarcastic tone.

***

Bradley entered the lab to find Dr. Ferrel partially sitting in front of Gabriel on the top of the lab bench. The surface of the bench was covered with tablet computers, printouts of schematics and hand-drawn flow diagrams describing Gabriel's experimental approach.

"Good morning, Dr. Ferrel," said Bradley as he removed his raincoat and placed it over Gabriel's.

"Hello, Bradley," Dr. Ferrel replied as he slid off the side of the bench and made his way toward the door. "I'd better be off, as I've got a first-year astrophysics lecture to deliver."

"It's about time," said Gabriel, casting a smile at Bradley to indicate he wasn't serious.

"I thought we weren't meeting until nine?"

"I couldn't wait. Look... I've already got everything programmed to go, and we just need to put the sensors in the chamber," Gabriel said as he lifted one of the tablets from the bench for Bradley to see.

"Excellent. Which exposure do you want to run first?" Bradley asked, trying to sound as enthusiastic as Gabriel.

"Let's start with the Argon first."

"Why Argon?"

"You don't know?" asked Gabriel while trying to maintain a straight face.

"No," Bradley replied, his face contorting under the strain of searching for an answer.

"It starts with A," Gabriel replied and burst into laughter.

"Oh I get it, alphabetical," Bradley said, cracking a smile at Gabriel's sense of humor.

Gabriel took two of the sensors from the bench and initiated their recording sequence. He walked over to the large metal door to the SAFE chamber and placed his finger on the security panel. A second later, the panel switched from grey to green and began flashing 'Safe To Enter.'

Gabriel placed the two fist-sized sensors on a small round table in the center of the chamber and positioned them so they would receive equal doses of radiation from the ceiling-mounted exposure port. They glistened like jewels under the bright lights of the chamber, but the data they would record was more valuable to Gabriel.

Gabriel and Bradley decided to measure the effect of different wavelengths of radiation on each individual gas composing the Earth's atmosphere in hopes of isolating and identifying the Ross radiation wavelength. In order to do this, they had built the SAFE chamber. This specialized room could be safely filled with a gas and exposed to different wavelengths of simulated solar radiation.

He knew it would be a long and tedious process, but he

was certain he could find the wavelength and prove Dr. Ross's theory.

Once the exact wavelength of Ross radiation was determined, Gabriel would replicate a mixture of the Earth's atmospheric gases prior to the onset of global warming and compare them to current atmospheric conditions under increasing levels of radiation. If he was correct, the chamber would fill with clouds, proving Ross radiation had caused the drastic changes in the Earth's climate and not human activity.

Bradley watched through the safety glass as Gabriel closed the chamber door and activated the safety lock on the small panel to the left of the door. The panel screen began flashing red: 'Chamber Activated—Do Not Enter.' Gabriel looked at Bradley through the glass and gave him a thumbs-up before he left the chamber area.

"Ready?" Gabriel asked, nearly running to the control desk where Bradley sat entering commands on the computer screen.

"You bet—been waiting all summer to start this. The argon has almost saturated the chamber, then I'll begin the radiation," Bradley said.

"All right," Gabriel replied, taking a seat next to him to watch the computer screen.

"I'm going to start with slightly above visible light first, say 750 nm, and we can increase by 10 nm, or do you want to start below the visible light range?"

"Above is fine," Gabriel replied, excited to have started.

They continued adjusting the wavelength for over an hour, each time peering through the glass to watch the inside of the chamber for the slightest sign of cloud formation.

Gabriel followed the progress of the experiment on the screen as well as information being sent to his tablet from the sensors he had placed inside the chamber. The data from one of the sensors appeared to be much lower than expected.

"Look at this; what do you think?" Gabriel asked while he lifted the tablet for Bradley to see.

"That's odd. Doesn't look like it's reading right to me."

"Me neither. I don't want to waste any more time if the sensor's faulty. I think we should change it before we go any further."

"I agree. I'll save this and then start the chamber evacuation timer."

"Okay, I'll get a new sensor while we wait."

The panel on the chamber door began to flash a five-minute countdown after Bradley activated the evacuation command on the computer. The instant he did this, a rattle could be heard coming from behind the glass originating from the ventilation system used to remove the gas from the SAFE chamber. The sound grew steadily louder, like an approaching chorus of drummers in a marching band, as the massive fans worked harder to lift the heavier than air argon out of the small room. Preoccupied by their work and with so little experience using the new equipment, neither Gabriel nor Bradley took notice of the sound.

Gabriel removed a new sensor from a shelf at the back of the lab. He carried it back to the desk and opened the package to inspect the sensor. Bradley saw the countdown near the one-minute mark, so he left the desk and walked to the chamber door. Gabriel removed the plastic packaging from the sensor and followed right behind Bradley. When the timer reached 0:00, the screen began to flash 'Evacuation Sequence Complete' in large green letters. Bradley entered the code to unlock the door and entered the chamber, followed closely by Gabriel.

Gabriel saw Bradley collapse before his own head began to spin. The light closed in from all directions around him, like during the opening of a movie in a theatre, until nothing was left but darkness. The background noise of the lab faded inside his head as if someone was turning down the volume until the only sound Gabriel could hear was the low rhythmic beating of his heart.

Then even that disappeared.

CHAPTER 13

ARGON

"Come quick!" Bradley shouted.

"What is it?" interrupted Derek's voice before the others could respond.

"He's not breathing. We're in the lab," Bradley told them.

Dr. Ferrel was standing at the front of the large auditorium lecturing his class when he suddenly stood frozen in midsentence. Confusion covered the faces of the first-year students; especially those sitting close to the front for only they could see clearly the blank stare in their professor's eyes. Gripped by fear, they remained motionless in their seats, hoping someone else would be the first to act.

The apparent seizure their professor was experiencing left them in shock, but before any of them could activate their VisText to call for help, Dr. Ferrel returned his attention to the class.

"I have an emergency I must attend to," said Dr. Ferrel, and he ran for the door to the left of the auditorium stage while calling for an ambulance on his VisText.

Sydney was working in the lab next to Dr. Ferrel's. The cringing sound of shattering glass filled the lab when she dropped the flask. Her statue-like pose remained intact despite the scattering shards of glass dancing off the concrete floor.

"I'm on my way," she responded and darted for the lab door.

"How's he doing?" Derek demanded.

"It doesn't look good," Bradley replied.

"Where are you?" asked Sydney, unable to see the bodies lying on the floor inside the SAFE chamber.

"Behind the glass, but I don't know if it's safe."

"What is it?" asked Sydney, slowing her pace.

"Argon. Use the respirator."

Sydney pulled the respirator case off the lab wall next to the SAFE chamber entrance. She snapped the suitcase-like case open and placed the mask over her face. The moment Sydney turned the regulator valve to the on position, cool air began to flow through the mask, momentarily fogging the clear plastic around her eyes.

"Hurry, Sydney, he's close!" shouted Bradley.

***

The darkness surrounding Gabriel lifted slowly like a valley fog rising from the warmth of the sun. His eyes flooded with a light so powerful it penetrated them even while closed. Gabriel felt he was staring at the sun, but instead of intense pain, he felt a soothing comfort from the bluish-white light. It was like floating in a gentle river, but instead of water, it was light that carried him.

Warmth raced through his body while the sensation of not being alone crept into his mind. He looked in every direction, trying to determine where he was and who was with him. No one was there, but he was certain someone was following him as he drifted through the light.

Out of the brightness, a woman's voice rose to his ears. The voice appeared to be of a young woman, soft and familiar yet one he'd never heard before. Certainty erupted inside his mind like finally finding the solution to a difficult problem when the voice called his name again. Instinctively he answered, "Mother," but no sound escaped his lips.

Suddenly, as fast as the darkness disappeared it returned,

quickly closing in on him from all directions. Gabriel didn't want to leave the place. He desperately wanted to see the woman; nothing was more important to him at that moment than finding the source of the voice, but the sound of the woman's voice was replaced by a slow beating drum that got louder with each beat. The warmth of the light no longer blanketed his body; it was replaced by a sharp burning pain in the middle of his chest.

***

Sydney had entered the chamber and grabbed Gabriel by the ankles, pulling his body off of Bradley's, which had cushioned his fall. She slid him out of the small room and into the main part of the lab.

A loud thud shook the entire lab when the lab door hit the wall. Dr. Ferrel swung the door open with such force it destroyed the floor-mounted stop, allowing the door handle to puncture the surface of the wall. Completely winded from his sprint down the corridor of the physics building, he struggled to regain his breath. Concerned only for Gabriel, Dr. Ferrel knelt down next to his body to see if he could assist Sydney.

Sydney ripped off the mask and began mouth-to-mouth respiration. Gabriel's cheeks were as white as eggshells, and his lips were blue and cold. She pressed hers tightly against his and forced as much air into his lungs as she could. Her first attempt felt like she was trying to inflate a tiny balloon; no matter how hard she pushed, nothing entered Gabriel's lungs. His chest remained still. Fully aware of the urgency of the situation, Dr. Ferrel called for the ambulance again. There was nothing else for him to do but watch.

Sydney continued to push harder with each subsequent attempt until finally on the fourth try, Gabriel's chest lifted. Sydney inhaled another deep breath and forced it into Gabriel. This last effort cleared the remaining gas from his lungs, allowing oxygen to re-enter his bloodstream. A tinge of pink grew in the center of his cheeks as the edges of his lips regained their color. Gabriel began breathing on his own, and then his eyelids started to quiver. Both his hands formed fists the instant he opened his eyes. The brilliance of their blue was a welcome sight for Sydney.

"He's regaining consciousness."

"Excellent! Was it the Vacare?" Derek demanded, the anger in the tone of his request was clearly evident.

"No, it was gas," Bradley replied.

"How?"

"Something went wrong with the exposure chamber."

"You're certain this was an accident?" Derek asked, still concerned that the Vacare may have discovered Gabriel and made an attempt to kill him.

"Absolutely," replied Bradley.

Derek turned his attention to Bradley.

"Dr. Ferrel, he's about to join us," Derek said.

Dr. Ferrel left Gabriel's side and raced into the chamber. Heavier than air, the argon had completely dissipated from the small room, replaced with air from the lab. Dr. Ferrel could breathe without the need for a respirator and immediately began artificial respiration on Bradley's lifeless body.

"He's still not responding," Dr. Ferrel replied.

"Don't stop."

Bradley's arms and legs began to shake and his chest rose with each breath Dr. Ferrel forced into his lungs. Just like Gabriel, color returned to Bradley's face.

"Stay with him," Derek commanded.

"Yes," replied Dr. Ferrel.

"We're on our way," said Derek, and he and Tanya left the mansion for the university.

Two security guards rushed through the open lab door, leading a pair of paramedics pushing a stretcher. One paramedic donned a pair of gloves and knelt down next to

Sydney to assess Gabriel's condition. The other asked Sydney to join him so he could ask her what happened. Sydney stood up and started talking to the paramedic when one of the security guards noticed Dr. Ferrel through the safety glass.

"Is someone else injured?" asked the guard, moving swiftly toward the chamber door.

"Yes, they were both working in the lab," Sydney replied.

"Is it safe to go in there?" asked the guard, looking down at the respirator on the floor.

"Yes," Dr. Ferrel replied.

The paramedic left Sydney and followed the guard into the chamber. Sydney knelt down to the right of the paramedic tending to Gabriel.

"Is he going to be okay?" she asked.

"He needs to go to the hospital; what's his name and can you tell me what happened?"

"Gabriel. They were both overcome by gas."

"What kind of gas?"

"Argon."

The small light on the paramedic's VisText began flashing, and Sydney waited as he relayed the information to the hospital. A moment later, the paramedic returned his attention to her.

"Did Gabriel stop breathing?"

"Yes, I had to give him mouth to mouth."

"How long wasn't he breathing?"

"I'm not certain... just a couple of minutes at most."

The paramedic looked up at the second security guard, who was watching him attend to Gabriel.

"A second ambulance is on the way, we can only transport a single patient at a time."

"Take Gabriel first," Sydney demanded.

"That depends on the condition of the other patient," replied the paramedic, taken aback by the tone of her request.

"Of course, it's just that he's my boyfriend," she said,

trying to explain her outburst.

"I understand. The second unit is almost here, so they'll both be going."

Gabriel was regaining more awareness of his surroundings while the paramedic covered his face with an oxygen mask. He tried to pull the mask off and speak, but the paramedic replaced the mask over his mouth.

"Gabriel, everything is going to be okay, please don't try to talk," the paramedic said in a firm voice.

Ignoring the request, Gabriel pulled the mask off and forced the words from his lips.

"What about Brad?" he said, and his eyes connected with Sydney's.

"Don't worry, Gabe," Sydney replied as she smiled.

"Gabriel, it's really important you leave the mask on and not try to speak. We're looking after your friend. Try to rest," said the paramedic, and he replaced the mask over Gabriel's mouth.

Fear and confusion overwhelmed him. The voices in the room became muffled as if he were hearing them from the end of a long tube. They began to combine, forming a single incoherent sound before they faded to nothing. Gabriel closed his eyes and begged for the white light to reappear and the chance to hear the voice again. However, when his eyes shut, there was only darkness.

"Go to the hospital. We're in the ambulance and we've left the university," Sydney said.

"We'll meet you there. How's he doing?" Derek asked.

"Resting right now."

Gabriel struggled to raise his eyelids until a faint voice gave him the strength to lift them. A pounding ripped through his chest and caused his heart to want to explode at the thought of seeing the source of the voice. When his eyes finally opened, they were blinded by an intense light. It was out of this light that the woman's voice grew stronger as it called his name. It was soft but completely unfamiliar, and his heart sank when the figure in front of him came into focus.

Dr. Fisher was a new resident at the hospital, having recently started in the emergency ward. Her petite frame made it difficult for her to look directly into Gabriel's eyes as she called his name from the side of the bed. She pushed the large round examination light away, allowing Gabriel to see. Her brown hair was pulled back and tied in a ponytail, giving him a clear view of her hazel eyes when he turned his head to the side.

The smell of antiseptic burned the back of his throat as it filtered under the oxygen mask still attached to his face. Dr. Fisher's voice disappeared behind the sound of each breath when inhaled though the mask. Gabriel's eyes left her and moved to the person standing in front of the pale green curtain. Sydney smiled.

"Hi, I'm Dr. Fisher. Gabriel, how are you feeling?"

He tried to answer, but the mask distorted his words. Gabriel slowly lifted his right hand to his face and pulled the mask below his chin.

"Not great. What happened?"

"Do you have any pain?" asked Dr. Fisher, unhooking the elastic bands from the mask so he could speak more easily.

"Only my whole body feels like it was hit by the Tube."

"You're a lucky man. If it wasn't for this young lady," Dr. Fisher looked over her shoulder at Sydney and then back to Gabriel, "you and your friend wouldn't have made it."

Gabriel's stomach rolled into a knot at the thought of the last thing he saw in the lab—Bradley's body collapsing to the floor. The heart monitor attached to his left index finger sent a signal to the display, causing a high-pitched tone to emanate.

"Relax, Gabriel…"

"How's Brad? Is he okay?" he interrupted, his concern resulting in another squeal response from the monitor.

"Yes, now please try to relax so I can let your grandparents in to see you."

"What, you called them?" he said while looking past the doctor toward Sydney.

Sydney lowered her eyes to mimic a young child's shame and cast a matching smile. Gabriel rolled his eyes and turned his head to stare at the ceiling while Dr. Fisher entered information on the chart tablet at the foot of his bed.

"You know they're going to be upset, especially Opa," he said, still staring upward.

"Yah, but what would you have done if it were me?"

"I would've at least waited a day or two," he said sarcastically.

"Right."

"Where are they?"

"On their way up."

"We're going to keep you overnight so we can monitor you just to make certain you're okay. After all, it's not every day you get to die and come back," Dr. Fisher said as she placed the tablet back in its sleeve.

"What are you talking about?" Gabriel asked, and he tried to raise himself a little higher on the bed.

"I'll let Sydney give you the details. I'll check in when your grandparents arrive," she said and grinned before pulling back the curtain to leave.

"Dr. Fisher," Gabriel called, panic evident in his voice.

"Yes?" she replied, holding the curtain so just her head appeared.

"Please don't mention the dying thing to my grandparents."

"I'll leave the details up to you."

CHAPTER 14

A DREAM

D
r. Fisher kept her promise, and Gabriel was allowed to leave the hospital the next day. Bradley had to spend an extra night, as his body was more seriously affected by the near suffocation.

Their release was conditional; they had to be observed on a twenty-four-hour basis for the next week. For Gabriel, this was a prison sentence. Sydney and his grandparents agreed the best place for him to recover was the mansion. Gabriel protested but to no avail and reluctantly returned to his old bedroom.

Gabriel noted the time on his VisText before pulling it off his ear; the early evening seemed too soon to go to bed, but he was exhausted.

The first night in his old bedroom began the same as the twenty years of nights he had lived in the mansion. He sat on the end of his bed and removed his shirt and pants, folded them in half and laid them over the headboard. After pulling his socks off, he rolled them into a ball and tossed them across the room in an attempt to get them to land on the large leather chair in the corner.

The moment the socks left his hand, a powerful memory shot through his mind, blinding him for an instant. Gabriel's chest heaved upward in a sigh at the memory of Andy and Sandy racing across the room to catch the socks. On a good night, he could toss the socks a dozen times before his grandmother called up the stairs demanding he go to sleep.

Until now, the loss of his childhood friends had never had a profound effect on Gabriel. He lamented, but only for their loss.

Gabriel pulled back the sheets and positioned himself in the middle of the bed; the room was stifling so he remained uncovered.

"Temperature decrease five degrees. Lights off," he commanded, and the room fell into darkness except for a dim radiance entering through his bedroom windows.

At the age of eight, like most young children, Gabriel was frightened of the dark and struggled to fall asleep. He stared at the ceiling for hours, trying to count the moving shadows of the yew tree leaves as they danced over top of his bed until sleep arrived. Unlike a decade ago, tonight's shadows brought him no closer to sleep.

No longer was it a child's angst of darkness that invaded Gabriel's thoughts. A seed of apprehension grew inside him; it flourished like a vine, creeping to every corner of his mind. Agitation overwhelmed him, and Gabriel's breathing became rapid as if he was climbing a steep trail. Sweat formed in the palms of his hands and crawled down the sides of his face.

Dr. Fisher's words repeated over in his mind, each time growing louder and clearer like approaching a waterfall: *"It's not every day you get to die and come back."* His thoughts turned to the light that surrounded him while he lay unconscious in the chamber and the voice calling his name. *Was it my mother? Was it God?*

Gabriel no longer wished for sleep; he begged himself to stay awake. Closing his eyes meant the light might return, and maybe this time he would not. Once again, fear choked Gabriel's mind as he tried to sleep, suffocating every thought but one—death.

Tanya knocked gently on Gabriel's door, but Gabriel didn't hear it. She slowly pushed the door open and crossed the floor to the side of his bed.

Gabriel turned his stare from the ceiling and faced his grandmother. Surprised by her appearance, he flipped the sheets over his body and pulled his back up against the headboard. The little bit of light was insufficient for Tanya to see any detail, but she could make out the position of his body.

"Is everything okay?" Gabriel asked.

"I was about to ask you the same thing. How are you feeling?"

"Fine," he lied.

"I thought for sure you'd be asleep by now."

"Why? It's early."

"You call midnight early?"

"Midnight?"

"Yes. What time did you think it was?"

"Nine-ish. I must've dozed off," he said, hoping not to draw attention to his inability to account for the last three hours.

"No, it's late, and you need to get back to sleep. It's cool in here; do you want the temperature up?" she asked and reached down to squeeze his hand.

Gabriel didn't see her movement and was startled by the contact. The instant Tanya placed her hand inside Gabriel's, she detected his warm, moist palm.

"Lights on," she demanded.

"Oma, what's wrong?" protested Gabriel while covering his eyes with his elbow.

"Derek, come in here," she called without speaking.

"You're covered in sweat; you're going back to the hospital."

"Oma, I'm fine, really, it's just that…"

"What is it?" Derek asked entering the room while tightening the belt around his housecoat.

"Great, now you're both here."

"Look at his sheets, they're soaked, and his palm felt like a wet sponge, and it's freezing in here!" Tanya protested.

"She's right, Gabriel. You're covered in sweat and the

121

room's not exactly warm. How are you feeling?"

"I told you I'm all right. It was just a dream," he said as his voice increased with agitation.

"I'm getting the Medi-scanner, if you have a temperature, we're heading straight back to the hospital," Tanya said while walking rapidly out the door.

"It's nothing. Oma, you're overreacting."

"If that's the case, then no harm done and we can get back to bed."

Tanya arrived with the handheld scanner all ready to go. She sat on the edge of the bed and pulled the sheets off of Gabriel.

"Oma!"

"Please, it's not like I haven't seen you before," she said without interrupting her scan of Gabriel's chest.

Tanya turned and faced Derek, who was standing at the foot of the bed. Her eyes displayed her displeasure.

"What is it?" Gabriel demanded while pulling the sheets back over his body.

"Nothing," Derek said.

"What does that mean?" Gabriel asked, confused by the single-word response.

"The Medi-scanner indicated you're perfectly fine," said Tanya, and she stood up from the bed while turning the device off.

"Can we go back to bed now before I die of embarrassment?"

"Good idea," Derek said, and he left the room first.

Tanya stood looking down over Gabriel. Using instinct only a mother has, she asked Gabriel one last time, "You're certain everything's okay? That must have been some nightmare."

"Nightmare? I didn't say it was a nightmare," Gabriel replied, forcing a smile to his face.

"Dream," Tanya said, knowing her surreptitious attempt to get Gabriel to talk had been discovered.

"Yah, dream."

"Good night then. Lights off," she commanded and turned to leave the room.

Thoughts bounced inside Gabriel's head similar to a rubber ball tossed in a wooden box. Like wanting to ask a parent about sex for the first time, uncertainty combined with awkwardness momentarily froze the words inside Gabriel's mouth. Gabriel's desire to talk to his grandmother quickly overpowered the emotions and freed the words from his lips.

"Wait."

"Yes?" she replied and turned to face the bed while a feeling of contentment swelled inside, knowing her plan to get him to talk had succeeded.

"Can I ask you a question?"

"Certainly," she replied and walked back to the side of the bed.

"Are you afraid of dying?"

"What?" Tanya snapped, caught completely off guard by the nature of the question.

"You know, do you ever wonder what happens after you die?"

Tanya returned to the same spot on the side of the bed where she was before and placed her hand over Gabriel's.

"So this was the dream," she said with understanding.

"It wasn't a dream," he confessed.

"Oh?"

"When I collapsed at the university, Dr. Fisher said I was dead, but I don't think I was because I saw something."

"What did you see?"

"Light, lots of light. I was surrounded by it. What do you think it was?"

Tanya's body went rigid, and her hand gripped tightly around Gabriel's wrist. Unable to see her face clearly, Gabriel waited for an answer.

"He's asking about death and Primoris."

"Now isn't the time," Derek replied.

"Oma, are you all right?" asked Gabriel, concerned about the unnatural silence after his question.

"Yes, I'm just gathering my thoughts," she answered and her body relaxed, as did her grip.

"It wasn't just the light, I heard a voice too. Was it God?" he said, feeling ashamed to ask.

"Who do you think it was?"

"I don't know; that's why I'm asking."

"Many people have had the same experience. It's more common than you think," she said, trying to downplay the experience.

"I've heard about it, but this was different."

"How so?"

"It was the voice. I'm certain it was my mother's, but I've never even heard her voice."

"You asked me if I was afraid of dying. I'm not, you know why?"

"No, why?"

"Because I believe there's nothing to be afraid of."

"What does that mean?"

"It's only what *you* believe that matters."

"What about God?"

"If that's what you believe."

CHAPTER 15

THE FUNERAL

Sleep continued to evade Gabriel; no longer did fear alone keep him up at night, now it was also his insatiable appetite to know more about the afterlife. Spawned by his midnight discussion with his grandmother and driven by his scientific mind, Gabriel had spent the past week searching for articles on life after death. Frustrated by the lack of scientific evidence, his obsession led him to the same conclusion; no factual research on the subject existed.

Article after article delivered great detail of the afterlife and what happened to one's soul based on their performance during their life. But none of the literature was scientific—all of it was religious. Each author went to great lengths to present their finds in a factual manner, but in the end, they were all based on faith. The more he read, the clearer it became to him that religion was the result of humanity's lack of understanding of death. This got him no closer to a definitive answer, so Gabriel decided he had no alternative but to ask Bradley what he had experienced when he was unconscious. Gabriel placed his VisText over his ear and called his friend.

"Hi, Brad. How you feeling?"

"Great, ready to get out of here though."

"Me too. Can I ask you a question, but you have to promise you won't think I'm crazy?"

"Sure, but you're not going to pop the question to Syd are

you? Because if you are, you're crazy."

"No," said Gabriel, and they both laughed. "Seriously, this is going to sound a bit strange but... did you see or hear anything strange when you collapsed inside the chamber?"

"He's asking about Primoris again. He sounds troubled," Bradley said in his head.

"He's searching for answers. Validate him by telling him you saw the same and nothing more," Derek commanded.

"Understood."

Gabriel held his breath in anticipation of a roaring laugh, but Bradley remained silent. The lack of a response left Gabriel feeling vulnerable, and regret rushed through his thoughts for asking the question.

"Brad, you there?"

"Yes, just a little stunned."

"I told you it was crazy," he replied, certain Bradley was searching for some way to end the call.

"No, no, it's not. I saw a light, but I thought it was just me."

"No way, that's what I saw! It was bright, and it felt like I was floating in it," said Gabriel, and an enormous wave of emotion receded from within him. His chest rumbled with exhilaration knowing Bradley saw it too.

"It was really strange; I didn't want to leave it."

"Same here. I also heard a voice. Did you?"

"I thought I did, like someone I knew calling my name, but that's when I woke up, so I didn't give it much thought."

"What do you think?" asked Gabriel, hoping Bradley would be the first to mention God.

"What do you mean?" Bradley replied, trying to end the discussion at this point.

Gabriel felt unsettled; his near-death experience had uncovered a part of his mind never exposed before. Since waking up in the hospital, a dull nagging had persisted in his thoughts, as if he had left something behind but didn't know what. Gabriel had relied on formulas, facts and science his entire life to explain the world around him, but now he struggled to understand what he saw. It was at that moment he realized how faith might fill the void left by science. Gabriel contemplated religion, something he knew nothing about, as a means of understanding what he saw and obtaining freedom from the reoccurring dream.

"You know, do you think it was God?" Gabriel asked, forcing the words past his lips.

"I don't know; guess it could be if you believe in that stuff."

"Yah, guess so. Have you told anyone else?"

"No way! Not something I want on my resume."

"Me neither. You're going to the lab tomorrow?"

"Yup. You?"

"Can't wait. I'm going to call Syd right now and see what the plan is for tomorrow."

"If you want a lift, Judie will be back, and she's coming to get me. We can pick you up on our way back."

"Where'd she go?"

"Her and an old girlfriend took the Tube south for a couple of days—for a short getaway."

"You mean away from you," Gabriel said with a laugh.

"Probably. I've been miserable stuck at home."

"Me too. That sounds good, but I've been stuck in here so long I'm going to see if Syd wants to walk back. Maybe Judie can drop her off on her way to your parents in the morning?"

"No problem, I'll let her know."

Knowing Sydney would be in the middle of preparing a lab for a first-year physics course, and she rarely answered her handheld while at work, Gabriel decided to send a text.

After sending the message, Gabriel decided to stop his afterlife research for the moment. Frustrated by a week's worth of reading leaving him with more questions than answers, Gabriel decided it was time to get back to science, and he downloaded a new paper recently published by Dr. Ross titled, *Does Oxygen 18 Hold the Key to Proving Ross Radiation?*

Gabriel's heart fluttered and his pulse pounded inside his veins. He began to question his research, giving him a sick feeling in the pit of his stomach. *Am I wasting my time? Has he already proven it and my research is useless?* Gabriel stared at his tablet but was unable to look at another word. Fear prevented him from reading any more. His eyes glossed over every time he tried. He threw the tablet on the bed and focused his thoughts on Sydney. This excited him to the point that no bad news could destroy the anticipation of returning to the flat the following day.

***

The next morning, his room filled with the aroma of freshly brewed coffee, and Gabriel arrived at the breakfast table before Derek. Tanya had prepared his favorite breakfast of French toast and strawberries and had a plate already waiting for him when he arrived.

"What's the occasion?" Gabriel asked, knowing full well why Tanya had made his favorite.

"No chance of convincing you to stay a bit longer?" asked Tanya with a girlish smile.

"Only if you promise to make this every morning," he said jokingly.

"We worry about you so much with all these religious terrorists attacking research labs, it's just not safe," she replied, the smile replaced with a mother's face of concern.

"Don't worry, Oma. The Catholic Church has requested an end to the attacks and..."

"That's not going to happen," Derek interrupted when he walked into the kitchen.

"Good morning," said Tanya, and Derek acknowledged her with a small grin before taking a seat at the table and continuing.

"It's more than just the Catholics. Many believe this to be the first step towards Armageddon."

"Why?" Gabriel asked, his mind filling with confusion.

"The discovery of the lost civilization on Mars destroyed the one thing most of humanity clings to for guidance— their belief."

"But the Pope said—"

"It doesn't matter what the Pope said, people are afraid."

"Of what?"

"Of finding out they're wrong."

Gabriel looked away from his grandfather's piercing stare, knowing exactly what he was thinking. A dam burst inside his mind and guilt flooded Gabriel's thoughts. He knew how much his grandfather wanted him to stay at the mansion and give up his research to run the family business, but the thought of it filled him with disdain.

His excitement to see Sydney paled in comparison to his burning desire to avoid rekindling the family business discussion with his grandfather. Desperate to change the topic, Gabriel faced his grandmother to thank her for such a great meal when she spoke first.

"How's Bradley doing?"

"I spoke to him last night, and he said he's feeling much better now."

"That's good. I spoke to his mother, and she said he's ready to go back to Judie's. You two are just like two peas in a pod," Tanya laughed and she looked up at Derek.

"Isn't that the truth?" said Derek, and he took a drink of coffee.

Gabriel quickly finished his breakfast, hoping to minimize his exposure to his grandfather, thus reducing the probability of an argument. Gabriel had stuffed the last piece of French toast into his mouth and placed his fork on his plate when Derek spoke, causing a knot to form in the pit of Gabriel's stomach.

"How you getting home?"

Not expecting this question, Gabriel stumbled over his words before answering.

"Judie's picking Bradley up, and she offered me a lift," Gabriel said, pausing before he finished his sentence in expectation his grandfather would redirect the conversation. "But she's bringing Sydney here instead so we can walk."

"That's a long walk, and it's really coming down today," Tanya interjected.

"I know, but I've been cooped-up in here all week, and I could use the exercise. Besides, they've already left."

"You're sure? I can arrange a lift," Derek said.

"Yah, thanks anyway."

"When will we see you next?" asked Tanya.

"I'll talk to Syd—maybe this weekend. Thanks for everything," he said, locking eyes with Derek before delivering a kiss on the cheek to Tanya.

Gabriel raced out of the kitchen and up to his room. He stuffed his leather satchel with his tablet and the few belongings Sydney had brought over for him and slung it over his shoulder. Jubilation lifted his spirits as he walked down the winding driveway of the estate in the pouring rain. He was uncertain if it was his departure from the mansion or the anticipation of returning to the flat.

Judie pulled the small electric vehicle onto the driveway in front of the iron gates. She rolled down her window and said "hello" to Gabriel while Sydney exited the passenger's side. Sydney popped open her umbrella and began walking around the front of the car.

"Thanks," Gabriel replied and raced over to meet Sydney.

"Hi, missed you," he said before stooping below her umbrella to give her a kiss.

"I saw you on the weekend," she replied, hoping to conjure a reaction.

"That's a lifetime in Gabriel years." He laughed and wrapped his arms around her, giving her a bear hug.

"Save it for tonight," she said, smiling while she pushed him away. "I've got to be at work by noon."

They began their walk down the empty sidewalks of the

wealthy Geneva suburb with Gabriel holding the umbrella in one hand and Sydney's hand in the other. The sound of the rain bouncing off the umbrella reminded him of popcorn cooking in a microwave. They walked briskly down the small hill, watching the road in front of them fill with a sea of red taillights.

The sidewalk was soon overflowing with people. The closer they came to the city center, the more crowded it became, making it impossible to walk side by side.

Gabriel followed Sydney, her umbrella acting like the blade of a bulldozer, separating the oncoming foot traffic. The noise of honking horns and the sound of tires racing over the cobblestones made it difficult to talk.

With his rain hood pulled tightly over his head, blocking his peripheral vision, Gabriel felt like he was walking in a tunnel. A row of vehicles was parked along the edge of the sidewalk with their taillights flashing. Sydney stopped to allow a group of people to walk in front of her. Gabriel watched as the procession passed, unaware of why all the sidewalk traffic was letting this group pass.

A thunderous clang resembling an ancient gong bellowed high above Gabriel's head, causing him to grab Sydney and pull her tightly against his body, shielding her from the impending harm.

"What's wrong?" Sydney yelled.

But before Gabriel answered, he snapped his head upward to locate the source of the noise. Embarrassment rushed through his veins, covering his cheeks with a crimson hue. Water rushed down the slate roof, pouring off the gothic sculptures crowning the corners of the stone building. The bell atop St. Mathieu Catholic Church released a second clang, the deep resonating tone momentarily covered the street noise, and Gabriel realized there was no danger.

"I'm so sorry; the bell startled me. With all the bombings and such, I thought…"

"It's just a funeral."

"I can see that now."

Gabriel struggled to peer above the rising stairs leading to the large wooden doors at the front of the church. The group of people who had passed in front of them stood between the massive stone columns in the entrance and shook hands with others waiting inside. Gabriel's thoughts turned to the hundreds of articles he had read over the last week. His immense curiosity overpowered his thinking, and he climbed the first step.

"What are you doing?" Sydney asked, confused by Gabriel's step.

"I've got to see this," he replied, pulling her toward him.

"Why, it's just a funeral. We don't even know who it is."

"I know, I just need to. Please, Syd, it's important to me."

Gabriel couldn't control the urge overwhelming his thoughts; he was compelled to look inside the church like a passerby gawking at a car crash. Desperate for an explanation of his experience, Gabriel needed to know more about religion to see if it could offer answers. He pulled harder on Sydney's hand, but she resisted his tug.

"I can't be late for work."

"Okay, go ahead without me. I'll catch up," he said, releasing her from his grip.

Sydney knew she couldn't leave him alone, especially in a Catholic Church.

"All right, but this is really freaky."

"Thanks so much. We won't stay long."

Sydney closed her umbrella and placed it in the ornate brass holder near the entrance while Gabriel removed his raincoat and hung it on the coat rack inside the foyer. Gabriel acknowledged the greeter with a small nod of his head and entered the church.

The smoke burned his eyes, and his nostrils tingled from the incense lingering in the air, forcing him to breathe through his mouth. The organ music reverberated through the stone building, covering the whispers of the mourners gathered near the front of the church.

They walked up the center aisle and slipped into the first empty pew behind the main group of mourners, hoping to be unnoticed. People continued to file into their pew, forcing them to the far side near the wall, as the church filled behind them. The steeple bell rang for a third time—the cue for the organist to stop playing.

Gabriel's heart raced with anticipation. This was his first time in a church and his first funeral. He leaned over to ask Sydney if she had ever been to a funeral when the entire congregation rose to their feet; instinctively, he followed. The priest began conducting Mass, and Gabriel remained glued to every word and action as it unfolded behind the altar. He held his curiosity in check until the priest split the Eucharist and drank the wine. Astonishment overcame him, and he couldn't hold his tongue any longer.

"Do people actually believe this?" he whispered into Sydney's ear.

"What?"

"That the bread is really someone's body and wine their blood?"

"Yes, why?"

"It makes no sense," he said loud enough so the young couple in the pew in front of them turned their heads to see who was speaking.

"It's religion, and that's what they believe. Now shhh," pleaded Sydney, concerned their conversation would be heard.

The stone walls of the church began to shake the instant the organist hit the first note of the next hymn. The stained-glass windows crowning the walls imploded, throwing shards in every direction. Gabriel's ears were numb from the explosion, making the screams of people running for cover appear miles away. The last thing he saw before complete darkness filled his eyes was the larger-than-life Crucifixion falling from the wall, crushing the priest against the altar.

Sydney tackled Gabriel to the ground, covering his body with hers. She screamed at him to stay under the pew while pieces of the ceiling crashed on to the floor next to them. The taste of the dust was bitter on his tongue, forming a chalk-like paste and making it hard to swallow. Breathing became impossible without coughing, and the smell of gunpowder replaced incense.

Gabriel remained completely still, petrified by fear. The weight on his chest was crushing, making it increasingly difficult to inhale. A warm liquid ran down his forehead, pooling in his eyes. Gabriel struggled to open them, too frightened by what he was about to see. It wasn't until he heard Sydney's voice that Gabriel finally looked at the carnage.

Like thousands of tiny crystal missiles launched at his face from the sky, the raindrops fell straight downward through the rising plume of dust, landing on his forehead and dripping into his eyes. Sydney rolled off his chest, freeing him to breathe normally. Pieces of the ceiling slid off her back onto the floor.

Adrenalin pumped through Gabriel's veins, firing his muscles into readiness. He lifted Sydney off the ground while scanning her for injury.

"Are you hurt?" he asked, unaware he was yelling because the power of the explosion had numbed his hearing.

"No, are you?" she asked, her voice barely a whisper to him.

"Just my ears; I can hardly hear."

"We need to get out of here. This whole place is about to come down," she said, looking up at the gaping hole in the roof.

"We have to help the others…"

"No, we have to leave; you're too important," she shouted and began dragging him toward the right side of the church, where the explosion had cut a ten-foot opening in the wall.

They stumbled through the debris covering the floor,

stepping over bodies in their race to escape the crumbling structure. Blood splatter painted the back of the mangled pews like children's art. The sound of crying and moaning rose out of the wreckage as Sydney and Gabriel followed the young couple who had been seated in front of them out the side of the church.

The heavy rain quickly washed the white dust from their face and arms as sirens grew louder with each step they took away from the building. People rushed to their side offering them assistance and covering them from the rain. The police were the first to arrive and began clearing people from the building when the remainder of the roof collapsed inside the church, followed by the wall they had been seated next to.

When the ambulances arrived, only a handful of people had made it out of the building before the roof collapsed. They attended to Sydney and Gabriel, insisting they go to the hospital to be examined by a physician. Sydney agreed but only if she could ride in the same ambulance as Gabriel. The paramedics reluctantly agreed, and put Sydney on the stretcher while Gabriel and a paramedic sat alongside her.

"He's been attacked," Sydney said to Derek in her head.

"Is he hurt?" Derek shouted.

"No."

"Where are you?" Derek demanded.

"On our way to the hospital."

"You said he wasn't injured. What's going on?"

"We're fine—it's only a precaution."

"Was it Vacare?"

"I don't know."

"Where were you?"

"St. Matthieu's Catholic Church."

"What were you doing in a Catholic church?" shouted Derek, not holding back his anger.

"I had no choice; he was going in without me."

"I'll meet you at the hospital."

"He'll be suspicious," Sydney said, reminding Derek that

Gabriel would wonder how his grandparents knew he was in the church.

"You're right. I want to be kept informed though," Derek demanded.

"Yes."

"Syd... Syd... Sydney!" called Gabriel as he shook her shoulder.

"Yes?"

"Are you sure you're okay? You were staring into space and I had to shake you to get your attention."

"I'm fine. My ears are ringing too."

"Whose funeral do you think that was?" asked Gabriel, trying to make sense of the disaster that unfolded minutes before.

"Why?"

"Obviously someone was trying to kill people at the funeral."

"It was those SnRs," barked the paramedic.

"Who?" asked Gabriel, his hearing still suffering the effects of the explosion.

"SnRs, they don't care about the funeral or anything else sacred. As long as it's religious, they'll destroy it," he hissed under his breath.

The ambulance rounded a sharp turn, requiring both Gabriel and the paramedic to brace themselves using the stretcher. Sydney spotted the tattoo of a cross on his right forearm first and used her eyes to direct Gabriel to the symbol. It was clear the paramedic was religious, and based on the bitterness in his tone, Sydney and Gabriel simultaneously came to the conclusion to stop their discussion.

The ambulance drove into the underground entrance of the emergency ward and backed up to the sliding glass doors. The paramedic in the back of the ambulance swung open the doors to find the attending physician waiting.

"You've got to promise me you're not going to tell your

parents, are you?" begged Gabriel, his back to the open doors.

"Yah, I promise, but I don't know how long we'll be able to keep it a secret."

Gabriel turned around to see Dr. Fisher's smiling face beaming back at him.

CHAPTER 16

ReFs and SnRs

Gabriel awoke the next morning to find the bed empty next to him. Even though the temporary deafness was waning, he couldn't hear Sydney preparing breakfast in the kitchen of their small flat. He was beginning to miss the absolute silence since it seemed better than the constant ringing in his ears. When he lifted his head to get out of bed, his entire body felt like he had fallen down a flight of stairs. Every muscle seemed to ache, and the stiffness rendered his movements slow and deliberate.

"Syd?"

"In the kitchen," she replied.

"How you feeling?" he asked while trying to pull his pants on without falling over.

"My ears are ringing pretty good, and my back's a bit sore where the ceiling tile hit it, otherwise not too bad. You?"

"I feel like I was hit by the Tube, and my ears are still a bit messed up. Have you seen my VisText?"

"You left it in the bathroom."

Gabriel retrieved it and headed into the kitchen to join Sydney for breakfast. They sat at the table eating and watching the V-screen. The entire morning broadcast on the WNN was devoted to the bombing of the church. The IGB confirmed a group calling themselves the SnRs had claimed responsibility for the terrorist act.

"What's next?" Gabriel said in disgust.

"Maybe you should take a little time off from your research—things are starting to hit closer to home."

"What? No way, I can't, I just started my experiments," responded Gabriel, caught off guard by her request.

"I'm worried. You're too important to me, and I just don't want to see anything happen to you, that's all."

The second she said the words, Gabriel's thoughts returned to the moment after the explosion, *"You're too important."* He'd forgotten about them until now.

"Can I ask you a question? It's kinda strange, but it's something you said in the church."

"Yah, what?"

"I wanted to help others in the aftermath, but you wouldn't let me, you said I was 'too important.' What exactly did you mean by that?"

"Did I? I don't remember, it must have been the adrenalin. I must have meant you were too important to me, that's all," she said, trying to explain away her slip.

"It's weird, you jumped on me before I even knew what was happening, and it was like you were expecting it. It all seems really odd, don't you think?"

"No, people always do crazy things under those kinds of situations; you're reading way too much into this, that's what I think. We better get going; we both have a lot of explaining to do for why we weren't in yesterday."

"I'm sure they'll understand, just tell your boss you had to stay home and help me recover from my lab accident."

They donned their rain gear and left early for the university. Sydney was hoping to make up for the unexpected day off and have all the labs ready for the day's lessons. Gabriel was anxious to get back into his lab to see what had gone wrong.

When they arrived at the university grounds, a group of more than thirty students had gathered in front of the entrance gate. The crowd was so large they couldn't see the entrance through the mass of umbrellas. Sydney approached a girl she was certain was a first-year student because she appeared to be no more than fifteen years old.

"Is there a problem?" Sydney asked.

"No, this is the line for the new enhanced security measures."

"Enhanced security?"

"Yup, everyone has to pass through a scanner before they can enter the grounds. I think it's because of all those bombings," said the student in a high mousey voice that matched her youth.

"Great, how long is this going to take? I thought we were going to be early—we'll be lucky if we're not late," Gabriel complained.

"It's moving quite quickly. I've only been here five minutes, and the line's already half of what it was," said the student.

"Are you sure you don't want to take a year or two off?" Sydney asked, hoping the new concern over security might help convince him.

"I'm not going to let a bunch of religious radicals screw up everything I've been working for," he replied in an unmistakable tone of assertiveness.

Once through the scanner, they walked toward the physics building without discussing the matter any further. The building was quiet and only the sound of their wet footsteps could be heard in the hall. Gabriel turned to kiss her good-bye when he saw Dr. Ferrel enter their lab at the far end of the hall.

"Wow, he's in early," Gabriel said.

"Who?"

"Dr. Ferrel. I saw him go into the lab."

"That's good, isn't it? You can discuss what you're doing next."

"What?" Gabriel replied, confused by the meaning of 'next.'

"I've got to go; I'll meet you in the café, okay?" she said, and Sydney raised herself onto her toes to kiss him and quickly escaped any further questioning.

"Bye."

Gabriel walked briskly down the hall to get to the lab before Dr. Ferrel could leave. When he entered the room, his heart sank and panic overwhelmed him. It was as if someone had shot him in the chest. He couldn't believe what he saw and rushed into Dr. Ferrel's office at the back of the lab.

"What's going on? Why is the SAFE room boarded up? How am I supposed to conduct my research?" he appealed.

"I'm sorry; the university health and safety committee has suspended your research indefinitely."

"Why? How can they do that?"

"The near death of two students is reason enough; there's no way they will reconsider."

"I don't believe this! Now what am I supposed to do? I've been planning this for years. We don't even know what happened."

"Blame it on the squirrels," said Dr. Ferrel in an attempt to relieve some of Gabriel's disappointment.

"What are you talking about?"

"After the accident, it only took Engineering and Maintenance about an hour to figure out what happened. They went on the roof and removed a large squirrel family from the exhaust system."

"Then what's the problem? We know what caused the problem, and they've fixed it. Why can't I continue?"

"The dean and the health and safety committee won't even consider it—it's done. Let's focus our attention on what you can work on next."

For the second time that day, a word triggered a memory around something Sydney had said to him, and this time it was only moments ago when she had said it. *"What you're doing next,"* the words echoed in his mind. *How'd she know?* The thought escaped him when Dr. Ferrel spoke.

"What do you think about collaborating with Dr. Ross's

lab in Rome?"

"What do you mean? We're already trying to prove the existence of Ross radiation."

"I know. I mean work directly with him on furthering his isotope work. Your background in physics combined with Bradley's background in chemistry will form an incredibly strong team."

"To do what?" Gabriel asked, upset over the loss of months of preparation and still not buying into the change of plans.

"If we collaborate, I'm certain we'll be able to further Dr. Ross's work and prove Ross radiation exists. And go one step further and prove it's the cause of the current atmospheric conditions gripping the planet."

Gabriel's eyes lit up at the thought of still conducting research to prove a natural phenomenon was responsible for the massive environmental shift the Earth was experiencing.

"Do you think Dr. Ross would be interested in collaborating with us?"

"Let's find out."

"Contact Dave," Dr. Ferrel commanded, and the V-screen in his office projected a blue screen with the words 'Contacting Dr. David Ross' flashing on it.

Gabriel's face contorted as if he had just bit into a sour candy when the realization entered his mind—Dr. Ferrel knew Dr. Ross. Before he could question Dr. Ferrel about his relationship with Dr. Ross, the V-screen projected a large bearded face.

"Two calls in one day, Mike! For what do I owe the pleasure this time?"

Dr. Ross's comment removed any doubt Gabriel had that Dr. Ferrel and Dr. Ross knew each other, and it was clear the reason for the call was not to ask Dr. Ross if he wanted to collaborate but rather to introduce him to Gabriel.

"Dave, I'd like to introduce you to a graduate student whom I think you might have quite a bit in common with."

Gabriel positioned himself so he could be seen by Dr. Ross.

"Hello, Dr. Ross, I'm Gabriel Muller."

"Hello, Gabriel. I understand you're interested, as am I, in putting an end to the nonsense about anthropogenic global warming?"

"Yes, sir," Gabriel replied, concerned Dr. Ross could detect his nervousness and resulting color change in his cheeks.

"Well, I think together we'll be able to do that if your current supervisor can come up with some funding?" Dr. Ross said while stroking his beard and raising his deep brown eyebrows before turning his large, nearly black eyes toward Dr. Ferrel.

"Of course I can. I got you the funding for the M3, didn't I?"

The butterflies slamming the inside of Gabriel's stomach faded into a tingling sensation like the first time he went on a date. Dr. Ferrel's last statement didn't have time to sink in; he was ecstatic and wanted to call Bradley right away.

"Are you certain?" he asked, wanting to make sure it wasn't too good to be true.

"Yes, why?" Dr. Ferrel asked.

"I'm going to call Brad right away and let him know."

"Yes, I'm certain. Go ahead and call him."

"Nice meeting you, Dr. Ross."

"I look forward to working with you," said Dr. Ross and his image disappeared from the screen.

Gabriel called Bradley, gave him the news and spent the rest of the day cleaning up equipment from the failed experiment. He and Dr. Ferrel lost track of the time as they planned numerous different approaches to Gabriel's new research. It was after nine o'clock when Gabriel left Dr. Ferrel's office to use the bathroom. He was about to send a quick text to Sydney to let her know he was late when he opened the lab door and heard a thud.

***

The soles of her work shoes released a high-pitched squeak as she advanced down the freshly mopped corridor. Classes had finished hours ago, and even the most dedicated students should have left for the night by now.

A low constant hum replaced the sound of her hallway footsteps, indicating she was near the mechanical room. She pulled the small plastic keycard attached to the lanyard out of the small breast pocket of her grey coveralls and swiped it in the reader next to the large steel door.

Once inside the room, the hum transformed into an ear-shattering drone like the engine room of a ship and she quickly closed the door to contain the noise. Unfazed by the clamor, she navigated through the labyrinth of pipes and valves with ease. Heat bellowed from the machinery, making the temperature unbearable and causing sweat to soak through the armpits of her powder grey uniform. She reached into her pocket, removed a small metallic egg and placed it on top of a large pipe where it stayed as if glued by the magnetism in its exterior. Exhausted from the heat, she raced back to the door.

Wiping the sweat from her forehead, she was hurrying back down the hall when the door to Dr. Ferrel's lab swung open, knocking her to the ground.

"I'm so sorry," Gabriel gasped, realizing what had happened while he bent down to help her.

"I'm okay, I didn't realize anyone else was still here," she said as she got to her feet.

Recognizing the woman's face and uniform, Gabriel felt even more embarrassment rush through his body.

"Angie, are you all right?" he asked with a look of concern gathering over his face.

"Fine, not to worry. Do I know you?"

"You cleaned up the mess I made in the cafeteria."

"I clean up many messes," she said with a smile.

"You're sure you're okay? You're soaked."

"I just finished mopping the floors—it's a tough job. What are you doing here so late?" she asked, desperately trying to change the subject.

"We're working on my new research project."

"We... you're not alone?" Angie asked, surprised to know others were still in the building.

"Dr. Ferrel's still here."

"You two should be at home—it's too late to be working. Especially you; you're too young to work so late. Get a girlfriend instead of wasting all your time studying. Go home."

"Yah, you're right. I'm heading home now."

"Good, have a good night," she said and began walking briskly down the hall.

Gabriel resumed his trip to the washroom and sent Sydney a VisText to see if she was still waiting for him at the campus café. She responded instantly with a 'yes' so Gabriel hurried back to the lab to pick up his tablet and go meet her. When he returned to the lab, Gabriel found Dr. Ferrel packing his things and shutting down the computer terminal they had been working on.

"I was just going to do that," Gabriel said, surprised to see him already closing things down for the night.

"Time for us to go home," said Dr. Ferrel with a smile.

"Yah, Sydney's waiting for me."

"At the café?"

"Yes."

"Good, I'll walk with you."

"That's all right."

"It's on my way."

"Okay."

A light drizzle was falling when they left the research building. Dr. Ferrel pulled an umbrella from the small briefcase he was carrying, and Gabriel covered his head with the hood of his raincoat. It was difficult for Gabriel to walk next to the doctor because the umbrella nearly knocked one of his eyes out with each of Dr. Ferrel's steps.

They were chatting about Dr. Ross's research when the breeze flooded their nostrils with a powerful scent. They both scanned the darkness for the source of the smell when Gabriel saw two figures moving next to the library building.

"What are they doing?" Gabriel asked, unable to make out what was going on in the darkness.

A second after the two people heard Gabriel's voice, they disappeared into the darkness. When Dr. Ferrel and Gabriel walked over to the library, they instantly knew what the smell was—paint. The two people had been writing graffiti when they were interrupted.

Gabriel read the words out loud, "'KILL ALL THE ReFs.' What's a ReF?" Gabriel asked.

"It means 'Religious Fanatical.'"

"What?" Gabriel asked, still not understanding the meaning.

"Ever since Pope John Paul IV condemned all of us who study science and technology as 'non-believers,' a movement has been growing around the globe. Groups of people have taken things to extremes. They're called ReFs—Religious Fanaticals—by others who don't share their religious views. The ReFs call anyone who doesn't follow the Word of God an SnR—Science not Religion. According to the ReFs, SnRs worship the advancements of science and not God."

When Gabriel heard SnR, he stumbled, remembering the paramedic. Thankful it was so dark that Dr. Ferrel didn't notice his reaction, he quickly regained his composure, hoping not to draw attention to himself.

Dr. Ferrel shook his head in disgust at the writing on the wall before continuing, "It looks like even our university can't escape the division shattering the world."

"I don't get it; why do the ReFs fear science?"

"They're blindly following the words of their religious leaders, who use fear to motivate them."

"Do they actually believe it when there's no proof God

even exists?"

"No belief is more powerful than one rooted in fear. Fact and proof as we scientists understand them are nothing more than grains of salt; tossed into a sea of belief, they just disappear like they never existed."

Darkness hid the confusion on Gabriel's face. Embarrassed to ask his professor but desperate to understand, Gabriel continued his questions while they walked to the café.

"Fear of what?"

"The afterlife of course," replied Dr. Ferrel, his voice full of intrigue.

"Oh," Gabriel replied, feeling stupid that the answer was so obvious once he heard it.

"The purpose of religion is to comfort those who crave the belief that there's life after death, but it's the fear of an afterlife that motivates the darkest side of humanity."

Gabriel couldn't shake the thought of the light, and the voice he had heard. It was eating away at him like the constant dripping of a tap; the need to understand what he had experienced was consuming his focus one thought at a time.

"If there's no proof of what happens after we die, then neither the ReFs nor SnRs are right," he said as they arrived at the front of the university café.

"That's just it," Dr. Ferrel said, and he waved to Sydney through the window while a large smile gathered on his face, made visible from the light over the entrance to the café.

"What is?" Gabriel replied, unsure of what Dr. Ferrel was referring to.

"It's not about proof; it's what they believe."

CHAPTER 17

THRESHOLD OF WAR SUNDAY

Scented candles cast an amber glow, partially illuminating the early-morning darkness inside St. Peter's Basilica. The Sunday crowd continued to file into the most sacred of all Catholic churches, hoping to catch a glimpse or receive a blessing from their supreme leader. It took less than an hour before the floor was crammed with the faithful. Their prayers echoed through the giant hall, filling it with a deep drone.

Like an elaborately staged theatre production, crepuscular rays illuminated the air above the altar the moment Pope Pius XIII arrived. The artificial Jacob's Ladder was made possible by rows of floodlights perfectly positioned outside the basilica windows.

Silence fell over the crowd when Pope Pius made the sign of the cross. Like an army of soldiers following their general's orders, billions of Catholics around the globe duplicated his actions on cue. This, his first public Mass, was being covered live for all to watch on their VisTexts and V-screens.

Father Black and Gino accompanied Tonino inside his office, where they sat watching the broadcast. Gino held a tablet in his lap while Father Black and Tonino sipped their coffee.

"He understands what I expect?" asked Tonino while gently placing his coffee cup on its saucer atop his desk.

"Yes, he'll deliver it," Father Black replied.

"Good."

The three men sat in silence staring at the V-screen and waiting for the Pope to address the crowd. The moment it began, Gino lifted the tablet from his lap and activated it. He read the screen simultaneously as the Pope delivered his speech, the words on the small screen were identical to those he heard coming from the V-screen.

"Once again, humanity stands on the threshold of war. Today I ask you to begin the next chapter in Christianity; one filled with tolerance and forgiveness. We must accept God's way and reach out to our brothers and sisters who have lost theirs. It is God's will to bring these lost and wandering souls back into the flock. I ask those who continue to engage in senseless acts of violence to put aside their anger and accept the differences He, our Father, created among us.

"Heaven has no room for those who continue to commit murderous acts, even against those who don't share our beliefs. It is His will, the will of the Lord, Our God, that we put aside our differences and help all mankind share in our unwavering belief. Let us pray that we all may one day be filled by the Holy Spirit, and that His power guide even the non-believers to true salvation. I stand here before Him as a humble servant and ask all the faithful to stop the assaults at once and begin to heal the wounds inflicted upon those..." continued the Pope.

"He's following it exactly as you've written it," said Gino, still reading the words on the tablet while the Pope spoke in the background.

"Wonderful, our new pontiff is working out quite well; V-screen off," Tonino said, releasing a small grin while turning to face the others. "Now, what's this pressing matter you wish to discuss with me?"

Father Black spoke first. "India and China are on the brink of collapse. The flooding continues to drive people into the cities. Shanghai, Beijing and even Hong Kong have established guarded perimeters; they're killing anyone who tries to enter without proof of a residence. The last estimate is that over two billion are in tent cities in China alone."

Tonino turned and cast his black and expressionless eyes toward Gino, "And you?"

"Sir, most of northern Africa is a military zone. The exodus of hundreds of millions of people from the low-lying countries into neighboring highlands has sparked new fighting daily. It won't be long before these skirmishes turn into a full-blown war."

Tonino lifted his coffee from the table and took a sip from the cup before speaking. "It is imperative they remain only that—skirmishes. A world war, or any form of genocide at this time would destroy everything. Tell the others it won't be long now, and they must do whatever it takes to keep the loss of life to a minimum."

"Sir, that's part of the problem..." began Father Black.

"What problem?" interjected Tonino, leaving Father Black hesitant to finish his sentence.

Father Black reluctantly continued, "The others, they don't understand. It would be easier to keep them in line if you would explain to them why all this is necessary. What good can come of this vile and repulsive population explosion? Most of the group thinks it's the end of all life, and the Earth will resemble Mars if we don't stop the growth rate immediately."

Tonino gently pushed his chair back from his desk and stood up. His sculpture-like face began to crack with rare-hints of emotion before he turned and took his usual position in front of the window. Gino glanced quickly at Father Black in an attempt to gauge his level of anxiety while the two of them sat in their seats waiting for Tonino to speak. Tonino clasped his hands together behind his back and cleared his throat.

"It was I who found the Vectors," said Tonino, his voice straining to contain his anger. "It was I who prevented them from destroying everything," his voice grew louder with each word. "And only I can rid the Earth of the Primoris once and for all!" he shouted while turning to face the two men.

Father Black glanced at Gino before addressing Tonino, knowing his words would further anger him. "The others have lost faith, they no longer believe you; they only see the collapse of their countries—the endless terrorist attacks by both sides."

"I'm fully aware of the escalation between the SnRs and ReFs. This is the reason for today's address, or have I missed something? Doesn't the Pope lead his twelve billion faithful anymore?" he said with sarcasm while approaching his desk.

"Yes, sir, of course, sir, but many are becoming radical, finding it more difficult to follow his requests. They live in tents and shanty towns, eat nothing but the food rations we provide," replied Gino, nearly stuttering to get the words off his lips under the fear Tonino would dispose of him for speaking out.

Relief spread over Gino the instant he heard Father Black take over the conversation. Tonino continued to stand behind his desk and directed his attention to Father Black while his agitation grew stronger with each moment of the conversation.

Father Black sensed Tonino's anger but knew he had to finish what he had started, so he went on, "It's becoming increasingly difficult for even the most faithful to watch as their land and homes are swallowed by the rising waters. Even our own researchers feel it's only a matter of time before we lose the battle against the cholera and other diseases threatening to spread across the globe. This could cost more lives than any war. Sir, if only we could tell the others how much longer this must continue, it would give them hope and purpose."

Unable to contain his rage any longer, Tonino blew up and began shouting while pounding his fist on his desk. The blows toppled the coffee cups from their saucers, spilling the contents. Neither Gino nor Father Black dared look away as

Tonino unleashed his anger.

"It may take a day, a week or another decade for that matter, but let me be absolutely clear, you tell the others they are to continue doing as I ask or they will be replaced."

"Yes, sir," responded Gino and Father Black simultaneously.

Tonino walked back to the window and briefly gazed outside before turning to face the men.

"Find these ReFs and SnRs, use whatever means necessary, I want to know everything about them."

"Eliminate them?"

"No, not yet, they may prove useful to us."

***

A thunderous echo resonated inside the hollow steel walls like the pounding bow of a ship plowing into a storm. The coffee-colored water slammed against the massive structure holding back the River Nile from submerging the Egyptian landscape. An extensive network of canals, dykes and pumping stations, easily rivaling those in the Netherlands, corralled the endless rainfall into the riverbed, keeping it from flooding the tropical Sahara green belt.

Covered by a blanket of lush green foliage, the once barren desert now teemed with life. Like the Arabian, Australian and Patagonian agrizones, the African desert had been transformed into the Earth's foremost outdoor agricultural area by constant precipitation and the endless heat.

Soya beans genetically modified to grow in saturated conditions and to produce high-protein yields dominated the produce from this area. Rows of rice thrived in the tropical humidity while date palm and coconut trees interrupted the perfectly flat horizon, all pointing eastward from the constant wind. The Sahara agrizone was blanketed by the thickest cloud cover and highest rainfall on the planet. These two atmospheric conditions combined to enable Egypt to feed over one third of the Earth's population, thus becoming the most important country on the African continent.

A pair of young women buried under raingear walked quickly along the top of the steel dyke, the echo of their footsteps overpowered by the waves. The taller of the two stopped to peer across the river. Sheets of rain whipped across the water, rattling the metal surface like a snare drum. Each woman removed a small object resembling a silver egg from beneath their raincoats.

"You certain they're working?" asked the shorter woman.

"Yes. We haven't got much time, hurry!" demanded the taller woman.

"I know,"

"Leave them here," said the taller woman. They bent down to place their eggs on the side of the metal dyke behind a large plastic sign stating 'Cairo's Dykeing Network – Another MBG Funded Project.'

"You sure this is the best location?" asked the shorter woman, shoving the small metal device in a gap between the sign and the top of the dyke.

"Yes, now let's go."

***

The early January rainstorm went unnoticed by the million or more residents of the small Alberta city of Manning. A steady wall of water raced down the outside of the thirty-eight solid glass skyscrapers erected on the banks of the reservoir formed by the massive MBG dam. The cooler temperatures of the Canadian north and the easy access to the Arctic Ocean shipping ports made Canada an ideal location for the Photo-Agricultural facility.

Named after the real luminescent brilliance that once danced across the night sky, the light from the fifty-story greenhouses and the MBG-Northern Lights Research

Laboratory could be seen for hundreds of miles.

The mid-afternoon darkness was lessened by the flash of lightning reflecting off wet concrete as the rainwater formed small streams on the sidewalk. The resulting thunder roared like a fighter jet taking off between the tall glass structures.

Cloaked under their raincoats three men moved swiftly down the sidewalk, their silhouettes visible in the headlights of the oncoming rush-hour traffic. When they approached the front of the MBG research building, one man entered the glass-covered front courtyard while the other men continued down the sidewalk.

Protected from the downpour, the lone man lowered the hood from his head while pausing to read the writing over the two etched glass lion heads on the entrance doors: 'Welcome to the Northern Lights Photo-Agro Research Laboratory – An MBG Initiative.' The words formed a circle around the lion's mane on each door. The man pushed the large door open and walked up to the all-glass desk sitting vacant in the lobby. The moment he stopped in front of the desk, a three-dimensional computer-generated digital receptionist appeared behind the desk.

"How may I help you?" asked the projection of a young woman wearing a lab coat and holding a tablet.

"I'd like to see Dr. Burrow," said the man.

"Is she expecting you?" replied the digital receptionist.

"Yes."

"May I have your name please?"

The man stuttered before answering, "Mr. Genesis."

"Please have a seat Mr. Genesis, I'm contacting Dr. Burrow now," replied the digital receptionist, pointing to a row of leather chairs along the wall to her right and appearing to operate her tablet.

The man took a deep breath and held his position, his hands fidgeting inside his coat pocket while glancing at the doors labeled 'Restricted Zone' on the far side of the lobby. The digital receptionist lifted her head from the tablet and repeated the exact same gesture as before.

"Please have a seat, Mr. Genesis. Dr. Burrow is on her way."

Again, the man held his position, but his movements became restless, like a child needing to use the washroom. Suddenly relief filled his face when the Restricted Zone doors opened and an elderly, grey-haired woman emerged.

"Dr. Burrow has arrived," announced the digital receptionist.

Dr. Burrow walked with intent across the lobby, her unbuttoned lab coat flowing behind her like a long white cape. She raised her hand to the man to offer a handshake. He pulled his hand from the inside pocket of his coat, cupping the small metallic egg-shaped object with his hand and discretely placed it inside her hand as they shook. The fire in his eyes cooled, and a large smile spread across his lips when he saw the hand-carved crucifix hanging from her neck.

"May God be with you, Mr. Genesis," said Dr. Burrow. She placed the hand carrying the metal egg into her lab coat pocket and turned toward the doors she had entered.

"Go in peace, Dr. Burrow," replied the man, and he pulled his hood back over his head before leaving the building.

Lightning reflected off the café window where the man sat waiting for his two partners to arrive. The small seating area was full of workers from the greenhouses spending their coffee break away from the heat and humidity of the growing floors. With no other option available, he took a seat at the bar near the back of the café.

Patrons' heads snapped toward the entrance when a clap of thunder rushed through the door opened by the two men rushing into the tiny restaurant. They removed their hoods while each took a seat on either side of the first man.

"What can I get you folks?" asked the bartender, wiping the bar surface in front of the three men.

"Coffee," they responded in unison.

The bartender pulled three mugs from below the bar and

reached behind him for the coffee urn. The men sat silently while he filled their mugs. The moment he finished, the bartender carried the urn to offer refills for those seated at the tables. The man sitting in the middle glanced at his partners in the mirror covering the wall opposite them.

"God's work went well?"

"The SnRs will suffer," replied the man to his right while the man on his left acknowledged the statement with a smile and nod.

CHAPTER 18

A VISIT

The gale-force wind lashed the rain against the bedroom window like a hail of gunfire. Wave after wave pelted the glass, and the endless tapping prevented Gabriel from closing his eyes. Through the partially closed curtains, he watched the sheets of water roll down in tiny swells. He knew this wasn't the reason for his lack of sleep, and he gently lifted his head to peer over Sydney's body to see the clock. Awakened by his movements, she turned her body to face his.

"What's wrong?"

"I want to visit your parents this weekend," Gabriel said.

"What? Why? I thought we were going to see your grandparents?"

"I know, but I think we should see your parents."

"Why?" asked Sydney again while sitting up so her back was against the headboard.

They had gone to London a few times to visit but only after a considerable amount of guilt from Sydney's mother. Gabriel didn't mind the short trip over to England, but he knew how much Sydney did, so he never asked to go. This was his first time he had requested to visit her parents, so it caught Sydney by surprise. Her mind raced for an explanation but with no success. Knowing Derek wouldn't want them to leave Geneva, Sydney searched for a reason not to go.

"You know how much I hate the Tube; can we put it off until the next weekend? We're supposed to go to your grandparents this weekend."

"No, I'd like to go this weekend."

"Why, what's the rush?"

"No rush, I just think we should visit them—we haven't been in ages."

"Just call them," she responded in a slightly sarcastic tone.

"It's not the same; we should see them. Don't you think?"

"Of course," she replied, having no other response ready.

A tingling sensation rolled through Sydney's body like a splash of ice-cold water on her skin. There could be only one reason he would want to see her parents in person. *He wants to marry me*, she thought. Uncertain what to do, she lay back down so the darkness hid her face and informed Derek.

"He wants to go to my parents this weekend," she said as Gabriel continued talking to her.

"Why?" Derek replied.

"He wants to speak to my parents, but only in person."

"He wants to marry you!" Tanya interrupted, a mother's exuberance unmistakable in her tone.

"That's what I was thinking," responded Sydney.

"I don't want him traveling, especially now with the increase in attacks," said Derek.

"I understand. I tried to convince him not to go, but he's adamant."

"Very well, but make sure he doesn't spend the night."

"I'll call and remind him we're expecting you on the weekend," Tanya said.

"Okay."

"Have you heard a word I said?" Gabriel asked, clearly annoyed by her total silence.

"Sorry, I dozed off for a second. What were you saying?"

"Nothing, get some sleep; we can talk in the morning," he replied with a tone of annoyance.

Gabriel rolled onto his back and battled to get some sleep.

The moment his eyes shut, it began. At first it was small, a well-defined point of light, like a single star appearing in the night sky, then it grew larger, and the longer his eyes remained shut, the closer the light came, consuming the darkness. He struggled to keep his eyes closed, knowing what would come next. Just as it had every night since his accident, a woman's voice called to him from inside the light. Gabriel felt himself yearning to enter the light, but it wasn't right.

His heart raced with anxiety, banging the inside of his chest and shortening his breath. He snapped his eyes open to escape the battle between his will to see the source of the voice and the feeling of fear keeping him from entering the light. He stared at the window, repeating this cycle a dozen more times before exhaustion overwhelmed him and he fell asleep.

The difficulty falling asleep hounded him the rest of the week, and Gabriel's patience grew shorter each day. By Friday afternoon, he was a kettle ready to boil over, banging the glassware on the lab bench while muttering to himself. Bradley was helping him set up some new equipment and noticed the agitation in his actions.

"What's up?"

"What do you mean?"

"You seem short."

"Nothing."

"Okay," Bradley replied, taking the hint that he didn't want to talk about it.

The office door swung open at the back of the room and Dr. Ferrel emerged with a frustrated smile on his face.

"What are you guys still doing here? It's Friday afternoon—go home," Dr. Ferrel demanded as he approached them.

"We're setting up for next week. Besides, I have to wait for Sydney to finish cleaning up the first years' teaching lab," replied Gabriel.

"Judie's meeting a friend, and then we're leaving. I'm

waiting for her to call."

Dr. Ferrel put his satchel on the top of the lab bench opposite where they were working and leaned against it. He was about to speak when the large beaker Gabriel was removing from the packing material slipped from his hands and bounced once on the concrete floor before shattering. The sound of the glass exploding on the floor was like the strike of a cymbal, and it made all three of them wince.

"Shit!" Gabriel shouted, and he slammed the empty box on the top of the bench before kicking a shard of glass across the room.

"Don't worry about it, it's only a beaker," Dr. Ferrel said, trying to calm Gabriel's overreaction.

"I'll clean it up," Bradley said while walking over to the corner of the lab to retrieve a broom.

"I'll do it myself!" Gabriel snapped.

"Whoa, what's going on?" said Dr. Ferrel, referring to Gabriel's inappropriately nasty tone toward Bradley.

"I'm sorry; I'm really tired and a bit short."

"Yah, I noticed..."

"Something I can help with?" asked Dr. Ferrel.

"No, thanks. I just need to get some rest that's all."

"Okay then, I'll leave you two to clean this up, and I'll see you on Monday," he said and grabbed his satchel as he left the lab.

"What's bugging you?" asked Bradley, using a much quieter and more sincere tone than his normal voice.

Gabriel was about to tell him why he wasn't sleeping at night when the light on Bradley's VisText began flashing. While Gabriel waited for Bradley to finish his conversation, he decided against telling him. As he continued cleaning the broken glass off the floor, the lab door opened.

"What happened here?" Sydney asked with a large grin on her face.

"I had a little accident."

"I can see that."

"Bradley and I were setting stuff up, and I dropped a beaker. I think he's talking to Judie now, so we can go any time."

"I just saw her; she's at the end of the hall talking to the cleaning woman."

"Great. I don't want to leave until this mess is all cleaned up, and I don't want Brad to do it; I was the one who broke it."

"Judie's almost here," Bradley said.

"Yah, Syd saw her, let's get out of here."

Gabriel finished sweeping up the broken glass and placed it in the disposal. They picked up their belongings and left the lab together, meeting up with Judie as she walked towards them.

"Hi, how's it going?" she asked, a large smile allowing her white teeth to glow.

"Great," Sydney responded.

"What are you doing this weekend?" asked Judie while leaning in for Bradley to kiss her on the right cheek.

"We're going to visit Syd's parents," Gabriel responded so fast that all three of them cast a look of surprise at him.

"I didn't think you liked going home," Bradley said while looking at Sydney.

"I don't, but Gabe really wants to," she said while forcing a grin at Gabriel.

"What?" Bradley snapped.

"We haven't been there in ages; I thought it'd be nice," replied Gabriel in a clearly defensive manner.

"Really?" Judie said, suspicion pouring from her tone.

"Great, I've never even met Judie's parents," Bradley said with a mischievous smile.

"What, you've never met them?" blurted Gabriel.

"I told you, they're very old fashioned. They'd kill me if they found out," she replied defensively.

"They don't know about you guys?" barked Gabriel in astonishment.

"They're Italian, and they wouldn't understand..." began Judie, but Bradley cut her off.

"They're traditional Catholics," he said while making quotation marks in the air with his fingers.

"Oh, religious," Gabriel replied in understanding.

"Let's get going," Judie snapped, clearly not wanting to discuss the matter any further.

Bradley remained silent with a clown-sized grin on his face, knowing better than to say anything more.

The four of them strolled to the end of the hall and stopped at the front doors to prepare themselves for their walk home. Gabriel's irritability shifted to anger when Bradley held the door open for them. He glanced at the MBG sign then at Gabriel.

It was like injecting acid into his veins; Gabriel wanted to rip the letters off the door. Bradley knew how Gabriel felt about the signage and felt bad for his innocent glance. Both Judie and Sydney stepped outside the building and popped open their umbrellas while Bradley and Gabriel followed, pulling their hoods over their heads. They lived on opposite ends of the campus, so they said their good-byes and began walking.

Sydney and Gabriel hadn't left the campus grounds when Tanya called Gabriel. He viewed the call display and debated whether to take the call, knowing his grandmother would ask when they were coming. Gabriel had no choice but to take the call, knowing she would call Sydney next. Since his lab accident, she called him every day.

"Hi, Oma," he said, turning to Sydney to let her know he was taking a call.

"Are you coming tonight or tomorrow?"

Guilt rushed through his mind while he searched for a way to tell her they weren't coming. His face filled with the warmth of a summer day from the blood pooling in his cheeks. He had avoided telling her all week of his plans to visit Sydney's parents, but now he had no option. Even though he was twenty, at that moment he felt like a ten-year-old; the possibility of disappointing a parent unleashed childhood emotions.

"I forgot to tell you, we won't be able to make it this weekend."

Tanya purposely paused for an extended period of time before responding.

"Really, why not?"

"We're going to visit Syd's parents."

"Oh, I see. That's nice," she replied in a disingenuous manner. "When are you going?"

"I was hoping we could leave tonight, but I haven't discussed it with Syd yet."

"How long are you staying?"

"I told you, I haven't had a chance to talk to Syd yet," Gabriel snapped, feeling the intended pressure from Tanya's precisely choreographed questioning.

"Okay, just give us a call if you find time for us this weekend," she said and ended the call before he could respond.

"Great!" said Gabriel with disgust.

"Who was it?"

"My grandmother."

"You didn't tell her, did you?" Sydney scolded.

"I'm not in the mood," he replied.

They continued to walk in silence. Sydney allowed Tanya's words to stew inside Gabriel before discussing it with him. Ten minutes passed, and they rounded the corner for their flat when Sydney decided to break the silence.

"Is she mad?"

"She's not happy, I can tell you that much."

"Can I make a suggestion?"

"Sure."

"You know my dad's tied up most of the day on Sunday, why don't we go tomorrow morning, have dinner and take the late Tube home so we can go to see your parents Sunday morning?"

"Do you think that's fair to your parents? We hardly go there."

"Trust me, they'll be thrilled to see us and won't think anything of it. Besides, I haven't told them we're coming either," she said in embarrassment.

"What? I don't feel so bad. Are they going to be home?"

"Of course they'll be home, they never go away. I'll call when we get in."

"Okay, I'll wait till you hear from them, and then I'll call my grandmother."

They entered their apartment and Sydney used the V-screen to call her parents. Her father answered the call.

"Hi, Dad."

"Hello, Reverend Grant," said Gabriel, struggling to contain his nervousness.

CHAPTER 19

FAITH SATURDAY

"Good evening, kids," said Reverend Grant, his smile filling the V-screen. As the Head Minister of All Saints Anglican Church, he couldn't help address his only child like he was welcoming a new member to the church. His deep voice projected across the small flat as powerfully as if he were standing on the pulpit.

"Lori, come here. It's the kids," he shouted.

Sydney's mother came into view with a smile equal in size to her husband's.

"Hi, Mom."

"Hello, Mrs. Grant."

"How many times do I have to ask you not to call me that? It makes me feel so old," she protested.

"Sorry. Hi, Lori," Gabriel said, feeling embarrassed.

"That's better."

"What's the occasion?" Reverend Grant asked.

"We'd like to come up for a visit tomorrow, will you be around?" Sydney asked.

"Of course. How long will you be staying?" asked Lori.

"We'll take the first Tube to London, and the last Tube home tomorrow night."

"What, you're not staying for Sunday to celebrate Holy Communion?" asked Reverend Grant, trying unsuccessfully to sound surprised.

"Sorry, Dad, we're leaving Saturday night."

"That's okay; I'll pick you up at the station. Give me a call if you're late."

"Thanks, we'll see you tomorrow. Bye," said Sydney, and Gabriel commanded the V-screen to turn off.

Friday night was the worst of the week for Gabriel. His anticipation of talking to Reverend Grant combined with his angst about his dreams left him sleep bankrupt. He was awake when the alarm sounded on Saturday morning, struggling to focus his thoughts as he lay in bed waiting for Sydney to get up first.

"Light on," she commanded.

"Are you going to get up or are we going to miss the first Tube?" she said while gently rubbing Gabriel's back.

"I'm awake," he replied and sat up on his side of the bed.

"I'm taking a quick shower; you want to join me?"

"You start, I'll be a minute."

"You feeling all right?" she asked while pulling off her oversized T-shirt.

"Fine, just tired, that's all."

"I can cancel; we can go another time…"

"No, I'm fine," he snapped and jumped off the bed. "Take your shower; I'll get us something to eat."

Gabriel skipped the shower and prepared a bagel and some coffee for them, which they ate on their walk to the station.

The streets were crammed with traffic, and the sidewalk had a steady flow of pedestrians even though it was early on a weekend. They joined a group of people waiting to enter the underground transit station. They rubbed shoulders with the other travelers, jostling for position down the long concrete stairs.

Armed security personnel lined the walls of the tunnel leading to the ticketing area. The crowd thickened when they neared the automated ticket dispensers. A chorus of high-pitched beeps screeched through the air, momentarily masking the din of the crowd before bouncing off the stone.

"What's with all the security?" Gabriel asked Sydney.

"I don't know. Do you think it's safe?"

"With all these guys, how could it not be?" he said, pointing to a female guard in an olive green military uniform.

They purchased their tickets from the machine and followed the long line of people waiting to enter the loading area. The large V-screens lining the top of the walls, which normally displayed advertisements, were now showing a security video describing the enhanced measures in place to ride the Tube. The message scrolling along the bottom of the V-screen indicated 'All passengers must be scanned prior to entering the loading platform.'

"That explains why we're moving so slow. And that noise," said Gabriel, and he directed Sydney to a body scanner.

"Perfect, I already hate riding this giant X-ray machine, and now we have to worry about terrorist attacks. Are you certain you don't want to go some other time?" she said, fishing for a response.

"It'll be fine. Come on, we're next," he said and he walked through the body scanner; the light at the top flashed green. Sydney took his hand so as not to get separated, and they made their way toward the front of the crowded platform, where they stood waiting for the next train. A moment later, the public address system announced its arrival.

"Now arriving: The Transcontinental—please step away from the doors."

The arrival of the electromagnetic train was preceded by a flush of cool air through the station, lifting Sydney's and Gabriel's hair from their heads. Its sleek aerodynamic design and brilliant silver exterior made it look like an enormous needle. When the large metal doors of the train opened, people flooded onto the already packed platform.

Gabriel waited for the last stragglers to leave before gently pulling Sydney toward the waiting train. They shuffled into the carriage as part of the crowd and jockeyed for a place to stand. This was a connector train, meaning the ride from

Geneva to Paris was only a few minutes so there were only a few seats provided for the elderly. Gabriel and Sydney held on to the waist-high polished brass bars running the length of the car, their shoulders rubbing against each other and the travelers next to them.

A rapid soft tone resembling the tapping of a crystal glass with a spoon filled the train followed by an announcement, "Please stand clear of the doors."

The doors of the windowless train lowered, sealing the compartment. A low rhythmic hum signaled the beginning of the trip, and the train levitated inside the iron tunnel. The interior walls sprang to life with animated advertisements. Gabriel watched the walls display different products without notice while trying to comfort Sydney.

"How you feeling?"

"I still hate this thing. Can't you feel the hair on your arms standing on end?" Sydney asked while lifting her hand from the rail and rubbing her arm.

"It's just a little harmless electrostatic electricity," Gabriel whispered, his voice barely audible over the background hum.

"I know, but doesn't it bother you how much we get bombarded by radiation?" she responded, her tone loaded with concern, but Gabriel didn't respond.

"Gabe? Gabe…"

Gabriel was oblivious to Sydney and everything else happening around him. His attention was focused on an advertisement. The video filled the wall with the latest bio-neural device—the V-chip. A beautiful young model in the advertisement turned her head and folded her long blonde hair over her ears, the text scrolling along the bottom of the advertisement stating, "Can You See The Chip?" referring to the absence of a VisText device.

"Did you see that?" asked Gabriel, unable to contain the excitement in his voice.

"What?"

"They've done it."

"Done what?" she replied, still annoyed by Gabriel's inattention to her earlier.

"The V-chip, it's a micro-sized VisText they implant. No more earpiece," he said like a ten-year-old describing a favorite birthday present.

"You're joking, right? Please tell me you're not thinking of getting one."

Gabriel quickly quelled his excitement and tried to erase the smile from his face. "Why not?"

"Really, you'd let them inject a chip in your head just so you don't have to wear a VisText?"

"It's just a tiny little chip, and they put it under your skin with a needle," he replied in an attempt to downplay the process.

"You're crazy, that's all I have to say." Sydney shook her head in disgust.

They changed trains in Paris and arrived in London less than twenty minutes after leaving Geneva. Sydney towed Gabriel up the escalator, thankful to see the dark grey morning sky and feel the warm drizzle on her face. The London streets were far more congested then Geneva's; there was no space between vehicles, and the constant sound of car horns made it difficult to speak.

They scanned the line of vehicles in front of the station for Reverend Grant's car without success, so they found shelter from the weather under a coffee shop awning across the street. Gabriel led Sydney across the street, weaving between the bumpers, when a loud blast of a horn startled them. Gabriel instinctively pulled Sydney toward him, thinking they were about to be hit, when she yanked his arm in the opposite direction.

"It's my dad," she said while leading him to a small green car two vehicles away from them. They entered the back of the car and exchanged hellos.

The trip to All Saints Anglican Church took longer than the

commute from Geneva. Lori was waiting to greet them on the steps of the rectory. Unable to contain her excitement, she left the cover of the entrance and met Sydney at the car, wrapping her in a bear hug as she stepped out.

"Wow, Mom, it's nice to see you too," Sydney protested, embarrassed by the scene Lori was making on their arrival. Reverend Grant remained calm and walked around the vehicle to join in the greeting.

"Let's get inside before we're all soaked," said Reverend Grant.

The four of them entered the small stone rectory and removed their wet clothes before heading into the living room. Gabriel removed his VisText as he walked in and placed it in his pocket, knowing Sydney's parents didn't care for the device.

The room was long and narrow and transitioned into a small dining area at the far end. A small bay window allowed what little daylight there was to enter the room, but it was the double row of ceiling lights that filled the area with brightness. Jasmine lingered in the air while faint creaks emanated from the hardwood floor with each step they took into the living room.

An ornate antique table circled by six matching chairs with crimson red seat cushions was positioned in the dining area. A large black leather loveseat and a modern bamboo recliner were positioned at opposite ends of an oval coffee table, making the living room appear smaller than it was.

Gabriel casually scanned the room. He still thought it odd that the home of a priest contained only one visible religious item, a small brass crucifix hanging over the entrance door. There was no shortage of décor on the walls or covering the small floating shelves, but they were all photos of Sydney and various other extended family members.

Sydney and Gabriel sat on the loveseat next to each other while Reverend Grant carried one of the dining room chairs into the living area, placing it opposite them.

"Can I get you kids anything?" asked Lori on her way through the archway leading into the kitchen.

"No thanks," Sydney and Gabriel said simultaneously.

"I'll have a tea if you're having one," Reverend Grant replied, and he took a seat on the chair he had carried over.

"How's work going, still enjoying the university?"

"Great, Dad, it's better than commuting to the research lab."

"Still don't like the Tube?"

"Nope."

"How's your research coming along, Gabriel? Make any earth-shattering discoveries?" asked Reverend Grant with an innocent smile on his face.

"Cole, leave the boy alone," Lori snapped from behind Reverend Grant before Gabriel could answer. She handed her husband a teacup and took a seat in the recliner.

"I was just having a little fun with him, he knows that."

"So why the sudden drop in?" asked Lori before blowing the top of her tea.

Sydney glanced at Gabriel before answering.

"We haven't been here in a while and thought we'd come and see you. That's okay, isn't it?" said Sydney, delivering a small jab.

"Yes, of course, you're always welcome," Reverend Grant replied.

They chatted for a couple of hours, discussing everything from the continual overcrowding of the world's major cities to the escalating terrorist attacks. Gabriel's stomach turned with the anxiety of an actor's on opening night. He desperately wanted to speak to Reverend Grant, but they had to be alone. Gabriel was losing the battle to hide his preoccupation, and it began to show on his face.

"Are you feeling all right?" Lori asked.

"Yes, fine. Why?"

"You look a little off, that's all."

Gabriel scrambled for a response.

171

"I'm just a bit hungry," he said and turned to smile at Sydney, who was staring at him with concern.

"No wonder, look what time it is," Reverend Grant replied.

Both he and Lori jumped from their seats and carried their teacups into the kitchen.

"I'll get lunch started; do you want to give me a hand?"

"Sure, Mom," Sydney said and pushed herself off the loveseat using Gabriel's lap.

Gabriel knew this was his chance, and he leaped from his seat and followed Reverend Grant as he carried the chair back to the dining room. He placed the chair back under the table and was surprised to find Gabriel standing next to him.

"Reverend Grant, do you have a moment?" Gabriel asked, his voice nearly a whisper.

"Is something wrong, son?"

"No, nothing's wrong, but I'd like to ask you something in private."

Like a child tasting ice cream for the first time, Reverend Grant's face transitioned from a cold concern to a warm delight. He too knew what was coming and why Gabriel wanted to ask him in private. Delighted with the prospect of his daughter getting married, Reverend Grant nodded his head.

"How about we go to my office?"

"Sure."

"Lori, how long before lunch?"

"Why?" she shouted from the kitchen.

"I need to run to my office."

"No more than fifteen minutes," she replied.

"Okay."

They left the rectory and walked briskly to the front of the massive stone cathedral. There were five sets of hand-carved wooden doors, a pair flanking each side of the largest entrance. Reverend Grant pulled a large steel key from his pocket and unlocked the door. The smooth marble floor glistened as if it was wet, and their footsteps echoed inside the empty church.

Walking toward the altar, Gabriel could see the deep red carpet and the rainbow of colors illuminated in the stained-glass windows. Hundreds of pews stood like perfectly aligned military troops on both sides of them. Gabriel struggled to keep up with Reverend Grant's faster gait.

"We have to hurry; she won't like it if we're late for lunch," said Reverend Grant.

"We don't have to go to your office, we can talk here," Gabriel said as they approached the first pew.

"Okay, what do you want to talk to me about?" Reverend Grant asked, his upper lip forming a slight grin as he strained to show no emotion.

"This is really difficult for me; I don't know how to begin."

"Relax, let's sit down."

They both sat in the first pew, and Reverend Grant waited patiently for Gabriel to collect his thoughts.

"Did Sydney tell you I had an accident in the lab?"

"No, what happened? Are you all right?"

"Yes… no… I don't know if I'm all right, that's why I want to talk to you."

The small grin disappeared from Reverend Grant's face and a look of concern now covered it. The sudden realization that Gabriel wasn't going to ask for his daughter's hand in marriage ripped through him like a jolt of electricity, but it was the look of anguish on Gabriel's face that sobered his jubilation. Reverend Grant's thirty years of helping troubled parishioners took over his instincts, and he instantly identified the look on Gabriel's face as that of someone who is questioning their beliefs.

"Tell me what's troubling you; I'm certain I can help."

"Like I said, I had an accident while working in the lab and I passed out, but the doctor said I didn't pass out—I died!" he said, expecting some type of reaction but not knowing what kind he would get from Reverend Grant. None was given, however.

"You saw a light?"

"Yes, how did you know?"

"What else did you see?"

"I don't know what I saw; it's all so confusing to me."

"What do you mean?"

"When I was dead," said Gabriel, lifting his hands to make imaginary quotations around the word 'dead', "I saw a bright light, like you said, but I also heard a voice. It was a warm comforting voice coming from the light. I couldn't see whose it was, but I'm certain it was my mother's. I've no way of knowing, as she died when I was an infant."

"What did the voice say?"

"It called my name, that's it."

Reverend Grant sat quietly staring at the altar. Gabriel felt uncomfortable in the silence and wondered how long he should wait before breaking it. Finally, unable to wait any longer, Gabriel spoke.

"Was it…"

"God?" answered Reverend Grant, still staring at the empty altar.

"Yah," Gabriel said, confused by Reverend Grant's aloof behavior.

"I wish I could tell you, but I can't. However, I can tell you that you're not the first person to experience this."

"Did the others have dreams too?"

"Dreams?" the reverend asked, turning his head to face Gabriel.

"I keep having the same dream every night. It starts the second I close my eyes."

"Then what?"

"The light and the voice, the same as when I had the accident, start coming closer and closer."

"This is what's concerning you?"

"Yes."

"Why? It's just a dream."

"I'm afraid I won't wake up."

"You mean you'll die?"

"Yes."

"Do you think it could be God?" Reverend Grant asked.

"I told you, I don't know what to think, and that's why I'm here. My entire life has been devoted to science. I only understand tangible things like equations, the laws of physics or proven facts. But since the accident, I've started to question myself; could there be something more, something we can't understand or science can't explain?"

"You can understand and it can be explained, just not the way you've been taught," Reverend Grant started. "You're looking for the answer in the wrong place, Gabriel; it's not a formula, equation or some kind of law of physics, it's far simpler than that. In order for you to understand, you only need to look inside yourself. The answer's always been there, you just need to release it."

"How do I do that?"

"You'll know when the time comes."

CHAPTER 20

I CAN FEEL IT

C hurch bells resonated through the Vatican as the rain blanketed Rome. The September afternoon sunlight struggled to reach the brightness of a December morning. Three years of continuous migration from the lowlands into the city had left Rome on the brink of collapse. The demands of ten million inhabitants had eroded the Roman infrastructure, rendering it unable to cope with the ever-growing population.

Tent communities covered every open green space that once existed within the city, forming cities within the city. Like all major urban centers on the planet, most of Rome remained high enough to avoid the waters flooding the countryside. Battles erupted among the tent dwellers, the civil unrest brought on by the lack of shelter and food. The IGB struggled to keep pace with the demands of a starving planet.

The stench of swamp gas created by rotting vegetation drifted through the Vatican hall where Father Black briskly walked to his meeting. He raised a small white handkerchief to his face to mitigate the stench. His long black robe drifted behind him like a cape following a horseback rider when he turned the corner toward Tonino's office. The sound of his footsteps on the stone floor could barely be heard, smothered under his robe. Tonino's office door was open, negating the need to knock. Father Black entered to an anxiously awaiting

Tonino.

"Good afternoon, Father Black," he said in a strangely pleasant voice.

"Sir."

"I think it's time we dealt with these terrorists. I'm concerned things could get out of hand. I don't want them to tip the balance. The last thing I need is a world war."

"This could prove difficult; their numbers have increased, and they've become well organized over the past three years."

"I don't want excuses, I want it done."

"Sir, we haven't been able to infiltrate all of the cells," Father Black replied, dropping his gaze to the floor.

"You of all people know my feelings about failure," Tonino replied in the same emotionless tone.

Father Black raised his eyes to meet Tonino's lifeless stare and cleared his throat.

"The ReFs are particularly covert, and we've only been able to fully infiltrate the South American and the Asian cells. We know virtually nothing about Europe and North America. If we begin the process without knowing the identity and location of all the cells, I'm afraid we'll make things worse."

"Then I suggest you find them soon or things will get worse—much worse—for you," he said, a toothless smile stretching across his lips.

Father Black stood motionless for an instant while still facing Tonino. He acknowledged him with a small nod before leaving the office.

***

Father Black's face was tired and pale; gone was its usual deceivingly friendly appearance. It was succumbing to age and the stress of heading the VSS. He sat silently in his office waiting for contact from two VSS operatives sent to track a lead on a ReF cell. It was Gino who had provided the information to Father Black based on some electronic messages he had intercepted. He waited with Father Black while working on his tablet.

"The information you mined was correct, but there's a fourth," said Father Black, smiling at Gino. "Just as you said, they've met in the station, and we're following them."

"Are they ReFs?" asked Gino.

"No confirmation, but they're leaving."

"Where?"

"They're taking the Intercontinental to North America," said Father Black as the color returned to his face, rapidly dissolving a decade from his appearance.

"Why?" asked Gino with an expression of concern and confusion.

"Don't know."

"You know it's possible they're not ReFs," said Gino adjusting his collar in a nervous twitch.

"They're ReFs," said Father Black emphatically.

"How can you be so certain? I don't think this is the time to make a mistake," said Gino, aware of Tonino's intolerance of failure.

"I can feel it."

***

The two VSS men walked down the crowded sidewalk unnoticed by the four women they followed. Their bodies were cloaked by jet-black raincoats and only their faces were visible under the brims of their hats.

Paulo Firenze, the senior VSS officer, donned a pair of eyeglasses with a built-in video camera, enabling him to record everything he looked at. He prepared for the first opportunity to video the women's faces in order to transmit them directly to Gino to search for their identification. Paulo remained in V-chip contact with his partner Vincenzo Dante while continuing to follow the women.

The women weaved through the approaching pedestrians, ducking and dodging beneath open umbrellas. They walked with purpose, but none of them spoke. Three of the four appeared to be in their early twenties, their faces young and wrinkle free, while the other was much older and could easily pass as their mother.

Walking side by side down the crowded Port Tobacco sidewalk was like trying to break through the scrimmage line in a football game. The quaint Maryland village of a decade before no longer existed, overcome by the same relentless urbanization as the rest of the planet. The group waited for a break in the traffic and pounced on the opportunity to cross the street when the traffic light turned red. They snaked through a sea of vehicles plugging Chapel Point Road as they rushed to make it to the other side before the light went green.

Paulo and Vincenzo remained unnoticed, shadowing the women from the opposite side of the street. It wasn't long before the women arrived at their destination—a tiny, red-bricked church. St. Ignatius remained the oldest Catholic church still in service in the United States. The Sunday morning Mass was long over, and the church parking lot was filled with pools of water reflecting the dark green images of the sugar maples and juniper bushes surrounding the pavement.

The cars halted again for the traffic light, allowing the two men to dart between them. They crossed the street and separated, approaching the church grounds undetected through the cover of the surrounding gardens.

The women paused for a brief discussion on the short driveway leading to the chapel then split up with the precision of a military special ops team. The older woman walked back to the foot of the driveway while the two younger women moved to the opposite sides of the church, unaware of the men already hidden in the gardens.

Father Black's face animated the instant he read the text.

"They're in the United States, at a church, St. Ignatius, Maryland," he shouted.

"I'll pull it up," replied Gino while Father Black gave orders to Paulo.

"This is it—I can feel it. Make no mistakes nor take any chances and use whatever means necessary, is that clear?" ordered Father Black.

"Yes, sir," Paulo replied.

Gino used his tablet and rapidly searched the Vatican database. The image of a young priest appeared on the tablet screen accompanied by a name.

"Father Adam Evenston," said Gino.

"Send me everything on him," demanded Father Black with the aggression of a drill sergeant.

***

Father Evenston was extinguishing the candles on the altar when he heard the church doors open. His short blonde hair, meticulously parted to the left and held in place with gel, seemed to glow atop his traditional black vestments. He placed the shiny brass candlesnuffer on the altar table and approached the woman entering the church; the warmth of his pastel green eyes spoke before he did.

"Hello, I'm Father Evenston. Welcome to St. Ignatius. How can I help you?" he asked with a firm but comforting voice while offering his hand.

"Hello, I'm looking for Eve," the woman asked, surprised to find herself talking to a young priest not much older than herself.

Father Evenston's eyes cooled, and his face became expressionless as he lowered his hand to his side.

"Who shall I say is calling?"

"Tell her it's Cap."

"Cap?" he said, his eyebrows lifting ever so slightly.

***

Shards of ruby red light refracted through the raindrops, resembling red spider webs floating in the wind. Paulo and Vincenzo fired their weapons simultaneously. The precision of the beams of light was lethal, silently piercing their victims' skulls without warning. The instantaneous death of the two women afforded them no opportunity to send a warning; as planned, the presence of the VSS operatives remained concealed.

They dragged the bodies from sight and tossed them into the bushes. They quickly made their way toward the woman on the driveway. Paulo approached from the sidewalk while Vincenzo waited behind the cover of some shrubs. Paulo continued to walk slowly toward the woman, his presence intended to capture her attention.

The woman's heart pounded the walls of her chest when instinct alerted her to the figure on the sidewalk. She initiated an alarm using her V-chip to inform the others when a loud ripping sound flooded her ears. Her head snapped backwards with so much force that it tore her raincoat open. A burning pain radiated from the back of her head.

Vincenzo clenched his right hand in the collar of her grey jump suit while gripping her hair with his left hand, forcing her to her knees. He released her collar, pulled a roll of shiny metal tape from his jacket pocket and forcefully wrapped her forehead with the tape. As if preparing a package for shipping, he continued to pull the tape around the circumference of her head until no skin was exposed between her hairline and nose. He completed the final wrap so it covered her mouth, preventing any chance of a vocal alert.

The metal tape established an impenetrable barrier. It prevented her V-chip from transmitting while allowing the VSS operatives to interrogate her. Paulo arrived with his weapon pointed directly at the woman's face.

Rain trickled down the steel tape, filling her warm brown

eyes with water, which resembled massive tears. Paulo grabbed a handful of hair from the top of the woman's head so he could look into her eyes then used his other hand to pinch the loose end of the tape next to her mouth. He yanked the tape off her lips with a snap of his wrist. The action ripped the skin off the top lip, causing blood to mix with the rain. It ran down her lower lip. The scarlet mixture dripped off her chin and onto the gold crucifix resting on her chest. Paulo began questioning her.

"What's going on? Who's your leader? Tell me what you're doing here."

The woman remained silent, her eyes fixed in space so as not to meet his.

"We're not going to get anything from her, take care of her then join me," commanded Paulo, and he released his grip on the woman's hair.

***

Father Evenston and the woman walked up the center aisle to the front of the church, both stopping to genuflect and complete the sign of the cross in front of the altar before making their way to his office in a small room behind the altar.

"Please have a seat," said Father Evenston, pointing to one of the chairs in front of the desk.

"Have you informed her I'm here?" she asked with a slight tone of concern.

"Yes, she knows you're here. She'll just be a minute. Do you mind telling me why you've come to see her?"

"I'm sorry, maybe this isn't a good time, and I'll come back later," said the woman, jumping from her seat.

"No, wait," shouted Father Evenston. "She's here."

"Where?" she asked and turned to look toward the door.

"I'm Eve."

"Thanks for your time, but I've got to get going," the

woman said, reaching for the door handle.

"I'll prove it to you," he said, using a much firmer tone.

The woman turned back to face Father Evenston while keeping her right hand on the door handle.

"Okay, you've got ten seconds."

"CAM 910," he said without hesitation.

Her eyes widened, and her hand released the door handle as her face filled with relief. The adrenalin rushed through her veins like a narcotic, signaling her heart to accelerate. A moment passed before its uncontrolled beating slowed, dissipating as rapidly as it arrived when she realized only another ReF captain could know the significance of CAM 910.

"And you? How can I be certain you're who you claim to be?" he demanded.

"MEG 1212," she said while nervously pulling back and forth on her necklace until the gold crucifix slid out from below her clothes.

Father Evenston smiled when he saw the cross.

"Good, but really, 'Cap' is the best you could do?" he said with a small chuckle, referring to her seemingly unimaginative shortening of captain for a nickname.

"Why Eve?" she snapped back.

"Adam Evenston, Adam and Eve…" he answered with a child-like grin.

"Of course."

"Well it's far more original than using 'Cap' for captain."

"That's not why…" she began, but her words were cut short by the warning alarm sounding in her head.

The rapid tone from her V-chip repeating in her head indicated they had been discovered.

"I've been followed," she shouted.

"Quick, this way," Father Evenston said, running for the door.

He pointed down the hall to an old wooden door near the far end.

"Go through that door and down the stairs. In the

basement, take the third door on your right. It will take you under the church to an old cellar, go in the cellar and open the hatch and you'll leave the church near the graveyard. Go!"

"What about you?"

"They'll be looking for Eve, remember? Quickly."

Father Evenston closed the door and walked over to his office window. He stood motionless, staring out the small panes of glass distorted with age.

The woman pulled the hallway door open just as Paulo rounded the corner. A shimmer of light reflected off the gold crucifix dangling outside her clothes. Its radiance caught Paulo's attention the instant before their eyes met. She slammed the door shut and leaped down the staircase three steps at a time to enter the basement door before he arrived.

Paulo threw open the hall door and ran down the steps, entering the first door to his left, the closest one.

Vincenzo kicked the office door open, throwing it off its frame, and entered Father Evenston's office with his weapon drawn. Father Evenston remained frozen in front of the window, ignoring the person rapidly approaching him. Locked like a bird dog's, his gaze remained glued to the graveyard, unwavering until he saw the figure darting through the field of tombstones.

"What's going on here?" Father Evenston shouted as Vincenzo smashed his face into the top of the desk.

"Where is she?" demanded Vincenzo, crushing Father Evenston's cheeks into the wood.

"Who?"

"The woman, where's the woman?" he forced through clenched teeth while jamming Father Evenston's face even harder into the desk.

A short yelp of pain carried down the back hall, followed by silence. Vincenzo left the office and began searching the back of the church. The heels of his boots tapped the old wooden floor like the ticking of a clock as he approached the open hall door. Exhausted from his frantic search, Paulo's heavy breathing preceded his arrival from the basement.

"She's gone," he said, expelling the words between breaths.

"I got nothing from the priest, a waste of time, all he muttered was 'It's God's will, Cap' and that's it. What about the other?"

"I recorded her face, that's it."

"Black's going to be furious," Vincenzo said.

"I'll tell him," said Paulo, and he activated his V-chip.

***

Gino didn't have to hear the conversation; the fire flooding across Father Black's face spoke louder than words. He stood up from his desk and kicked his chair over. His eyes roared with anger as he faced Gino.

Gino placed his tablet on the desk and cringed before asking, "What happened?"

"They failed."

"How?" said Gino, and his face relaxed.

"The target escaped; we'll never find her now," he said, interlocking his fingers together and placing his hands on his head.

"Her?" said Gino, sounding surprised to know they were searching for a woman.

"Yes, a woman. It appears she may've been their leader. Paulo got her face, and that's it," snarled Father Black while lowering his hands.

"What about the others?" asked Gino, his voice slightly subdued.

"They're sweeping them now. He'll send the video directly to you."

"They're dead?" he asked as he turned his attention to his tablet.

"What did you expect?" replied Father Black with a tone of surprise.

"Of course," Gino said and he began tapping his tablet while whispering a prayer.

"I need the leader," demanded Father Black.

"Don't worry, I'll find them," Gino replied. "Once we know who the others are, we'll find her."

"Failure isn't an option," stated Father Black. The peril in his tone unnerved Gino, who lifted his tablet from the desk and scurried from the office.

CHAPTER 21

A NEW TAG

The small white appliance sitting in the fume hood resembled a miniature coffee grinder but was a hundred times louder. Its high-pitched whirl combined with the drone of the fume hood fan made speaking impossible. Bradley was pulverizing a sediment sample while waiting for Gabriel to prepare the chemicals for extracting the isotopes from the sample. The smell of the reagents was similar to vinegar but stronger, burning the inside of his nose. Gabriel poured the contents of the beaker he was working on into a small flask and placed it in the refrigerator until Bradley was ready for it.

Silence returned to the lab when Bradley turned off the machine. He removed the flour-like grey powder from the pulverizer, spilling the dust onto his fingers. He wiped his hands on his stark white lab coat, leaving a pencil colored stripe, and took it to the bench where Gabriel was working. This was the last of a dozen soil samples they had been preparing for the past six months.

"What do you think? Fifth time lucky?" asked Bradley, referring to the number of times they had worked up samples over the last few years without finding even a trace of a change in the oxygen 18 levels.

"I certainly hope so because this is getting a little bit monotonous, don't you think?"

"I'd say so, but that's research," said Bradley in a manner

meant to imitate Dr. Ross's voice, since this was a saying they had both heard hundreds of times since starting their collaborative research.

Gabriel chuckled at Bradley's poor attempt to imitate Dr. Ross and went to the fridge to retrieve the flask he had prepared.

"Should we call him and Dr. Ferrel to let them know we're ready to run the sample?" Bradley asked.

Gabriel viewed the time on his VisText and then had another thought.

"It's almost five o'clock, what do you think about leaving it here and starting the analysis in the morning?"

"It's Friday."

"Oh yah, I totally forgot; all the more reason to leave it so we don't have to come in on the weekend. I hate dealing with security after hours."

"Me too," Bradley replied, and he and Gabriel began cleaning up the lab bench for their departure.

"What are you guys up to this weekend?" asked Gabriel.

"I'm spending it at my parents' place—Judie's gone away."

"Where?"

"Visit her parents."

"Really, with all the bombings and the flooding and stuff?"

"That's happening everywhere. Anyway, I told her she was crazy and she should stay home, but she never listens to me..."

"You mean anyone," Gabriel interrupted.

"What are you guys doing?"

"Going to my grandparents' place again."

"Finally going to learn the business?" asked Bradley, returning the jab with a half smile.

Gabriel's face instantly dissolved of emotion, becoming statue-like. His heart accelerated, pushing the heat boiling in his blood to every part of his body. He knew Bradley was only teasing him, but hearing the words was like igniting a fuse; Gabriel felt as though he was about to explode. He clenched his teeth to help suppress the immediate urge to snap at Bradley and sealed his mouth shut, avoiding any chance of saying the wrong thing.

Bradley saw the internal struggle Gabriel was poorly trying to conceal and quickly attempted to diffuse the situation.

"How's your grandfather doing?" Bradley asked, the concern evident in his tone.

Gabriel paused before he answered, allowing the acid in his thoughts to dissipate. "Not so well."

"Sorry to hear that. Anything I can do?"

"No, but thanks, not much anyone can do, he's really slowed down over the last couple of years."

***

"Stop it! We're not going to do this again. Don't come with me if you're that concerned," Gabriel snapped.

"Well, I am concerned, really concerned, and you should be too. It's getting worse every day. Have you forgotten already? We almost died," Sydney pleaded to no avail.

"You sound like my grandparents. I'm not ten, I can go by myself; it really doesn't matter to me," he replied and pulled on his raincoat.

"Why can't you just give it a break for a while and see if things settle down?"

"I told you before. You just don't understand; it doesn't work that way. It's not something I can just take or leave, it's like in the old days when diabetics had to take insulin; they didn't want to but had to in order to stay alive. That's what it's like for me, I can't explain it, but without it, something's missing inside me—here," he said making a fist and holding it to his heart.

"I can't believe what I'm hearing. You're a scientist, a physicist. What you're talking about isn't real, it's what my father tells people who refuse to believe the Earth was created by the Big Bang," she said reaching out to touch his forearm.

"I don't know what to believe! I just know there's something more than science. I can't explain it to you... there's no one who can explain it to you; you just have to believe..."

"You've been like this for years—since that visit to my parents! I don't know what my father said to you, but you've never been the same since then, and it worries me," she said, reaching out to pull both his arms toward her body in a failed effort to show how strong her worry was.

"I told you a hundred times, he didn't say anything," Gabriel said, pulling away from her. "I've got to go or I'll be late—Saturday night Mass always starts on time."

"I'm coming," she said, putting her jacket on and grabbing her umbrella from the stand next to the door.

***

Gabriel used his VisText to transmit the code to open the large steel gates of the Muller estate. Protected under her umbrella, Sydney offered him her free hand as they strolled up the driveway. Water rushed down the steepest section with such force it poured over the toes of their boots. The smell of the wet grass and rustle of the leaves on the trees lingered in his childhood memories.

Unable to resist, Gabriel glanced at the scars left on the yew tree as they walked past. His mind raced back to the hospital and the moment he found out his grandfather was injured. A surge of emotion welled from inside his chest, knowing he had caused the death of his closest companion; the pain burned a hole in his heart that had never been filled. Watching his grandfather's health deteriorate over the past two years resurrected the same uncontrollable ache in his heart, causing him to dread these Sunday get-togethers more each week.

"You're awfully quiet, what's up?" Sydney asked, trying to peer out from under the umbrella to see his face.

"Nothing."

"Really, I thought maybe you were talking research with Bradley."

"He's at his parents' too—Judie's on another weekender," he said, not withholding any of the snideness in his tone this time.

"Doesn't it bother him?"

"I don't think so; he's never said anything to me."

Gabriel let go of her hand so they could climb the stone steps leading to the door. Before Gabriel could turn the door handle, Tanya swung it open and greeted them with her usual soft-spoken voice and beaming smile. She pulled Gabriel into the house first and then waited for Sydney to collapse her umbrella. Once they had removed their rain gear and Sydney had wiped the condensation from her glasses, Tanya hugged them individually.

"You're early; I didn't think you'd be here for another hour," she said with delight. "But why didn't you call? I would've sent a driver," she continued but now pretending to be angry.

"We like the walk," Sydney said.

"Come in, come in! Your grandfather will be happy to see you."

Gabriel and Sydney followed Tanya toward the media room when Gabriel asked his grandmother, "How's he doing?"

She stopped and faced them, causing Sydney and Gabriel to halt their progress. Tanya's blue eyes drifted from Sydney's to Gabriel's without displaying emotion. She inhaled deeply before answering just above a whisper.

"He's getting on—eighty-three this year. It's getting tougher for him to do even the most basic things like shower or shave. He now has trouble getting around, so I got him a power chair—of course, he refuses to use it. I told him this week it's getting too hard on me, and I'm going to need some help."

"I'm sure that must've set him off," Gabriel said, knowing his grandfather's refusal to have house staff.

"It riled him for a couple of days..."

"That reminds me, please don't bring up the church topic again," Gabriel demanded.

"You're still going?" she said in disbelief but knowing full well, as did Derek, that Gabriel and Sydney had been attending church for the past two years.

"Please don't start again. It's hard enough for me to listen to Opa go on about it."

"You know he doesn't care what you believe—it's your safety he's concerned about."

"The IGB has more security around the churches than they do at the Tube! What's the world coming to when you've got to have your body scanned to go to church?" he said with disgust.

"I don't care how much security they have. These SnRs have blown up hundreds of churches and killed thousands— it's just not safe!" she protested, glaring at Gabriel first then turning her eyes on Sydney before resuming their walk to the media room.

"I'm getting some tea; do you want some?" Tanya asked before heading for the kitchen.

"No, thanks," Gabriel replied.

"Sure, I'll have some. Would you like a hand?" asked Sydney.

"No, thanks. I'll bring it in," Tanya replied before disappearing into the kitchen.

It was only two weeks since they last visited, so Gabriel wasn't prepared for the shock of seeing the change in his grandfather. He sat in the large recliner chair watching the V-screen with the volume so loud he couldn't hear them arrive. His skin was pasty and cheeks sunken. Tiny veins were visible through his skin around his nose, creating a red spider web, and his eyebrows glowed as white as snow. Every part of his body seemed to have aged years in the past two weeks except for his eyes—they radiated with the same brilliant blue they had always had.

"V-screen off," Tanya commanded.

"Hi Opa."

"Hello, Mr. Muller," Sydney added.

"Hello, kids," Derek said while struggling to lift his body out of the chair.

"Don't get up," said Gabriel, and he and Sydney took a seat on the couch.

"Is it lunch already?" asked Derek, who was slightly confused by their early arrival.

"No, Opa, we're a bit early."

"Early, I thought you'd be watching that space stuff."

"I forgot; were you watching it?" Gabriel asked, unable to contain the excitement in his voice.

"I was, they're on final approach to the station."

"V-screen on," Gabriel commanded.

"That's rude," Sydney whispered in his ear so Derek couldn't hear.

"I just want to watch for a second—it's better than if I watch it on my VisText, isn't it?" he said, trying to make it sound as if he was doing her a favor.

"I guess?" she said with a roll of her eyes.

The rest of the morning was spent watching the M3 mission come to an end and discussing how it had changed the world. Gabriel felt like he was walking on eggshells every time there was a lull in the conversation, dreading the possibility his grandfather would bring up his going to church.

He couldn't bring himself to explain it, how Reverend Grant had helped find a way for him to stop the dreams and end the paralyzing hold they had over his sleep. Gabriel found comfort listening to the priests, in particular their description of the afterlife. For reasons he couldn't comprehend, listening to the sermons offered understanding where none existed. He had learned to stop analyzing the things he didn't understand and had begun to accept them without question.

Sydney protested every time Gabriel said he was going to church, and her attempts to stop him were agitating him. She knew the SnRs were increasing their attacks, and there was real danger associated with being in a church, but she still always accompanied him.

Despite the escalating danger, it always surprised Gabriel how many people risked a terrorist attack to attend church. The small Anglican church near the university overflowed on Sundays, so they normally attended the less crowded Saturday evening sermon. This also allowed them to free their Sundays to walk to the Muller estate for lunch.

***

"Thanks again, Mr. and Mrs. Muller."

"Yah, thanks, Opa and Oma. That was the best lunch ever."

"You're leaving so soon?" protested Tanya, walking them to the door.

"I talked to Bradley, and we want to get an early start on our experiment tomorrow."

"It's Monday, and I have a ton of work to do too," replied Sydney.

Derek slowly made his way to the door while they were dressing. "You can't fool me, you want to get home so you can watch the rest of that space stuff," he said with a large smile, which made his wrinkled face appear younger.

Sydney smiled back at him before turning to face Gabriel with a look of 'I told you so' written across her face.

"Good-bye, Opa," Gabriel replied, and he pulled the door open.

They enjoyed the walk home better than walk to the Muller estate mainly because it was downhill and because the lights of the city twinkled through the rain, which reminded them of the star-filled nights of their youth.

They followed their usual route home, which took them past the entrance to the Tube. Only partially illuminated by the dull light cast from the streetlights was some new graffiti. The two-foot high crimson letters were obscured by the branches of a large maple tree to the right of the entrance.

"What's that?" Gabriel asked, pointing to the brick wall.

"Looks like more graffiti," she said, squinting to read it through her glasses.

"Yah, but what does it mean?"

"I can't read it from here, my glasses are all fogged up," she complained.

Gabriel struggled for a moment before he could make out the writing, "It says: CAM 910."

Chapter 22

Mr. Optimistic

T he WNN anchorman's voice was filled with the excitement of a World Cup soccer announcer. Gabriel remained glued to his seat as if he were watching the final match while Sydney prepared for bed. Their Sunday walk usually left them ready for sleep, but tonight nothing could move Gabriel from the V-screen.

"Good night," she said, but it fell on deaf ears. She looked at Gabriel, who continued to follow the events unfolding on the screen like a cat stalking its prey and knew she was wasting her breath, so she went to bed.

Excitement rushed through his mind and his skin tingled with every second that passed. His thoughts flipped between childhood dreams of becoming a space traveler and the real-life events unfolding in front of him. The hope of one day moving amongst the stars, discovering new galaxies or witnessing the birth of new worlds drove his unwavering commitment to science. The return of the Frontier paled in comparison to the earth-shattering discovery it revealed; but its arrival back to Earth continued to unleash a flood of emotions inside him. A hot-flash raced through his body every time the screen filled with the space station, its exterior glowing white in the deep blackness of space.

Gabriel watched as they floated crate after crate of artifacts and samples into the space station for transfer to Earth. He couldn't wait until they were done analyzing them in hopes they would be placed on public display. It was well after midnight when he finally succumbed to the gritty feeling in his eyes and gave in to common sense, making his way to bed.

He gently slid into the bed, trying not to wake Sydney. Just the thought of seeing or maybe someday touching an artifact from Mars overwhelmed him. Like the rapid fire of a pistol, his mind shot images of the ancient Martian civilization through his thoughts while he lay in bed struggling to sleep. It took a full hour for Gabriel to wind down his mind and slip into asleep.

***

"You need to get up," Sydney called from the bathroom, but there was no movement.

"You're going to be late!" she said forcefully, but with the same outcome.

She finished brushing her teeth and walked over to his side of the bed to shake him. "It's quarter to, and we've got to leave in fifteen minutes."

"What?" Gabriel said without opening his eyes.

"It's quarter to, and you haven't even showered yet. We're going to be late."

His eyes burst open and he sat up, throwing the blanket off his body.

"Why didn't you get me up?" he snapped. "I've got to meet Brad early this morning."

Sydney just smiled and continued to get ready.

Gabriel skipped his morning shower in favor of getting dressed and leaving right away. He wasn't worried about being late for Bradley as much as he was excited to talk to Dr. Ferrel about the samples they were going to analyze.

The walk to the university went especially fast, with Sydney complaining that she couldn't keep up. When they neared the university entrance, they both puckered their faces like they'd bitten into lemons from the pungent smell of solvent hovering in the air. The smell was overpowering, causing their eyes to sting and forming a tickle in their throats.

Two university maintenance men, their faces hidden behind masks, scrubbed the smooth plastic surface protecting the University of Geneva sign hanging from the stone block wall. The hastily painted crimson writing was three feet high and left thin trails of paint resembling blood snaking down the wall. Gabriel pulled his ID out of his raincoat and swiped it over the reader before walking through the body scanner. Sydney followed right behind him, her attention focused on the graffiti.

"What does 'CAM 910' mean?" asked Gabriel, pointing to the wall. The security guard turned and looked at it before answering him.

"Don't know, but the IGB investigators have been here all morning. They think it has something to do with the whole ReFs-SnRs attacks, but they're tight-lipped," she said without cracking a smile.

"Oh, great," Sydney said.

"Don't worry, nothing's getting by us," said the guard with confidence.

"Unless they're painters," replied Sydney under her breath while turning her head to the workers removing the writing, which was only a few yards away from the guard post. She glanced back at the guard before racing to catch up with Gabriel, who was already making his way across the courtyard.

They entered the science building when Gabriel turned and kissed Sydney good-bye.

"How late are you working?" Gabriel asked, walking down the hall to the lab.

"Not sure, why?"

"We might be late."

"Okay, I'll come by the lab."

Anxious to get started as soon as possible, he pulled his raincoat off while walking toward the lab. When he opened the door, he was surprised to see Bradley talking to Dr. Ferrel outside the office. They both turned and smiled in unison when he entered.

"I was certain you would've run the samples by now; it's almost nine o'clock," Bradley snickered.

"Good morning, Gabriel," said Dr. Ferrel, holding back his laughter at Bradley's comment.

"Good morning. What are you doing here already—you're not an early riser?" Gabriel said, directing his question to Bradley with his eyes.

"You said you wanted to start early so…"

"I don't think so," said Gabriel, not buying into Bradley's reason. "It's more like Judie kicked you out."

"Close, she didn't get in until early this morning. I couldn't get back to sleep, so I decided to come in."

"That sounds more like it." Gabriel laughed.

"You don't look much better," replied Bradley. "Up all night?" he said with a large grin.

"As a matter of fact, I was up late last night, but it's not what you think. I was watching the M3 return, and then I couldn't get to sleep."

"Of course you were," Bradley said with a quick roll of his eyes.

"Really, I was," protested Gabriel before he was rescued by Dr. Ferrel from further ridicule.

"What a perfect segue for some news I have for you. Do you have some time to come into my office this afternoon, or are those samples begging for your attention?"

"We've got time. When?" Gabriel replied, suspecting some good news by the tone of Dr. Ferrel's request.

"After my afternoon lecture; meet me back here around half past two. Now go start your analyses; I'm interested to see the results," he said and headed for his office.

Gabriel removed the dozen small glass vials from the

refrigerator and placed them on the lab bench next to Bradley, who was preparing the mass spectrometer to conduct the analyses. Their search seemed in vain, trying to find a link between solar radiation and a rare isotope of oxygen. Their years of fruitless labor had been exhaustive; Gabriel had begun to question his research, suspecting it was futile.

"Here goes another six months of wasted time," he chirped while dispensing some of the chalk-like sample into a small glass injection syringe.

"That's research," replied Bradley in an overly cheerful manner and trying to imitate Dr. Ross's voice.

"Why are we even bothering? There is no connection; this is hopeless, it just doesn't exist."

"Just think of it, if... no, I mean *when* we find it, we'll be famous."

"Famous? I think you were up too early today—you're delirious."

"Okay, maybe I was stretching it a bit... we'll be famous among our peers at least, but if we're right, our research will finally prove the sun is causing these changes and..."

"And the Earth has been through these atmospheric changes before. Yah, yah I know, you don't have to remind me. I know why we're doing this, but don't you think, maybe, we could be wrong?"

"Nope, not even for a second."

"Just start the analyzer, Mr. Optimistic, we don't have all day," Gabriel said through a smile and remembering they had a meeting that afternoon.

It was a little past two o'clock when Bradley injected the last of the twelve samples into the analyzer. They had worked right through lunch in order to get all the samples done so the computer could complete the analysis of the data in time for their meeting with Dr. Ferrel. Gabriel's oversleeping had left him without a lunch, and Bradley didn't want to risk waking Judie, so he hadn't prepared one either. The two of them walked over to the cafeteria to buy lunch while the samples finished running.

They left their rain gear in the lab, choosing to use the building overhangs to make their way across the campus courtyard to the cafeteria. The sound of water clapping on the pavement made it difficult to talk, so they walked in silence. They entered the large open sitting area to find a sea of empty tables covered with used food containers and uneaten food resembling the aftermath of a wedding reception. What looked like a first-year student dressed in kitchen whites, including a well-soiled apron, was clearing a table near the back of the room.

"Wow, looks like a bomb went off in here," Gabriel said.

"No kidding," Bradley replied as they proceeded to order their food from the attendant behind the counter.

"Is there a strike we didn't hear about?" Gabriel jokingly asked the woman as she handed him a sandwich.

"Cleaning staff a 'no-show'," barked the woman, looking at the cook clearing the tables.

"Oh," they replied in unison and took the hint from her tone that she wasn't happy about the no-show situation. They headed over to the cashier to pay.

They retraced their route back to the science building, and as food wasn't permitted in the lab, they sat in the foyer of the building watching a V-screen while eating their lunch. Unaware of the time since they had both left their VisTexts in the lab, it wasn't until a steady stream of students exiting the main lecture hall had filled the once quiet corridors with cackles and chatter that they realized it must be two thirty. The class leaving was from Dr. Ferrel's first-year astronomy lecture. Dr Ferrel's bald head and dark glass stood out among the crowd of students filing out of the room even though he was a full foot shorter than the surrounding mob.

"You're so anxious that you came to meet me?" he asked in a tone of humor and disbelief.

Gabriel and Bradley both laughed but couldn't speak with

their mouths full of food. Gabriel pointed to the sandwich in his right hand and smiled while Bradley lifted his like he was performing a toast. Gabriel quickly swallowed his bite so he could speak.

"We wanted to get all the samples in the analyzer before we took lunch so we could go over the results together."

"Wonderful idea! Shall we head back to the lab?" Dr. Ferrel replied, his large smile slightly lifting the glasses off the bridge of his nose.

They both scoffed the rest of their lunch quickly and joined Dr. Ferrel for the walk back to the lab. Upon entering the lab, the doctor went straight into his office while Bradley checked on the samples and Gabriel got his tablet.

"Another minute or two and the data should be ready," Bradley said.

"Make sure it's on 'auto-send' so I can combine it with Dr. Ferrel's solar event calendar before we view it."

Bradley hit the auto-send key then followed Gabriel into Dr. Ferrel's office, a large windowless room that Dr. Ferrel always kept dark so he could remove his glasses. A wall of clutter covered his oversized wooden desk, making it impossible for anyone seated in front of it to see him. Now aware of this, he pushed a small plastic box and a three-dimensional model of the solar system to the side, opening a view while at the same time knocking a stack of old journals to the floor.

Gabriel bent down to help Dr. Ferrel retrieve the papers from the floor. He gathered the pile at his feet, which had spread across the floor like a deck of cards. His eyes were immediately drawn to the large MBG letters embossed in gold along the top of the first document he lifted; underneath them read the words '*Grant Renewal Application.*'

"Ah, they were rubbish anyway. You can publish anything nowadays if you have the right corporate backing," he said with a smile and placed his glasses where the pile of papers once sat.

It was as if a sword had ripped through the center of Gabriel's chest when he read the words. Anger raced from deep inside him, excluding all other thoughts. The anticipation of discussing their research evaporated from his mind, and his thoughts turned to disdain. Dr. Ferrel had never told him where he received his funding, and his mind filled with the lustrous gold MBG letters on the paper, matching those on the glass doors. His emotions plummeted like a meteor, falling from enthusiasm to resentment so quickly it left him momentarily catatonic.

"You okay?" Bradley asked.

"What?" Gabriel asked, completely unaware that Dr. Ferrel was speaking to him.

"I was asking you if the results were complete," repeated Dr. Ferrel, unaware that Gabriel had seen the document.

Gabriel hoped the dim lighting in the room masked the embarrassment covering his face. He opened the cover to his tablet and turned it on. The thought of seeing the new data quelled his anger, allowing the excitement to reappear.

"I'm just overlaying the radiation data with the isotope results. If you activate your V-screen, I'll transfer the images there so we can all see it."

"Good idea, I've got to make a call soon anyway. V-screen on," commanded Dr. Ferrel, and the room filled with a blue hue from the light of the empty screen.

"It should only take a few seconds, and we'll have the results," said Gabriel.

The instant he finished speaking, the screen filled with columns of numbers on the left side and colorful charts on the right. The three of them sat silently, like watching the beginning of a movie, while the information scrolled across the screen. Gabriel slid a little farther toward the edge of his seat with each passing sample. His hands tightened their grip on the tablet, and his eyes began to water from the intensity of his stare. A warm sensation formed inside his stomach with each passing sample.

They watched as six months of work scrolled past with no meaningful results. When the negative results for the eighth sample rolled off the screen, a ball of fire raged in his belly, causing him to squirm in his seat. He placed the tablet on the edge of the desk in order to put his hands on his head. Gabriel undid his ponytail and shook his head, releasing his shoulder-length hair so he could run his hands through it before lowering his head into them. Overcome by frustration, he sat holding his head, refusing to watch the last three results.

"Hold it! Go back," Bradley commanded, unable to contain the excitement in his voice.

Gabriel lifted his head and hit the tablet screen with his finger to stop the scrolling. He dragged his finger upwards and stopped the data at sample number eleven.

"Would you look at that," Dr. Ferrel announced, sounding surprised.

The ball of fire exploded inside Gabriel, ignited by the flurry of elation ripping through his body. He instantly recognized a large peak in the chart that none of the other samples had. He dragged the chart for sample eleven across the screen and placed it in the upper right corner so he could put all the other sample charts on the screen at the same time.

"What do you think, Dr. Ferrel? Could it be?" Gabriel asked.

Dr. Ferrel stood up and walked closer to the V-screen for a better look.

"It looks like a match to me, and there appears to be a pattern," said Dr. Ferrel, and he counted the reoccurring peaks and valleys in the data. "There's a sharp increase in both radiation and the isotope every four thousand years. How far back does this sample go?"

"At least a hundred thousand years," Bradley replied.

"What wavelength was this?" asked Dr. Ferrel, excitement building in his voice.

"It's UV," Gabriel replied.

"We need to repeat the analysis, but if I was a betting man, I'd say we've found what we're looking for. There's clearly a match with the last few major solar eruptions."

Bradley and Gabriel leaped out of their seats and slapped hands together.

"Hold the excitement, boys," Dr. Ferrel said, using a tone of concern. "Make this area of the graph larger so I can see the scale better."

Gabriel did as he was asked, enlarging the last hundred years of data so it filled the screen. Dr. Ferrel pointed to the far side of the graph where the isotope levels began to rise sharply. The peak started in the late eighteen hundreds and continued to the early nineteen sixties, the last data point on the graph, before it went off the scale.

"What isotope are we looking at?" asked Dr. Ferrel, realizing he hadn't bothered to ask earlier.

"Oxygen-18, all our samples do that. We think the O18 levels have been increasing," said Gabriel as a knot formed in the pit of his stomach. "Is this a problem?"

"This isn't possible. The levels of O18 have remained relatively stable from the beginning of the Earth's creation," Dr. Ferrel said, the shock in his voice fueled by disbelief.

"No, that can't be, look at the data..."

"I can see it, but I don't believe it," Dr. Ferrel exclaimed.

"I'm certain it's correct," Bradley said, compelled to respond since he had run all of the chemical analyses.

"Why didn't you tell me this?"

"We didn't think anything of it. It just looked normal to us, you know—cyclic," Gabriel replied, and the knot inside him tightened its grip.

"I assure you, this isn't normal. I know of only one theory that could explain this, but it's been scoffed at and completely discredited over the years. It's an old paper published way back in 2014 by a scientist called 'Tent' or something like that."

Dr. Ferrel raced over to an old steel file cabinet in the

corner of his office and pulled the top drawer open. He rifled through the file folders and pulled a bright yellow one from the back of the drawer. He placed it on the top of the cabinet and opened the folder, removing a paper from it.

"Trent, that's his name, Dustin Trent. I don't know how he did it, but he got this paper published entitled 'Galactic Clouds.' Trent suggested that our galaxy is filled with massive clouds made of elements drifting through the cosmos. These clouds could be the size of entire solar systems, and they float through space like an invisible fog. Every once in a while, a solar system, like ours, passes through one of these clouds."

"You think we're passing through a cloud right now?" stated Bradley.

"A cloud of O18?" Gabriel added.

"Maybe, if he was right, and just maybe these clouds don't randomly float through the galaxy but are cyclic and our solar system passes through on a regular basis—"

"Like a comet returning to Earth," said Gabriel, starting to understand where Dr. Ferrel was heading with his train of thought.

"This could explain the sharp increases in O18 occurring now and in the past," said Dr. Ferrel, the large grin forming on his face was barely visible in the dim light.

"Of course!" said Bradley and Gabriel in unison.

"We must be absolutely certain before we know anything definitive, and we'll need a second lab to confirm... Damn, what time is it?" Dr. Ferrel asked in a panic.

Gabriel looked at the corner of his tablet, as he wasn't wearing his VisText.

"Ten after three, why?"

"We're late. Call Kim," Dr. Ferrel commanded, and the V-screen switched to blue and displayed large white text 'Contacting Dr. Kimberly Biggs, Massachusetts Institute of Technology, Space Program.' A few seconds later, the face of a middle-aged woman filled the screen with her cheerful smile and flaming red hair.

"Mike, nice to see you. I was getting concerned you weren't going to call," said Dr. Biggs, holding back her laughter.

"You'd have to be dead to miss a once-in-a-lifetime chance like this."

Dr. Biggs laughed and turned her attention to Bradley.

"You must be Gabriel and Bradley?" she asked, looking at Bradley first then Gabriel.

"Actually, I'm Gabriel."

"And I'm Bradley."

"Oh, I apologize. You all look excited to me; Mike must've told you already."

"No, not yet," Dr. Ferrel interjected.

"Well then, I've some exciting news. I understand you're using oxygen isotopes in core samples in your research?"

Gabriel and Bradley simultaneously looked at Dr. Ferrel for any indication that they were permitted to break the news of their recent discovery, but he offered none so Gabriel answered.

"Yes."

Dr. Biggs turned to face Dr. Ferrel. "Which one of these boys is the space nut?"

"That would be me," Gabriel replied.

"You'll be especially excited about this. I understand you two are experts at isotope analyses. How would you like to analyze a couple core samples for me?"

Already twice its normal rate, Gabriel's breathing doubled again as his heart tried to catch-up with his adrenalin rush. *'Massachusetts Institute of Technology, Space Program,'* he thought, and he looked at Bradley's face now covered with a smile, and Gabriel anticipated what was coming.

"Sure."

"Great, because I shipped them about an hour ago; you should have them any minute."

Gabriel looked at Dr. Ferrel who pointed to a small sealed plastic box sitting on the corner of his desk.

Tormented by the smiling faces and unable to contain himself any longer, the words burst from Gabriel's lips. "Where are these samples from?"

"Oh, I'm sorry, didn't I mention that? These are Martian samples..."

It was like standing next to a bolt of lightning. Acting out of reflex, Gabriel and Bradley closed their eyes from the blinding white light emitted from the V-screen. When they opened their eyes a second later, the only light remaining was the warm blue of the V-screen.

CHAPTER 23

THE SUMMIT

"Contact Kim," repeated Dr. Ferrel, but the V-screen failed to connect.

"What happened?" Gabriel asked.

"I've never seen that before," Bradley said.

"Gabriel, get your VisText. I want to check something."

Gabriel quickly left the office and returned wearing his VisText.

"Contact, Gabriel," commanded Dr. Ferrel and instantly Gabriel's VisText identified the call.

"End call. Contact Kim," commanded Dr. Ferrel, but the V-screen displayed 'Kim Unavailable.'

"Something's wrong on her end," Dr. Ferrel said just as Sydney entered the office.

"Display WNN," she commanded and the V-screen displayed a chaotic scene of smoking rubble and burning debris. Flashing lights and screaming sirens emanated from the screen as the first responders arrived from multiple directions. Injured people wandered the disaster area like zombies from a bad horror movie, appearing from clouds of billowing grey smoke, most covered with blood and nursing injuries.

"What happened? Where is this?" demanded Gabriel.

"The University of California," Sydney replied.

"How do you know?" asked Bradley.

"The students were following it in the lab."

"What's happening?" Gabriel asked.

"They're speculating it was a ReF attack. Gabe, that's one of the U of C science buildings," Sydney said, pointing to the remains of a large building in the background of the image. Concern flooded across her face, made visible by light from the V-screen in the dark office.

"What?" snapped Gabriel, straining to hide the concern in his voice as the realization of what Sydney was thinking arrived in his mind.

A new image appeared on the V-screen of a building engulfed in bright orange flames and billowing dark black smoke.

"This is incredible!" shouted the WNN announcer. "The scene you are now witnessing isn't the University of California but the main science building at MIT, more than twenty-five hundred miles away. It appears there has been a second explosion, but we haven't received confirmation if the two are related."

"Was Dr. Biggs at work?" Gabriel asked, raising his voice to speak above the sounds of screaming students and shouting voices coming from the V-screen.

"Volume mute," commanded Dr. Ferrel. "Yes, I'm afraid she was," he replied in a solemn tone while looking toward Sydney.

Hidden from Gabriel by the poor lighting, Dr. Ferrel, Sydney and Bradley slipped into a coma-like state, their eyes motionless and fixed, staring into space when the commanding voice entered their minds.

"Get him out of there now—it's not safe!" demanded Derek, concerned there may be further attacks.

"Yes, at once," Sydney responded and she snapped back to life as if turned on by a switch.

"Gabe, I'm nervous about being here right now, I think we should go," she pleaded.

"I agree," chimed in Dr. Ferrel, followed closely by Bradley's support.

"I think we need to get out of here."

"Go? Why?"

"Because they've blown up two universities, that's why," Sydney said without holding back the obviousness in her tone.

"They haven't confirmed if they're attacks yet, it could be just a terrible coincidence," Gabriel responded.

"Look at that!" stated Bradley in disbelief and pointing to the screen.

"Volume increase," Gabriel commanded.

Splashing water exploded from the surface of the wet grass as debris fell from the sky onto the University of Alaska campus while hundreds of students fled across the lawn, darting around fallen bricks and twisted pieces of metal. The main science building crumbled as if a wrecking ball were pulverizing the walls from inside.

The announcer's voice began to crack as he watched the mayhem unfold at a third university. He cleared his throat as if preparing to make a speech, regained his composure and continued his coverage of the breaking news.

"I feel there's no doubt any longer about what we are witnessing. These horrible events are cowardly attacks orchestrated against the scientific community. They are nothing more than terrorist attacks, yes, that's what they are. They were not random, as all three occurred at exactly the same time..." said the announcer, his commentary cut short when an alarm sounded over the science building security system, overriding the WNN broadcast.

"This is not a drill. Please evacuate the building at once," commanded the holographic security officer projected into the middle of the office. The digital voice was three times louder than the V-screen, making it impossible to speak. The holographic officer was repeating the evacuation notice for a third time when a university security guard entered the lab.

Gabriel and Bradley glanced at the guard while continuing to gather their belongings. They recognized the guard's aggressive walk as an indication that they would be forced to leave without them if they stopped at that moment. The guard passed directly through the holographic image like a ghost passing through a wall and approached them.

"I have to ask you people to please evacuate the building at once. Gather your belongings and leave the campus immediately," the guard demanded.

"We've just come to the same conclusion," Dr. Ferrel said, casting a friendly smile toward the guard.

Bradley picked up his VisText from the lab bench as they left the lab together. They swiftly moved down the hall and out of the building, escorted by the guard while the voice of the holographic security officer could be heard repeating the alarm throughout the building.

It was early evening, and there were many students on campus for evening lectures. The low murmur of hundreds of people could be heard over the pounding rain on the steel rooftops. The night air was stagnant, and raindrops sparkled as they fell through the beams of light coming from the security post like a shower of diamonds.

Gabriel walked slowly, preoccupied with watching the events as they unfolded on his VisText while Dr. Ferrel, Bradley and Sydney walked silently alongside him. The day's steady deluge had done little to dissipate the odor of the cleaning solvent lingering around the exit gate. The workers had left for the day but had only partially removed the writing. Gabriel went through the gate first and stood staring at the letters, trying to make sense of their meaning while he waited for the others to make their way out of the crowd of students flooding the sidewalk.

"Has he left the campus?" Derek asked.

"Just now," Sydney replied.

"Keep him away from there."

"Do you think he knows?"

"If he doesn't, it won't take him long," Bradley replied, walking up to where Gabriel was standing.

"I'll see how long this lock-down lasts, but we need to keep him away from here until we know what's going on. I'll contact security," Dr. Ferrel interjected.

***

"Security must have some record of her," demanded Father Black, his patience growing shorter by the second.

"IGB's scanning their database but it's going to take some time," Gino replied, pulling a second tablet from the drawer in his desk.

"That's the one thing we don't have!" barked Father Black while tapping his fingers in sequence on the antique wooden desk in front of him. Gino's office was large and cluttered with electronic equipment, bookshelves and half a dozen V-screens. Father Black pushed his wheeled chair away from the desk and stood up.

"We are working on gathering details for two of them. Their travel documents were false; we're trying a facial recognition search, but we're talking about scanning billions of records."

"You're telling me that with all this equipment, you can't identify four women, four Catholic women?"

"As far as we can tell, they didn't even know each other—there's nothing linking them to each other."

"Impossible!" Father Black shouted, kicking the chair hard into the front of the desk.

"Impossible? I can only surmise you're referring to your chances of finding the ones responsible for these attacks," stated Tonino as he walked into Gino's office, his Italian accent doing nothing to lessen the anger in his tone.

"Sir, we've got some substantial leads, and it's just a matter of time," Father Black claimed, the color running from his face with each word he spoke.

"Unfortunately, that's the one thing we don't have," said Tonino, repeating father Black's words as if he had been in the room the entire time while staring down Father Black with his empty black eyes.

"The IGB security team is working on it, and we'll have names any time," Gino added, his voice cowardly but trying to support his colleague.

"I don't care about the IGB," Tonino snarled, his voice gaining volume with each word. "I don't care about anything but stopping these attacks!" he continued, bellowing the words with each step he took towards the window. "They must stop now!" he shouted, his head bowed toward the floor while he placed his hands against the glass as if he were completing a standing push-up.

Tonino lifted his head and gazed at his reflection in the glass for an instant then turned and faced Gino and Father Black. Fire replaced the blackness in his stare. Tonino inhaled a deep breath as if to blow the flames out and forced a closed-lip grin across his lips before speaking.

"They're pathetic; the IGB have been impotent in their efforts to quell the attacks. Things are getting worse, unraveling much faster than even I could have predicted. If I don't act swiftly, we'll have a war on our hands—something mankind cannot..."

"We'll find them, sir. A little more time, and we'll have them. I'll take care of them personally," pleaded Father Black, knowing what had happened to those who had failed him in the past.

"Calm yourself, Father; I've no intention of dispatching you, as I still have need for your services. However, we must change our approach before it's too late. Timing is critical," he said with a trailing voice while walking past Gino's desk to peer out the window.

The silence in the room remained unnerving for Gino and Father Black while they waited for Tonino to continue. It was unclear to Father Black if Gino had positioned himself on the same side of the desk as Father Black out of solidarity or for protection, but the farther away from Tonino he was, the safer he felt. They waited an uncomfortable amount of time before Tonino spoke.

"Since these attacks began from religious belief, then we must use religious beliefs to stop them. Inform the pontiff he'll be hosting a summit tomorrow of the world's religious leaders."

"Tomorrow?" answered Father Black, the surprise unmistakable in his tone.

"I would have demanded it today, but Gino and I have a speech to prepare for his Holiness. I suggest you inform him so the Vatican can send the request at once. I want every leader in attendance. Is that clear?"

"Absolutely," Father Black replied, making his way to the door.

"Excellent, I trust you won't find this 'impossible'?"

Father Black left the office without turning back or acknowledging Tonino's final comment.

Gino and Tonino worked through the night and most of the next day on the message the world's religious leaders would deliver to their faithful.

Tuesday evening arrived, and all but the Ayatollah and the Australian Anglican Dean had gathered at the Vatican. Tonino grew anxious awaiting their arrival. He knew in order for his plan to work the religious leaders must address their congregations as soon as possible. With the entire world's attention focused on the attacks, and the images of the maimed and dying still fresh in the minds of the public, the impact of their request would be at its strongest. Tonino beckoned Father Black to Gino's office.

Gino and Tonino waited in silence for Father Black to arrive while watching the WNN coverage of the Religious Summit occurring a few hundred feet from where they sat. The V-screen display cycled through images of yesterday's attacks with brief interludes of experts attempting to analyze the reason for each of the targets. The V-screen was filled with a live image of the gathering crowd erecting tents in St.

Peter's Square. 'Attacks Bring World Religions Together' scrolled across the top of the V-screen as Father Black entered the office, his rapid breathing drowning the commentator's voice.

"Are they ready?" Tonino asked, not waiting for Father Black to catch his breath.

"Yes, the Ayatollah has arrived and the Australian is on her way," said Father Black, alternating each word with a breath.

"They offered no resistance?" Tonino inquired in a tone of surprise.

"At first, but it took little to convince them; they're all on board," he replied in a normal tone, having finally caught his breath.

"I see you've done an excellent job gathering the media."

"It didn't take much; they're clamoring over this unprecedented gathering of the world's religious leaders." Father Black inhaled deeply and cast his eyes toward Gino for an instant before continuing, "Are you certain this is the…"

"I've never requested your opinion on these matters in the past, and I won't be starting today."

Gino turned his head to gaze out the window in an attempt to distance himself from Father Black.

"Yes, sir. It's just that I expect some out there may not be prepared to accept this information. Won't that make matters worse?" continued Father Black, knowing his comment would escalate Tonino's anger.

"Thank you for your concern," Tonino said, straining to keep from yelling. "Right now, I think it best you focus your attention on the Pope and ensure he delivers the message. I can assure you it would be disastrous for all us if he was to follow in his predecessor's footsteps," he said, cracking a smile before delivering a penetrating stare at Father Black.

"I'll return to the pontiff and personally see to it that all the leaders deliver the message."

"Excellent. Gino and I will follow the WNN broadcast."

Father Black climbed the steps that ended at the opposite end of the long stone hallway which led to the meeting room. The smell of incense lingered into the hall from a candle burning next to an old wooden crucifix hanging in a small cove at the top of the steps. Voices echoed through the ancient halls like the sounds of partygoers in a ballroom. The dimly lit corridor hid the media scrum gathered in front of the door at the far end of the hall.

Father Black approached the crowd unnoticed until he nearly slipped on the smooth marble floor; a pool of water had collected off their rain gear. The crowd descended on him like a pack of wolves thrown a piece of meat, their recording devices pointed at his face like weapons.

"Father, when can we enter? Why are they here? Who requested this summit?" asked voices from the media in a relentless effort to get information about what was going on behind the large wooden doors.

Father Black collected himself from the near fall and proceeded to push his way through the scrum. When he arrived at the doors, he turned and addressed the group. The crowd went instantly silent.

"Each of you has been selected to cover the summit based on some form of affiliation your media outlet has with one of the world's major religions. This was agreed to by each of the individual leaders, thus ensuring equal coverage for each faith. As you were informed, the most powerful and respected religious leaders of every major religion on the planet have gathered here to deliver a message. In a show of solidarity, each has agreed to deliver the exact same message. No questions will be addressed until after all of the leaders have spoken. When I open the doors, please remain in the area marked 'media'."

Father Black pushed the large doors open, flooding the hallway with light. Two Swiss guards stood at attention on either side of the entrance; their brightly colored uniforms stood in contrast to the solid white of the walls. The large, windowless room was long and narrow with a set of double doors at each end. Enormous frescos covered the ivory white walls, compensating for the lack of an exterior view. A bright white tablecloth draped to the floor over the length of the meeting table, which was positioned a few feet away from the wall on the side of the room opposite the media. In the center of the table, a plain black pulpit was positioned for the leaders to present their statements. Pope Pius XIII slowly approached the pulpit while Father Black closed the doors.

CHAPTER 24

CARDINAL SIN

The pungent aroma of garlic lingered in the small kitchen as Sydney and Gabriel prepared their dinner. A flash of lightning was reduced to a dull flicker by the condensation blanketing the window of their flat while a distant roll of thunder permeated the walls. A sharp metallic clash startled Sydney when Gabriel accidently dropped their eating utensils on top of the glass plates he was placing on the table.

Like the pasta on the stove, anger boiled inside Gabriel, causing him to lose focus. His mind was occupied with thoughts of the attacks and how it frustrated him that events occurring on the other side of the globe were affecting him. *How could this happen now, right when we had our first real breakthrough?* His thoughts jumped from anger to guilt for thinking of himself when people had been killed. *We're lucky it wasn't us.*

Sydney carried the pot over to the table and placed some food on their plates while Gabriel filled their glasses with water.

"V-screen on, volume low," Gabriel commanded, and they took their seats at the table. They had just begun to eat when it occurred to him that he hadn't told Sydney about their discovery. The attacks had been so distracting that Gabriel had forgotten to mention the good news.

"I forgot to tell you..." started Gabriel, his tone happier

than it had been all day. His words stopped midsentence, and his eyes locked on the V-screen while he twirled the pasta on the end of his fork. The image of the Pope standing behind the pulpit captivated him, overwhelming his urge to eat. Sydney was equally interested and they both stopped eating to watch.

"Volume up," Sydney commanded so they could hear the Pope's address. He made the sign of the cross and completed a silent prayer before commencing his speech.

"God has blessed us today, for this is a historic event. He has sent us representatives from all of the world's major religions. We may have arrived separately, but we gather here as one, united as a single voice—speaking for each and every member of mankind. It is with great sadness I must inform you that humanity rests on the brink of yet another war, a war where none will survive. It is for this reason we gather in order for the Lord, our Father, to guide us to the path of salvation. Through prayer, He has shown us the future; our future must be preserved so we can continue to complete the work He has put us on this Earth to do.

"As your leaders, we have decided tolerance will no longer be given to those whose wish it is to destroy the peace our world has been given by our maker. This peace will not be squandered by the few who continue to wage attacks against their fellow man. From this moment forward, I declare it a cardinal sin for anyone to engage in acts of terrorism in the name of the Catholic Church, and I commit the full resources of the Church to search out and find the sinners who commit these acts. I do this so mankind can continue to do the Lord's bidding without the threat of war. Not since the dark days of the Inquisition has the power of the Church come to bear on those who choose to commit these atrocities against the Lord. Let us pray."

The Pope recited another silent prayer followed by the sign of the cross and left the pulpit, taking a seat to the right while the next of the dozen leaders approached the pulpit.

"Volume mute," Gabriel commanded. "What do you think that means?" he asked.

"I'm not sure, but it sounds like they're going after their own in an attempt to stop the attacks," said Sydney, her forehead compressing with thought.

"What good is that going to do? The IGB hasn't been able to stop them, why do they think they can?" Gabriel replied sarcastically.

"The mention of the Inquisition makes me think these religious leaders may have more power and be able to do more than we think."

"Yah, I guess so. I just can't see what difference it's going to make."

"Those people," she said, pointing at the V-screen, "are the most powerful people on the planet. They have more control over what goes on in our lives than anyone else, including the IGB. I think if I belonged to one of these terrorist groups, I'd think twice before doing anything. You don't know if one of your loyal members has now had a change of heart—not wanting to spend the rest of their eternity in hell for committing a cardinal sin."

"Really, do you think they have that kind of influence?"

"Gabriel," she said in astonishment. "You tell me, you're the one wanting to go to church every Sunday."

Gabriel's heart fluttered as he processed her words. The skin on his face burned from the rush of blood streaming through his veins. His thoughts turned instantly to the relief he gained from going to Mass on Sunday and how listening to the sermons opened new thoughts in his mind, thoughts he never realized were even there. Gabriel understood for the first time how someone could be motivated by belief. The sheer power of faith seemed limitless if one truly believed.

His stomach rolled and released a growl as he felt Sydney's uncomfortable stare cut right through his eyes like she could see his every thought. A slight panicky sensation rippled through his body while the urge to change the subject rose inside him. Sitting like a schoolboy in class who was just asked a question he didn't know the answer to, Gabriel squirmed in his seat.

"That was my stomach—I guess we better eat something," he said, hoping this would be enough to deflect Sydney's question.

Like a wave of cool air passing over his body on a hot summer day, relief arrived when Sydney changed the subject. His face calmed, and his once tense muscles relaxed, returning Gabriel to the point where he was about to tell Sydney of his research.

"What were you going to tell me before the Pope came on?" she asked, having sensed his discomfort.

"I totally forgot to tell you about our discovery, but you've got to keep it to yourself until we finish," he said, his face beaming with excitement.

"I promise," she forced through a childlike giggle.

"It looks like Brad and I did it," he said, pausing for her rhetorical answer.

"Did what?"

"We're pretty sure we know what's been causing these crazy climatic changes over the last few decades," he said, unable to contain the excitement in his voice.

"You're joking!"

"Nope, really, I think we did it."

"Tell me."

"Dr. Ross was right. It's radiation."

"Okay, I'm listening, but you're not telling me anything new," she said, trying to play along with Gabriel's attempt to build the suspense.

"It's solar radiation, and it's never been measured before, and here's the cool part—it correlates with O18," Gabriel said, expecting to hear her unleash a wow, but Sydney remained silent.

Gabriel's face filled with puzzlement at the lack of any reaction. He threw his head back and stared at her for a couple of seconds. Sydney's face showed no sign of emotion as she stared back at Gabriel.

"What's the matter with you? Don't you think that's amazing?" he said in disbelief of her non-reaction.

"Sorry, but I don't get it. How can that be? O18 is about 0.2% of all the oxygen on Earth—I suspect that's not enough to even form a good thunderhead let alone blanket the Earth with rain."

"That's because I haven't told you the most interesting part. The level of O18 has been steadily increasing since the late eighteen hundreds and is now over five percent. Dr. Ferrel thinks we may have proved a theory first published back in 2014—something to do with Galactic clouds."

"What?" she shouted, displaying the type of reaction Gabriel was expecting before.

"Yup, we've compared our data to his solar calendar, and there's a correlation."

"You're certain?"

"We're going to re-run the samples and send some to another lab to verify our results, but I'm confident we're right."

"Do you have any idea what this means?" she asked with the same level of excitement as Gabriel.

"Yah, we think it's the O18 in the Earth's atmosphere causing the temperature to rise, and it has something to do with the sun. I just knew it had to be a natural..."

"I meant... you guys will be famous."

Gabriel ignored Sydney's statement; he shunned center stage and avoided all media attention, having grown up in one of the most famous banking families in the world. Gabriel was immune to the call of fame.

"I haven't even told you the best part," he said like a salesman attempting to seal a deal.

"What could be better?"

"Dr. Ferrel has arranged for us to analyze some Martian samples."

The moment the words left his lips, Gabriel's expression turned to stone; the colorful laughter of a moment ago dissolved from his face, leaving it a palette of grey. The sick feeling rushing through him was driven by sadness. Dr. Biggs' effervescent face was etched inside his mind, making it impossible to maintain his excitement as he told Sydney the news. The chance of a lifetime opportunity given to him by Dr. Biggs was marred by her death. Gabriel found his thoughts returning to anger and frustration toward the people who had perpetrated the attacks.

"What's wrong?" she asked, taken aback by his sudden swing in emotions.

"Nothing," he lied, not wanting to talk about it.

Respecting Gabriel's refusal to talk about what was bothering him, Sydney revived the conversation by asking about the Martian samples.

"Are you really going to work on Martian soil?" she asked in a perky tone.

"I can't wait; I didn't even get to see it before the evacuation. When do you think they'll clear the campus?"

"It's going to be a while—especially our building."

"I can't spend another day sitting around here; do you want to go and visit your parents?"

"No!" Sydney shouted, surprising Gabriel with the intensity of her response.

"Okay, I thought I'd at least ask—it's been a while since..."

"I don't want to travel with everything that's going on," she said, regaining some composure. "We can go to your grandparents if you want."

"I'll call Brad and Judie after dinner; let's see what they're up to before we try my grandparents."

"Okay."

Sydney commanded the V-screen to change to a music-only broadcast before taking their plates to re-heat their food. They finished their meal, cleared the table and sat in the living room to call their friends on the V-screen.

"Call Brad," Gabriel commanded, and a few seconds later the image of Bradley and Judie filled their V-screen.

"Hi, G. Hey, Syd," said Bradley, who was sitting next to Judie on their living room couch eating dinner.

Sydney and Gabriel turned and faced each other the moment they saw Judie; they shared a look of shock but didn't speak before quickly turning back to face the V-screen. They hadn't seen Judie since last week, and despite viewing her through the V-screen, they could see her pale and sunken face. Gabriel continued talking, hoping neither Judie nor Bradley had noticed their reaction.

"You're still eating," Gabriel said apologetically. "Call us back when you've finished your dinner."

"Don't worry, we're just finishing," Judie said, poking her head out from behind Bradley and struggling to smile.

"All right, we're wondering if you guys have plans for tomorrow."

"Gabe... I really thought you'd notice of all people," said Judie, still donning a fake smile.

"We didn't want to say anything. You okay?" asked Gabriel timidly, not wanting to embarrass himself.

"I'm fine, just really tired. Look," she said and pointed to her ear.

"Tell me you didn't," Sydney scowled.

"Yup, and it's fantastic," Judie replied referring to the V-chip she had implanted the week before.

"Did you know she was getting one?" asked Gabriel, looking directly at Bradley.

"Nope. She surprised me too."

"When did you get it? How do you like it? Did it hurt? How much...?" Gabriel fired, but his questioning was cut short by Sydney.

"Don't be getting any ideas; your grandparents will kill you, and then me for not stopping you," Sydney stated.

Gabriel's face sparkled with the excitement of a child handed a gift. He couldn't wait to talk to Judie about her V-chip and had forgotten the reason they had called.

"Gabe," Sydney said in a manner a mother would use to scold a child. He quickly returned to the reason they called.

"Yah, tomorrow," he began, but Bradley interjected.

"My parents are coming. Sorry, you're on your own tomorrow," said Bradley with a grin.

"Thanks," said Gabriel sarcastically. "We'll catch up with you guys later. End call," Gabriel commanded.

Gabriel looked at Sydney, a massive grin covering his face, negating the need to speak. The idea of getting a V-chip wiped his mind clean of everything but finding a way to call Judie without Sydney knowing. He knew it wasn't his grandparents Sydney was worried about; she was most concerned for him. She tolerated Gabriel's VisText, but loathed the idea of him getting a bio-neural implant and would remind him of it every time the subject came up.

"Now, don't go and do something stupid," she scowled, knowing exactly what he was thinking.

CHAPTER 25

A PRAYER

The navy blue panel van arrived silently in the dark, parking at the rear of the high-rise apartment complex. A man and a woman left the vehicle and walked briskly to the main entrance at the front of the building. Their heads were protected from the rain by military style berets, and all but their faces were hidden beneath long black rain cloaks. The man stood a few feet in front of the automatic sliding glass doors, diligently canvassing the front of the building, while the woman entered the lobby and approached the concierge—a young man who resembled a massive egg with legs. The concierge snored lightly with his head cradled in his arms on his desk, which was positioned behind a chest high counter. His slumber continued unabated; he wasn't expecting anyone to arrive at four a.m.

She lifted the right side of her cloak with her left hand and pulled an identification card from an inside pocket, placing it on the counter. Using her right hand, the IGB officer dragged her fingers up the length of her cloak to gather some water, which she flicked over the counter and onto the face of the concierge. The shock of the warm droplets hitting his face startled the man awake. The force of his overweight body lunging out of the chair caused it to topple backwards, filling the vacant lobby with a crashing sound.

Embarrassed by his actions, his dark brown cheeks

showed a hint of rose.

"How I help you?" the concierge asked, using broken English while reading the identification card.

"We're looking for this couple; do they live here?" asked the woman officer, handing him a tablet with a photo of a young man and woman while returning her identification to her pocket.

"Yes, yes, that is Renata and Antomi," he said, shaking his head nervously.

"Are they home?"

"I think yes?"

"Give me your key," she demanded.

"I am forbidden to…"

"Do I look like I care?" the officer replied as five other IGB officers carrying weapons scrambled to take up position to secure the lobby.

She had already alerted the rest of the IGB team using her V-chip so they could finish securing the perimeter of the building. When the rest of the South American special operations team arrived, her partner and two others joined her, and they rode the elevator to the 46th floor. One of the officers carried a camera to document the operation.

Armed with the element of surprise, the female officer swiped the credit-card-sized plastic key over the security panel on the outside of the apartment door, and they stormed inside the unit.

The tiny living room was set aglow by the lights mounted on the officers' drawn weapons. The wail of the interior security alarm was deafening as the team scoured the unit.

The female officer entered the bedroom followed closely by her partner and the officer recording the arrest. Their lights flooded the empty bed, reflecting enough light to illuminate the back of the couple holding hands and jumping out the large bedroom window.

After capturing their leap, the cameraman turned his recording device to the image of the large Star of David hung over the bed before ending the recording.

***

"You're certain it's been recorded?"

"Yes, it was part of the deal."

"When will it be broadcast?"

"The moment the senior IGB officers have given their final approval."

"It's imperative this happen immediately, or it will have little impact."

"They're fully aware of that, and I made it clear the Vatican wouldn't supply any more names unless they do it as requested," said Father Black in a matter of fact manner.

"Good. If this goes as planned, the public will have renewed their faith in the IGB's ability to find these terrorists, and we will have shown them the power of the religious faithful. The Pope's delivery will have these ReF leaders wondering which one of their own is going to turn them in next," Tonino said, showing a rare bit of delight at the thought of his plan coming to fruition.

"Excuse me, sir," Father Black said, lifting his finger in the air to indicate he was receiving a message on his V-chip.

Tonino stood up from his desk and walked toward the window, not hiding his annoyance at the interruption.

"There's a small problem," Father Black said, his tone diminished from a moment ago.

"You know how much I like small problems," Tonino replied without facing Father Black.

"The arrest didn't go as planned," said Father Black.

"How could they screw this up? We gave them everything they needed, names, photos... we even gave them the apartment number. How could they get away?"

"No, sir, it's not that, please let me finish. They didn't escape; they were unable to question them..." he tried to continue, but Tonino's anger flared, cutting Father Back's words off.

"They shot them?"

"No, sir. They jumped out the window of their apartment."

"Together—how sweet," Tonino said in a vile tone.

"They did record some of it, and WNN is broadcasting it."

"V-screen on," Tonino commanded.

The V-screen in Tonino's office projected the WNN coverage—a continuous loop of the image of two dead bodies covered with a large red plastic tarp, the IGB team entering the apartment followed by the couple jumping from the window before fading to the Star of David. The caption scrolling at the bottom of the screen read 'Religious Leader's Pleas Pay Off.' The announcer urged viewers to remain on WNN as the story continued to develop.

"Volume mute," Tonino commanded. "This isn't as bad as I expected," he said, looking at Father Black with approval.

"The IGB also have a lot to gain by working with us; this is their first big breakthrough, and they don't want to jeopardize our new partnership."

"It would have been nice to question our ReF friends, but seeing as that's no longer possible, the IGB did manage to salvage as much as they could," Tonino said, returning to his desk.

"Do you want me to give them the Asian leaders?" Father Black asked.

"It appears you may have to. These terrorists are far more faithful than I expected. The others may decide to follow this couple's lead, and we may end up with no one to help us find the others. I trust you've made some progress?"

"The North Americans and Europeans are far more organized and advanced than the others, but Gino has assured me it's only a matter of time before…"

"I told you, we don't have any more time!" Tonino lashed out. "I suggest you use yours more wisely."

Father Black understood the meaning of Tonino's statement and entered the hallway without looking back.

***

The hallway appeared deserted, and except for the trail of wet boot prints covering the concrete floor, there was no sign of life. It looked more like a Sunday morning than a Friday morning. Used coffee cups and sandwich wrappers remained in the sitting areas along the side of the hallway, and two of the trashcans were nearly overflowing, having not been emptied for some time.

"Wow, looks like even the cleaning staff haven't been in for a while," Gabriel said, leaning over so his lips could meet Sydney's.

He kissed Sydney good-bye and began walking the short distance to Dr. Ferrel's lab, leaving his own trail of water. He didn't give her a second look because he knew this would give her the opportunity to try and convince him one more time to stay at home until Monday.

He could hear his own footsteps squeaking on the floor and the sound of the leather pouch containing his tablet rubbing against his raincoat. The unusual quiet replaced the chatter of students that normally filled the hallway. It was evident from the state of the science building and the lack of students that most people were thinking like Sydney and considered it too soon to come back to campus.

Gabriel entered the lab, pulled his rain gear off and hung it by the door. Expecting to be the first in the lab, Gabriel stumbled, nearly dropping his leather pouch, and his heart nearly jumped out of his chest when Bradley said good morning. Although unexpected, the sound of Bradley's cheerful voice was comforting, as he thought he would be working alone.

"Wow, a little jumpy?"

"I didn't think you'd be coming in. I guess Judie let you?"

"Yah, why?"

"Sydney did everything short of forbidding me to come.

She thinks it's too soon."

Sydney had already informed Bradley and Dr. Ferrel that she had been unable to convince Gabriel to stay away from the campus until Monday, so they had both arrived ahead of Gabriel. Bradley had begun the preparation of the Martian sediment core for analysis while Dr. Ferrel attended his first-year lecture.

"Funny, Judie didn't mention it; is that a good thing or bad thing?" Bradley asked with a smirk.

"You know; 'visiting her parents'," Gabriel said, lifting his hands in the air and making the 'quote' symbol with his fingers while laughing.

"Oh, I never thought of that," he replied with a silly look.

"And she did look terrible the last time I saw her—has it been a while since the last time you guys…?"

"Okay, that's enough," Bradley said, choking back a laugh. "We're doing quite all right. Why do you think I'm in so early anyway?" he finished with a smile.

"The sample of course," Gabriel responded as if there was no other answer.

"Of course, the sample," Bradley agreed.

"Seriously, Brad, is she okay? She looked really awful the other day. Were you guys fighting?"

"No, that's just it, something's really bugging her, but she won't tell me. She refuses to talk about it and gets really angry when I ask. I can tell she's been crying forever, but she gives me nothing. You know what she's like."

"Yah," Gabriel said, feeling uncomfortable and not knowing what to say.

The memory of the call to them reminded Gabriel that he hadn't spoken to Judie about her new V-chip, and since they weren't allowed to wear them in the lab, he decided to ask Bradley, hoping to change the subject.

"I haven't been able to call her about the V-chip; does she like it?"

"I don't know, I don't want to get in the middle of this,"

Bradley said, the worry in his tone unmistakable.

"What do you mean?"

"Sydney will kill me if she finds out I even talked to you about it."

"I'm a big boy; if I want to get one, I'll get one. I just want to know if she likes it or not," Gabriel said, annoyed with Bradley and Sydney treating him like a child.

"Fine, but you didn't hear it from me—she absolutely loves it."

"I thought so, I can't wait to—"Gabriel started but thought twice before finishing his sentence.

"Great, I'm dead."

"Forget about it. Have you started the sample?" Gabriel asked, walking over to the lab bench where Bradley was working.

"What else would I be doing?"

"I thought you might be re-running the last batch to confirm the results?"

"Are you kidding? That'll only take a few days to do, running the Martian sample's going to take months."

"Great idea. Did you let Dr. Ferrel know?"

"Yes, just before he went to his lecture."

"Is that it?" Gabriel asked, pointing to the small clear plastic tube filled with bright rust-colored earth.

"Yes, sir."

"I thought it'd be more..."

"Red?" Bradley replied before Gabriel could finish his sentence. "Me too," he said, and his eyes glazed over while he stared blankly at the tube in his hand.

Derek's voice entered Bradley's mind, interrupting his discussion with Gabriel.

"I've suffered a heart attack, and I'm in an ambulance with Tanya. We've sent a driver, and Tanya has sent a message to the university to inform Gabriel. Sydney, accompany him," Derek commanded.

"I'm on my way to his lab," Sydney said.

"Brad, Brad, are you okay?' Gabriel asked, trying to get Bradley's attention when the holographic security system activated in the lab.

Gabriel turned to face the digital security guard projected in the center of the lab.

"Urgent message for Gabriel Muller—Please call Tanya Muller at once. I repeat: Urgent message for Gabriel Muller—Please call Tanya Muller at once. I repeat..."

"Message received," Gabriel commanded, and the holographic image disappeared.

"What's going on?" Bradley asked.

"Something's wrong. I've got to call my grandmother," he said, running to get his VisText from his leather pouch.

Gabriel placed the device over his ear and commanded it to call his grandmother.

Tanya answered the call on her handheld while still traveling in the back of the ambulance. Gabriel began to talk when Sydney entered the lab.

"What's wrong, Oma?"

"It's Opa; he collapsed in the kitchen. We're on our way to the hospital right now," Tanya said. She was obviously concerned at how Gabriel would take the news from the tone of her voice.

A massive lump formed in Gabriel's throat, making it difficult to swallow. His legs became weak, and he leaned back on the lab bench for support. He could hear the pounding of his own heart in his head, and his mouth dried, making it difficult to speak. He pushed the next words out of his mouth.

"Is he going to be okay?"

"I don't know. I've sent a car to the university to bring you and Sydney to the hospital. It'll be waiting for you."

"Thanks," he said and ended the call.

Gabriel looked over at Sydney; she was removing his raincoat from the hook. A second of confusion passed through his mind, *How did she know?* The thought escaped his mind as fast as it entered, and he ran to the door to get his coat on.

"It's my grandfather," Gabriel said to Bradley as he was leaving with Sydney. "He's on his way to the hospital—I'm heading there now."

"I hope he's all right."

"Thanks," he said, and they left the lab.

***

Tanya greeted Gabriel and Sydney in the emergency ward. Her warm smile instantly reduced the anxiety coursing through Gabriel's veins. He hugged his grandmother unusually long as if never letting go would prevent him from knowing. Gabriel refused to release his embrace, not having the strength to look into his grandmother's eyes when he asked, "Is he okay?"

"They've stabilized him and are running some tests," she said, holding Gabriel in her arms while looking at Sydney.

Not hearing the words he most feared, Gabriel left his grandmother's arms and faced her. The pressure inside his head from the tears he was holding back subsided and he took a deep breath.

"Where is he? I want to see him," Gabriel demanded, regaining his composure.

"They'll come and get us as soon as we can go in. Let's have a seat," Tanya said, and they began walking over to the cluster of lounge seats in the waiting area when a petite, brown-haired woman entered the waiting area through the swinging doors. Her hair was cut short and her hazel eyes were partially hidden behind gold wire-rimmed glasses.

"Are you Derek Muller's wife?"

"Yes."

"Hello, I'm Dr. Fisher," she said, extending her hand toward Tanya.

"Nice to meet you," Tanya responded while shaking the

doctor's hand.

Gabriel had just enough time to send a glance toward Sydney before Tanya began to introduce them.

"This is Gabriel and Sydney," said Tanya and both Sydney and Gabriel shook Dr. Fisher's hand.

"Have we met?" asked Dr. Fisher, still holding Gabriel's hand and attempting to make eye contact.

"I don't think so, but our family name is common," replied Gabriel, hoping to deflect further questioning.

Dr. Fisher's face crumpled with confusion; she was certain they had met and was surprised Gabriel had denied it.

"How's he doing?" Tanya asked.

"He's resting at the moment…"

"Can we see him?" Gabriel interrupted.

"You can, but I must warn you he's suffered at least one serious heart attack, maybe more, and the next couple of days are going to be critical for…"

"What do you mean 'critical'? Is he going to be okay?" interrupted Gabriel again, his concern for his grandfather erupting inside him.

Dr. Fisher turned and faced Gabriel before she spoke.

"Listen to me, your grandfather is seriously ill. Right now, I can only make one promise to you, I promise you I'll do everything I can for him—the rest is up to the good Lord."

It was if a dagger had pierced his chest. At that moment, Gabriel realized that all the science and technology in the world couldn't save his grandfather. Dr. Fisher's last words released a warm surge that radiated from his heart and continued to permeate every part of his body. A tidal wave of faith flooded over him like being lost then looking at a map only to realize you are where you needed to go.

Gabriel prayed.

CHAPTER 26

SIX MONTHS

T he young woman covered her mouth and nose with a cloth as she forced her way through the mass of people, towing her four-year-old daughter through the crowd with her other hand. The wind carried the stench of urine through the thin canvas walls, its pungent smell unabated by the pelting rain. Nauseated by the lingering illness, her daughter vomited what little food she had eaten that evening. Her mother's struggle to the front of the food line became increasingly futile as the hordes of hungry people formed a wall. Frustrated and exhausted, she made her way outside the tent to fill her container with water from the river of rainwater pouring off of the roof of the tent.

This dramatic image on the V-screen was replaced by a new one; the image of a gang of young people fighting over food rations thrown from the back of an IGB military truck. The scene switched again, this time to an aerial view displaying the enormity of one of the thousands of tent towns expanding up the hillside; this one stretched as far as the eye could see. The makeshift colonies were erupting overnight to escape the ever-rising water.

Transfixed by the disturbing scenes, Sydney paused for a moment while making their lunches and then commanded the volume to increase.

The WNN announcer's voice was slow and methodical as he described the scene like he was narrating a nature documentary. Sydney listened to him deliver the breaking news while she prepared the food.

"It's becoming clearer that the IGB is losing its struggle to maintain order in tent towns like this one popping up across the continent. The global exodus to higher ground continues to accelerate the strain on our planet's resources. As you can see by our coverage, the lack of food and proper housing coupled with the incredible number of individuals forced to live in such a cramped area has spawned the resurgence of historical diseases like cholera and diphtheria. We are broadcasting live from the foothills mere miles from where Las Vegas once stood, but the scenes you're witnessing could be from anywhere in the world. Now submerged under millions of square miles of water, the once water-starved desert interiors of Africa, Australia and Asia resemble this Nevada desert—nothing more than inland seas. I can only quote one nameless individual I spoke to earlier this evening: 'Not since Noah has the Earth seen such flooding,'" said the reporter with dramatic flair.

The V-screen image changed to a line of fifty or more sick people lying on cots while attended by medical personnel.

"By their own admission," continued the announcer. "The IGB has confirmed that limited access to modern medical resources and the lightning-fast spread of disease under these crowded conditions has exposed more than ten percent of the world's twenty-one billion people to squalid conditions not seen since the Dark Ages. Unrest is leading to anarchy, and death is rampant. These tent towns are nothing more than powder kegs on the verge of exploding, so the IGB continue to reinforce them with additional military troops to try to maintain peace," reported the WNN announcer before pausing to allow the image of the mass of people to fill the V-screen.

"Volume mute," Sydney commanded, not wanting to hear any more of the coverage. She sliced a bagel in half and placed it in the toaster, expecting Gabriel to join her in the kitchen at any moment.

***

The smell of bagels in the toaster drifted through their tiny flat. The aroma signaled Gabriel to open his eyes and focus on the time scrolling along the bottom of his solar system clock. The room was filled with darkness, which made it seem like it wasn't time yet to get out of bed. He tossed the sheet off his body and left the bed for the bathroom. While standing in front of the mirror, he grabbed the back of his long wavy hair in his fist and formed it into a crude ponytail. Subconsciously he looked in the mirror to ensure his birthmark remained concealed. He slipped two elastics around his hair to hold it in place before taking a shower. Gabriel quickly dressed, his hunger drawing him to breakfast.

"What's this all about?" Gabriel asked, referring to the V-screen as he walked into the kitchen.

"The flooding and how the tent towns are becoming unlivable," Sydney replied while walking over to the kitchen window. "One guy said the Earth's not seen anything like this since Noah," she said in a comical tone.

"Well, it's getting bad around here too. I saw some tents going up outside the campus, and they don't know how much longer the dykes will hold back the Rhone."

Sydney lifted the blinds of their small kitchen window and peered out their third-floor window to the front courtyard. She searched for any sign of movement in the early December darkness.

"They there?" Gabriel asked, not holding back the resentment in his voice.

"I don't see anyone," she replied and turned back to face him.

"Great, I'm really sick of them, they're like vultures waiting for some road kill to die."

"I know, but it's their job," she replied, trying not to sound too sympathetic.

"I'm sick of it; I've had to deal with them all my life. Usually I can ignore it, but this has been going on for months. I'm just tired of it, that's all."

Sydney was looking out the window for any sign of the media. Since Derek's near fatal heart attack, tabloid reporters had been hounding Gabriel for an interview—waiting outside their apartment building and following him to campus. His refusal to address their constant questioning left them no alternative but to concoct their own fictitious headlines, including his grandfather's death. This headline angered Gabriel to the point of swearing at a group of reporters the morning after the article was broadcast.

They finished breakfast and left the flat as quickly as possible, hoping to avoid contact with any reporters. No one was waiting at the door, but two men under umbrellas stood ten yards away at the edge of the sidewalk, leaving the front of their building unusually vacant this morning. Instead of his usual morning snarl at the frenzy of reporters waiting for his arrival, Gabriel smiled until he saw their faces. Having become familiar with the normal scrum of men and women greeting him each morning, Gabriel quickly recognized one of the men the moment his face was visible from behind the umbrella.

It was Kendal Toews, a young and particularly annoying and aggressive reporter who had been pestering Gabriel from the moment the news of his grandfather's ill health had been leaked. Kendal's boyish face, curly blonde hair and charming smile lured his prey like the light of an anglerfish, allowing him to get close enough to his victim to capture a career-ending misquote. The moment Sydney and Gabriel stepped onto the sidewalk, the two men approached them aggressively and identified themselves as reporters.

"Are you Gabriel Muller, heir to the MBG fortune? Can we have a moment of your time?" asked the reporter Gabriel didn't recognize.

"Gabriel, can you confirm if your grandfather is in fact still alive?" Toews chimed in.

Gabriel stopped dead in his tracks. His insides filled with acid as he stared into Toews' eyes. Sydney felt his hand squeeze hers until it hurt. She knew he was about to erupt and pulled him down the sidewalk with all her might. Gabriel resisted and tried to pull his hand out of hers, which she now held as tightly as she possibly could.

"Ignore them, please, let's just get going," she pleaded, tugging him like a child trying to pull an overloaded wagon with one hand while holding her open umbrella with the other.

"I can't," he snapped.

"You've got to, think of your grandparents; they'd ignore it, and you can too. Keep walking."

Sydney's pleading worked. The few seconds of convincing cooled Gabriel's anger enough to allow him to regain control of his emotions. She lifted her umbrella over both their heads and rested it on her shoulder so it covered their backs, acting like a shield to prevent the reporters approaching them from behind.

They walked briskly toward the campus while the two reporters followed, trying to regain Gabriel's attention with additional questions to no avail; they gave up their pursuit a short time later.

"Thanks," Gabriel said, looking down at her with a forced smile.

"Don't worry about it; they're starting to get to me too."

Their walk to the university came to an abrupt halt when they neared the main security gate. A small crowd of students milled around the entrance, making it impossible for them to see the security checkpoint. As they approached the entrance, it became apparent why the crowd had gathered. A line had formed because the body scanner was sealed off. Students were waiting for the security officers to manually check their bags before permitting them to enter the campus.

The reason for the sealed scanner became clear when

Gabriel and Sydney approached the front of the line. The left side of the device was spray painted with three large letters and what appeared to be the beginning of a fourth letter. The letters were written in a column and formed the word 'MEG.'

The instant Sydney saw the writing, she contacted the others.

"Why didn't you tell me about the message?" she demanded, the tone of her voice inside Dr. Ferrel's and Bradley's minds indicated the urgency of her request.

"What message?" they both responded.

"At the entrance. There's going to be another attack, and we're standing in the security line up at the moment."

"I'm not there yet," Bradley replied.

"I came in the north entrance," Dr. Ferrel said.

"Don't let him on campus," Derek ordered, the tone of his voice filled with alarm.

"There's nothing I can do; we're already on campus, and he won't listen to anyone right now. He's obsessed with finishing the Martian sediment sample. That's all he's talked about for the last three weeks," Sydney replied.

"I don't want him anywhere near the campus; it's just too dangerous," Derek demanded.

"I'll call and tell him you're not doing well, and he's to come see you as soon as possible," Tanya interjected.

"Excellent idea," Derek agreed.

Gabriel approached the screen post and handed his leather satchel containing his tablet and lunch to the security guard.

"This has to be a bit embarrassing," Gabriel said, unable to hold back a smirk.

"Let's just say the night guard now has all the time in the world to sleep," the security guard replied.

"Oh." Gabriel sighed as if he was in pain.

"Although, to his credit, he did almost catch her."

"Her?" exclaimed Gabriel, not expecting the graffiti artist to be a female.

"Yah, he saw her on the camera and bolted after her before she could finish."

"What do you think she was writing?" asked Sydney, who joined Gabriel after having her bag checked by the second guard.

"Her name?" responded the guard while lifting his shoulders to indicate it was only a guess. "Who knows what any of the things these nutcases write really means?"

They had walked a few yards into the campus when Gabriel received the call from Tanya. It was like a cold winter wind blowing over his body when Gabriel's VisText displayed his grandmother's incoming call. Ever since his grandfather's hospitalization, the sight of a call from his grandmother sent a chill of fear up his spine. He had mentally prepared for the day the news would come in order to lessen the shock, but the idea of getting 'the call' was like a kick in the stomach knocking the wind out of him.

Not a single day had passed since his grandfather's heart attack that Gabriel didn't start his day with a prayer; he thanked the Lord for another day of life for his grandfather. Derek remained in their bedroom at the estate, confined to a bed with twenty-four-hour care. Gabriel considered each day his grandfather lived as another gift from God. Gabriel buried the upwelling of emotion deep inside his body so he could tell Sydney about the call.

"Syd, I just got a call from my grandmother. She's sending a driver to take me to the estate," he said in an artificially calm manner.

"Your grandfather?" she asked, but her eyes spoke more than her words. "I'll come with you."

"Sure, if you want, but what about your lab?"

"I only have Dr. Ferrel's lab today; I'm certain he'll understand."

Gabriel sent a message to Bradley to inform him as well as to let Dr. Ferrel know while he and Sydney walked back through the main entrance to wait for their ride.

***

A faint white light bled through the partially open bedroom door in the Muller estate. Gabriel held Sydney's hand as they walked down the upstairs hallway. The low hum of medical equipment could be heard through the opening. Like he had done many times as a young boy frightened by a midnight clap of thunder, Gabriel stood in front of his grandparents' bedroom door listening for the sound of their voices. Fear rose up from deep inside him, tearing at his emotions. The fear which gripped him was a hundred times worse than his childhood fears; no longer did he want to burst into the room to find the comfort of his grandparents' arms. Gabriel wanted to run away and avoid what was waiting behind the door.

"What's wrong?" Sydney asked, surprised by his inaction.

"Nothing, I was just preparing myself for the worst," he said, looking despondent.

"Come on," she said, pushing open the door and leading him in by the hand.

The master bedroom was bigger than Gabriel and Sydney's flat. Floor-to-ceiling windows filled one entire wall while the other walls were decorated with exquisite oil paintings. Two beds were positioned against the wall in the center of the room. Derek lay partially prone in one bed surrounded by the flashing monitors of medical equipment and attended to by a nurse, who stood at his right side.

Tanya sat on a chair to Derek's left, holding his hand in hers. The nurse was the first to acknowledge their arrival with a sudden turn of her head and a nod followed by Tanya, who also faced them, her mouth filled with a welcoming grin.

"Look who's here," Tanya said to Derek.

Derek labored to move his head to see Gabriel and Sydney approaching his bed. The wires and tubes connected to his face made it difficult for any movement, but he still managed to produce a smile from beneath them.

Tanya looked at the nurse, who immediately took her cue and began walking toward the door.

"Please try not to excite him," the nurse said before leaving.

"How are you doing?" Gabriel asked, his eyes shifting between Derek's and Tanya's.

"Okay, just had a little scare, that's all," Derek said, struggling to get the words out between breaths.

"What happened?" Gabriel asked, his eyes locked on Tanya's.

"His blood pressure was dropping and we were afraid..."

"Why didn't you call an ambulance and take him...?"

"No ambulance, no hospital," Derek said, trying unsuccessfully to say the words with authority.

"He won't go back to the hospital; this is where he wants to..."

"Don't!" Gabriel shouted, not allowing Tanya to finish her sentence.

Gabriel never let go of Sydney's hand and was unaware that he was nearly crushing her fingers in his attempt to hold back his tears. Sydney took her free hand and rubbed it up and down his arm. Her touch loosened his grip, allowing her to free her hand.

"Come here," Derek demanded, lifting his hand from Tanya's in an attempt to motion Gabriel to sit on the edge of the bed.

Gabriel approached the bed nervously; worried he would disrupt one of the wires or tubes snaking along the side of the bed. He sat on the side while keeping both feet planted on the floor. Derek reached out for Gabriel's hand, placing his own on top.

"The time draws near for me to move on, but please," he begged before inhaling as much air as he could through the clear plastic oxygen tube taped under his nose. "Don't be sad for me—for I am looking forward to the future."

Gabriel's teeth clenched as the lump formed in his throat. Swallowing became impossible, and his bottom lip quivered from the strain of fighting back the tears. He turned to look for support but found he was alone. Gabriel opened his mouth to speak, but Derek shook his head while struggling to grip Gabriel's hand.

"I'll do the talking, you'll do the listening," he said with a hint of a small grin. "You mustn't think of dying as the end of existence, but as the beginning."

"What?" replied Gabriel, his face filled with confusion.

"Quiet, just listen. Inside you is a tiny bit of existence. Think of it as your consciousness," Derek said and then paused to catch his breath before continuing. "When your time here comes to an end, your consciousness will join a much larger one called 'Primoris.'"

Gabriel opened his mouth to begin to speak, but Derek lifted his hand while raising his index finger to silence Gabriel.

"So you see, you mustn't think of dying as the end of my time. Time doesn't move in a line, where you start here and end over there," he said, pointing to an imaginary line in front of him. "There's no beginning or end," he continued before lowering his hands and resting to gain more breath. Derek paused to let his words settle in Gabriel's mind.

Overwhelmed by a surge of sadness, Gabriel's mind was suffocating from the thoughts of his grandfather's death. Dark images of an empty void ran through his mind, rendering him unable to process what Derek was trying to explain to him.

Seeing the struggle in Gabriel's eyes, Derek decided to end the discussion, knowing it wouldn't be long before Gabriel would understand.

"Gabriel," Derek said, looking deep inside Gabriel's glossy blue eyes.

"Yes," he replied in a scratchy whisper.

"Stay home for a while—give an old man some company."

Derek knew he had broken down Gabriel emotionally, and

it would be impossible for him to refuse. This would keep him away from the campus and safe at the estate.

"Absolutely. I'll let Syd know."

Without speaking, Derek called Tanya and Sydney back to the bedroom. Gabriel let his eyes meet Sydney's for an instant before facing his grandmother.

"Do you know how long?" he asked, unable to face his grandfather.

"They can't say; could be a day, a week or a month—but they're certain he won't last more than six months," Tanya said.

CHAPTER 27

THE SNOW DOME

T he evening darkness transformed into brilliant color from the thousands of red and green Christmas lights hung from the lampposts along the sidewalk where Sydney and Gabriel were walking home. Their colors reflected in the puddles scattered along the pavement resembled balls of shimmering candlelight. The cool December air made the rain feel like ice pellets hitting their faces.

Gabriel quickened his pace, anxious to return home. He had been at the estate for nearly a week. Derek had tried everything to keep him longer, but nothing short of his death would have stopped Gabriel from returning to his research. Gabriel had tried to leave earlier that afternoon so he could attend Mass, but Tanya asked Sydney to come early and help her prepare dinner, so Gabriel felt obligated to stay. The most frustrating part of the last week had occurred every afternoon when Bradley called him with a daily update on the progress of the sample analyses—this had been nothing but torture for him.

No longer was it a casual walk back to their apartment, for they struggled to stay on the sidewalk as they navigated through a gauntlet of moving bodies. Geneva was bursting at the seams from the continuous influx of people escaping the flooding. The constant sound of heavy machinery could be heard twenty-four hours a day as workers rushed to shore up the banks of the Rhone and Arve rivers. Gone were the deep blue waters of Lake Geneva, once Switzerland and France's jewel. The blue had been replaced by a dirty brown color, the result of constant erosion.

One person walking toward them didn't move like the others to avoid a collision, but instead approached them with intent. The individual was a tall woman with long dirty blonde hair which hung out of the sides of the large piece of orange plastic she wore wrapped around her entire body.

When the woman approached Sydney, with an outstretched hand, Gabriel pulled Sydney to his side and they both stepped off the sidewalk to avoid contact with the beggar.

"They were talking about the food shortage on the WNN broadcast. They said it's been more than two decades since there have been this many homeless and hungry on the streets," Sydney said, pulling Gabriel's hand to lead him back onto the sidewalk.

"I've never seen anything like it," Gabriel replied, unaware he was beginning to walk too fast for Sydney to keep up.

"I think we'd better get used to it," she said, pulling back on Gabriel's arm to slow his pace.

"Why?"

"They said the IGB is struggling to keep pace with the demands facing the world's population. They're limiting the distribution of food around the globe because they can no longer monitor the migration of entire populations as they search for food and shelter."

"What about all those photo-agro-places?"

"They can't keep up."

"Great, what's next? Flood, famine, disease—all we need now is a war," he said with a great deal of sarcasm as they entered the front door of their apartment.

***

Gabriel reached up to remove his VisText in order to prepare for bed when Bradley called.

"Hi, Brad," Gabriel said while he fidgeted with the device behind his ear.

"Sorry I'm calling so late. Can I put you on V-screen? Judie's here too."

"Sure."

"How's your grandfather doing?" Judie asked, her eyes still filled with sadness.

"Better."

"Good. Is Syd there?" she asked.

"She's just getting ready for bed; I'll get her while I switch you over to the V-screen."

Gabriel informed Sydney of the call as he walked into the living room to put them on the V-screen. Sydney pulled a housecoat on and joined him.

"Hey, Syd, what's your day like tomorrow?"

"I have a morning lab to prepare and another just after lunch. Why?"

"Can you go for coffee after you're done in the afternoon?"

"Sure," Sydney said, glancing at Gabriel with a look of confusion.

"Perfect, I'll meet you in the cafeteria. What time?"

"Three thirty."

"Have a good night, you guys," Judie said, and she disappeared from view.

Gabriel looked at Bradley then turned to face Sydney, who raised her shoulders and lifted her hands to gesture her confusion.

"Are you going to be in early tomorrow? I really want to get the sample finished," Gabriel said, unable to contain the excitement in his voice.

"If you guys are talking research, then I'm going to bed. Good night, guys," Sydney said, walking out of the room.

"Night, Syd," they replied in unison.

"What was that all about?" asked Gabriel, referring to the

late call just to ask Sydney to go for coffee.

"I don't know. She still looks like she's been crying and is still acting strange. Something's really bugging her; she's up half the night, and she's been miserable."

"You guys have a fight?"

"No, nothing. I don't get it. Can you and Syd do me a favor and see if you can find out what's up? Don't let on that I asked though."

"Of course. I'll talk to Syd tonight."

"Thanks."

Gabriel joined Sydney in their bed where she was sitting up looking at the solar system clock.

"Why would she call at nearly eleven only to ask me to go to coffee? Does that seem a bit strange to you? She looks even worse than the last time I saw her," Sydney said, completely bewildered by Judie's out of character actions.

"Did you see her while I was at my grandparents?"

"No, why?"

"Brad said she hasn't been herself lately, and he's asked us to see if we can find out why."

"I'll let you know tomorrow," she said, and they went to sleep.

***

Gabriel pulled open the lab door to find the room filled with the high-pitched squeal of the sediment grinder. He would have been surprised to see Bradley had beat him to the lab again, but their discussion the previous night provided a good explanation for Bradley's early arrival. The real surprise for Gabriel was Dr. Ferrel standing at the top of a small stepladder at the back of the lab. He was pulling down the old solar event calendar. Gabriel lifted his lab coat off the back of the stool and replaced it with his rain gear. He placed his VisText on the lab bench in front of the stool and walked to the back of lab. On his way, Gabriel passed by Dr. Ferrel's office when the sight of his disheveled desk awakened the anger sleeping inside him for months. The opportunity to work on the Martian sample had rendered the anger dormant—until now.

"Good, you're just in time to help. Could you please hand me the end of the new calendar and hold the other side while I pin it to the wall?" Dr. Ferrel asked while he tore the old one off the wall, letting it drop to the floor.

"Here," Gabriel said as he handed him the end of the poster-sized paper, which was rolled up to form a tube.

Dr. Ferrel fastened the paper to the wall while Gabriel unrolled it as he slowly walked backwards. The new calendar looked like the old one except for the end, which Gabriel held in his hands waiting for Dr. Ferrel to make his way over to him to secure it.

Gabriel's head felt like it was about to explode; he couldn't hold it in any longer, and without premise, he blurted out his thoughts.

"How could you do it? Why did you lie to me? I trusted you!" he fired at Dr. Ferrel, which caught the man by surprise and he nearly fell off the stepladder.

"Wow, slow down. What are you talking about?"

"The funding, you lied to me about the funding," Gabriel said, trying to restrain his voice.

"What about the funding?"

"I saw it, months ago, it fell off your desk, and I picked it up when we were talking to Dr. Biggs."

"Saw what?" the doctor asked while stepping off the ladder to address Gabriel.

"A grant renewal form; all of this is funded by corporate money—the worst corporate money of all—MBG," he protested, his voice nearly yelling.

"I haven't lied. You've got to trust me. None of the funds for the work you or I do has come from corporate coffers."

"What about the renewal?"

"The Science Department sends that to everyone; I simply

added it to the pile when I should've discarded it," replied Dr. Ferrel with a grin and climbed back up the stepladder.

Embarrassed by his overreaction yet relieved he wasn't funded with corporate dollars, Gabriel's mind raced to change the subject as he looked at the large poster in his hands.

"Why the new one?" he asked, referring to the calendar.

"I've analyzed some new data I received last week from the research satellites. Take a look for yourself," Dr. Ferrel said, pointing to the area of the calendar that represented the previous week.

"What's all this?" Gabriel asked, unable to understand the meaning of the data.

"Some unusual solar activity occurred last week; it was strong enough to interrupt the power grid from China through India. The activity appears to be getting stronger and more frequent—that's what those lines represent," he said, pointing to some bright red lines rising above the bottom of a graph. "If they continue like this, the solar flares predicted early next year will be off that chart. I've not finished my analyses yet, but it appears to me to be part of a four-thousand-year solar cycle. The Earth hasn't seen anything like this since biblical times."

"How bad will it get?" Gabriel asked with some apprehension.

"That really depends on the type of solar particles erupted and the position of the Earth relative to the sun. Don't worry yourself too much about it, the Earth's gone through these events before; I'm certain it will survive the next one. Now, go back to what you really want to do," he said, smiling so much that it lifted the glasses on his nose.

"Thanks."

"Oh, I'm sorry, I forgot to ask—how's your grandfather doing?"

"A little bit better, thanks," he said and quickly made his way over to Bradley, not wanting to talk about it.

Shouting over the noise of the pulverizer to say hello to

Bradley would likely startle him, so Gabriel let him continue to work in the fume hood while he gathered the chemicals for extracting the samples. The moment he opened the chemical storage container, the lab filled with the pungent smell. He quickly dispensed the brightly colored liquids into separate vials, capped the tops of the vials and returned the rest to storage.

The chemical aroma immediately gained Bradley's attention, and he turned around to find the source of the smell. "You finally made it," he said with a smile, and he turned off the machine so they could talk.

"When did you get here?" Gabriel asked, astonished with the amount of work Bradley had already completed.

"Oh, about an hour and a half ago."

"What? You okay?" Gabriel replied, clearly in shock over Bradley's early arrival.

"It's not me, Judie was pacing again, and I couldn't get back to sleep—so here I am."

"I'll have to thank her; you've got almost everything ready for the extraction."

"I just finished, we can start adding the reagents."

"Let's get 'er done," Gabriel replied, the excitement spilling out of his words.

***

Sydney was five minutes late when she entered the cafeteria and stood frozen with amazement. Students finished cramming for final exams rushed past her on both sides, knocking her shoulders as they tried to exit through the doors. She had forgotten it was finals. Bodies occupied every possible open space throughout the campus, some trying to stay awake, while others tapped the screens of their tablets madly. Every table was overcrowded with people, and the combined din of the thousands of voices made the room louder than an auditorium before the start of a play.

She scanned the cafeteria looking for Judie, stopping her eyes on each table in hopes of catching an arm waving in the air. While slowly weaving her way deeper into the room, she heard Judie call her name through the chatter. Sydney pushed her glasses up the bridge of her nose in an attempt to increase the clarity of her vision and searched for Judie. Sydney heard her name a second time, and before she could turn to look behind her, she felt a tug on her arm.

"She's over there," said the student sitting at a table next to Sydney, and he pointed with his other arm through the crowd to Judie, seated at the table opposite him.

"Thanks," Sydney said and made her way over.

Judie pulled back a vacant chair she had been saving for Sydney and lifted her raincoat and bag off of it.

"A little crazy in here," she said with a smile but her eyes were still filled with sadness.

"A little," Sydney replied, looking at the five other people crowded around the small round table.

"I didn't think you'd have time to leave. Do you want to get something?" Judie asked, holding her empty coffee cup.

Sydney looked at Judie with surprise and tried to ascertain if her question was serious, while at the same time searching for a way to ask about her strange behavior of late.

"I can't even see the end of the food line from here; I think I'll be fine."

"Okay," Judie said, and she paused while looking into Sydney's eyes, trying to find the right place to start the conversation.

"Have you ever been to the Snow Dome?" Judie asked as lightheartedly as she could.

Sydney's left eyebrow lifted above the rim of her glasses. "No, never. Why?"

"It's incredible in there. It's over two square miles of everything winter. The entire place is filled with snow, ice skating, horse-drawn sleigh rides—even a ski hill," Judie said as if she were reading a travel brochure.

"Ski... I've never even seen snow," Sydney replied, wondering where Judie was leading with the conversation.

"Tomorrow they're beginning their twelve days of Christmas display when they turn on millions of colored lights on almost every tree under the dome. It's magical."

"I've heard of it, but there's no way you'll get tickets for that—they're sold years in advance," Sydney said, even more confused.

"I've got four," Judie exclaimed. "And not just entrance tickets but tickets for a sleigh ride to view them, but..." she said, forcing the excitement into her tone.

"But what?"

"There's a catch," Judie said, and her face transformed instantly from one filled with excitement to one riddled with seriousness.

"Okay," Sydney replied in expectation of what would follow.

"You know, I come from a traditional Italian family." She paused for a moment while her mind search desperately for the right words to continue. "I told my dad about Brad, and he insists I need to get married," she blurted out as if she was holding her breath.

"Married?" Sydney said with a massive smile growing on her face.

"I know it's really old-fashioned, but that's the Italian way..."

"I take it you haven't spoken to Bradley about this yet?" Sydney asked, now aware of the reason for Judie's recent odd behavior.

"No, and there's more. The reason I wanted to talk to you," she said, lifting her deep brown eyes from the coffee cup to meet Sydney's. "Have you ever thought about you and Gabriel?"

Sydney's smile waned, and she pushed herself to the back of the chair without answering.

"I know his grandparents are also traditional, and his

grandfather's health is failing; this may be his only chance to…"

"Nobody gets married anymore, it's so… old-fashioned," Sydney said, still suffering from the initial shock of Judie's question.

"It'll be fun," replied Judie as relief filled her body.

"Let me think about it."

"That's just it; I need to know today…"

"Today! Are you nuts?"

"I'll lose the tickets otherwise," Judie said in a tone reflecting the need for a quick decision.

"Tickets?" Sydney said. The shock of Judie's request sidetracked her thoughts and she had momentarily forgotten about the Snow Dome.

"I thought we could propose together, on the sleigh ride— it'll be so romantic."

"Now I get it, it's all starting to make sense, of course," Sydney said, realizing the need for Judie to sell the Snow Dome adventure to her.

Judie said nothing, but her face spoke volumes.

"I've got to know tonight or my friend who's getting me the tickets will have to release them to someone else."

"All right."

"Oh, don't say anything to *anybody*; it has to stay a secret, promise?"

"Promise."

"I'm late, I've got to get back to my class; it started ten minutes ago," Judie said, and she grabbed her bag and raincoat and started making her way through the crowd.

Sydney remained at the table and began talking to Derek, completely unaware that a student was asking for the vacant seat next to her.

"Judie wants me to ask Gabriel to marry me."

"When?" Derek asked.

"Immediately."

"Excellent idea! We should've thought about this sooner.

The timing couldn't be more perfect."

"Why?" Sydney asked, confused by Derek's response.

"I'm concerned. There's too much at stake—if he fails, the code must survive."

"I understand, but I don't think he will marry me."

"If you must, tell him you're already pregnant—just say anything to keep him away from the campus."

"I'm not sure even this will be enough," Sydney said, knowing the strength of Gabriel's conviction to complete the Martian sediment research.

"Convince him," Derek demanded.

"Is anyone sitting here?" said a voice in a clearly annoyed manner after asking Sydney several times and getting no response. "I hate those stupid V-chips. You can never tell when someone is using them," he said to the other students at the table.

"I'm sorry. No, you can have this one too," Sydney replied, standing from her seat.

"Thanks," said the student as he and a friend sat at the table, pulling out their tablets.

Sydney removed her handheld from her pocket and called Judie, hoping to get her before she made it back to class.

"That didn't take you long," Judie answered.

"I'm in," Sydney told her.

"Fantastic. Here's the really hard part. We have to be at the Snow Dome no later than nine on tomorrow morning. If we are even one second late, we won't be able to get in. The guys aren't going to be happy about not going to the lab, being so close to finishing the Martian sample."

"You're right about that. Any ideas on how to convince them to leave without telling them?" Sydney asked.

"None, I'm just going to tell Brad the truth. I have once-in-a-lifetime tickets, and he has to go—the samples can wait for another day."

"I'll say the same, but Gabriel's going to flip out. He spent all of last week at his grandparents. I don't think I'll tell him until the morning, otherwise he'll find a way to squirm out of it. Did you get Brad a ring?"

"I thought about it, but that's too traditional even for me—I drew the line at rings."

"Good," Sydney said, the relief evident from her tone.

"Good luck with Gabe. I'll pick you guys up at eight—don't be late."

***

Bradley lifted the last of the Martian sediment samples out of the grinding machine and carried them over to the lab bench, where Gabriel added the reagents to them. Gabriel dispensed some liquid into the vials and placed them with the rest of the samples to digest overnight. They both started to clean their work area and prepare for the final stages of analyzing the samples the following day.

"I can't wait to run these samples," Gabriel said.

"Me either."

"Maybe you can stay all night, the way you've been sleeping lately?"

"Real funny," Bradley replied, showing his lack of humor with Gabriel's statement.

"Wonder how coffee went? I'm certain Syd will be by soon, and then we can find out what's going on."

"I hope so; I can't take many more nights like last night."

The door opened and Sydney entered the lab to find both of them smiling at her in anticipation of receiving some news. She walked over to them and leaned against the lab bench without an ounce of expression on her face.

"Well?" they both blurted.

"I got nothing for you; she just wanted to chat about some girl issues."

"That's it, really?" Gabriel asked in disbelief. "She needed to call immediately because of some girl issues? Is she pregnant?" he blurted out.

"No!" Bradley shouted, casting his eyes from Gabriel to Sydney.

"I'll never understand how women think," Gabriel said, and he placed the last piece of clean glassware onto the bench for the next day. "Shall we leave?" he said, reaching for Sydney's hand, and they walked to the stool to retrieve his stuff.

"I'm leaving too—could be another long night," Bradley said with a fake laugh, and they shouted a good-bye to Dr. Ferrel, who was working in his office.

***

Sydney woke up the next morning to the sound of the shower. She reached for her glasses on the nightstand next to her bed and read 2036 Wednesday December 10 – 06:36:22 scrolling along the bottom of Gabriel's clock. Her stomach clenched knowing Gabriel wasn't an early riser, which meant he was even more excited about completing the samples than she anticipated. She stripped her clothes off and decided to break the news to him after she had followed Derek's orders.

Water vapor flooded out the bathroom door when she pulled it open. Gabriel's face was completely hidden behind his hair as he worked the shampoo into lather. Sydney quietly slid the glass shower door to the side and stepped in behind him. She wrapped her arms around his torso and pressed her cool body against his. Her unexpected presence released a scream of surprise from Gabriel, causing both of them to laugh uncontrollably.

Sydney gained control of her laughter first and asked, "What are you doing up? I thought you'd still be sleeping."

"Are you kidding? Brad and I left the samples running overnight, and with any luck, they'll be downloaded to my tablet right now. I'm trying to get there before him so I can be the first to see the results," he said and turned to face Sydney while leaning his head backwards into the flowing water.

Sydney pulled the few remaining strands of his hair lying

across his face out of the way and stood on her toes to kiss him before whispering in his ear, "I can guarantee you Bradley won't beat you to the lab this morning."

"How do...?"

Sydney placed a finger across his lips with her left hand to silence him and lifted the bar of soap with her right. She slowly dragged the bar down his chest, lathering every inch of his body. Gabriel struggled to talk a few more times before finally giving in.

***

Gabriel sat on the end of the bed, trying to sneak a look at the time without Sydney noticing while she dried his hair. She wrapped the towel around his head and rubbed it like a mother would do with a small child before gathering his hair with her hand.

"Bend your head down so I can dry the back," she commanded, and he obeyed, allowing her to squeeze the water from his hair. Sydney smiled when she saw the birthmark and then let go of his hair.

"How do you know Bradley won't be at the lab before me?" he asked, finishing his earlier question.

"He's not going to the lab today," she said, wrapping the towel she used to dry Gabriel's hair around her body to reduce the chill she was feeling.

"How do you know that?"

"The same way I know that you're not going to the lab today either," she said through a forced smile.

"Are you joking? I've been waiting for this day forever," he said in denial, now beginning to understand the reason for the unexpected shower experience.

"It can wait one more day," she said in a stern manner.

"Why?" he asked, sounding despondent.

"Judie has gotten us tickets to the Snow Dome Festival of Lights; it's a chance in a lifetime, and we're not going to miss it. Your sample will be there tomorrow," she said, sounding a little like a mother scolding a child.

"Wow, what a way to ruin a fantastic morning," he said, throwing his back onto the bed in a display of disappointment.

"Get dressed, we've got lots of time; Judie and Bradley are going to pick us up at eight. Seeing as you were up so early this morning, let's not waste the rest of it worrying about the samples. I'll make us a special breakfast."

Lots of time, thought Gabriel as he jumped off the bed and hurried to get dressed.

"Forget about breakfast," he shouted to Sydney, getting ready in the bathroom.

"Why?" she asked.

"If I've got to spend the day in the freezing cold, I at least want to know the results of the analyses. We've got plenty of time to go to the lab and get my tablet," he said with excitement, knowing it could be done.

"No way! Judie said we can't be one second late—we can't take the chance," Sydney pleaded, now pulling her clothes on in the bedroom.

"It's really important to me, and I've agreed to go today. Besides, the main entrance is right on the way to the Snow Dome—if anything, we'll be saving time."

Sydney saw the look on Gabriel's face; it was the same one she had seen before he led her into the church or when he dragged her to London to visit her parents. She knew he was going with or without her, so she quickly got dressed and they left the apartment.

"Do you want me to call Judie and let her know to pick us up at the campus main gate?" Gabriel asked as they walked toward the campus at a feverish pace.

"No, I think she'll flip out. Let's wait until it's almost eight; like you said, she has to drive right by here, so it won't make a difference."

They cleared the security checkpoint at the main entrance

and shuffled through the groups of students walking through the campus. Even though all the lectures had finished for the Christmas break, there were an exceptional number of students on campus preparing for and writing exams. The science-building corridor was filled with first-year students milling outside the main examination room. Gabriel forced his way through the crowd to get to the lab.

He unlocked the lab door since it was too early for Dr. Ferrel to be in his office, and he and Sydney made their way to the analyzer. He lifted his tablet from the port on the side of the machine and hit the power button.

"What are you doing? We don't have time to look at it now, it's almost eight," Sydney scolded.

"Okay," Gabriel replied. He reluctantly unzipped his raincoat and put the tablet inside his breast pocket.

"Let's go," Sydney demanded, concerned they would be cutting it too close.

"It's a minute to eight. I'm calling Judie."

Sydney and Gabriel struggled to move through the crowded hall as the doors had just opened to allow the hundreds of students in to take an exam. Sydney pulled Gabriel out of the hall and into the fire exit stairwell, thinking it would be much faster than trying to make their way through the people to the main stairs.

"Hi, Judie," Gabriel said, but before he could continue, she yelled at him.

"Where are you guys? It's eight o'clock."

"We stopped by the lab to…"

"No!" Judie screamed with her voice, even though she was using her V-chip. "Get out of there!" she continued to scream, causing Bradley to search outside the moving car for an indication of what was causing the outburst.

Judie stopped the car on the side of the road a few hundred yards from the main entrance as an incredible flash of light brightened the morning sky.

She then started to weep uncontrollably.

CHAPTER 28

JUDAS

Without warning the stairs disappeared beneath his feet. For the briefest instant, Gabriel recalled the sensation he was experiencing—it was the same feeling he had the moment he flew off his skateboard as a teenager. It was the euphoria of total weightlessness one could only get from free falling, or in outer space. The thrill was so short-lived that he wasn't certain he had actually experienced it.

A thunderous blast preceded an ear-piercing roar as the pressure wave from the explosion shattered the stairwell window. Like staring into a bolt of lightning that never fades, Gabriel's eyes felt as though they had been poked with a hot needle, the pain so severe it blinded him. He felt as though he had fallen face first into a pit of fire when the intense heat radiated across his exposed skin. There was no relief from the fierce burning on his face, and the rotten stench of singed hair filling his nostrils.

As if someone had flipped a switch, the pain vanished the instant the piece of falling metal collided with the back of his head. For a moment, there was nothing but absolute quiet and darkness. Then fear arrived like a freight train, stronger than any fear he had ever known. It overwhelmed him. His mind raced with the images planted there by the years of attending Sunday Mass. Gabriel could feel every beat of his heart as though he were holding it in his hands while it raced uncontrollably. He realized what was happening and where he was, and it was worse than how they had described it, worse than how he had imagined it. He was in hell.

"Help!" Sydney yelled, and Derek immediately responded while his body remained asleep.

"What is it?"

"He's hurt."

"Where are you?" Derek demanded.

"There's been an attack—we're on campus."

"I'm almost there," responded Dr. Ferrel, who was on his way to the lab when he heard the attack from the far side of the campus.

***

Bradley looked at Judie sobbing like a small child, her head slumped over the steering wheel.

"I'm on my way," Bradley replied. "How'd you know?" he asked Judie before he sprang out of the car and began running toward the entrance gate.

Debris and bodies littered the campus grounds. The force of the blast had sent pieces of the science building in every direction. Clouded by thick grey smoke, the remains of the structure were hidden from view. Cries for help pierced the ball of smoke, but it was impossible to know exactly where they were coming from. Bradley stood helpless in front of a large section of the science-building roof, wondering where to look for them.

***

Sydney had survived the blast in better condition than Gabriel. Her face and hands were also burned, but her body had been thrown under the metal staircase by the blast, providing her protection from the falling debris. She tore a large piece of material already ripped from the blast off the bottom of her shirt and rolled it into a tight ball. She held it tightly against the back of Gabriel's head to slow the bleeding.

"Can you see anything?" Dr. Ferrel asked from the opposite side of where the building had once stood.

"Nothing," Bradley replied.

"Where are you?"

"The east side fire stairwell," Sydney shouted. The stairwells reinforced structure had been sufficient to keep it intact. "He's hurt quite badly and needs help," she pleaded, desperate to get some assistance for Gabriel.

Both Bradley and Dr. Ferrel moved to where the east side of the building had once stood, but the smoke remained too thick for them to start searching.

Wailing sirens grew louder as they approached the campus and more people shouted for assistance.

"I'm here," Derek said, and he instantaneously arrived with Sydney. "We've got to get him to a hospital," he told the others.

The steady rain began to cleanse the air of the floating dust and the smell of burning plastic. A moment later, the top of the stairwell came into view like the steeple of a church; its rust orange metal glistened against the dull sky.

"We can see the top of the stairwell. We're on our way."

Bradley and Dr. Ferrel moved slowly through the smoke, pulling the top of their shirts from beneath their coats to cover their noses and mouths. Dr. Ferrel stuffed his glasses into his pocket and led the way. The scene became more gruesome with every step they took. Dead bodies and body parts littered the area. The smell of burned flesh was nauseating; they both gagged and choked back vomit while climbing over the debris and pushing pieces of the building out of their path.

The smoke and dust cloud continued to dissipate when Bradley spotted a brilliant translucent blue glow like a massive flame from a gas stove hovering over the first landing of the stairwell. They both rushed toward the light, where Sydney knelt over Gabriel's body holding his head.

"Can you walk?" Bradley asked.

"Yes," Sydney replied.

"We'll carry his body while you hold his head with the cloth."

They lifted Gabriel's limp body off the landing. A small pool of crimson blood stained the concrete landing where his head had rested, and the three of them shuffled down the remaining steps to the ground. Unable to protect themselves from the lingering smoke, all three coughed and choked as they scrambled back the way Bradley and Dr. Ferrel had come.

When they finally emerged from the plume, the campus looked like a battlefield. Hundreds of first responders had descended on the disaster scene. Police officers shouted commands to other officers, and firemen in self-contained breathing suits swarmed the area.

Bradley, Sydney and Dr. Ferrel carried Gabriel past the makeshift triage area forming along the inside wall of the entrance gate to one of the waiting ambulances outside the campus.

Two paramedics pulled a gurney from the back of their ambulance and rolled it over to meet the group carrying Gabriel. The three of them lifted his body on to the gurney with the aid of the paramedics.

"It's his head. He's bleeding quite badly from the back," Sydney said, still holding the cloth to Gabriel's head.

"Keep the pressure on it, and we'll take a look in a second," said one of the paramedics, and he pulled a clean bandage from his medical bag to dress the wound. The paramedic used his handheld scanner and passed it over the entire length of Gabriel's body before stating, "Non-responsive."

***

Father Black paced in the quiet hallway, his long black robe swirling with each turn he made while the clicking of his heels on the polished marble floor echoed in through the empty Vatican corridor. He monitored the morning WNN coverage on his V-chip, wishing it wasn't such a nightmare.

Steeple bells rang in the distance, indicating the nine o'clock Mass was about to begin. His hands trembled when he finally mustered the courage to enter Tonino's office, for no one knew more than him that bringing bad news to Tonino was life-threatening, but there was no way of hiding the information. The morning broadcasts were already displaying video, and it was only a matter of time before Tonino found out.

When Father Black entered Tonino's office, he found him sitting calmly behind his desk watching the broadcast on his V-screen. He quickly placed his hands under his robes to shield their shaking from view. The aroma of jasmine from the herbal tea Tonino was drinking filled the tiny office, its calming effect unlikely to subdue the man's temper. Father Black's body chilled when Tonino moved his eyes away from the V-screen and cast them into his.

"You're here to bring me good news this morning?" Tonino asked with a devious grin.

"No, sir."

"I didn't think so, but I don't blame you for today's attacks. I'm certain the VSS is doing everything it can to put an end to them?"

"Sir, I didn't come here to inform you of this morning's ReF attacks, I'm afraid I have worse news..."

"What could be worse?"

"I received news from the IGB this morning. Their preliminary census data indicates population growth has reached a plateau and may actually be declining, but the IGB is far more concerned over their ability to feed the current population and keep the peace. They've indicated that if the Vatican doesn't immediately release additional food stores, there will be nothing they can do to prevent the world from plummeting into war. The fighting over what remains of the planet's resources has already begun, and if allowed to continue without intervention, it will be catastrophic."

Tonino's face turned to stone, and his eyes never moved from Father Black's. It was as if Father Black had swallowed a block of ice; Tonino's stare ripped through his chest like falling on a frozen icicle. Like a childhood staring contest, Father Black feared moving his eyes first and waited for Tonino to turn his gaze away. It felt like an hour to Father Black before Tonino walked away from the desk.

"Give them the food," Tonino commanded in a low voice while standing in his typical location in front of the window.

"But that'll leave us with nothing," Father Black replied sheepishly.

"I'm well aware of the consequences—do it! And tell me, how is your search for the leader of the ReFs progressing?"

"Gino is tracking down a lead, and I assure you that I'm doing everything I can to find these ReFs."

"Good, but I blame these latest attacks on my own poor judgment; I should've seen it sooner."

"What do you mean?"

"It's obvious. They've been targeting only our facilities," replied Tonino, his patience with Father Black growing short.

"I only see them focusing on random science or technology facilities—the genetics lab in Manning, a dyke in Egypt, some universities. There's no way they could know of our involvement..."

"You see nothing!" Tonino shouted to prevent Father Black from continuing. "That's why you can't see what's happening right under your nose. There's a Judas in your ranks! Someone among you is giving these ReFs information," he said, staring with accusation.

"Never! I can assure you I've been nothing but loyal to your every request," Father Black snapped.

"University of Alaska, California, MIT and now Geneva—

this is no coincidence."

"Impossible. Only the other members of the Vatican Council and ourselves could know," Father Black protested.

"I suggest you start looking under your nose."

"Right away, sir," Father Black replied and turned to leave the office when Tonino spoke again.

"Father Black, we're not finished," Tonino snarled.

"Yes, sir." He turned back to face Tonino.

"I'm afraid these attacks will launch us into war long before the food runs out. We need to stop them."

"Understood. I'll keep working on finding them."

"Excellent, but I've got another idea. I want you to host another meeting."

"Sir, we just..."

"Shut up! Listen to me carefully. I want you to gather the religious leaders again, but this time I also want you to assemble a meeting, no... call it a summit of all our project leaders."

"That'll only make matters worse; the people will be confused—they won't know who they can trust."

"I'm fully aware of the risks, but I see no other choice. There's too much at stake. If these attacks don't stop, everything will be lost."

"But, sir, some of our people have no idea where their funding originates, and getting them all here on such short notice could take weeks if you want everyone," Father Black protested, unable to see the purpose of such a gathering.

"Then I suggest you get started. It's time the world knew how long science and religion have been married."

CHAPTER 29

MY COAT

Medical equipment cluttered every corner of the room. White wires and thin plastic tubes hung from shiny metal holders like the tentacles of a giant jellyfish. The ceiling lights in the room were off, and the window blinds were closed tight so the only light was coming from the flashing red and green indicators on the life-saving machines. Their reflection off the chrome bedrails resembled the twinkling of a Christmas display. A steady rhythmic chirp originated from the monitor at the foot of the bed, and it pierced the otherwise silent room.

Tanya raced into the room and took up a position to the right of the bed, lifting Gabriel's unusually cold hand in hers. The idea they could lose him when they were so close wore heavy on her mind.

"Is he breathing on his own?" Tanya asked, looking for any sign of life in the unconscious body lying before her.

"No," the nurse replied.

"How long?" she said without emotion.

"The doctor is estimating days," the nurse said in a soft and understanding voice.

Tanya's heart filled with anguish, and her glacial blue eyes displayed a deep sadness as they stared blankly across the dimly lit room to communicate with Derek.

"Keep him alive," Derek ordered.

"Understood," she replied and turned her head to face the

nurse.

"I understand things must be incredibly difficult for you right now. I'm sorry, but it doesn't look good at the moment. I really don't think he will..."

"Stop!" Tanya shouted. "Do not give up on him. I want you to do whatever it takes to keep him alive; I'm certain you understand that money's not a concern for us. He must not die."

The nurse lifted the tablet from the holder at the foot of the bed and scanned the data displayed on the screen. The poorly lit room hid her expression of concern for what she was about to say.

"I sympathize with your feelings, but there's no amount of money that can help now. I strongly suggest you consider how long you wish to continue. Without the equipment, it wouldn't be possible for him to even breathe," she said in a quiet and compassionate tone.

"I know what you're trying to say, but I want to make this clear—do whatever is necessary to keep him alive until I say otherwise," Tanya said without the slightest hint of compromise in her tone.

"Yes, absolutely, this is your decision, and I'll respect it."

"Thank you," Tanya replied in a noticeably calmer voice.

***

For three days, Tanya kept a vigil at his bedside like a Swiss Guard protecting the Pope, and she remained steadfast in her resolve. On the fourth day, Tanya entered the room and opened the blinds to allow the dull morning light to enter the room.

She watched as the nurse came in to change the sheets. Her years of experience enabled her to expertly maneuver his body, which looked more like a storefront manikin than a human being, lifting and repositioning every limb as if they were going to don him in a new piece of clothing while never interfering with the cables and tubes keeping him alive.

The nurse finished her duties and began briskly walking to the door when the entire room filled with a dull glow. Confused by the green hue and unexpected brightness, Tanya and the nurse immediately cast their attention to the medical equipment, fearing one of them was malfunctioning. It only took a second for them to realize that the light was coming in through the window, and they crossed the room to investigate its source.

Standing at the window, the two women were mesmerized by the color of the sky. The normally deep grey sky glowed like the surface of an ocean as waves of turquoise light filtered through the clouds. Resembling the Northern Lights but a thousand times brighter, the intensity of the color changed as the wind shifted the blanket of clouds across the sky. Their view of the natural phenomenon was interrupted when the medical equipment emitted a brief loud chirp before falling silent.

Tanya darted to the side of the bed first, followed closely by the nurse. The white noise drone of the medical equipment had vanished, and it was evident from the lack of any form of indicator lights on the machines that the power had failed.

"The power's failed," the nurse stated. "The battery back-up should've kicked-in by now... something's wrong; this shouldn't be happening."

"The ventilator—he's not getting air, we've got to get him some air!" Tanya shouted.

"I'll start mouth to mouth. Find the hand ventilator," said the nurse as she pulled the cables and tubes out of his mouth before covering his lips with a plastic mouth shield she kept in her pocket. She forced a large breath into his lungs.

Tanya looked frantically inside the stand next to the bed before spotting the small blue pouch labeled 'Ventilator.' She handed it to the nurse, who immediately placed the mask portion over his mouth and nose and began to squeeze the balloon-like ball with her right hand as she held his wrist with two fingers of her left.

"His pulse is dropping," she stated and climbed onto the bed, straddling his chest to administer chest compressions.

"We're losing him!" Tanya shouted. "Nothing's working. The CPR isn't helping; you'll have to get him."

"I'm already there."

***

Derek found himself moving down an unfamiliar path—one he hadn't seen before. The way ahead was flooded with light. He could sense the brightness even though he hadn't opened his eyes. The warmth of the light carried him down the path like a fallen leaf drifting in a warm October wind. His emotions bubbled inside him, rising to the surface to explode and release an unimaginable contentment. Derek's only desire was to remain where he was—forever.

His tranquility disappeared at the sound of a voice. He didn't recognize the voice, but unlike the path, the voice seemed familiar. Although the sound of the voice was familiar, he couldn't understand what it was saying. Unaware he was no longer moving, Derek listened as the voice grew louder and clearer—it was calling his name.

"Derek," the voice called.

"Mother?" he asked.

"Son," said the figure of his mother, materializing from the light in front of him. She offered her hand to him.

Derek reached out and placed his hand inside hers. The instant they touched, they began to move.

"Where are we?" Derek asked.

"We're on a bridge," she answered.

"Where does it go?"

"The other side of course."

"Can we stay here?" he asked, afraid to lose the wonderful feeling filling his mind.

"That depends."

"On what?"

"You of course," she said, and they stopped walking. "The choice is completely yours—you can stay or follow me."

"I'm coming with you," he said, and he followed her.

His mother disappeared the moment he took his next step, and without warning, the bridge ended, leaving Derek falling as if he had jumped off a towering cliff. At first, a blissful sensation surrounded his body like a giant bubble carrying him to the ground. Derek knew he was falling, but his heart didn't race with fear, instead it was filled with an inexplicable joy that radiated through him. The farther he travelled, the more the joyful feeling grew, and the bright light once surrounding him now completely enveloped his body until there was nothing but a beautiful bluish-white light everywhere. Derek knew he had stopped falling the moment he saw nothing but the light. The light continued to grow brighter, and when he opened his eyes, he realized he had joined the Primoris.

"I'm sorry, Mrs. Muller. He's gone."

***

"I don't believe this! His eyes blinked open—I think he's conscious!" yelled the nurse, unable to contain her excitement.

Sydney stood next to the bed with an enormous smile forming on her face, and she leaned over to make certain Gabriel knew she was there.

"Gabriel!" called the nurse in a tone usually reserved for small children.

Like military scouts, each of Gabriel's senses reported in sequence to his brain, beginning with his smell. The pungent odor of disinfectant swept through his nostrils, tingling the inside of his nose and triggering a rush of childhood memories of skinned elbows and knees.

"Gabriel!" the nurse called again.

The sharp sting originating from his right hand was quickly overpowered by the rapidly increasing pressure in his head. The dull ache started at the base of his skull and covered the entire back of his head; the intensity of the pain grew with each passing second as if it was being squeezed in a vice. With no saliva to swallow, the bitter taste of the plastic tubes once keeping him alive lingered on his tongue.

"Gabriel!" repeated the nurse.

Still not conscious, Gabriel was certain he could hear his mother's voice. Her voice was faint, like it was far off in the distance. Gabriel listened with as much intensity as he could but failed to hear her speak again. He tried in vain to speak to her.

Gabriel lay motionless with both eyes shut, but his vision was filled with a spectacular blue light as he desperately tried to listen for his mother's voice. The light was mesmerizing as it gently floated in the air. Gabriel was overcome by the urge to reach out and touch it as it swirled in front of his face; its edges remained diffused, and the light gently faded into the darkness. *God?* he thought.

Suddenly, a new and unfamiliar voice entered his ears; this voice was much louder and he knew it was close. When the nurse's third call entered Gabriel's mind, it awoke the last of his senses. He opened his eyes.

Gabriel struggled to focus on the objects hanging from the ceiling in front of his face. The lack of lighting combined with his blurry vision made them impossible to identify. He tried to turn his head and find the source of the calling, but he froze in place as the pain of a thousand bees stinging him at once shot through his body. Moving the only part of his body he could without causing additional agony, Gabriel shifted his eyes toward the nurse.

"Gabriel, can you hear me?" the nurse asked.

He tried to form a word, but the dryness in his throat made speech impossible. Frightened to move, Gabriel answered by slowly closing his eyes and re-opening them. The nurse recognized his response immediately and smiled.

"There's someone here who's been waiting for a long time to say hi," the nurse said, and she moved out of Gabriel's field of view so Sydney could be seen.

"Gabriel, I'm so thankful you're alive," Sydney cried the instant their eyes met.

Gabriel forced a small grin to his lips before closing his eyes to hide the pain circulating through his body. Weakness overwhelmed him, and he couldn't find the strength to keep his eyes open any longer, so he closed them again to get some rest.

Three days had passed since the solar storm had first struck the Northern Hemisphere. The solar eruptions continued to interrupt power and communication, paralyzing large portions of the planet without warning. It was the morning of the fourth day, December 21ˢᵗ, when the unnatural green glow that penetrated the cloud cover began to fade. The solar storm raged, but Gabriel was unaware of its impact even though he remained awake longer each day. He gained strength with each passing day, but his mind was troubled by the re-occurring voices he heard in his sleep. It reminded him of the first time he had heard similar voices in his head, and that he hadn't attended Mass for some time.

Tanya and the others continued to keep Derek's death a secret, fearing the devastating effect it could have on Gabriel's frail condition. She demanded the cremation occur in the middle of the night with only the owner of the crematorium present. Tanya knew time wasn't on her side; it wouldn't take long for the media to get wind of the story. The death of one of the world's richest men coupled with his only living heir a near fatality at the hands of the ReFs formed irresistible fodder for the tabloids. She savored the current freedom, knowing it would end when the reports launched continual attacks on their privacy.

***

A small package the size of a coffee cup, meticulously wrapped in sparkling gold and silver Christmas paper and adorned with an emerald green bow with the letters 'GM' hand-written on the top, sat on the table. The smell of fresh-brewed coffee filled the kitchen as Bradley prepared breakfast for Judie and himself while she was getting dressed in the bedroom. He placed half of a toasted bagel on two plates and positioned them on the table next to the package along with two cups of coffee and some preserves.

"Jude, your breakfast is ready," he called.

"Coming," she replied and entered the kitchen.

"Why are you up so early?" Bradley asked.

"I'd like to come with you this morning. I'd like to see Gabe, and I have something for him," she said in a sheepish tone.

"It's a waste of time; he's only conscious for a few minutes at best."

"I don't care; I want to give him a Christmas gift."

"He can't even talk, he'll never be able to open it," Bradley said, trying to keep his anger in check.

"I just need to see him, okay?"

Bradley couldn't hold back any longer the anger that had been boiling inside him for the past four days, so he unleashed it.

"How'd you know?" he snapped.

"Know what?" she asked while pulling a chair from under the table and taking a seat.

"The attack, you knew about the ReF attack."

"What are you talking about?" she said, turning her eyes away from his to lift her coffee cup to her mouth.

"The trip to the Snow Dome, trying to pick them up, and the call..."

"What call, what are you going on about?" she asked, sounding confused.

"You screamed out loud at Gabe right before the explosion. You knew it, didn't you? You knew it was going to happen."

"What, are you crazy? How would I know anything? I saw images on my V-chip of the destroyed research facility in Canada and the blown-up dyke in Egypt, and I knew it would be too dangerous to be on campus—that's why I screamed. It was horrific, and I was frightened for him."

Bradley's temper quickly dissipated when their eyes reconnected. Judie's face was riddled with sincerity, so he decided it best to let it go, as he needed to get to the hospital. They sat through a moment of uncomfortable silence eating their breakfast before Bradley decided to change the topic.

"What did you get him?" he asked while lifting the small package from the table.

"It's a surprise."

***

Judie and Bradley arrived in Gabriel's room to find him conscious and sitting up in his bed. Sydney had slid the chair she was sitting on next to his bed so she could feel his fingertips touch hers. Gabriel's eyes widened when he spotted the two new guests arriving in the room. His heart raced, and he wiggled the tips of his fingers to indicate his pleasure.

With his pain under control, Gabriel could now stay awake most of the day. This increase in consciousness was bittersweet, for the longer he was awake, the more he struggled to communicate. Like trying to talk with tape over his mouth, the words left his mind, but there was no way to form the sounds. Every attempt to speak so far was preceded by intense pain in the back of his head, so Gabriel quit before the words could leave his lips. Today Gabriel's mind was like a teakettle on the verge of reaching the boiling point, his thoughts trapped inside him wanting to scream out.

Following a moment of intense frustration, the words rose to his lips and escaped his body like the kettle's whistle. Although weak from days without eating, as chewing also resulted in massive agony, Gabriel gained enough strength to speak his first word since the attack.

"Ferrel," he said in a scratchy whisper so quietly that even Sydney, who was only a few feet from him, was unable to hear exactly what he said.

"What?" she asked and stood up, leaning over the bed to put her ear closer Gabriel's mouth.

"Where's Dr. Ferrel," Gabriel managed but winced when he attempted to move his body a little higher in the bed.

"Take it easy," Sydney demanded, watching his struggle. "He's fine. Now rest."

"Hey, I'm so happy you're doing so well," Judie said as her eyes welled with tears.

Gabriel saved his energy and responded with only a smile.

"I've brought you a little gift," she said and lifted the small shiny package so he could see it.

Judie looked down at his hand, which was covered with dressing and tape so that only the tips of his fingers could be seen.

The color in her cheeks flushed a bright rose red as embarrassment flooded her thoughts. Thinking quickly, she spotted the small nightstand next to the bed and covered her blunder by handing it to Sydney to place on the top. "I'll leave it here; you can't open it until Christmas."

"Thanks," he said and lifted his lips to form a grin.

CHAPTER 30

MY HAIR

His fingers slid across the smooth surface of the tablet as if he were finger-painting on canvas. The screen flashed as it scrolled through the thousands of images looking for a match. Father Black paced back and forth inside Gino's office, hoping the Vatican supercomputer would finally find a match for the ReF captain.

"How long is this going to take?" Father Black asked, growing impatient with the lack of any progress.

"Even with all our computer resources dedicated to this, it may not happen," Gino replied without lifting his attention from the tablet screen.

"Don't tell me this," Father Black stormed, stopping in his tracks to face Gino. "He wants this taken care of, and all I have to go on are the faces of four women!"

"Be patient. I told you I'll get them, but it's going to take some time..."

"We don't have any more time."

Gino looked up at Father Black and indicated with his eyes that he was displeased at his inclusion in the word 'we.'

"I promise you, you'll be the first one to know if I find something. Now let me work," Gino said in retaliation, his words not a subtle hint for Father Black to leave.

"Very well, I'll leave you to it. I have a meeting with him anyway," Father Black said as he stormed out of Gino's office.

Father Black entered the office and found Tonino waiting

at his desk. Weary from the years of these meetings and prepared for another outburst, Father Black no longer faked a smile when he walked toward the desk. His face was sunken and aged, and the expression in his eyes resembled an old dog's that was about to be whipped.

Tonino's brilliant white hair stood straight up like a military cadet's so the skin on his skull glistened under the bright office light. Unlike Father Black's, Tonino's face remained untouched by time except for the blackness in his eyes; they now seemed to cast their darkness into the entire room as they stared, emotionless, at Father Black. Tonino lifted a hand toward the empty chair in front of his desk and waited for Father Black to sit.

"I see the media has dubbed our meeting as the 'Christmas Summit.' Amazing what the media can do, isn't it?" said Tonino but not expecting a reply. "I trust everything's in place?"

"Yes, sir, but only seventeen of the twenty-three will attend tomorrow," Father Black said.

"You informed the no-shows their Vatican funding would be terminated?"

"Yes."

"Very well, I think we have enough to make our point."

"Sir, I still don't understand—what do you expect...?" Father Black began, unable to contain his frustration but knowing this would certainly agitate Tonino. However, he was desperate to know why Tonino had ordered him to gather every research scientist the Vatican funded, many of whom were the world's leading scientists in their field.

"Don't you see it? These ReFs and SnRs are fighting over who's right; there're killing each other based on what they believe. It's all the same!" Tonino said, his voice increasing in volume. "There's no difference between science and religion; right from the beginning the two have been married. Over time as humans evolved, the things they could explain became science, while those they couldn't remained as religion."

Tonino paused for a moment and then continued, the tone

of his voice and the darkness in his eyes mesmerizing Father Black. He had never seen Tonino speak so passionately and with such conviction, as if he were delivering a sermon.

"Why do you think the early Greeks and Romans worshiped gods? Why do you think religion still exists today? Because they're still searching for the answer to the one thing that concerns them above all others—death."

Father Black sat silently, knowing Tonino wasn't finished. Tonino stood up and walked over to his favorite place in the office, his eyes fixed on a droplet of rain. He watched as gravity pulled the single drop down the smooth surface. It accelerated as it converged with other drops until it grew so large it formed a pool of water at the base of the window.

"There's one thing I'm certain of; humans haven't changed from the moment they were created... they're the same now as they were then, and only in death will they discover that science and religion are the same."

Father Black struggled to understand the meaning of Tonino's last statement but dared not ask for clarification. Tonino turned and faced Father Black, his face less angry than it was concerned.

"My friends?" Tonino asked, referring to the religious leaders.

"All will make it but the pontiff will lead Mass and give his Christmas address in St. Peter's Square."

"We won't require much of his time, but I would like to meet with them all before we address the researchers and media. Have them gather in the usual place."

"Yes, of course," Father Black replied, and he stood up to leave, filled with relief to be escaping without an outburst. His stomach clenched and the hair on the back of his neck stood on end at the sound of Tonino's voice.

"Oh, there's one more thing."

"Yes?"

"Have you found our Judas?" Tonino asked.

"Not yet."

***

Christmas Eve morning arrived and Gabriel awoke to find Sydney sitting next to his bed. The palms of her hands were bandage free, but two small dressings remained on the back of her hands to allow the skin to completely heal from the burns. She ran her fingertips down the edges of a small plastic device, blatantly teasing him. Gabriel looked at her and recognized the device at once—it was his tablet.

Guilt riddled his mind; the images flashed between the fiery explosion and the comforting blue light he had seen a few days ago. The long hours trapped in the hospital bed left him no escape, and he dwelled on what he saw. The inability to rationalize what it was and his unwillingness to discuss it—even with Sydney—compounded the uncertainty festering inside him. His heart pounded with anxiety when he looked at Sydney, realizing how close they had come to dying. *I couldn't live without her*, he thought. Gabriel made a decision. *I can't go back to the university*. The desire to see his data began to slip from his mind like a handful of sand escaping a closed fist. At that moment, Gabriel resolved to never put the one he loved in harm's way again.

"You okay?" Sydney asked, noticing the anxiety in his face.

"Great," he said sarcastically. "Are you here to feed me or just to torture me with my tablet?" Gabriel asked while pushing himself up in the bed without the expected jolt of pain.

"Just to torture," Sydney laughed.

"Nice."

"I've got good news," she said in a bubbly voice.

"Tell me, or are you going to torture me with that too?" he asked with yet more sarcasm.

"Dr. Fisher is coming in this morning, and she's going to remove your dressings. If everything looks good, you can feed yourself and…"

"And use the bathroom?" he blasted out before Sydney could complete her sentence.

"Yes," she laughed. "But that's not what I was going to say."

"Sorry, it's just that I'm going crazy stuck in this bed. No VisText or V-screen, all I do is talk to you guys and the nurses. I'm ready to go nuts."

"If you'd let me finish. If everything looks good, you can come home today."

Gabriel couldn't believe what he had just heard. The last two days had felt like he was in a prison cell and not the hospital. His body ached more from its captivity in the bed than the injuries it had sustained in the explosion. His heart monitor screamed as the adrenalin triggered his heart to race above the warning limit set by the medical staff. He squirmed in the bed, wanting to leap from under the sheets.

"Now you did it," Sydney said, looking at the heart monitor.

"What's going on in here?" said Dr. Fisher as she entered the room with a large grin and walked over to the monitor, tapping the screen to silence the alarm.

"Is it true? Can I go home today?" Gabriel asked with the excitement of a child given permission to open a Christmas gift.

"Only if I like what I see," Dr. Fisher replied, struggling to sound stern. She unwrapped the dressing from his hands and examined the skin grafts that had replaced the most severely damaged portions of his hands.

"Open your hands fully," Dr. Fisher instructed.

Gabriel complied and lifted his hands so he could see them clearly. The wounds had healed closed but felt stiff as though they would rip open when he stretched his fingers forward.

"How does that feel?" she asked.

"Tight."

"You're going to need some physio, but the grafts look

good. I'm going to get the nurse to put a small dressing over them to protect the new skin for a while longer."

"That sounds fun," he said while holding back the rest of his sarcasm in fear it may affect Dr. Fisher's decision.

"Now, let's check that nasty blow you took to the back of your head." Dr. Fisher walked to the front of the bed to remove the bandages wrapped around Gabriel's head.

The moment she removed the material holding the pressure on his head, Gabriel's heart sunk deep in his chest. His forehead wrinkled as if he were in pain, causing his eyes to squint while Dr. Fisher examined the wound.

"What's wrong?" Sydney asked.

"Did that hurt?" Dr. Fisher asked, looking at Sydney's reaction, as she was unable to see Gabriel's face.

"No," Gabriel snapped. "Nothing hurt... it's just..." Gabriel said, struggling to hold in his emotions.

"What is it?" asked Dr. Fisher, her tone slightly concerned.

Gabriel reached his right hand to his left shoulder and moved it across the bare skin. He lowered that hand and repeated the action with his left hand. His eyes drifted slowly toward Sydney, who now understood what was happening. There wasn't a day in his entire life that Gabriel could remember when he didn't have hair touching his shoulders. The lightheaded sensation tore through his body like stepping naked out of the shower in front of a crowd; the panic consumed every other thought he had and, like Samson, weakness rippled through his body.

"You look fine," said Sydney, reaching for his right hand.

"What's wrong?" Dr. Fisher asked again.

"His hair, he's always had long hair. He uses it..."

"My hair, I use it to cover the birthmark," Gabriel said.

"Oh, I'm sorry, Gabriel, we had to cut it. You had a six-inch cut in the back of your neck right above your birthmark. We needed to remove your hair so we could fuse the skin closed, but if you're that concerned about the birthmark, it can be removed when you're a hundred percent."

Mark Sekela

Dr. Fisher replaced the large dressing previously wrapped around his entire head like a turban with a much smaller one that only covered the wound.

Gabriel looked at the doctor with anticipation, but she ignored him and walked to the foot of the bed to read his medical chart. Like a poker player holding a winning hand, Gabriel was unable to contain his anxiety any longer and squeezed Sydney's hand as the words sprang from his lips. "Can I go?"

Dr. Fisher tapped the tablet repeatedly and then lifted her eyes from the chart, her face emotionless.

"How do you feel?" she asked in a serious tone.

"What do you mean, is this a trick question?"

"I mean, other than your hands and head, how have you been feeling?"

The jubilation of leaving began to wither like catching a fish only to have it fall through a hole in the net. Gabriel and Sydney could tell by her tone and the serious expression in her eyes that something wasn't right.

"What's wrong?" Sydney asked.

"There's something odd on his chart. When the nurse arrives to dress his hands, I'd like to check something."

No sooner had Dr. Fisher said this than a nurse entered the room carrying a small container of dressings.

"Do you have a Medi-scanner handy?" Dr. Fisher asked the nurse.

"Yes." She reached into her uniform pocket and pulled the small device out, handing it to the doctor.

She scanned Gabriel's body with one hand while watching the tablet screen. Her eyebrows raised high above her eyes when she finished the scan. The reaction piqued the interest of all the spectators watching her.

"Is there a problem, Doctor?" the nurse asked.

"I noticed this when he first arrived," said Dr. Fisher, pointing to the tablet screen so the nurse could see. "It looks like it's increased to me, but he hasn't exhibited any ill effects."

"We've been monitoring it but felt it was just a common cold," the nurse replied.

"Yes, it does appear to look like that, doesn't it?" said Dr. Fisher and her face relaxed.

"What is it?" asked Gabriel.

"It's a virus, similar to one you get when you catch a cold. The virus has been steadily increasing in your cells since you were first admitted, but I don't think it's anything to be too concerned about, and your vaccines are working, as you have no symptoms."

"So can I go?"

"Yes, I think we can let you spend Christmas at home, but you must take it easy for the next few days and be careful. It won't take much to split the wound on the back of your head open or tear that new skin on your hands."

"Yes!" Gabriel shouted as he threw the sheet off his body and moved his legs to get them on the floor.

"Slow down there, what's the hurry? I still have to dress those hands," the nurse said, the humorous tone of her voice making the others laugh.

"I'm not peeing in another bottle," Gabriel replied, and he made his way to the bathroom while the nurse and Sydney steadied him.

CHAPTER 31

VECTOR

A flash of light penetrated the stained-glass windows and illuminated the Vatican hallway for an instant, its brilliance sufficient to stimulate the rich colors of the ancient tapestries hanging from the stone walls. The subsequent crack of thunder echoed through the Vatican corridors, its noise so loud it momentarily drowned the constant resonance of church bells signaling the arrival of Christmas morning.

Father Black stood in the corridor with Paulo Firenze discussing security matters when they paused for the noise of the thunder to subside. Father Black left Paulo in charge of the other VSS operatives so he could focus his attention on gathering the religious leaders in the cafeteria. They parted ways and Paulo joined the other VSS operatives escorting the half dozen reporters and first of the Vatican-funded research scientists to the large meeting room.

Tonino remained in his office watching his V-screen and monitoring the media coverage. He knew it was critical that the entire planet focused on the event, so he scanned the different broadcasts to assess how many media outlets were covering the story. A grin showed on his face when he realized all the major media players were following the story, telling their audience to stay tuned for the full live coverage starting in the early afternoon.

***

Once again, his mother's voice along with many others filled Gabriel's dreams while he slept. They were more vivid and clearer than the night before, but he still couldn't make sense of the snippets of meaningless conversations he heard. Their realism and perceived closeness caused his heart to flutter, and he woke up covered in sweat.

The aroma of fresh-brewed coffee taunted him to get out of bed, but the vivid dream kept him recovering a little longer. He sat up and caught his breath, thankful Sydney was in the kitchen making breakfast so she couldn't see the state he was in. He peered over to his nightstand to get the time, but his solar system clock was obscured by the small gift Judy had given him. The sight of the unopened package resting on top of his tablet triggered a melancholy thought; it was Christmas morning, and he hadn't got Sydney a gift.

"Merry Christmas!" Sydney said, entering the bedroom carrying a tray of food.

"Wow!" he said, referring to his breakfast in bed. "Merry Christmas to you too. Now, you realize I'm not in the hospital anymore, and you don't have to feed me anymore either," he added with a chuckle.

"Yah, I know, but it's Christmas, and after all that's happened, I forgot to get you a gift," she said, placing the tray on his lap and casting a puppy-dog look of sadness.

Gabriel's face lit up at hearing her words, and he couldn't hold back the large smile on his face.

"What's so funny?" she asked.

"I'm happy to hear that because I didn't get you anything either," he said then reached over to the nightstand and picked up the package. "Well, we can open this one together if you like. These bandages would make it difficult anyway."

"Sure."

Sydney pulled the tail of the ribbon and partially lifted some of the wrapping paper off the outside of the small plastic box to make it easier for Gabriel's bandage-bound hands to pull the rest off. With the last of the metallic paper removed and lying on the floor next to the bed, Gabriel couldn't believe his eyes.

"You're not using it," Sydney scowled. "I can't believe she did this," she continued, and her voice rose in anger.

"Me neither," Gabriel replied, his voice filled with excitement.

"I forbid you to inject that death-chip into your skull," Sydney demanded, staring at the small plastic box containing the V-chip.

Gabriel knew her feelings and didn't want to ruin their Christmas or his first morning home, so he placed the box back on his night table on top of his tablet.

"Relax, please, let's not ruin our Christmas by arguing. Have some breakfast with me," he said, offering her a piece of toast.

Sydney's anger dissipated while they shared the last of the food and coffee on the tray. She lifted the tray off Gabriel's lap and carried it back in to the kitchen. When she returned to the bedroom, she found him staring at the V-chip.

Gabriel looked up at her and smiled.

"You really want to, don't you?" she asked sounding deflated.

Gabriel instantly recognized the reason for her unfriendly tone and quickly explained.

"Not the V-chip, I want to call my grandparents; I was looking at my tablet."

"Oh," she said, feeling guilty for assuming it was the V-chip. "Go ahead."

"Thanks, Syd," he said and reached over to the nightstand, removing the V-chip from his tablet and placing it next to his clock.

He powered on his tablet and began clumsily tapping the screen with the ends of his fingers sticking out from his dressing. Unnoticed by Gabriel, a large smile spread across

Sydney's lips.

"I'm going to take a shower; I'll call when I get out," she said, and Sydney raced to the bathroom as she alerted Tanya to the reason he was calling.

Overflowing with determination, Gabriel couldn't think of a better Christmas gift to give his grandparents than telling them he would finally leave his studies and work in the MBG. He scanned the screen for the small communication icon in order to initiate the voice command feature, but his bandaged fingers accidently launched the icon to the right— the Martian data filled the screen.

The data ravaged his mind like a junkie receiving a long overdue hit; the power of his resolution was no match for the years of research—data was his heroin, and he had to look at it. His heart raced and his mind awakened with each new data point he saw. The pain and suffering of the past week vanished under the escalating high he was getting from the results.

Gabriel studied the information on the screen, looking at the different graphs with such scrutiny it felt as though he were trying to identify a person's face in a crowd of thousands. His partially bound fingers cramped as he dragged the images across the screen. Gabriel commanded the computer to run an analysis to compare the Martian data with the samples collected from Earth. It only required a few moments before the screen displayed a match.

His heart skipped a beat when his eyes spotted the results. He pushed his body upright in the bed and re-read the screen in disbelief. Certain there must be an error, he repeated his analysis, carefully double-checking each step of the process to be absolutely positive the results were valid.

There was no mistake; the data clearly indicated the level of O18 on Mars also began to increase about a hundred years ago. When Gabriel combined the two sets of data, the historical increases in O18 also matched—the two were identical. The longer Gabriel looked at the data, the more a sinking feeling grew inside his stomach. *The patterns are too similar*, he thought as he continued to stare at the screen.

The images of the ancient Martian civilization captured by the M3 kept popping up in his mind—the remains of life on a lifeless planet. *Is the Earth going to suffer the same fate? Is civilization on the verge of ending?* The sinking feeling rapidly progressed to the urge to vomit. His hand began to shake to the point that it became difficult to properly work the tablet. Gabriel forced his fingers to drag the data on the screen. His hand trembled like a player about to pull the trigger in a game of Russian roulette, and he closed his eyes as he tapped the screen.

It was if the gun had fired; the image that filled the tablet screen was as painful as a bullet piercing his temple. The current trend in O18 levels matched exactly those that had occurred nearly eight thousand years ago on Mars. If the data was correct, why wasn't life destroyed on Earth at the same time? He struggled with the thought when Dr. Ferrel's words entered his mind: *"That really depends on the type of solar particles erupted and the position of the Earth relative to the sun."*

Gabriel grabbed his solar clock and placed it on the bed in front of him. He commanded it to change time to December 25th 6000 BC to estimate the same year as the peak in the data on his tablet. All the planets in the solar system disappeared for a moment and then reappeared in different locations. The Earth and Mars were on the same side of the solar system relative to the sun but quite a distance apart.

He changed the time to December 25th 2000 BC and watched the planets realign. Mars and Earth remained on the same side of the sun, but this time the Earth was significantly closer to where Mars had been eight thousand years ago. The location of the Earth would have only resulted in a partial hit by the solar eruptions of that time. Images of tent towns and masses of people fleeing the rising waters released another memory. *"Not since the time of Noah has the Earth seen such flooding."* He began to think about his weekly trips to church and the sermons. *This would explain Noah's flood and why life continued after that time.*

Gabriel changed the date to the present and his heart nearly exploded inside his chest when the clock displayed the current position of the planets—the Earth moved to exactly where Mars was in relation to the sun nearly eight thousand years ago. *The Earth is about to take a direct hit from the solar eruptions.*

Panic rendered his muscles like jelly. The shaking spread from his hands to his legs, and fear ravaged his mind. *I've got to talk to Dr. Ferrel*, he thought. He tossed the sheet off his body and placed his feet on the floor. Breathing became difficult, like a car was parked on his chest, and the room began to spin.

"Get control of yourself. You're hyperventilating," he whispered to himself.

Desperate to talk to Dr. Ferrel, he grabbed the V-chip from the night stand and popped open the lid to the plastic box. He unfolded the instructions and glossed over them. Gabriel looked at the small applicator and removed the plastic tip covering the end. He placed the tip on his left temple and pushed down on the end, firing the spring-loaded needle, which pierced his skin, placing the nano-chip into his forehead.

It only took a few seconds for his body to recognize the device, and it sent a message to his brain that it was activated. Gabriel started to get dressed while repeatedly commanding the device to contact Dr. Ferrel, but there was no reply. He also tried Dr. Ross without success. Concerned it wasn't working properly, he tried Bradley next with the same result. Frustration exasperated the panic rolling through his thoughts, and out of futility, he called the next person that came to mind.

"Merry Christmas, Gabe! How's the new…?" asked Judie, but before she could finish, Gabriel interrupted her.

"Where's Brad? I need to talk to him," Gabriel snapped, panic evident in his tone.

"What's wrong?"

"Where's Brad? Why isn't he answering?" Gabriel yelled.

"He left his VisText here. He's gone to get us a coffee—he won't be long. What's happening?"

"I need to speak to Dr. Ferrel and can't contact him, I thought Brad might know why," he said in desperation.

"It's probably because he's at the Christmas Summit. It's all over the news," she said matter-of-factly.

"The what?"

"The Christmas Summit—turn on your V-screen. The Pope has requested a meeting between a bunch of the world's leading scientists and religious leaders. Nobody knows why, but they're all in Rome at the Vatican. And, Gabe, I'm really sorry to hear about your..."

He terminated the call before hearing the rest of Judie's sentence. Gabriel pulled his pants on at the same time he heard the water shut off in the shower. In a split second, he had made the decision to leave; he had to show the results to Dr. Ferrel or Dr. Ross. They were the only ones who could verify his findings. He only had a few minutes to exit the apartment before Sydney would come out of the bathroom and forbid him to go. Gabriel grabbed his tablet, removed an old raincoat from the closet by the door and left the apartment for the Tube.

The combination of weakness from days lying in a bed and the enormity of what was about to happen left Gabriel struggling to hurry. He walked as though he were waist-deep in water, forcing his legs to lift his feet with each step he took. The knowledge of the future hung like a cross on his back. Even though it was Christmas morning, people crowded the sidewalk and most cast a stare at him as he struggled toward the station.

***

Gabriel was boarding the Tube when Bradley entered the apartment carrying two cups of coffee. Judie rushed to the door, a look of concern covering her face.

"You need to call Gabe right away," she said.

"Why, has he found out about his grandfather?" Bradley asked as he placed the cups on the small table next to the door and began to undo his coat.

"No, it's something to do with Dr. Ferrel; I think he's going to Rome."

"What?" Bradley shouted, and he paused for a moment to contact Sydney.

"Is he there?"

Sydney opened the bathroom door and saw the empty bed. She called for Gabriel, but there was no answer.

"He left while I was in the shower."

Gabriel could hear their conversation in his mind. He pressed a finger to the spot where he had injected the V-chip. *It must be faulty. I'm hearing other people's conversations*, he thought when his V-chip indicated an incoming call from Bradley.

"What are you doing? Where are you?"

"I'm on the Tube; I need to talk to Dr. Ferrel," he replied, but there was a few seconds of silence before he heard a voice inside his mind. "He's headed for Rome."

"What? Brad, who are you talking to?" Gabriel asked, thinking the voice was coming from his V-chip.

"Stop him! It's too dangerous!" said Animus, his voice much louder inside Gabriel's mind.

"What's dangerous? Who are you talking to?" Gabriel demanded.

"Gabriel, listen to me. You've got to come home," Bradley demanded, but before Gabriel could respond, three more voices entered his mind.

"I'm already running to the station," Sydney said.

"We'll meet you at the Tube," Bradley responded.

Gabriel struggled to make sense of the multiple conversations rolling through his mind. Confusion momentarily strangled his cognitive abilities, leaving him open to doubt and despair. If he was certain of his data, there was no point in continuing; life on Earth was going to end whether he spoke to Dr. Ferrel or not. He began to regain mental focus, and he fought back the growing urge to give up. *I could be wrong*, he thought. *I have to know.*

Standing in the middle of the overcrowded train, the hair on his arms lifted and a tingling sensation crawled across his skin. Small beads of sweat dribbled down his back and the sides of his torso from his armpits. The bodies around him began to distort, and his surroundings started to rotate. Gabriel closed his eyes tightly, attempting to force the dizziness away when a searing heat rose from inside his chest as if he had swallowed a raw chili pepper. The virus multiplying in his body began migrating, leaving the nucleus of his cells making its way into his bloodstream. Gabriel's body tried to fight back, but the fever stimulated by his immune system had no effect; the virus continued to fill his veins.

The dressings covering his hands combined with his light-headedness made it difficult to hold the handrail, and he stumbled when the Tube slowed to a stop in Rome Station.

Hundreds of thousands of people from around the globe were gathering in Rome to hear the Pope's Christmas address from St. Peter's Square. Rome Station was jammed with travelers rushing to the Vatican to secure their spot in front of the Basilica. Gabriel was moving down the narrow sidewalk with the crowd when Sydney called.

"Your grandfather. You've got to come back. Do you want to end up back in the hospital?" she pleaded to no avail.

The sound of her voice unleashed a tide of emotion. It swelled from deep inside his heart, rising to the surface in the form of uncontrollable crying. Gabriel leaned against the brick wall surrounding the Vatican and wiped the tears flowing down his face. The image of losing Sydney burned his mind like acid. He sobbed for a moment before regaining his composure.

"No, it's the data; I need to confirm something with Dr. Ferrel. What's wrong with Opa?"

"Can I tell him?" Sydney asked, but before Animus could answer, Gabriel responded.

"Tell me what?" he asked, using his V-chip.

"He can hear us," Animus replied. "He's getting confused."

"Who is that? Syd, did you hear a voice? I think this V-chip Judie gave me is screwed up—I keep hearing voices."

In an act of desperation, Sydney didn't wait for a response from Animus and decided to tell Gabriel his grandfather was dead, hoping it would shock him into returning.

"I've terrible news for you. Your grandfather is dead—come home."

Gabriel bit his lip in an effort to fight back the tears. Anguish moved through his body like a winter wind, spreading sorrow as it passed. He thought of his grandfather lying in bed with his grandmother holding his hand. That's the way he would want to die, with Sydney at his side. The chill of his grandfather's death passed instantly; like being injected with a narcotic, the feeling of relief passed through his veins.

"That's wonderful," he said.

"What, are you okay?" Sydney replied in disbelief.

"I'm fine. It was his time. Better he go now."

"I'm worried about you. Please stay where you are; we're coming to get you," she demanded.

Gabriel arrived at the entrance to St. Peter's Square without a clue where to find Dr. Ferrel. The growing tide of people was so thick it was difficult to move. He was locked shoulder to shoulder with the religious faithful, and like a piece of wood carried by a river, he had no choice but to file into the square with the moving mass.

A throbbing sensation pounded the inside of his head as

though he could hear his own heartbeat. Gabriel searched above the sea of people for a sign of where to go, turning his eyes in every direction. The crowd of people closed in on him, creating the feeling that he was lying in a coffin and the lid was shutting. An uncontrollable panic awoke within him, the kind experienced by a claustrophobic stuck in an elevator. His body unleashed a surge of adrenalin, and out of desperation, Gabriel began to ask people next to him for help.

At that moment, the virus passed out of his bloodstream and into his lungs. His body continually released the contagion, delivering millions of viruses with each breath he took. Gabriel was a vector, infecting others with a virus of unimaginable virulence. His every word passed the virus from his body to the people surrounding him, entering them like an invisible spirit.

CHAPTER 32

SHATTER

The flow of people halted when the square filled to capacity. Gabriel had only progressed a hundred yards into St. Peter's Square. He was unable to move forward, so he turned around and fought his way back to the street. Exhausted and shaking from the fever ravaging his body, he sought refuge from the rain and the crowd.

Gabriel rested under an awning over a small café across the street from the square. A battle raged inside him, distorting his mental focus and leaving him dejected and overcome with failure. He squatted against the stone wall of the café, fighting back the urge to quit. Images of Sydney raced through his mind. *I should be with her*, he thought. He had just decided to call her when he received a call from Dr. Ross.

"Merry Christmas, Gabriel. I'm happy to know you're doing well, and I'm sorry to hear about your..."

"Dr. Ross, I've got to see you right away."

"Why? What's wrong, is there a problem?"

"Yes, there's a problem—a really big problem—and if I'm right, it may not matter in the end anyway," he shouted, hoping to convey the severity of the situation to Dr. Ross.

"What are you talking about?"

"The data, it's about the data—you must see it."

"All right, you can send it to me, and I promise to look at it the moment I leave the summit."

"No!" Gabriel shouted. "You've got to see it now; that's

why I brought it to Rome."

"You're here?" Dr. Ross asked, clearly surprised that Gabriel found it important enough to make a trip to Rome.

"Yes, I'm outside of St. Peter's Square. Can I meet you somewhere?"

"Of course, I've just arrived at the Vatican myself. Where are you?"

Gabriel read the writing on the glass door of the café. *"Café Piazza."*

"I know exactly where that is. I'll be there in a minute."

The moment he finished his call with Dr. Ross, Sydney called him again.

"Where are you? Our Tube arrives in a few minutes. I want to know where we can meet you."

"I'm in a café near St. Peter's Square. Dr. Ross is on his way—I see him now, I'll call you later, I've got to go," he said, and he finished the call before she could ask any more questions.

It only took a few moments of looking at the data for Dr. Ross to turn chalk-white—with an expression of horror one can only get when they foresee their own death. The look was frozen on his face. The terror in his eyes confirmed Gabriel's worst fear—his analysis of the data was correct. Gabriel put his head in his hands and closed his eyes. The roar of the milling crowd in the square disappeared, leaving only the sound of his own words; he prayed inside his head. He finished his prayer and lifted his head.

"How long?" Gabriel asked.

"I don't know, but I'm certain Mike will know. We need to get to the summit."

Dr. Ross had little trouble forcing his way through the people; his massive frame easily carved a path for Gabriel to follow. Gabriel continued to ignore the incoming calls from Sydney, Bradley and Judie but froze his progress the instant he saw the call from his grandmother. The crowd swallowed the small opening blazed by Dr. Ross, forcing Gabriel to fight his way through bodies on his own while speaking to his grandmother.

"Hi, Oma, I'm so sorry about Opa," he said, fighting back tears again.

"I'm worried sick about you. Where are you?"

"Don't worry about me, I'm fine. I'm with Dr. Ross; we're going to talk to Dr. Ferrel."

"Listen to me carefully, it's important. Do not go into the Vatican," she implored.

"Why? I've got to. We need to see Dr. Ferrel right away. You don't understand... I love you," he said and ended the call.

"Animus, he's going into the Vatican."

"Hello, who is this? Who's Animus? Oma, can you hear me?" Gabriel asked, thinking someone was communicating with him on his V-chip.

Dr. Ross led Gabriel around the outside of the Vatican to a separate entrance leading to the back of the Basilica. Gabriel struggled to climb the stone steps of the administrative building while Dr. Ross approached the VSS operative manning the door. He showed the guard his identification and asked him to permit Gabriel to attend as a student.

The guard contacted Paulo for clearance before allowing Gabriel to enter the building. Paulo left the meeting room and walked the short distance down the corridor to the entrance. He examined Dr. Ross's identification first and then Gabriel's. He stared at Gabriel's name on the identification card and then looked up at him.

"You're not *the* Gabriel Muller?" asked Paulo, raising one eye higher than the other to look at Gabriel.

"Yes."

"Oh, sorry about your father," he said, handing Gabriel back his identification.

"Grandfather, and thanks."

"It's okay," said Paulo to the guard, and Gabriel followed Dr. Ross down the corridor, which was filled with the noise of chatter emanating from the open meeting room door.

***

Father Black sat beneath the life-sized crucifix at the far end of the table sipping his espresso while he waited for the last of the religious leaders to arrive in the Vatican café. He finished the last bit of coffee in the small cup and placed it on the saucer in front of him. The crowded room went silent when he stood up.

"I understand you're all anxious to know why you're here—it won't be much longer," Father Black said, and he left the room for Tonino's office.

Tonino stood behind his desk and watched the V-screen with the volume turned off while sipping his tea. A serene look covered his face when Father Black entered the office.

"Look at this," he said, pointing to the V-screen with his teacup. "We're on every broadcast."

"I'm happy you're pleased that everything is going as planned," Father Black replied while he took a position next to Tonino's desk so he could see the images on the V-screen.

"The religious leaders are assembled?" Tonino asked before taking another sip of his tea.

"Yes, they're anxiously awaiting your arrival," he replied when he noticed something odd about the image on the V-screen.

Tonino noticed it at the same time and pointed to the figures filling the screen as they entered the meeting room.

"Who's that?"

"I don't know," Father Black replied, his eyes glued to the screen. "The one on the right is Ross, but I have no idea who the younger one is."

The image on the screen moved off of Gabriel and Dr. Ross and back to the scientists seated behind the brilliant white tablecloth covering the table, which stretched the full length of the room.

***

Dr. Ferrel was seated when he saw Gabriel. "Animus, he's here," he said.

Gabriel paused for a moment, startled by the voice, when Dr. Ferrel approached him.

"Gabriel, what are you doing here? You shouldn't be out of bed let alone traveling. You need to return home at once and..." scolded Dr. Ferrel.

"Mike, you need to see this," Dr. Ross interrupted and handed him the tablet.

Dr. Ferrel looked at Gabriel for a moment longer while ignoring the device.

"Please, Dr. Ferrel, forget about me. You've got to see this data," Gabriel pleaded.

"I'll only look at it if you promise you'll leave the moment I finish."

"Fine, whatever, just look at it," he replied disingenuously.

Dr. Ferrel looked at the data and scrolled quickly through the results as if he had seen the data already.

"What do you think, Mike?"

Dr. Ferrel looked at Dr. Ross for a second, his eyes hidden behind the dark glasses and then handed the tablet back to Dr. Ross without speaking. He then turned and faced Gabriel before removing the dark glasses from his face so his blue eyes could lock on Gabriel's.

"You need to go now, Gabriel!" he demanded.

"You already knew, didn't you? You've known for a while—how long have you kept this from us?" Gabriel yelled, the sound of his voice attracting the attention of the scientists seated at the table and the media corralled in the room.

"Hey, it's him, that's Gabriel Muller!" shouted a voice from the media scrum stationed behind the roped-off area in front of the speaker's podium.

Kendal Toews forced his way to the front of the reporters. The result of his identifying Gabriel was instantaneous, every reporter and camera in the room focused their attention on him.

The familiar sound of Toews's voice paralyzed Gabriel for a second. Stunned by the unexpected meeting, Gabriel knew there would be no escape. Like a school of sharks swimming in a pool of blood, the media were in a frenzy, surrounding him. They fired question after question at Gabriel about his grandfather's death and the MBG empire. There was nowhere to hide.

"Volume on," Father Black commanded.

Tonino and Father Black watched and listened to the V-screen in an attempt to understand what was going on.

Gabriel's weakened physical state and mental anguish left him vulnerable to the reporter's attacks. The final blow arrived with Kendal's question.

"Gabriel, is it true you're really Derek Muller's lovechild from a sordid affair he had with an office assistant?"

Kendal's question hit Gabriel like a shotgun blast, penetrating his body and instantly releasing a lifetime of pent-up disgust toward the media. A violent hatred erupted in Gabriel's mind, leaving only emotions and no words.

"What's wrong with you people? Is this what the world wants to know? The world's leading scientists and highest-ranking religious leaders have gathered here to deliver grave news to the world, and your only concern is who this boy's father is!" shouted Dr. Ferrel, hoping to draw attention away from Gabriel with the news of the impending disaster.

"What's he talking about? This'll ruin everything! Stop him!" Tonino yelled.

The gossip-hungry reporters ignored Dr. Ferrel's words and remained focused on the tabloid news in front of them. Gabriel panned the mob of reporters, desperately looking for someone to break ranks and ask about his research. No one spoke. Like a free-floating balloon, the weight of decades of keeping a secret soared from within Gabriel. Raw emotion formed his words.

"You really want to know?" he said, staring through the wall of faces directly into Kendal's eyes. "I'll tell you. I never had a chance to know my parents," he said, shifting his eyes from Kendal to the floor. "My father was murdered... my mother was killed in a car crash, but before she died, she named me..."

Pausing to take a deep breath, Gabriel searched for the strength to say his name for the first time in public. He kept at bay the lump forming in his throat with a hard swallow and exhaled through pursed lips as if he were about to jump from a high-diving board.

"Gabriel... Shannon... Anderson!" he stated with pride.

Tonino and Father Black faced each other for a brief instant, their faces mirror images of horror. The teacup trembled from Tonino's hand as he stood, paralyzed with disbelief.

"It can't be," he whispered, approaching the V-screen to get a better view.

Father Black stumbled, his legs turned to rubber and the loss of balance forced him to lean on the corner of Tonino's desk to prevent himself from falling.

"It's impossible," he kept repeating over and over while shaking his head back and forth.

The cameras focused on Gabriel's face as the media bombarded him with questions.

Dr. Ferrel fought his way through the mass of reporters and grabbed Gabriel's shoulder. He turned Gabriel away from the wall of cameras and carved a path toward the door. Like a disgraced politician publically resigning, the scrum followed Gabriel's every move as he navigated through the bodies, their cameras still locked on him, removing any lingering doubt the instant Gabriel's birthmark filled the V-screen.

The sound of the teacup exploding on the tile floor resonated in the small office, but its impact triggered no response from either man. Hundreds of tiny shards of glass moved across the smooth surface, scattering the way ants do escaping a rainstorm. Like the remnants of the broken teacup spinning at his feet, Father Black saw Tonino's composure shatter.

"Get him!" Tonino screamed in a tone so vile it didn't sound human.

The sound of Tonino's voice erased the weakness paralyzing Father Black. He leaped off the desk and raced toward the door, his black robes flying in the air behind him like a stallion's mane. Father Black alerted the VSS SWAT team already deployed to secure the Vatican and protect the religious leaders.

"I don't care how… or if he's dead or alive, just bring him to me!" Tonino shouted as Father Black vanished through the door.

Chapter 33

The Apophis

Hidden beneath umbrellas, the VSS operative guarding the door struggled to keep his attention directed toward the three people approaching. He preferred to monitor the commotion occurring down the hall through the open meeting room door. Bound by orders to remain at his post, the lure of the commotion was distracting, but he opened the door and stepped onto the covered entrance to intercept the approaching group. Bradley led the way up the stone steps while Sydney and Judie closed their umbrellas. The guard met Bradley at the top of the steps outside the building.

"I'm sorry, you're not allowed in this area," the VSS guard said.

"We're here for the summit," Bradley said.

"Really," replied the guard, indicating his disbelief.

"Yes, we're with Dr. Ferrel's lab," Sydney said.

"He's already arrived and didn't indicate anyone else would be coming."

Sydney continued to speak to the guard while Bradley contacted Dr. Ferrel to request his assistance to get them past security.

"We need you at the door," Bradley requested.

"Impossible, I'm trying to get him out of here," Dr. Ferrel replied.

"We can't get in."

"You must," Dr. Ferrel said, aware the situation was rapidly deteriorating.

"Did you call Dr. Ferrel?" Judie asked, thinking his focused state was the result of a call on his VisText.

"What?" Bradley said, confused for a second by her question. "Yes, I spoke to him, but he indicated it's impossible for him to get us through security. I'm worried about Gabriel; we really need to get in there."

"He's not going to let us in," Sydney interrupted, turning to face Bradley.

"I can get us in," Judie said.

"How?" Sydney and Bradley asked in unison.

"I need to make a call," was all she said.

They waited outside the glass entrance doors while the guard directed his attention back to the large mass of bodies moving in the entrance of the meeting room. A few moments later, Bradley watched through the glass as a short, fat, disheveled-looking man arrived inside the door. He spoke to the VSS guard for a moment then disappeared. The guard opened the door and called them inside.

"I'll need to see identification please," he requested.

The three of them began to get out their identification when the guard, clearly uncomfortable with the orders he was just given, contacted Paulo. Unhappy to leave the events unfolding in the meeting room, Paulo ran out of the room in such a hurry he didn't see Gino scurrying past the open door. Their shoulders collided, stopping their progress instantly.

"My apologies, Signore Capozzi," said Paulo, checking to see if Gino was okay.

"I'm fine," Gino replied, not stopping to return the gesture.

Paulo arrived at the entrance door to find the guard holding the three identification cards in his hands. Paulo held out his hand, and the guard gave him the three cards.

He bowed his head and scanned the photos on the cards one at a time, starting with Bradley's. After confirming Bradley matched the likeness of his photo, Paulo moved

Bradley's card to the back and scanned Sydney's in the same fashion.

Paulo directed his attention toward Judie, his gaze drawn to the shiny gold crucifix hanging from her neck. Judie froze the instant she saw his face. The next three seconds passed like hours while the memory of a small church hallway scrolled through both their minds. Judie acted first and disappeared out the door. Like a bolt of lightning hitting the ground, the glimmer of the gold combined with the name on the identification card ignited Paulo's memory and the connection was made.

"Judie Capozzi," he whispered in astonishment and lifted his eyes from the identification card to find she was gone.

"Cap!" he shouted, and he threw Sydney to the ground in an effort to lunge out the closing door. "Stop them!" he commanded to the guard while on his way after Judie.

Unaware of what was happening but thankful for the opportunity, Bradley took advantage of the guard's moment of confusion.

"Run!" Bradley yelled, and he dove onto the guard like a leopard in for the kill. Bradley's tackle caused them both to collapse to the floor, allowing time for Sydney to jump up and dash down the corridor to the meeting room.

A crimson flash of light reflected off the white polished marble floor; the lethal light delivered by the commander of the VSS SWAT team. The guard rolled Bradley's body off his chest and onto the marble while the four SWAT team members continued past without missing a step.

Chaos filled the once-organized meeting room. The room resembled a theatre lobby during intermission. Scientists who had been seated patiently awaiting the commencement of the meeting now mingled in small groups watching the media frenzy unfold around Gabriel and speculating about what was happening. Sydney entered the room and fought her way through the crowd, pushing violently on the wall of bodies to make her way to Gabriel and Dr. Ferrel.

"They're coming! Get to the other door!" Sydney shouted.

Gabriel immediately looked around as the words resonating inside his head sounded like they were shouted by a person standing right next to him.

"Did you hear that?" he asked Sydney, who ignored his question. "Who's coming, what's going on?" Gabriel demanded as Sydney grabbed his wrist and pulled him in the opposite direction while Dr. Ferrel acted like a linebacker carving a path through the bodies.

Gabriel pulled his arm back, causing Sydney to stop and allowing the reporters to reform a mob around them and begin asking more questions.

"What's going on? I'm not leaving; people need to know..."

Before Gabriel finished his sentence, a blinding white flash of light filled the room, followed quickly by an ear-popping explosion. Unable to see or hear for the next three seconds, every person in the room was paralyzed for an instant. When they regained the full use of their senses, they found the room filled with darkness and the sounds of coughing. The doors of the windowless room were sealed, and a thick fog choked their lungs. Sydney pulled Gabriel to the ground by his shirt to find the remaining clean air.

"Follow me!" she shouted to Gabriel in the darkness.

Overwhelmed by the speed of the events unfolding around him Gabriel no longer resisted and did as he was told. Sydney pulled him along by the shirt as they hobbled on their hands and knees in the direction of the table.

Protected by the breathing apparatus inside their helmets and assisted by computer-aided vision, two of the SWAT team took position in front of the doors at either end of the room while the other two raced through the disoriented bodies wandering in the darkness. They methodically scanned every person as they made their way through the crowd in search of their target.

Sydney felt the white tablecloth hit her forehead as she and Gabriel continued along the ground. Gabriel felt as if he were crawling on broken glass every time he put his bodyweight on his hands. The skin grafts under the bandages tore open a little wider with each movement, and he could feel the warm sensation of blood pooling in the dressing. Sydney pulled him under the tablecloth.

"We're under the table, heading to the far door," said the voice inside Gabriel's mind.

"I'm almost there," Dr. Ferrel replied. "Wait for my signal."

Gabriel could hear the conversation in his mind as clear as if he were speaking but fought desperately to ignore it. Sydney crawled under the table, leading Gabriel like a small child. She reached out to the side and touched the tablecloth every few yards to use as a guide in the darkness. Completely undetected by the SWAT team, they continued to crawl their way under the table until Sydney felt material brush her face. They had arrived at the far end of the table, which was only a few feet from the second door and the SWAT team member guarding the exit.

Slowly, individuals in the crowd regained their vision. Desperate for fresh air, they looked for a way to escape. Like moths flocking to a streetlight, people gravitated toward the only light in the room. It came from the corridor, penetrating the darkness from the gap between the doors and the doorframe.

The SWAT officer remained diligent and guarded the door, not allowing anyone to leave.

Dr. Ferrel crawled along the floor, stopping every few feet to wipe the tears flooding from his eyes. He made his way toward the light unimpeded until a body stumbled over the top of him. The impact halted his progress immediately.

"I'm in position. When I give the word, you'll only have a second," Dr. Ferrel said.

"I'll tell him," Sydney replied. She reached down and found Gabriel's hand in the darkness.

Afraid the SWAT members might hear her, Sydney had no other choice but to communicate directly with Gabriel without speaking.

"I know you can hear me. I'm going to squeeze your wrist, but don't make a sound," she said and squeezed.

Gabriel instinctively yanked his hand away as if he had just placed it in a fire. He clenched his teeth in an effort not to yell in fear. Sydney reached in the darkness and found his arm again.

"Listen to me. You're okay, but I don't have time to explain, you just have to trust me. Can you do that? Lift your arm to let me know."

Gabriel lifted his arm to acknowledge.

"Those guys out there are looking for you, and they'll do anything to find you. We've got to get out of here, do you understand?"

He lifted his arm again.

"Good. When you hear 'now,' lift the tablecloth and run as fast as you can, do you understand?"

Gabriel lifted his arm one more time, but confusion and fear rose inside him like a bubble racing to the surface of a pond, and his need to know what was happening grew larger until it broke his silence. Unable to contain his words, Gabriel unleashed a flood of questions.

"What's happening to me? Why can I hear voices in my head? Why are they looking for me?" he said barely above a whisper.

Before Sydney could answer, Dr. Ferrel gave the command.

"Now!" shouted the voice in their minds.

Dr. Ferrel launched himself from the ground onto the SWAT team member guarding the door. Not expecting the attack to occur from below his knees, the SWAT officer fell backwards through the closed doors.

Sydney lifted the tablecloth, allowing Gabriel to see the open doorway and flood of corridor light entering the room.

Gabriel sprang from beneath the table and bolted toward the open door, followed closely by Sydney.

Gabriel froze in shock, the sight of Dr. Ferrel rolling on the ground and fighting with a SWAT team member unhinged his mind. This unraveling was short lived as Sydney pushed Gabriel past the struggling men, returning his thoughts to the immediate urgency to run.

The sudden exit from complete darkness to the dim light of the corridor was enough to release a shot of pain from his eyes to the top of his forehead. It subsided quickly to be replaced by a welcomed sensation. Like returning to the surface from a deep dive, cool fresh air rushed into his lungs, filling his body with renewed life. Adrenalin coursed through his veins and fueled Gabriel's weakened muscles. He sprinted as fast as he could down the corridor, unaware of where he was heading.

Sydney kept pace with Gabriel, running alongside him. She yelled continuously at Gabriel, encouraging him to keep going. Excitement rose inside him. *We're going to make it*, he thought as the path ahead seemed clear, but as they ran for the glass doors in the distance, a silhouette appeared like a shadow from the dimly lit corridor between them and the door. The thick red rope keeping Father Black's robe closed emerged into view first, glowing like a ring of embers in a fire pit as he walked toward them. He took two more steps then stopped.

Father Black's action caused Sydney and Gabriel to stop, and before Gabriel knew what was happening, Sydney stepped directly in front of him. The flash was so quick that Gabriel wasn't certain if he had actually seen it or imagined it, but the sound of Sydney's body hitting the stone floor confirmed that it was real.

The SWAT team member had emerged to their right from the other meeting room door and fired a single perfect shot.

It was as if someone had reached inside his chest and ripped out his heart. Air couldn't enter his lungs no matter how hard he tried to breath. Anguish, not oxygen, bathed every cell in his body. His adrenalin rush vanished, and his legs buckled at the knees. He fell to the ground next to Sydney, a river of uncontrollable tears cascading off his cheeks. Gabriel lifted her head with one hand and pushed her broken glasses off her face with the other before he brushed the hair out of her eyes. Gabriel screamed in agony when her glacial blue eyes faded to grey.

His will to live vanished. A SWAT team member drove his knee into Gabriel's back, pinning him to the ground. Gabriel offered no resistance. A second SWAT team member lifted his head off the cold marble floor and tightly wrapped his forehead with metal tape, preventing any communication using his V-chip. The first member got off of Gabriel and pulled a small plastic strap from his belt while the other member grabbed Gabriel's hair and the back of his shirt, lifting him to his feet. They tied his wrists together with the plastic strap and waited for Father Black to give them orders.

Father Black walked up and faced Gabriel. He ran his eyes slowly up and down him as if he were his commanding officer performing a military inspection. Father Black slowly walked behind Gabriel without lifting his gaze. The instant he spotted the birthmark, astonishment covered his face.

"I don't believe it," he said to himself, and he lifted his fingers to touch the mark as if feeling it would confirm its authenticity.

"Sir?" asked the SWAT team member.

"I'll take him," Father Black said.

"Yes, sir."

"I want you to go and get me the traitor and bring him to the cafeteria while the rest of you clean up this mess before the media gets out here," Father Black snarled while pointing to the two bodies lying in the corridor.

"Right away, sir," the SWAT team leader said.

There was nothing left inside him; every emotion drained from his body, leaving him hollow. Gabriel fell to his knees when the SWAT team member threw Sydney's lifeless body over his shoulder to carry her away. He couldn't take his eyes off her, and Father Black grabbed the back of his shirt to lift him back to his feet.

"Let's go, my friend. There's someone anxious to meet you after all these years."

Gabriel struggled to walk, his legs nearly buckling with every step as if he were carrying a massive weight upon his shoulders. A tiny trail of blood trickled down the side of his forehead where the metal tape dug into his skin. When they passed the SWAT team member dragging Dr. Ferrel's body out of the corridor, Gabriel collapsed to his knees again.

Father Black prodded him in the back forcing him to his feet. "Keep moving," he barked, not withholding his pleasure in watching Gabriel suffer.

Stupefied by what had occurred, Gabriel began to emerge from the shock incapacitating his every thought. Nothing could explain what was happening around him. Gabriel dragged his feet down the corridor while staring at the polished floor when it came to him. He knew why this was happening. *Opa's dead and they think I control MBG.*

"Is it money you want?" Gabriel asked, his words soft and broken.

"What, money? You think this is about money?" laughed Father Black. "We don't need money."

"Then why, why are you doing this?" Gabriel begged, stopping his progress to look Father Black in the eye.

Father Black pushed Gabriel to keep him moving. "You really don't know?"

"No."

"He says you're the one."

"One what?"

"The Apophis. The one who'll end it all."

CHAPTER 34

THE CRUCIFIXION

A single place setting remained unoccupied at the far end of the long table. The uncomfortable quiet in the Vatican cafeteria was broken by the clanking of flatware on a porcelain plate. Tonino sat at the head of the large wooden table spinning the silver steak knife like a propeller on the surface of the bleached white tablecloth. His cruel black eyes never moved from the life-sized Crucifix hanging above the opposite end of the table. Tonino's weathered expression and chiseled look rendered words unnecessary to communicate the anger festering inside him, and the religious leaders cowered with fear while they ate their lunch, refusing to break the silence.

"I'm afraid we won't be able to wait for the pontiff to finish his Christmas address," said Tonino with a malicious grin. "There's been an unexpected change of plan, as we have a special guest arriving."

The table of religious leaders halted their lunch and stared at Tonino in anticipation of his next words when Father Black arrived with Gabriel through the small wooden door of the cafeteria. His entrance transformed Tonino's expression to one of excitement. A large smile melted the age lines around his mouth, and his eyes glistened with darkness at the sight of Gabriel. He pushed his chair away from the table and stood up.

"Show them the mark," he commanded.

Father Black grabbed a handful of Gabriel's hair and wrenched his head down and to the side in order to display the birthmark for the entire room to see. The force of the movement sent a shower of Gabriel's blood flying off his forehead and onto the tablecloth.

Uncontrollable gasps and murmurs of disbelief rippled around the table.

"How's this possible? You said he was dead," said the Ayatollah, and others at the table chirped in agreement, gathering confidence from his strength to break their silence.

"It's not wise to dwell on the past when our future rests on the cusp of destruction," Tonino snapped, his words crushing the group's feeble attempt to question his authority. "Put him over there," Tonino said, pointing to the end of the table. "I want them all to see."

Father Black escorted Gabriel along the full length of the table. Unable to use his hands, Gabriel stumbled to his knees again when he tried to move between the wall and the oversized table. Father Black shoved his fist into Gabriel's back and demanded he get up. Gabriel used the last remnants of his strength to raise his body from the floor. His struggle went unnoticed by the group as their attention turned back to the cafeteria door.

Gino entered the cafeteria. Like Gabriel, his hands were bound at the wrists in front of his body with a thin plastic strap. He was followed closely by the SWAT team leader who held his weapon aimed at Gino's back. Gino never lifted his head from the floor as he proceeded so he didn't notice Tonino's head shaking with disappointment.

"Put him with the other," Tonino said in disgust and nudged his head toward Gabriel.

The SWAT team leader passed Gino to Father Black and left the room. Gino slowly shuffled over to the end of the table and stood to the right of Gabriel when Paulo entered the room. His arms were filled with what appeared to be an oversized doll. It quickly became clear it wasn't a toy but a woman. Her long brown hair nearly touched the ground where as it draped over Paulo's right arm while her legs dangled over his left, swinging with each step he took into the room.

"Who do we have here?" asked Tonino.

"The ReF we've been searching for," Paulo replied, and the instant he finished saying this, Gino lifted his head to view the body.

"On the table," Tonino demanded, and he pointed to center of the table a few feet in front of him.

The sound of plates cracking and glass shattering resonated off the plaster-covered stone walls like a rock tossed through a window. The noise gathered the room's attention to the body tossed onto the tabletop like a large stuffed toy. A few of the leaders turned their heads while most of the others mouthed a prayer for the deceased.

"No!" screamed Gino when Judie's lifeless head became visible. He faced Tonino and yelled, "First my Angela, now my Judie. You're monsters!" He then faced Father Black and spit on him. "Your time is near—God will get his vengeance," he said and continued to cry.

Gabriel glanced at his friend's pale and broken body strewn across the top of the table. He had no emotion left to spill and no strength left to go on. He collapsed to the floor.

"Put our guest in his proper place," said Tonino while he slowly walked toward the other end of the table. "Like father, like son. It's only fitting he replace the other who failed," he said, unable to hold back his laughter.

Paulo and Father Black slid the crucifix off the steel bar and tossed it on the floor. They walked back to Gabriel and positioned themselves on opposite sides of him, lifting his body off the floor by his arms. They struggled to position his torso high enough while trying to keep his arms pointed upward. After two unsuccessful attempts, they hung him from the metal pole by his wrists. Gabriel's body swung like a carcass hanging in a meat locker.

Positioned between Gabriel's swinging body and Gino,

Father Black used his right hand and pulled down Gabriel's legs to stop his movement and to magnify his agony.

Scorching pain raced down Gabriel's arms as the flesh tore his wrists where the plastic strap penetrated his skin. The tendons and ligaments in his shoulders began to fail, separating the bones from their sockets. His head felt as though someone was pushing it toward the ground, and he quickly relinquished the effort of trying to lift it. A salty mixture of sweat and blood escaped from under the metal tape crowning his head and slowly leaked into the corners of his eyes.

When Tonino spoke, the whisper quiet gasps of horror and disbelief disappeared, leaving only the sound of Gino's sobs.

"Give me your weapon," Tonino demanded, now standing directly in front of Gabriel.

Father Black reached inside his robe with his left hand and handed the laser to Tonino.

"Thank you, Paulo," said Tonino, using an artificial tone of gratitude which left no doubt in Paulo's mind that he was to leave.

Tonino looked at the small shiny silver weapon in his hand and activated it. With his back to the petrified audience frozen in their seats, Tonino lifted the deadly weapon and pointed it toward the end of the table. Gino's swollen and red eyes never blinked when Tonino began to speak. "I must admit, I'm disappointed in you. You've been a faithful and useful member of my team, but you, of all people, understand... I have no tolerance for failure."

The red light penetrated the black robe, passing through his chest and disintegrating his heart instantly. Father Black collapsed to the floor; the impact of his body on the ground was inaudible over the horrified sounds coming from the onlookers around the table. Gino turned his head and looked down at the crumpled mass strewn on the floor next to him.

The revolting smell of burned flesh rose to his nostrils,

carried by the plume of grey smoke rising from the hole in Father Black's chest. A large smile arrived on Gino's face, and then he lifted his gaze and looked lovingly at his daughter's body before he locked eyes with Tonino.

"I am ready, God," said Gino, and a second flash of light reflected off the white walls of the cafeteria.

Tonino turned and faced the group. He placed the weapon on the table in front of him with Gabriel's body hanging above him. He was about to speak when the absolute silence in the room was broken by a whisper. It was a single word, "Why?" said so faintly that no one knew where it had come from.

Tonino scanned the faces, attempting to out the dissenter, but he saw none of them utter a sound. No one moved or dared utter a word when the voice spoke again.

"Why are you doing this?"

His face covered with disbelief, Tonino took a knife from the table setting in front of him before turning to address Gabriel.

"You don't know? They haven't told you?" Tonino asked with a tone of surprise in his voice.

"Why?" Gabriel repeated, each breath releasing more viruses into the room.

"You've got the mark... You're the one, the Terminal Vector. Created by the Primoris, destined to bring life to an end," Tonino replied as anger rose in his voice. "But just like your predecessors, you have failed!" he shouted and shoved the knife into the side of Gabriel's body, twisting it left and right like a doorknob before pulling it out and tossing it on the table.

The bloody tip of the knife left scarlet dots on the pure white surface as it began to skip across the table. Rapid vibrations rattled the utensils left on the plates, and the floor trembled. Large pieces of plaster fell from the ceiling. Smashing glass and the low rumble of collapsing buildings could be heard coming from the hall. The stone walls shook as if it were an earthquake, sending the entire group racing for the cafeteria door.

Tonino followed the leaders to the exit but hesitated before leaving. He turned back and faced Gabriel, searching for a sign of life, when the power of the next explosion shook the building so violently it sent Gabriel flying off the metal bar and onto the tabletop. Tonino left the room to escape the building.

Massive explosions devastated St. Peter's Square and the surrounding Vatican buildings. The SnRs attacks were precise and perfectly timed, killing thousands of religious followers, and like the ReF attacks, the bombings occurred at multiple locations destroying the Western Wall and Mecca.

The carnage was broadcast live to the world, including the death of the Pope during his Christmas address. The retaliation attacks by the SnRs on the holiest of sites were like tipping the first domino in a row of thousands. Once started, nothing could prevent the events that cascaded the planet into war.

***

Tanya asked the two IGB security officers accompanying her to wait as she leaned her petite body against the partially open wooden door. She strained to push it open, the difficulty caused by the mound of ceiling plaster piled on the other side. Her actions caused a dull scraping noise as the door moved the debris across the floor. Dust still floated in the air of the cafeteria, forcing her to cover her nose and mouth with a handkerchief. This wasn't enough to keep the particles from tickling the back of her throat, and she coughed as she stepped over the debris littering the room. Drops of water bounced off the marble floor and the wooden tabletop, its constant rhythmic dripping resembling the sounds of a percussion section in an orchestra.

"He's here, Animus," she said.

"Alone?" Animus asked.

"Yes."

"He's afraid, he's fighting it. Speak to him," Animus commanded.

Tanya walked over to the end of the collapsed table where Gabriel's body lay on its side, his birthmark partially hidden by a spot of blood caked with plaster dust. She pulled his left shoulder toward her, causing him to roll onto his back. Unable to contain her emotions, tears seeped from the corners of her eyes when she saw the thin streaks of dried blood snaking over his face and the large patch of fluorescent red tablecloth below his ribs. His chest barely moved with each sporadic breath.

She leaned over him and placed her mouth next to his ear. Tanya gently placed her left hand on his face just below the crown of metal tape and kissed his cheek. Her breathing was labored, and her chest filled with fire as she struggled to catch her last breath.

"Don't be afraid," she whispered, and with all her remaining strength, Tanya pulled the edge of the tablecloth over Gabriel to shroud his body before collapsing to the floor.

Her soft and familiar voice kindled the most incredible light Gabriel had ever seen. Like the lights he had seen in the past, this one glowed radiant blue, but its intensity was thousands of times brighter. Its brilliance could only be compared to the sun's, yet there was no pain as he stared at it. On the contrary, the more he looked at the light, the less he wanted to turn away.

Uncertain if the light drifted closer or if he was moving near to it, Gabriel could see the shimmering mass grow larger. As it approached, a feeling of warmth flooded over his body like an August breeze, and a level of happiness never experienced before erupted from every cell inside him. His mind filled with euphoria and the tranquility of a mountain meadow; Gabriel unknowingly released all concept of time. Nothing mattered anymore but the urge to touch the light before him. His every thought focused on entering the light, but he hesitated.

"Don't be afraid," said the same voice Gabriel had heard in his mind many times before.

"God?" he whispered.

"If that's what you believe."

Gabriel paused before he answered even though 'God' arrived in his mind instantly, he gave a different answer.

"I don't know. I've heard your voice before in my head, and there were other voices, they spoke to you..." It took Gabriel a few seconds to recall the name he had heard, "Animus, you're Animus?"

"Touch me."

Gabriel looked at the light then the back at his hand. They were only inches apart. His heart raced with excitement. Like finally making the decision to leap off the dock into an ice-cold lake, Gabriel slowly placed his hand into the light.

An explosion of serenity swallowed Gabriel. At first, the only thing he could see was light; he was surrounded by it, nothing but warm blue light.

"Is this heaven?"

"That depends," Animus replied.

"On what?"

"If that's what you believe."

"Is she here?" Gabriel asked, his voice cracking with desperation.

The instant Gabriel finished his question, Sydney walked out of the light and stood before him. She raised both arms and offered her hands to him. Gabriel placed his hands inside hers and pulled Sydney into a hug. His mind was bathed in endorphins, and Gabriel released an extended sigh, signaling his overwhelming desire to never let go. But his emotions quickly unraveled when she loosened her grip and started to push away. Sydney faded back into the light without speaking.

"Don't go!" he begged, and she smiled before disappearing completely.

"She's not gone," Animus said.

"Where is she?"

"Primoris."

"Where's Primoris?" Gabriel demanded, still hesitating to follow her into the light.

"Sydney has joined the others, and you will too."

"I'm afraid," he said, forcing himself to admit it.

"You've nothing to fear."

"What about those people, the ones torturing me?"

"There are no Vacare here," Animus replied, trying to reassure him he was in no danger.

"Why did they want me?"

"You're the Terminal Vector, the nexus to expanding Existence—it's hidden in your DNA."

"What are you talking about?" Gabriel responded, and confusion tightened its grip on his mind.

"The Vacare have hunted the Vectors from the moment of human creation, seeking to destroy them and end all Existence."

Unable to comprehend the enormity of what he was hearing, Gabriel could only focus his mind on one question. "Why me?" he asked in disbelief.

"You're the final recipient, the last human to hold a genetic code concealed inside the DNA given to the first human created, and it's been passed on to you from your ancestors. The code remained hidden from the Vacare for millennia—until now."

Gabriel held back the barrage of questions erupting inside him; he still couldn't comprehend what this had to do with him. He paused for a moment, hoping some understanding would finally arrive, but none did, so he was forced to continue his questioning.

"What do I have to do with Existence?" Gabriel asked. That word triggered his memory of a few hours before and the foreboding discovery he had made with the Martian data.

"Everything," said Animus. "The genetic blueprint for a virus was hidden within your DNA, programmed to remain dormant until awoken by the sun's radiation."

Anxiety quickly filled his thoughts, and like the focusing of a telescope on a distant star, an image began to form in his mind of what once seemed to be unrelated events. Animus continued even though Gabriel struggled to keep pace with the tide of information flooding his mind.

"The virus you unleashed holds the key to releasing the incredible energy locked away in all human DNA. But like an explosive without a fuse, the energy is trapped, unable to be released. Only the virus can set free the energy the instant it is ignited..."

"The sun, the massive solar flares every four thousand years, it's the sun; radiation will ignite it," interrupted Gabriel, beginning to make the connection.

"Yes," Animus replied. "But the timing is critical; unless the virus is spread to enough human DNA before the solar flares erupt, expansion cannot occur."

"Why?"

"The Vacare. Their sole purpose is to prevent the expansion of Primoris; they seek to create the opposite of Existence—an absolute vacuum. Destroying you before the virus could be released would have assured their success. Without the virus, the energy within human DNA is trapped; instead the solar flare would unleash an implosion, the energy forever falling inward and forming the perfect vacuum the Vacare quest."

"A black hole," Gabriel retorted.

"Yes, this is how you would understand it."

"*I had the virus when I left the hospital,*" he remembered.

"Gabriel, it's time."

The invisible wall of fear impeding him from moving forward collapsed, and Gabriel felt a warm wind surge over his body. Like standing on the bow of a ship, the wonderfully pleasant sensation beckoned him to close his eyes and inhale deeply. An unimaginable nirvana intoxicated him.

Gabriel stepped into the light and vanished into Existence.

CHAPTER 35

ABSOLUTE SUCCESS

T he massive event went unnoticed for the first few minutes, its size so enormous the research scientists manning the International Solar Observatory failed to detect it. Four thousand years had passed since the sun had erupted with such force. Conceived deep inside and nourished by time, a cloud of muons grew larger below the sun's surface with each passing millennium. Its gestation complete, it tore through the corona, giving birth to a plume of cosmic rays. Recent solar activity had been responsible for disrupting large areas of the planet and increasing Ross radiation, but this eruption was different.

Travelling at the speed of light, the invisible wall of muons mushroomed, expanding thousands of times wider than the sun as it hurled through the solar system. The subatomic particles instantaneously passed through matter unimpeded as they approached the unsuspecting Earth. Like a gigantic abstract painting hung high above the planet, the atmosphere exploded with light. The waves of pastel green, pink and violet spread across the sky and ignited it in a magnificent palette of color.

***

The dark grey clouds above the Rome skyline provided a perfect backdrop to reflect the flashes of yellow and orange light. Sparked by the SnRs retaliation on the Vatican and fueled by the homeless and starving masses, the fighting had spread quickly to the tent towns. IGB intervention failed to control the unrest, and war continued unabated.

For the past two months, a field of plastic tarps and makeshift tents covered the ground where St. Peter's Basilica had once stood. Teams of workers continued to sift through the mountains of stone and bricks left behind from the collapsed buildings. Tonino stood in his office where he always did, staring through a shattered pane of glass, the cracks covering the window like a spider web. A smirk formed across his lips, knowing it was pointless for the workers to continue searching the debris for artifacts.

Still frozen like a statue with his hands tightly clasped behind his back, Tonino listened to the V-screen without shifting his attention from the window. The WNN announcer described the most recent fighting sweeping the planet. Tonino gazed skyward, patiently watching as he had done every day since the fighting began; his coal black eyes glistened in the dull afternoon light like the body of a black widow spider.

An ear-piercing tone filled the tiny office from the V-screen, followed by three equally loud rapid peeps. The WNN announcer's voice was interrupted and a familiar warning message scrolled across the solid blue screen: 'Solar Flare Detected 14:27:36—Prepare for Imminent Power Failure.' The sky filled with a rainbow of color, and the smirk on Tonino's face transformed into a malevolent smile.

In less than two months, the virus spread by Gabriel had infected the entire human population. When the muons reached Earth they passed unimpeded through every form of matter except for one—human DNA. And like igniting the primer within a bullet, the muons triggered the virus to release the energy within the DNA.

At precisely the same instant, the emptiness within Tonino's eyes erupted producing an unfathomable implosion.

It was so powerful it tore a small hole in space. The newly released energy created by the Primoris did not accelerate deeper into the cosmos, but instead it began twisting and swirling like water falling through a drain.

The energy spun slowly near the outer edges but gained speed quickly toward the middle, creating an unstoppable vortex as it entered the hole. Like the mouth of an incredible beast, the Vacare swallowed planets, solar systems, entire galaxies and Existence. Nothing remained but a void in—a perfect vacuum.

The dark force was so powerful it altered time, causing it to bend upon itself to form a circle. The Vacare had succeeded.

***

It may have been six days or six oons before the energy within the black hole converged. This convergence ignited a cataclysmic explosion, hurling energy through the universe in every direction. Primoris expanded farther than ever before, extending Existence to the outer reaches of the cosmos, where a small planet circled a medium-sized star.

This planet was like countless others scattered throughout the universe. It teemed with life. Lush green forests formed a perfect canopy over the ground, extending to the edge of a rugged shoreline.

The turquoise ocean cast gentle swells upon the rocks, the sound muffling the call of the shore birds darting across the receding waves. Silky white sand gathered in the gaps between the massive rocks protruding from the warm water.

A thin veil of clouds drifted through the cyan sky, partially blocking the amber sunset glowing across the horizon. Two young lovers held hands as they stood near the water, their naked bodies gilded bronze from countless days beneath the tropical sun.

A majestic white bird soared unnoticed above the young

couple, watching them intently as though eyeing seeds upon the soil. The evening breeze was filled with the fragrance of blossoming flowers. It gently brushed the hair from the back of the lovers' necks, exposing their matching birthmarks. Enamored by the beauty before them, the young couple closed their crystal blue eyes and kissed.

The Beginning.

ABOUT THE AUTHOR

 As a young boy growing up in the Okanagan Valley in beautiful British Columbia, Canada, Mark spent most of his youth roaming the surrounding hills looking for the next perfect fly-fishing opportunity. His love of nature and the outdoors influenced his education, and Mark went on to complete a Bachelor of Science degree from the University of Windsor and a graduate diploma in Environmental Toxicology from Simon Fraser University.

Now a senior scientist working for the Canadian government for more than twenty-five years, Mark conducts cutting-edge research on new and emerging environmental issues. He has traveled the globe extensively, speaking at scientific conferences and presenting his research. Mark has published many scientific papers but *The Convergence Series* represents his first work of fiction. When asked what made him want to write fiction, Mark replied, "Because my sons asked me to." Mark still resides in British Columbia with his two boys, where they enjoy trolling the waters of the Pacific Northwest in search of that elusive Tyee.

THE CONVERGENCE SERIES

Please visit www.MarkSekela.com for details about the other books in the Convergence Series.